GALLOGLASS

Also by Scarlett Thomas

Worldquake Sequence
Dragon's Green
The Chosen Ones

GALLOGLASS

WORLDQUAKE BOOK THREE

SCARLETT THOMAS

CANONGATE

First published in Great Britain in 2019 by Canongate Books Ltd,
14 High Street, Edinburgh EH1 1TE

canongate.co.uk

1

British Library Cataloguing-in-Publication Data
A catalogue record for this book is available on
request from the British Library

ISBN 978 1 78211 933 3

Typeset in Horley Old Style MT
by Palimpsest Book Production Ltd, Falkirk, Stirlingshire

Printed and bound in Great Britain by Clays Ltd, Elcograf S.p.A.

MIX
Paper from
responsible sources
FSC® C020471

For my family

'The effect of the successful adventure of the hero is the unlocking and release again of the flow of life into the body of the world.'

Joseph Campbell

'No man can swim unless he enters deep water. No bird can fly unless its wings are grown, and it has space before it, and courage to trust itself to the air.'

H. P. Blavatsky

'And the botanist who finds that the apple falls because the cellular tissue degenerates, and so on, will be as right and as wrong as the child who stands underneath and says that the apple fell because he wanted to eat it and prayed for it.'

Leo Tolstoy

1

The elderly headmaster of the Tusitala School for the Gifted, Troubled and Strange sighed and walked stiffly into the staff room. His own dark office, which he rarely left, smelled comfortingly of books, tapestries, good wine and cigars. The staff room, however, was a displeasing miasma of forgotten lunch-boxes, cheap coffee, red ink, tragic perfume and all the unique aromas of the fugitive ex-class-pets.

There was, by now quite a large selection of small mammals and birds that had momentarily forgotten themselves and bitten children (although never that badly) or eaten their own young (although rarely in public) and had, therefore, officially left the school.

'Hide the guinea pigs,' hissed someone. 'And cover Petrov.'

Mrs Beathag Hide (owner of the tragic perfume) tossed a pantomime vampire's cape over the cage containing the parrot that was supposed to have been removed after swearing at the school inspector. Dr Cloudburst and Mr Peters started putting the guinea pigs' cages into the Lost Property cupboard. Luckily the elderly headmaster moved slowly enough that there was plenty of time to do this.

The school cat, Neptune, uncurled from a hairy cushion and stalked off in the same direction, in the hope of finding himself shut in with the guinea pigs. He was quite deft at undoing their hutches. Mr Peters shooed him out into the main corridor. At least Neptune no longer had to be hidden. His last misdemeanour had now been forgotten, and so he had recently begun to reappear in the School Prospectus and annual newsletter. Parents liked cats.

Today, though, the headmaster was uninterested in the pets and their ignoble pasts.

'It is time,' he said slowly, once he eventually arrived in the centre of the room, 'to finalise our plan for the Winter Fair.'

Everyone groaned. It wasn't that people didn't like the Old Town Winter Fair. They did. But things always went wrong during fairs, fetes and open days. It was far better, in all the teachers' opinions, to keep things well-structured and predictable. Get the children in, lock the doors and try to teach them something – anything – before the end of the day. That, translated into Latin, was the school's motto, pretty much. Or it would have been if anyone had ever thought to have a motto.

'We do, presumably, have a plan?' said the headmaster.

'We're sending five children to the university,' said Mrs Beathag Hide. 'Some first-years expressed a desire to learn creative writing and, as you know, we have forged some links with the new Writer in Residence there. There will be workshops, I believe, for the lucky children.' The way she said 'lucky children' didn't make them sound very lucky at all. Quite the opposite, in fact.

The Old Town University traditionally held its Open Week during the Winter Fair. There were workshops for children, and public lectures for people who couldn't afford to go to university and wanted to learn things for free. The beautiful old butter-stone buildings were, for one week only, covered with colourful balloons.

'Ah yes,' said the headmaster. 'A Terrence Dark-Heart, I believe?' He gave Mrs Beathag Hide a searching look, or as much of one as he could manage at his age.

'Terrence Deer-Hart,' corrected Mrs Beathag Hide. 'Yes. A dreadful, sentimental children's writer now apparently working on some dire epic for adults.'

'Remind me again why we are sending the children to him?' said the headmaster, wearily.

'The other lecturers in the department are rather *interesting*. Dora Wright is now there, of course. The new Head of Creative Writing is Professor Gotthard Forestfloor. He's the Scandinavian novelist we talked about last week, if you remember. There's also Lady Tchainsaw, the Russian avant-garde poet. The visiting professor, Jupiter Peacock, is also a rather intriguing person. You may recall that he claims to carry around with him the spirit of the ancient writer Hieronymus Moon in a small ceramic bottle stoppered with a cork. The children are bound to learn something. And we're only sending five of them. The others will be doing Winter Fair crafts with children from the Mrs Joyful School.'

'What about Blessed Bartolo's?' asked Dr Cloudburst, peering at a test-tube which had something dry and black stuck at the bottom of it. It looked a bit like tea that has been left in the staff room over a long weekend, but was probably more dangerous than that. 'We won't be sending any more children there, surely?'

It seemed no one could remember what the arrangement was with the Blessed Bartolo School, or what had happened to the children who'd gone there last year. Had they ever come back? Perhaps not.

'It'll all be fun,' said Mr Peters, the Head of P.E. 'The children like a bit of fun.'

Everyone looked at him as if he was a complete simpleton.

But he was right. Most children did like a bit of fun, and if you counted as fun seeing bad men ripped apart by demons, hearing prophecies about your best friends' deaths, almost dying because you have run out of magical energy, having to confront your worst fears, being expected to fight evil, and travelling to other worlds from which you might never return, then yes, some of the children in this school knew all about fun.

'Everyone loves the Winter Fair,' said Dr Cloudburst.

This *was* true. During the Winter Fair, stalls sprung up all over the Old Town selling hot chestnuts, fermented doughnuts and marmalade made from foraged fruits. Every well-known shop had its own stall. The Esoteric Emporium brought out some of its dustiest vintage wines and oldest jars of sauerkraut to sell by the warmth of its little ovens, in which fresh sourdough bread baked gently. Madame Valentin brought her exotic snakes, all of which were planning to escape again this year. The Puppet Man displayed his very best marionettes – many of which were too frightening for children under ten to look at. Luckily there were also roasted marshmallows and lots of glittery decorations.

The main thing was that the Winter Fair made people forget

the cold and the dark, as the northern hemisphere hurtled unstoppably towards the shortest day, and the various Midwinter celebrations that would keep people cheerful until the Turning of the Year, when mass depression would set in again, as it always did. It was almost as if our world – or at least, this part of it, for it was Midsummer elsewhere – became a bit more like the Otherworld, just for a time. Not that most people believed in the Otherworld, of course.

Alexa Bottle closed the door of Mrs Bottle's Bun Shop and began walking the hundred or so yards to the house where she lived with her mother and father. She was slightly late, which was unusual. Normally she was very late. It wasn't her fault – she just found her after-school job making magical remedies extremely absorbing and never quite remembered to look at the clock. At the moment she was also revising for various M-grade tests, and trying to remember the differences between all the old apothecaries' systems of weights and measures. By Monday, Lexy had to know how many granums went in a scrupulum, and how many of those made a drachm. How many minims were in a fluid scruple? Twenty. At least she'd remembered that. Maybe Dr Green would even be pleased with her for once.

Lexy was still in her school uniform, but in less than ten minutes she was supposed to be wearing her best dress for dinner with the Bottles' important houseguest. What was his name again? Jupiter something. He was a famous writer and philosopher in town to give a public lecture at the university as part of

5

the Winter Fair. Lexy's family had won a raffle, which meant they got to host their very own visiting personage and they had been assigned Jupiter Whatshisname.

Lexy's mother Hazel was taking her responsibilities as host very seriously. For far too long, she'd said, she had simply been seen as the flower-power, hippy-dippy wife of the local yoga teacher. No matter how hard she tried, Hazel had never appeared quite like other, normal mothers. She had never hosted a successful dinner party (the last one had featured bean hot-pot and group chanting). She wore the wrong things. She had crazy hair. She went barefoot in summer, and in winter sometimes wore homemade skis to go shopping. She smelled of patchouli and herbal tea. She had never ironed a sheet in her life.

Until this week. This week, Hazel Bottle had declared, their houseguest was going to sleep on clean, ironed sheets, and in the morning his toast was going to be served in one of those little metal racks. Everything was going to be normal, just like it was in other people's houses. And Lexy was not going to ruin it by being late, or by letting any of her remedies catch fire, or by making the whole house smell of burnt clove and scabious ointment, and she was going to tidy up her room and remove all her medicinal plants from windowsills around the house, and make sure the new kitten, Buttons, didn't do anything too embarrassing . . .

Lexy's mind returned to the three drachms of powdered water-lily in the jar in her school bag. *Culpepper's Herbal*, a book Lexy was studying for yet another one of her tests, said that the herb 'cools and moistens, just like the moon itself'. Lexy was going to use the water-lily to make a new remedy for sports injuries and battle wounds. Her friends Effie Truelove and Wolf Reed always needed things like that. Lexy had also promised her friend Maximilian that she would make him some enchanted ear-drops to enhance the sound of music. And Raven had asked for some magical hoof-balm for her horses. It was going to be a busy weekend.

Lexy opened the front door to her house and found that the whole place smelled of the beeswax the Bottles used on the rare occasions that someone decided to do some polishing. Something was cooking, and it wasn't bean hot-pot. There was some other new smell in the air too. Sort of like Earl Grey tea mixed with lavender and lemons and . . . Buttons ran to greet Lexy, which he did by clawing his way up her school tights and then her back, until he was sitting on her shoulder.

'And who is this charming young lady?' came an unfamiliar deep voice, as Lexy walked into the main living space of the house, an open-plan kitchen, dining-room and sitting-room area that looked a good deal cleaner and tidier than it usually did.

'This is Professor Jupiter Peacock,' said Hazel, removing Buttons from Lexy's shoulder and then taking Lexy's coat and bag and putting them in a cupboard where they did not usually go. Usually they just hung off the bannisters with everything else that people couldn't be bothered to take upstairs. 'Professor Peacock, this is my daughter Alexa.'

Professor Jupiter Peacock stood and held out his hand. He was a tall, broad man dressed in a pair of indigo jeans and a black velvet shirt with a yellow polka-dot cravat around his neck. His hair was swept up in an extravagant pompadour style, like the ones men had in really ancient films. He looked like the sort of person who didn't normally wear jeans. The Earl Grey smell was his aftershave.

'*Enchanté*,' he said, taking Lexy's hand and winking. 'You must call me JP. *All* my friends call me JP.'

'And I'm Lexy,' said Lexy.

Jupiter Peacock's hand was hot, and his handshake was very firm, much firmer than any normal handshake Lexy had experienced. She winced, and took her hand away as quickly as she could before he broke one of her fingers. She'd have to take an arnica tablet after that. Or maybe even try out her new remedy on herself, once it was ready.

'What a delightful child you have,' said Jupiter to Hazel Bottle.

Hazel blushed. The visit was going so well so far. At the end of the Winter Fair all the visiting personages were invited to rate their hosts, and the one with the highest score got a bunch of flowers, a box of chocolates and had their name engraved on a silver plaque mounted on the wall of the Town Hall. And Hazel Bottle was going to win this year; she was sure of it.

'Thank you,' she said.

As Lexy went upstairs to get changed a small bruise started to form on the outside of her hand. She decided to avoid shaking hands with Jupiter Peacock again. Of course, he hadn't meant it. He was just one of those people who had no idea of their own strength.

When Lexy came down the stairs five minutes later, she was wearing her best pink tutu-style dress with matching ballerina shoes. Somehow this seemed like the wrong outfit in which to be spending the evening with JP. Lexy wished she had something that looked more grown-up, although she wasn't sure why. Maybe it was because her parents seemed to be acting so much more like grown-ups themselves. Her mother was using her most serious voice, which was a couple of octaves lower than normal, and Lexy's father Marcel had on an ironed shirt. An *actual* shirt, rather than a crumpled, long-sleeved T-shirt with some 'amusing' yoga message on it such as *Yoga Dad, There's No Place Like Om*, or *Shake Your Asana*.

As Lexy reached the bottom of the stairs, she heard her father laugh in the way he did only when there were other adults around and he'd just said something he found very funny.

'That's if any of us survive Midwinter, of course,' he said.

Jupiter Peacock now laughed as well. The sound was loud and strange, like a bittern calling for a mate.

'Don't scare our guest,' Hazel Bottle was saying to her husband.

'Oh, I'm not easily frightened,' said Jupiter Peacock. 'But I must say I am a little unnerved by the idea of the world ending while I'm in the middle of my lecture. That would be most unfortunate indeed.'

'The world never ends when people say it will,' said Marcel Bottle. 'I wouldn't be too alarmed.'

So *they* were talking about the prophecy as well. It had been all over Mrs Bottle's Bun Shop that afternoon. There were often weird prophecies flying about nowadays, but most people ignored them. Of course most people also thought that magic didn't exist and there was no such thing as the Otherworld. Magical people, on the other hand, believed in everything, and took prophecies quite seriously.

Apart from this one. Even magical people thought this prophecy was a bit of a joke, as it had come from Madame Valentin. She'd been cleaning her crystal ball, she'd said, and it had gone off. The thing hadn't functioned for years, and Madame Valentin had used up the last of her M-currency long before the worldquake. But suddenly the crystal ball had activated itself (this is not at all how crystal balls work, which was yet another reason to pour scorn on the whole story) and that was when Madame Valentin had seen it all unfold before her.

It was Midwinter, on the dot – this year that meant 8.12 p.m. on the 21st of December, which was this Monday evening – and the sky had gone pink, and then green, and then completely black, a black Madame Valentin had never seen before. There were hundreds of cats flying through the sky. And then – a massive explosion. The End.

'I'm sure when the world does end it will be in a way we haven't even thought of,' said Hazel Bottle.

'All those cats,' said Jupiter Peacock. 'How inventive.'

'Madame Valentin works in a pet shop,' said Marcel. 'So that's probably where she gets her inspiration.'

'She's completely doolally,' said Hazel. 'Has been for years.'

'In the nicest way, of course,' added Marcel. He always hated saying nasty things about people.

'But the end of the world, though . . .' mused Jupiter Peacock. 'How fascinating that would be. Imagine surviving it.'

'Yes,' said Marcel Bottle uncertainly. 'Just imagine.'

2

Euphemia Sixten Bookend Truelove, known as Effie, had been in the Otherworld since the end of school. Time worked differently there; three days in the Otherworld (they called them moons) only took 57.3 minutes of Realworld time, which meant it was always possible to slip off for a long weekend there if you had an hour to spare.

But it took M-currency – also known as lifeforce – to stay in the Otherworld. People from the Realworld couldn't store very much of it, and Effie's seemed to run out particularly quickly.

So she always had to leave too soon.

Today (in Otherworld time) Effie had woken up early in the large, comfortable bed in her lovely light room in Truelove House. This room always had fresh linen and clean towels, unlike in her Realworld home in the suburbs of the Old Town, where if Effie wanted anything cleaned she had to do it herself, and where it never got fully light at this time of year anyway. She'd looked at her watch – it told the time in both worlds – and calculated that she'd have to leave the Otherworld by early evening if she wanted any chance of being back in the Realworld in time for supper.

But there was still a whole Otherworld day to enjoy, and Effie was going to spend it in the nearby town of Froghole with her cousin Clothilde. She was sure she'd have enough lifeforce for that.

As usual, the morning was warm and bright. After eating the lavish breakfast that Bertie the maid brought for her – a massive bowl of creamy porridge with maple syrup and fourflower jam, and soft toasted muffins with peanut butter, banana, chocolate chips and marshmallows, and a pot of tea – Effie dressed in the blue silk jumpsuit that Clothilde had made her. She brushed her hair and scraped it into a slightly more tidy ponytail than usual. Then she put on the long necklace that held a vial of deepwater that her friend Maximilian kept topped up for her. She didn't have to put on the golden necklace that held her Sword of Light, because she never took it off. She'd stopped wearing her Ring of the True Hero lately, because it seemed to drain her in ways she didn't understand. She'd threaded it on a string to wear around her neck, but she usually didn't even bother with that.

Soon there came a knock at the door, and her cousin's voice. 'Are you ready?' Clothilde asked.

'Nearly,' said Effie. She took her wooden caduceus from where it was propped against the wall and used her magic to shrink it to the size of a hairpin. She admired the two snakes wrapped around it, and the wings carved into it. It had been a gift from her Otherworld cousin Rollo. She tucked it into her hair at the back. 'But do come in.'

Clothilde entered the room. She was wearing a long, flowing dress in one of the Otherworld colours that was close to what we would call yellow. It was something like summer parties and pale marzipan and the middles of soft cakes all mixed into one.

'So, are you *very* excited about going to Froghole?' Clothilde said.

'Yes,' replied Effie, grinning.

'And getting your consultation at long last?' Clothilde raised an eyebrow.

'Double yes,' said Effie. 'I mean, I don't think they're going to tell me that I'm *not* a true hero-interpreter but . . .'

'It's good to have it confirmed,' said Clothilde. 'And there's your shade, of course. I guess you'll already know all about it. I know what you're like with *The Repertory of Kharakter, Art & Shade*. You must have read it fifty times by now.' Clothilde smiled. 'Do you already know what you think you are?'

Effie shook her head. 'No. I heard that if you find out too much about the shades in advance it can distort the results of the test. So it's all still a complete mystery to me. I've saved that part of the book for after today.' She smiled. Clothilde squeezed Effie's arm gently. Effie knew how excited Clothilde was for her. It was so wonderful having someone who understood her so well.

In all the time she'd been visiting the Otherworld, Effie had still not actually been to an Otherworld town. People kept meaning to take her, but Pelham Longfellow – the other traveller who regularly visited Truelove House – was always being called away urgently to investigate 'the Diberi situation in Europe', and Clothilde couldn't leave the Great Library for very long. But today, at long last, it was finally going to happen.

'And you'll be getting your Keeper's mark as well,' said Clothilde.

'I know,' said Effie. 'I can't wait to be able to help you all in the Great Library. To be actually allowed to go in, and—'

'Oh no!' Clothilde suddenly put her hand to her mouth. 'We're supposed to do a sort of official induction in the Great Library before you get your Keeper's mark. I can't believe I forgot. I think it'll only take five minutes. We'll do it before we go. Is that all right?'

'OK,' said Effie. But somewhere nearby the sun seemed to go behind a cloud. It wasn't that Effie was scared of the Great Library exactly – she wasn't afraid of anything – but the last time she'd been in there she'd almost died.

'I'll go and get my things and wait for you downstairs,' said Clothilde.

Effie found Clothilde in the entrance hall, carrying a large wicker basket that seemed to be full of tissue paper and colourful striped boxes. Her cousin now put these down and took from around her neck the brass key that opened the Great Library.

'Ready?' asked Clothilde.

'Yes,' said Effie, frowning slightly. 'Definitely.'

'Are you sure?'

'Yes.'

'Is something wrong?'

Effie shook her head. She couldn't lie and say no out loud. She couldn't tell Clothilde about the slight headache that had just started. Was it because she was remembering what had happened last time she'd been in the Great Library? Or did it mean that she was running out of M-currency? Effie blinked and tried to put it completely out of her mind. Lexy had once told her that something between 90 percent and 100 percent of pain was in the mind. Which meant you could control it – if you knew how. The first step was not believing in it, apparently.

The wooden panelled doors to the Great Library were just underneath the large sweep of the grand staircase that went up to the gallery, where Effie's room was, and the doorway leading to the staircase to Cosmo's private study. Clothilde approached with the key. Effie gulped silently. Would it be like it had been before?

'All right,' said Clothilde. 'You first.'

'Really?' said Effie.

'We're not going very far in,' said Clothilde. 'I just want to map your version of the Great Library onto mine, so that we can go together in future. While you're being initiated it will help you to go into my version until you build up enough strength to go to your own. Eventually we'll be able to merge our versions in order to be in there together. And then you'll be able to visit your version on your own too. Does this make any kind of sense at all?'

'Yes.' Effie nodded. 'I think so.' She already knew that the Great Library was in a different dimension and in order to become real here it had to be sort of folded down into three dimensions. Everyone did this in their own way, which meant the library looked different to each person who went in. Generating the library took lots of lifeforce. That was only one of the reasons it was dangerous.

Clothilde opened the door.

'OK,' she said. 'Step inside. Just a small step. Concentrate – but not too hard. Get your brain onto the frequency you use to do magic.'

'All right,' said Effie.

'Now tell me, what do you see?'

It was the same as the last time she'd been in here. Effie described to Clothilde the small country-house library she saw in front of her, with its old-looking bookshelves and dark polished-wood floor. There was a wooden filing cabinet that held the classification system. And, of course, the books, all shelved so neatly, with their spines in dark, sober Realworld colours: red, blue, brown. Effie described the yellow wallpaper, with its faint mint-green-stripe pattern. There was a small reading table with a chair next to a window on the right-hand side. Last time Effie had been here it hadn't had a little lamp. But today there was one.

'Is it supposed to change?' Effie asked Clothilde, when she got to that bit.

'It will change a little for a while at the beginning, as you get used to it,' she said. 'It's normal. There's no need to worry unless it changes a lot. Right. Take my hand.'

Effie held Clothilde's hand. It was small, dry and soft.

'Now close your eyes. And listen. My library is similar to yours, but different. There are all the same books, for one thing: we don't get to decide that bit. But my library is arranged around a central spiral staircase. There is a gallery rather like yours, but my shelves are all around the main walls. In the middle of the room are four reading desks. They are all made of old wood – again similar to your library. Each one has a pen pot containing

16

a fountain pen and a pencil, and each one also has a little jar of peacock blue ink. And on each desk there's blotting paper . . .'

Effie saw Clothilde's library take shape in her mind. Clothilde described the turquoise and gold wallpaper and the vast paintings of various birds from the Otherworld that were all large and pink.

'Open your eyes,' said Clothilde.

When Effie did, it was Clothilde's library, not hers, that she saw. She took a step forward, but Clothilde pulled her back.

'We won't go any further today,' she said. 'I know Cosmo's already told you that what we have in here is the blueprint for all existence. There are books on geometry, physics, music theory, harmony, perspective and so on. Everything that's real has a corresponding book in here. Books can't be removed, for obvious reasons. Well, they can, but it's very unusual and . . . You probably don't need to know that bit now. New books can be put into the library, but again it's very complicated, and . . .'

Clothilde was good at many things, but explaining wasn't one of them. As she talked about something called a Wizard Quest, and the Great Ritual needed for a book to be accepted into the library, and where they put the book on the Great Split, and the problems of visualising the two different halves of the library, Effie's stomach started to grumble. So soon after such an amazing breakfast, too. This lecture about the Great Library was very interesting, but Effie was particularly looking forward to getting to Froghole and doing some shopping. And having lunch out. She wondered what she'd order. Everything that was chocolatey here was *really* chocolatey. And the marshmallows came in

17

colours that didn't exist in the Realworld, and they were much softer and sweeter . . .

'Sorry,' said Clothilde, and blushed. 'I've been babbling on and on. I've never initiated anyone before. I'm probably boring you stiff. We can do the rest next time.'

'No, it's—'

Clothilde laughed. 'You're very sweet,' she said. 'But we should go.'

'Are you sure?' said Effie.

'Yes, we've covered most of it, I think. And there's no test. You just have to learn by doing it all really. OK. Are you ready to go?'

'Yes,' said Effie. 'Absolutely.'

But as Clothilde locked the library door behind them, Effie felt weak suddenly, and strange. Was it going to be like last time all over again? She'd had to go to London, where a powerful doctor had given her golden tablets, and . . .

'Are you OK?' asked Clothilde, seeing Effie hesitate.

'Yes, fine,' she replied.

Effie was determined to remain excited. She absolutely wasn't going to ruin today by thinking about the Yearning or worrying about what happened when you ran too low on lifeforce. It would be all right. Maximilian would get some new deepwater for her when she got back. It was just . . . she *couldn't* run out of power again here. She'd had the Yearning once and it had been the most awful experience of her life. Well, except for losing her mother and her grandfather, that is.

Effie didn't understand why her lifeforce seemed to run out so quickly when she was in the Otherworld, even without

18

draining trips to the Great Library. She knew one reason was that Realworlders weren't really designed to be here. But she was a traveller, and someone had once said her energy was more Otherworld than Realworld. So what was going wrong? And the Ring of the True Hero was supposed to help, but it just seemed to make things worse. Effie used to think that it turned used-up physical energy into magical energy and that playing tennis for a long time while wearing it was the key. But recently it hadn't been working. Playing tennis just seemed to drain her as well. And she hadn't even been playing well lately. Coach Bruce kept telling Effie she had to get back in the zone, whatever that meant.

She put it all out of her mind. Her headache began to fade. Maybe it was in her imagination, like Lexy said.

'I'm all right. Let's go,' she said to Clothilde.

Back in the Realworld, in the dim silvery light of the rising moon, this almost Midwinter evening was full of slow, delicate intrigue about which most humans knew nothing. More than half the Cosmic Web was in hibernation of course, and so at this time of year those who didn't want to be seen started creeping about, safe in the knowledge that news of their activities wouldn't spread very fast.

Most people ignore the constant sounds of the animals around them: the hooting, clucking, meowing, barking, howling, baying and so on. More fool them. This, of course, is the sound of the Cosmic Web in action: it is the way that animals talk to each other, spreading all sorts of news and gossip and warnings and prophecies.

So it was that the Northern Lights were on holiday with the Bermuda Triangle, resting before the big display they always put on for the various Winter Fairs around the northern hemisphere. Even the Luminiferous Ether had given itself some much-needed days off and had gone to join them.

Later this night there would be snow. Everything would be white and everything would be very, very silent. And, just after midnight, in the basement meeting room of the Old Town University, Terrence Deer-Hart would be presenting himself for the first time to the secret meeting of the Fifteenth Order of the Diberi, originally based in Vienna but lately moved to new head-quarters in the Old Town.

Which meant he had to take special care doing his hair with his heated comb, and so he had already started, just as the moon came up, which it did so early on these last days of the year. Terrence had already given up writing for the day. He had too many flipping projects on the go and his head was spinning.

Terrence Deer-Hart was a famous children's writer who unfor-tunately hated everything about writing. He hated paper, and pens, and pencils, and words. For Terrence, even one project was one project too many. And yet here he was with three different flipping piles of paper on his desk, each in its own different way thin and pathetic and ridiculous.

The nearest pile was the beginning of his first novel for adults. Now that he was allowed to swear as much as he liked, and write without limit about violence and kissing, he suddenly didn't want to. He had only got three pages in, although he'd been telling everyone it was going to be a great epic with multiple volumes.

The second pile looked like a school project that had been left on the bus, damaged by rain and half-chewed by a dog. A lot of work and thought had gone into it, and it interested Terrence far more than his novel. These pages formed Terrence's dossier on the children who'd killed his beloved Skylurian Midzhar. They had buried her alive, the flipping brutes! Terrence was intending to get revenge, but as he was very afraid of blood, and violence, and, if we're honest, children, he was relying on the Fifteenth Order of the Diberi to get his revenge for him. That was one of the main reasons he intended to join them. They were properly evil, and would be able to come up with a suitable death for each one of the revolting brats who had been involved with dear Skylurian's death. Sadly, whenever Terrence tried to think of, say, boiling Effie Truelove alive, he got a migraine.

Anyway, their names and addresses were all here. Euphemia Truelove. Alexa Bottle. Raven Wilde. Maximilian Underwood. Wolf Reed. Terrence had already given a copy to the Diberi, who had been pleased, as it turned out they were looking for children to use in some kind of evil spell. Was one of the children to be sacrificed somehow? Maybe on Midwinter's Eve? Terrence couldn't quite remember.

Terrence ran the heated comb through his dense curls and tried to think himself into his third project, the one Lady Tchainsaw had said would be a work of immense genius. He quite liked Lady Tchainsaw. You couldn't always tell what poets meant, especially not when they were Russian, but she had come quite close to him – close enough that he could smell her perfume, the top notes of which were dead things and violets – and whispered straight into his ear. What she had said sounded something like, 'Your abundant locks, they are so beautiful, darlink.'

Then she had asked him to write the blueprint for a whole new universe.

This was the project Terrence was having most trouble with. Given that he couldn't even manage to get going on his epic adventure for adults, how the flip was he supposed to author an entire universe? He just couldn't face it today.

So once he'd finished his hair, he began changing slowly into the special outfit the Diberi had given him: a dangerously tight yellow jumpsuit with a small red cape. Did this ensemble suit him? It did not. It did not make him feel remotely diabolical or magical. It made him feel like something from early evening Saturday night TV shows from the olden days.

And he was ready five hours too early, like some kind of flipping teenager attending their first flipping ball. Still, once he was part of the Diberi, everything was going to be different. Terrence would be officially evil! In return for his initiation, and for promising to kill the children, Terrence would give the Diberi all the information he had on the location of Dragon's Green, in which they had seemed extremely interested.

Then, somehow, the Diberi were going to take control of the entire universe. And Terrence, once a mere children's writer snubbed by big prize juries and reviewers despite selling millions of copies of his books, was going to be the author of this universe. If only he could get started on the flipping thing.

How did you write a whole universe? Lady Tchainsaw had given him some tips, as had Professor Gotthard Forestfloor. The main thing, they'd told him, was that this universe had to depict only the Realworld, and that this world should be extremely magical and controlled by the Diberi. There was to be no Otherworld. They'd both been very insistent about that.

'Write the Otherworld out of existence, *darlink,*' Lady Tchainsaw had said, 'and you will be celebrated for ever.'

Being celebrated for ever sounded quite nice, and Lady Tchainsaw was very pretty, in a harsh sort of way. Terrence already knew he was going to do everything she told him.

3

Just as Clothilde was about to open the door there was a small scuffling noise and then the sound of Bertie's familiar soft voice.

'I thought perhaps you girls might want to use this,' she said.

Clothilde and Effie turned. In her arms Bertie was holding the most beautiful rug Effie had ever seen. It had been carefully woven in soft Otherworld yarns, and its unusual colours were interspersed with gold, turquoise and pink. It looked both brand new and a million years old. From the way Bertie was holding it, it seemed a lot more important than other rugs.

Clothilde gasped and put down her basket.

'You didn't!' she said. 'How long have you been working on this?'

'Oh, only the last year or so,' said Bertie shyly. 'I had a fancy that you could be using one, especially when I heard you had plans to take the young one out more often. Do you like it?'

'Like it!' said Clothilde. 'Oh, Bertie, I simply adore it! But it must have taken you much longer than a year. It's exquisite. Look at all the perfect little stitches. Did you do it all on your own?'

'I did,' said Bertie, nodding proudly. 'Course, it was the magic that took the longest. But anyway, now it should be fully charged with around a hundred or so moons of flying time. That'll be enough to last a good long while. When it starts to wane, bring it back to me and I'll recharge it for you.'

'A flying carpet?' said Effie.

Clothilde nodded. 'Yes, made especially for us! Isn't Bertie magnificent?'

'Absolutely!' said Effie, grinning. 'Can we try it out now?'

'Of course,' said Clothilde. 'I might just go and get my— Hold this!'

Clothilde gave Effie the rug and ran lightly up the stairs. When she returned she was wearing a necklace with a large shiny green gemstone in it.

'What's that?' Effie asked.

'Greenstone,' said Clothilde. 'Perhaps you call it jade, or *pounamu*.' She touched it, and it almost seemed to glow.

'Is it a boon?' asked Effie.

'Yes,' said Clothilde. 'I hardly ever get to use all my explorer boons, because I so rarely go out. I mean, I do use them in the Great Library but that's in quite a different way and . . .' She blushed. 'I've always dreamed of having my own magic carpet. Only explorers can fly them, you see.'

'I didn't know you were an explorer,' said Effie. 'Why didn't you tell me?'

Effie had gone through a phase of being quite obsessed with everyone's *kharakter* and art. She'd quizzed all members of the

25

Truelove household – including Bertie and the gardeners – and knew that Rollo, Clothilde's brother, was a scholar engineer and Pelham Longfellow was a hunter witch. Bertie was an elysian hedgewitch. Cosmo was a wizard, of course, which meant he was now every *kharakter* and art at once, but Effie had got him to tell her about his time as a young cleric guide. Her cousin, however, had always found some way of avoiding having this conversation with Effie.

Clothilde shrugged. 'Everyone laughs when I tell them I'm an explorer because all I do is stay at home. And my art is elysian, which no one really understands, and some people even find quite funny. Elysians give pleasure to others, you see, but they also like pleasurable things themselves, and so people worry they'll become lazy and self-centred, which is obviously a terrible thing. When we were young, Rollo said I was useless, that I'd never be any good as a Keeper. Once he said that all I was good for was making chocolates and helping in the kitchen. And that one day I'd be so fat I wouldn't be able to leave the house!' Clothilde laughed at the end of all this. But Effie could tell that she hadn't always found it amusing. Perhaps she didn't even now.

'He was such a cruel child. He's a lot better now,' added Bertie.

'Anyway,' said Clothilde brightly. 'We mustn't hang around here all day! We've got a magic carpet to try out.'

'Here's a little something for the child, too,' said Bertie, holding out another package. This one was wrapped in turquoise tissue paper. 'In case it's cold up there.'

Effie took the package from Bertie and unwrapped it. Inside was a beautiful, shimmering light gold cloak, much finer and softer than Effie's heavy school cape, which had come from the second-hand basket and had always smelled of whisky and moth-balls. This gold cloak smelled of flower petals and clear blue skies. It had a large, loose hood and two patch pockets. It did up with a big gold button at the neck.

'I believe all the young girls in the towns have them,' said Bertie, 'so you won't look out of place.'

'You're so kind,' said Clothilde, touching Bertie's arm gently.

Bertie seemed embarrassed. 'Right, well,' she said, 'the cakes won't make themselves. Will you both be back for your afternoon tea?'

'I don't know,' said Clothilde. 'We'll try. We're definitely out for lunch, though. Pelham's booked Anastasia's. We're meeting him there later.'

'My my! You girls won't be needing any tea after that. But I'll save you some anyway, just in case,' said Bertie. 'Good luck with the carpet!'

'Thank you,' said Clothilde.

Effie followed Clothilde out of the front door of Truelove House and all the way down to the guarded gates.

'You can't arrive or leave without going through them,' Clothilde explained. 'Otherwise our enemies would be arriving on magic carpets all the time.'

But once they were through the gates, Clothilde unrolled the carpet and put it down on the warm, dusty pavement.

'Now,' she said, 'I last practised this a few years ago, so . . .'

She seemed to be using her hands to pull the rug up into the air via an invisible force. Effie didn't say anything while this was going on. She understood now that magic needed your whole concentration. She'd been practising quite a lot lately.

27

Clothilde soon got the carpet to rise up into the air. She and Effie got onto it. Immediately it seemed so much bigger than it had on the ground.

'OK,' said Clothilde. 'Try not to fall off!'

'I will,' said Effie.

'Probably best to lie on your front. That way you can look over the edge and see the view, but I can hold on to you if it gets bumpy.'

'Bumpy?'

'Air currents,' said Clothilde. 'They're quite safe. Well, sort of. Ready?'

'Of course,' said Effie.

Apart from a couple of jolts when the air current changed as they flew over a large blue lake, it was a completely smooth ride. Effie felt that she could have stayed on the magic carpet for ever. It went pretty fast, but you could still see everything perfectly laid out beneath you. There were forests with little cottages in them, and two large castles.

Effie had only been in an aeroplane once, and this was completely different from that. It felt a bit like how she imagined it might feel to be a bird. Waves of air lifted the carpet gently in little steady puffs. Soon there were more normal-looking houses below, and Effie could see people walking down wide, tree-lined streets. Then, suddenly, at the base of a hill, began the thick, white stone wall that seemed to hold in the vast number of brightly coloured shops, houses, bazaars, markets, people, carriages, animals and complex passageways that made up the higgledy-piggledy town of Froghole. At the top of the hill was a castle covered in masses of tumbling pink flowers.

'We can land in Anastasia's courtyard,' said Clothilde. 'We'll get a drink while we're there and store the carpet in their cloak-room until later. Right, hold on!'

Landing was quite a complex procedure, made even more complicated by the sheer amount of things in the air above the town. As well as the many people on carpets, broomsticks and flying bicycles, there were also a number of miniature flying dragons, cats with wings, pink parakeets, hummingbirds and large glowing insects. Effie tried to be quiet while Clothilde navigated her way down.

Everything was so lovely. One shop was displaying golden urns in a pleasing jumble just outside its blue wooden door; another had hardback books with the most handsome covers; another had the most intricate, ornate cakes. Everything sparkled. Above one of the shops a long-haired man on a balcony played the saxophone as if he had been paid to do it for the entertainment of everyone below. It was the most pleasant sound Effie had ever heard.

Down in the streets there were all different kinds of people: old, young, fat, thin, male, female and everything in between. Most of them were a sort of light brown colour, but some were very pale white and others almost completely black. A few – Effie had to look twice to check she wasn't seeing things – had extremely well-groomed fur. On closer inspection, Effie realised that several of them also had elegant-looking tails. And quite a few had small pointed cat's ears, rabbit's ears or whiskers. One man seemed to have a variety of small flowering shrubs growing out of one of his arms. It was like a complicated tattoo, but real. Everyone, without exception, was extremely beautiful.

Effie saw some girls about her own age standing in a group by a fountain at the end of the road. They all had animal ears of one sort or another, almost as if it were the height of fashion. Maybe it was. They were wearing capes a bit like hers, but theirs were white and tied with ribbons of different colours. Effie suddenly felt as if she might stand out in her gold cape, with her decidedly human ears.

Clothilde landed the carpet expertly on a sort of landing pad in the courtyard of Anastasia's café. No one seemed at all surprised to see a magic carpet landing. The people sitting at the courtyard tables were drinking cups of thick dark coffee or hot chocolate, or sipping pink, white or mint-green drinks through paper straws. Every table had a bunch of flowers in its centre. There were flowers everywhere, scrambling over the walls wherever Effie looked. She watched one of the large, plump insects go right inside one bell-shaped flower and then have to wriggle out backwards. Everything smelled heavenly.

'So,' said Clothilde, smiling, 'do you want a fourflower tea or a nut-cream frappé before we – as I think you might put it in your world – hit the shops?'

'What's a nut-cream frappé?'

'It's sort of cold chocolate milk with edible flowers. They make the milk from nuts and then put whipped nut cream on the top.'

'I'd love one of those,' said Effie.

She sat down at a table with Clothilde, who ordered two large frappés and some macarons.

'The macarons here are probably the best in the whole world,' said Clothilde, when they arrived. 'They're made from a very ancient blend of aquafaba and magic.'

Effie had never tasted anything like them. They w
round filled meringues in every possible colour, includi
not seen in the Realworld for many years, and each o
sprinkled with edible gold and rose petals. Effie chose a yellow
one. When she bit into it she found it tasted a bit like banana
and custard, and the white cream filling tasted of chocolate and
vanilla. The most delicious things Effie had ever eaten had been
in the Otherworld, but this was the nicest of them all. She immediately ate another one, and then another.

'Save room for some lunch,' giggled Clothilde.

As usual in the Otherworld, they didn't pay. Effie noticed
how happy the waitress looked when Clothilde thanked her and
complimented her on the food and the service. Effie realised that
even Otherworld waitresses were very different from the ones
at home. This young woman was wearing a pristine white linen
apron over a soft black velvet playsuit and her hair was in perfect
blonde ringlets. Effie noticed that she had a single blue flower
growing out of one of her eyebrows. She had the air of someone
doing her dream job.

'I always love meeting other elysians,' said Clothilde. 'It's just
so nice to get out, don't you think? I love meeting new people.
Oh, it's all so exciting! I'm so glad we came, aren't you?'

'Yes,' said Effie, trying her best to ignore the fact that her
headache had begun to develop again. It wouldn't be long before
they were back, and she'd be able to go home and recharge.
Maybe she just needed more food? Effie ate another macaron
and told herself everything would be all right.

After rugby practice, Wolf went straight to Leonard Levar's Antiquarian Bookshop. He didn't exactly think of it as *his* bookshop yet, even though he held the only set of keys. At some point he would need to call a meeting with his friends and tell them about how he'd been using it. But no one had asked, and so it wasn't as if he'd lied. He just hadn't said anything.

He'd been hoping to keep it a secret from the entire world, but that was difficult, given that the bookshop was on one of the main streets in the Old Town. The blinds were down most of the time, and he'd tried to disguise his comings and goings, but it wasn't long before the neighbours began asking what was happening. Or, to be more specific, one neighbour in particular.

Monsieur Valentin was quite old – at least fifty – and French. He always wore green corduroy trousers, for which he was a bit too tall, and walked with enormous strides even in a small place like the bookshop. He had a short, unkempt beard and smelled strongly of onions and kittens. If you think that kittens do not smell of anything, you have clearly never owned a pet shop. Monsieur Valentin did not exactly own the pet shop, however; he just lived in it. The Exotic Pet Emporium belonged to his wife. He did the accounts and worked, when he could, as a theatrical director, a profession in decreasing demand these days in the Old Town.

'And you are habsolutely sure you are 'ees nephew?' Monsieur Valentin was saying to Wolf. 'And you say you are looking after 'ees shop until 'ee comes back from Hantarctica? Mmm. I am beginning to hunderstand. But surely 'ee would 'av told you of our harrangement?'

Monsieur Valentin had a habit of leaving *H*s off the start of

32

words that required them, and then adding the spare ones freely to words that did not.

'No, he didn't say anything,' said Wolf. 'He . . .' Wolf did not find it easy to lie; he never had. But of course he couldn't tell Monsieur Valentin what had really happened to Leonard Levar, or how Wolf had ended up with the keys to his bookshop, as well as all his other property and money.

''Ee lets me borrow any of 'ees books I like,' said Monsieur Valentin. 'For my programme of self-himprovement. 'Ee some-times borrows hanimals from my wife's shop in return. You are of course welcome to do the same, as long as you return them hun'armed . . .'

'No,' said Wolf quickly. 'I won't need any animals.'

'Well, I need my books,' said Monsieur Valentin. 'When did you say your huncle would be returning?'

'I don't know,' said Wolf. 'Not for a long time.'

'And you are sleeping on this camp-bed, I see.'

Monsieur Valentin started walking around the shop, the slightly flared bottoms of his green corduroy trousers flapping around his long legs as he did so. He only needed to take three steps to cover the whole area, then he came back. Wolf hoped he'd stop, but he didn't. He started again, this time looking at things.

At some point Wolf would also need to tell Effie what had happened to her grandfather's old flat. He wished he hadn't had to leave. Until two weeks ago, Wolf had been secretly living in it, and had held what he'd thought were the only set of keys (and, indeed, the deeds to the whole building, which he'd found in a filing cabinet in Leonard Levar's bookshop). But then a tall

American woman had turned up while Wolf had been at school and moved in. Just like that.

Miss Dora Wright, who had once been Wolf's teacher, and had lived below Effie's grandfather, had returned to the flat below at exactly the same time. So Wolf had moved permanently into the bookshop. He was never going back to his cruel uncle, so he had no choice. He certainly couldn't risk adults or teachers finding out he was living on his own, or they'd probably put him in care. And now here was this annoying French neighbour asking him questions for the second time that week.

'What is this?' Monsieur Valentin asked Wolf.

He'd discovered Wolf's notebook open on his bed and had picked it up. Wolf rushed over and took it from him. He closed it.

'Nothing.'

'Nothing? Hah. I see you are also hinterested in the self-himprovement.' He winked, and as he did so his beard seemed to crawl halfway up his face, like a creature desperate to escape.

How much of the notebook had Monsieur Valentin seen? Adults could be so nosey. Wolf kept all his lists in the notebook, and he made a lot of lists. They were all very private.

In the notebook, Wolf had a five-year plan, a list of goals for this year, a list of targets for each week, and a To Do list and a Training Plan for every single day since he'd moved in here (which was when he'd found the notebook, unused and dusty, on the desk). Every morning and every evening Wolf did fifty press-ups, fifty sit-ups, fifteen pull-ups (there was a convenient old beam for this) and three one-minute planks. He did sets of bicep curls and triceps dips and one-arm rows, using big books

34

– the Bible and the Koran worked well – as weights. Every morning he ran two miles around the quiet streets of the Old Town.

Wolf's list of MAJOR LIFE GOALS, which was written out neatly on the first page of the notebook, went as follows:

1. FIND NATASHA
2. DEFEAT THE DIBERI
3. BE A GOOD FRIEND TO EFFIE, LEXY, RAVEN AND MAX AND PROTECT THEM FROM DANGER
4. GET TO THE OTHERWORLD
5. BECOME A PROFESSIONAL RUGBY PLAYER AND/OR A MAGICAL SOLDIER OF SOME SORT

Natasha was Wolf's younger sister. He had no idea where she was, or what she even looked like. All he knew was that she was around nine years old, probably even ten by now. His mother had taken her when she'd left Wolf's father many years before, and Wolf hadn't seen her since then. But now Wolf was going to find her and give her a good life. In order to do that, he needed to be strong, and he needed to be prepared.

And he needed to keep what he was doing a secret.

'You do a lot of hexercise,' commented Monsieur Valentin. 'You seem like a tough boy, no? I wonder what you are doing, then, in a bookshop. Although I see you 'ave already removed all the major volumes that deal with war.'

It was true. Wolf had been digging through Leonard Levar's extensive collection of books on Napoleon, as well as reading Sun Tzu's *The Art of War*, and anything else with the word 'war' in the title, and anything with pictures of battles on the front. He'd read the *Bhagavad Gita, How to Use Your Enemies* and the *Tao Te Ching*.

'And a lot of philosophy. What a strange boy you must be. I still think there is something hodd about you being 'ere, but I will hoverlook this for now, as long as you don't mind me taking a few books. You can tell your huncle that I will return them as halways.'

'OK,' said Wolf.

He wasn't going to argue. He needed somewhere safe for Natasha to live, once he found her, and since he'd lost the flat this would have to do. It was awkward, though, having Monsieur Valentin prowling around. Wolf would have to find some subtle way of stopping it happening. Perhaps using advice from Machiavelli or another great strategist. Leonard Levar's Antiquarian Bookshop was a very useful resource, and Wolf wasn't going to give it up in a hurry. It had a connected phone that sometimes worked, and an ancient computer on which Wolf could call up BBS pages, although nowadays these usually crashed after about ten seconds. But he'd found some useful numbers to call about Natasha.

There was also a good supply of paper, envelopes and stamps for writing to Official Records in London. Wolf had also found an extremely ancient microfiche system and various collections of plastic slides, many of which were creepy but fascinating, with titles like 'Records of Lost Children' and 'Missing Orphans of the North'.

It turned out that lots of children went missing every year, and Leonard Levar had taken an unhealthily detailed interest in many of them. There were examples of children lost at sea, children lost on the moors, children lost in Quirin Forest, children who had been kidnapped by strangers or (more commonly) deranged family members, and a small but significant number of children who'd never returned from the Blessed Bartolo entrance exam.

The one thing all the missing children had in common was that someone had actually gone to the trouble to report their disappearance. No one had reported Natasha missing. But she had definitely gone. Wolf had been in touch with every school in the district, and not one of them had a Natasha Reed. Only one of them even had a Natasha, and she was the wrong age. Wolf's mother must have taken her a long way away. But why? And where?

''Ere you go,' said Monsieur Valentin, returning from the back of the shop. He dropped a large, well-thumbed paperback on the desk. 'This will get your tough little brain going. You can thank me later.'

The book was called *The Answer*. It was not unfamiliar. Wolf had seen it before in the Military Strategy section. It frightened him in some way, although it was impossible to say what this was. He'd read much more frightening-looking books, after all. He'd even dipped into the massive books he used as weights, and they were both terrifying in their own ways.

Monsieur Valentin was holding three dusty hardbacks. Wolf couldn't quite see what they were, but one seemed to be called *Preventing Apocalypse*, and another was called something like *Home Remedies for a Malfunctioning Crystal Ball*. But perhaps Wolf had read it wrong. It had been upside down, after all.

The door tinkled and Monsieur Valentin was gone. Only a slight smell of onions and kittens remained.

Wolf blew out most of the candle-lamps and found a book of hard Sudoku puzzles to take to bed with him. Great warriors needed to train their minds, too. And he found Sudoku strangely comforting.

4

After she had eaten the last of the macarons, Effie followed Clothilde into the street. The saxophone still played above them, the musician seemingly lost in bar after bar of the smoothest jazz. The sun shone, but didn't feel too hot. A man came out of one of the shops with several small dragons on his arm. They clucked and hooted and whistled. Their eyes were all silver or gold.

'Flying dragon?' he said to Effie. 'I got a rare albino here if you want it.'

Effie gulped. Imagine actually owning a flying dragon! But they were probably very expensive. And not something she could easily take back to the Realworld with her either.

'Or how about a nice cake, luvvie?' offered a woman with black curly hair, coming out of the cake shop. 'I got the softest, densest, most delicious chocolate cake you've ever had, with a fresh cashew cream filling. Or maybe you'd like an iced bun? A fourflower horn? Oh, what about a nice big slice of *flan Parisien*?

Made it just this morning, I did, with silken cloudcurd and fresh vanilla. Bright blessings to you anyway, child.'

'Are you interested in *kharakter* studies?' asked a stout man coming out from another shop. 'You must be, as you're an interpreter. Oh yes, I can tell from the caduceus in your hair. I've got a very wide selection of books and charts on *kharakter*, art and shade in my basement. Any of them is yours if you want it . . .'

Effie looked around her. One shop was full of silver and turquoise jewellery. Another sold dark wooden violins. Another sold fountain pens. A dark little basement shop sold strange-looking pamphlets and a bright boutique sold capes in holographic colours. One shop was full of aventurine, bloodstone, onyx and every other kind of gemstone. Lexy would love it here, Effie thought. Something flapped past Effie's head. Another flying dragon. And then a little pack of white fluffy kittens ran down the narrow cobbled street. No; they weren't kittens. They were an animal Effie had never seen before.

Clothilde had said something to Effie, but she hadn't been listening properly. Something about going upstairs to see the saxophonist perhaps? She'd gone, anyway. Before Effie knew it, she had accepted a box containing two fourflower horns and a slice of *flan Parisien*, as well as a brand new copy of *The Repertory of Kharakter, Art & Shade*, three notebooks, a silver bracelet with turquoise charms hanging from it (a dragon, a cat and a moon) and, finally, a new fountain pen.

'Did you lose your pen?' said Clothilde, coming out of a door to the side of the bookshop just as Effie thanked the shopkeeper again.

'No,' said Effie. 'Of course not.' She felt bad suddenly, because

Clothilde had got her a lovely fountain pen not long ago. 'I liked this one, though, and they always say you can't have too many pens. And everything is free here, after all.' It was true. No one had asked for any money. And each shopkeeper had seemed very pleased when Effie had chosen something to take from them. She'd very nearly ended up with a dragon as well.

Clothilde frowned, which was unusual for her.

'Well, don't get so many things that you can't carry them home,' she said. 'And be careful. You don't have as much lifeforce as we do. When I said "hit the shops" I meant a little more gently. Most people only take one thing home with them from a shopping trip like this. One special thing that they really need, and don't already have.'

Before Effie had a chance to ask her what she meant about lifeforce, the little door opened and the saxophonist came out. He was holding a striped box with its lid off. He had a single white flower growing out of his top lip, and his eyes were a deep shade of green, one that Effie had never seen before. He was definitely a man, but seemed quite feminine. Effie realised it was because he was wearing electric blue eyeshadow and black eye liner. And his ears! His ears had fur on them! But they were also studded with many tiny diamonds. He was a like a man-woman-cat.

'These are so beautiful,' he said to Clothilde, taking a pair of hand-knitted red woollen socks from inside the box. 'Thank you.'

Clothilde often knitted in front of the fire in the evenings, creating long soft scarves or complex-looking socks using four needles at once.

'Well, thank you for the music,' said Clothilde. 'We all enjoy it so much.'

'Not that you come to hear it very often,' he said.

'I know,' said Clothilde, sighing.

'And who's your friend?' said the man, looking at Effie.

'Oh, sorry!' said Clothilde. 'This is my cousin Effie. And Effie, this is Bo.'

'From the island, I see,' said Bo. 'How *exotic*.'

The way he said this wasn't entirely friendly, although he gave Effie a big smile afterwards. Effie already knew that some Otherworld people were very suspicious of her world, which they always referred to as 'the island'. They called their own world the mainland.

'She's not a typical islander, I promise,' said Clothilde.

'What does she make?' said Bo. 'What do you do?' he asked Effie.

Effie didn't quite understand, so she simply said, 'Oh, I'm still at school,' which didn't seem to answer his question at all.

Clothilde said her goodbyes, and she and Effie walked off down the street. Effie soon became aware that although everyone was friendly and offered her beautiful, free things, quite a lot of people avoided catching her eye. More than once she heard someone whisper something like 'From the island, you can tell!' or 'Islander!' just after she'd passed. People looked her up and down without even disguising what they were doing. A few of the windows had posters in them calling for 'Mainland Liberation', whatever that was.

Soon they came to the fountain where the group of teenage girls was still standing. They all turned to look at Effie. Clearly, no one had ever told them it was rude to stare. Mind you, it was hard for Effie not to stare right back. The girls were so incredibly beautiful. Clothilde got another one of her striped boxes out of her basket and told Effie she'd just be a moment. She walked off to a house beyond the fountain.

'Hello,' said Effie to the girls, who were still staring at her.

'*Allora*,' said one girl to another, raising an eyebrow. '*Un estraneo*.'

It was a language that Effie didn't immediately recognise. Effie was fluent in Rosian, and if she needed to understand any other languages she just had to hold her caduceus. Effie was just reaching into her hair for it when the girl switched to Rosian.

'Who are you?' she said to Effie. She had long, straight, blue hair and sharp, thin limbs. Her pointed cat's ears were white.

'Effie,' said Effie.

'Why are you wearing a gold cloak?' said a girl with pink curly hair and a flying dragon on her shoulder. This girl was much rounder than the first one. Her body was covered with a layer of the most beautiful pale fur.

'Um . . .'

'And aren't you supposed to *die* if you come here from the island?' said the first girl.

'We'd die instantly if we went to your world, because it's *really* horrible and *really* dangerous and your air is completely toxic to us.'

Slowly, the group gathered around Effie.

'I don't like the cloak,' said the girl with the pink hair.

'Me neither,' said a girl with yellow eyes.

'It's from thousands of moons ago,' said the first girl.

43

'I see she's done a lot of shopping,' said the girl with the blue hair. 'It's just like what they say about the island. They're all so greedy.'

'They never do anything for anyone else. They just take,' said the girl with pink hair. The dragon on the girl's shoulder sort of nodded, as if it agreed with everything she was saying.

Effie felt like crying. Wasn't everyone in the Otherworld supposed to be nice? But of course she'd hardly been anywhere in the Otherworld and knew barely anything about it. Her headache intensified. And her arms started to ache from carrying all her wonderful free things. She felt like a complete idiot standing there in her gold cloak, unable to put anything down. She wanted to run away. But Effie never ran away.

'We might be greedy on the island,' she found herself saying, 'but at least we don't all look the same.'

'You think we look the *same*?' said the girl with yellow eyes. 'How? We're all completely different.'

'Yes, do go on,' said the girl with the blue hair. 'How? We're just dying to hear how someone from the *island* would choose to judge us.'

'Your cloaks,' Effie said. 'They're all the same colour.'

'That's because it's our school uniform, you jar of cloudcurd,' said the girl with the dragon.

Somewhere nearby a bell tinkled and the girls turned and left, their long, pastel-coloured hair swishing behind them. Effie realised that she would have loved to have been friends with them, but that was never going to happen now. They all hated her. Effie wondered how to explain to Clothilde what had happened, and how sad she felt, but she didn't have to.

44

'Were they very blunt?' said Clothilde when she came back. 'Teenage girls here are encouraged to say exactly what they think without holding anything in. They can be a bit too honest sometimes.'

Effie didn't say anything.

'Right,' said Clothilde. 'Time for your *kharakter* analysis. Are you excited?'

Effie nodded. 'Yes,' she said. She still had an awkward feeling inside from her encounter with the girls, but that faded as she followed Clothilde down a thin cobbled lane and up some stone steps until they reached a large brown wooden door in the wall with pink flowers growing out of a large pot next to it. A tiny brass sign said: *Consultations*.

'Do you want me to come in?' asked Clothilde.

'Not if you've got something else to do,' said Effie. 'I'll be all right.'

'OK. I'll be back for you in an hour, then,' said Clothilde. She squeezed Effie's hand. 'Good luck. Oh, and let me look after all these.' Clothilde took Effie's shopping from her and arranged it expertly in her basket. Effie felt a lot lighter, suddenly.

She slowly pushed the door, which made a small bell ring gently. Inside, the large, cool house smelled very faintly of roses, wood and warm spices. There was a tiled hallway leading to a reception desk. The receptionist smiled at Effie and led her through a courtyard to a consulting room lined with bookshelves and filled with old-looking books. It also had a desk, a chair, and a view out onto the courtyard. Effie watched as a flying dragon stretched its wings on a window ledge.

'Here's the test,' said the receptionist. 'The consultant will be

45

with you in fifteen minutes. You're seeing . . .' She looked at her clipboard. 'Dr Wiseacre. She's new. But very good.'

Effie had done this test before, but in quite different circumstances. This version had some extra sections. Of course, there was no doubt about Effie's *kharakter* – true hero – and her art – interpreter. She had boons to match those. But the main thing that needed to be decided now was her shade. One of the extra sections had pairs of statements, with instructions asking you to put a cross next to the one that described you best. Effie confidently chose statements like *I will always help my friends* and *I will always fight my enemies*.

She finished filling in the paper test and waited for Dr Wiseacre to arrive. On the wall she saw a big chart that looked vaguely familiar. Yes – it was the map of the shades that she'd seen in *The Repertory of Kharakter, Art & Shade* but had not let herself look at too closely.

The chart had a circle painted on vellum in faded but attractive Otherworld colours, close to the pinks and purples Effie knew from home. It was like a clock face, with the number 12 at the top, and the number 6 at the bottom. By the number twelve were the letters *Ph*. At two o'clock were the letters *Ae*. At four o'clock the letters were *Ar*, at six o'clock the letters were *Pr*, at eight o'clock there was simply the letter *G*, which somehow looked bigger and more menacing than the others. Then at ten o'clock was the letter *S*.

Soon the door opened and Dr Wiseacre came in. She was young and had something about her that reminded Effie of the schoolgirls she'd met before, although her ears were only slightly pointed. Her eyes were very big and very green, and her hair was short and black. Her eyebrows were finely shaped and pink.

'Greetings and blessings, young hero,' said Dr Wiseacre.

'Greetings and blessings returned,' said Effie, remembering how to politely greet people in the Otherworld.

Dr Wiseacre picked up the test Effie had completed and looked at it hard, nodding here and there, and then frowning before smiling and then frowning again.

'Right,' she said. 'I just have a few more questions. First of all, can you tell me about your trip to Froghole today? What happened before you came here? Did you speak to anyone or do any shopping, for example?'

Effie told Dr Wiseacre all about her morning.

'You came here on a flying carpet?' said Dr Wiseacre, smiling.

'Yes,' said Effie. 'Our maid Bertie made it.'

'Your maid?' Dr Wiseacre looked confused, as if she'd never heard the word before. 'Oh,' she said eventually, 'do you mean like a servant?'

'Yes,' said Effie. 'And she made me this cloak as well.'

'Very nice,' said Dr Wiseacre, looking Effie up and down. 'Now tell me something of your life on the island. It sounds like a very fascinating place. I've never been. I am not a traveller, sadly, so it would kill me.'

Effie told Dr Wiseacre about her life back home. She couldn't help making it sound a bit miserable, though, what with her step-mother Cait and her constant diets, and her father Orwell with his long days working at the university. The family virtually lived on takeaway because Cait was always throwing out all the real food. Effie far preferred the Otherworld, and started talking

47

about that, but Dr Wiseacre steered her back to her life on the island.

Effie told Dr Wiseacre about the Tusitala School for the Gifted, Troubled and Strange, with its leaking roof and strange cruel-but-kind teachers. She talked about how she was captain of the Under 13 tennis team, and her friend Wolf was captain of the Under 13 rugby team. As they were both only eleven, this was quite an achievement; but then they did have quite a lot of magical strength to draw on, since Wolf was a warrior and Effie was a hero. Effie told Dr Wiseacre about her other friends – Lexy, the healer, Raven, the witch, and Maximilian, the mage-scholar.

'We're all going to help out next week at the university,' said Effie. 'Actually, I've got to go in this weekend to help my dad set up for the Winter Fair. But he's giving me some pocket money for that, which is good. Then next week I'm going to be in the Creative Writing Department with my friends. Which is better than the rest of my class, who are stuck helping children from the Mrs Joyful School do papier-mâché or learn to knit and cook and develop "life skills".'

'Tell me more about this Mrs Joyful School,' said Dr Wiseacre. 'It sounds delightful.' She raised a pink eyebrow.

'I promise you, it's not,' said Effie, smiling. She told Dr Wiseacre about how rough it was there, with all the impoverished children who couldn't even afford lunch and ate sweets instead and then beat each other up. She would have gone there herself had she not passed the test to get into the Tusitala School.

Effie found herself talking in a way that didn't quite sound like her, but she didn't seem able to stop doing it. It was partly because of the way Dr Wiseacre responded, smiling and laughing when Effie complained about something at home. And everyone here hated the Realworld, it seemed, so Effie found herself playing up to it and making it sound much worse than it really was. She felt like an Otherworlder – a mainlander – at heart and always had done. If that meant hating the island as much as they all did then she could do it.

She could maybe also get a pet dragon, and dye her hair blue, and try to grow a cat's tail and ears, and perhaps just have a single pink flower growing out of the back of one of her hands . . .

'All right, Effie, thank you,' said Dr Wiseacre. 'We should probably start to review everything now. You're quite right that you are a true hero and an interpreter. That's all confirmed now. Quite an unusual combination, especially here. So all that remains is the matter of your shade. Tell me, what do you know about the shades?'

'Not very much,' said Effie. 'I've got a book with a chapter on the shades, but I didn't read it because I didn't want to influence my result.'

'So, do you even know what the six shades are?'

'Philosopher?' said Effie. 'That's the one at the top?'

'That's right. Go on.'

'Then . . . No. I've forgotten. I've been saving it up to read after this, so I've only ever glanced at the picture really. Sorry. Oh – protector is at the bottom of the circle, I think?'

'Yes. You'll have noticed it's structured as a clock face. It's *Philosopher* at twelve o'clock, then *Aesthete* at two o'clock, *Artisan* at four o'clock, *Protector* at six o'clock, *Galloglass* at eight o'clock, and *Shaper* at ten o'clock. They all merge into one another in different directions, but mainly clockwise and anti-clockwise. Where do you think you might go on the clock?'

'I'm not sure,' said Effie. 'I don't know enough about what each shade does.'

'It's not really about what they "do". The *kharakters* concern what you do. But the shade tells you *why* you do it. Everyone is a blend of all six shades, but most people fall between two shades in particular. It's up to them to develop themselves in one direction or another. Philosophers ask the big questions about life. Aesthetes prioritise beauty. Artisans create useful things. Protectors keep things safe. Galloglasses, well, we don't have any of them here. We expel any that we find. They are individualists who act for their own profit – completely out of place here on the mainland. Shapers are people who change things. Obviously we prefer shapers who end up on the philosopher side than the galloglass side. Any questions?'

'No,' said Effie. 'Well, actually, what are you?'

'I'm between shaper and artisan.'

'But they're not next to one another, are they?'

Dr Wiseacre sighed. 'You're observant, aren't you? It's far too complex to get into now, but it's possible in rare cases to move across, rather than around, the circle.'

'Oh. That sounds interesting.'

'It is. Now, any more thoughts on what you might be?'

'Probably a protector. I mean, I want to defend Dragon's Green and my friends and . . . But I don't really make things, so that must mean I'm going towards philosopher rather than artisan? I do think a lot about how the world works.'

'Interesting. Not many philosophers left on the island, so it's fairly unlikely. And, as I said, it's extremely rare to move across the circle.' Dr Wiseacre got up. 'I need to go and consult with a colleague. I'll be back in a few minutes.'

While she was gone Effie looked at the chart again. She thought about her friends. Maximilian would probably be somewhere between philosopher and aesthete, she supposed, what with all his Beethoven tapes and trips to the Underworld to learn deep secrets about life. Raven, with all her spells and witchy ideas, would probably be a philosopher-shaper. Lexy would definitely be a protector-artisan, with all her homemade healing remedies. Wolf? Effie wasn't so sure. He was probably a protector like her, but what direction would he be going in?

After a couple more minutes, the door opened and Dr Wiseacre entered again. She was not alone. With her was a man in a very black cloak who looked as if he had never smiled in his life. His face was etched with hundreds of deep wrinkles and more than one massive scar. He had what looked like a large thorn growing out of each ear.

'Mr Greyday, here is the galloglass,' said Dr Wiseacre, not catching Effie's eye.

Effie didn't understand at first that she meant her.

'What?' said Effie, when she realised. 'But . . . No, that's—'

'Take her away, Frank,' said Dr Wiseacre.

The man in the cloak – Frank Greyday seemed to be his horribly appropriate name – walked towards Effie and took her firmly by the arm – right by the shimmering letter *M* that meant Effie could travel through portals to the Otherworld – and yanked her to her feet.

'But I'm a Truelove,' said Effie. 'I'm going to be a Keeper at Dragon's Green. You can't—'

'Lock her up,' said Dr Wiseacre. 'We'll let the town council work out what to do with her. She'll need to be sent back to the island, of course, but she must have that mark removed first. And any boons that help her to get here will need to be confiscated. We might have to surgically remove all her memories about being here, too.'

'But . . .'

'Come on, *islander*,' said Frank Greyday.

'Where are you taking me?'

'To the dungeon, where we put all the monsters.'

'But my cousin—'

'She won't ever want to see you again when she knows you're a galloglass,' said Dr Wiseacre. 'You can forget about her, and anyone you ever met here. It's all over.'

5

Lexy was pretty sure that everyone was asleep when she crept down the stairs holding a small hessian bag full of healing gemstones that she was going to steep in the light of the full moon. This was how you recharged them. She had several pieces of greeny-blue aventurine, which she used for Effie's remedies, and some bloodstone for Wolf. She was almost running out of Maximilian's black onyx, though, and . . .

'Hello, little lady.'

Lexy jumped at least a foot in the air, while her heart felt like it had dropped to the bottom of her stomach.

'Oh my God, it's you, JP!' she said. 'You gave me a fright.'

He was sitting at the kitchen table wearing a pair of red silk pyjamas and reading a book of what looked like poetry. His hair was still swept back in its extravagant pompadour style. It didn't look as if he'd been to bed at all. Buttons, the kitten, was on JP's lap, but didn't look that happy about it. Indeed, he would certainly have jumped down by now, had JP not been holding him by the neck.

'Sleeping's overrated,' he said. 'Wouldn't you agree?'

'Um . . .' said Lexy.

Buttons now managed to jump off JP's lap and up onto the table, where Lexy could stroke him. Lexy put down her bag of gemstones and picked him up. He climbed onto her shoulder as usual, and nibbled her ear.

'Do your parents know you go sneaking around in the middle of the night?'

Lexy shook her head. 'No. You won't say anything?' she said. 'My mum worries enough as it is.'

'Of course not. Your secret's safe with me.'

'Thank you.'

'On one condition.'

'What condition?'

'I want you to keep me company for a while. I like you. You're not like normal little girls. I'd say you're much more mature. What do you think?'

'Um . . .'

'Sit,' said Jupiter Peacock. 'I want to read something to you. It's called "Galloglass". It's a very old poem that I have recently translated into English. It contains some extremely important philosophy, from the days before the Great Split, when all worlds were one. But I expect you don't know anything about that. Anyway, sit. SIT.'

Buttons jumped off Lexy's shoulder and went back to his basket. He didn't like shouting.

Lexy had no choice. She had to sit down. She calculated that she could listen to him for five minutes, but then she'd need to get outside before the moonlight faded. It was at its strongest right now – which was why she'd come down at exactly this moment.

Jupiter Peacock began reading.

'*In days of yore, when brave and true, the heroes of the day shone forth* . . .'

As Jupiter Peacock continued to read, Lexy felt her mind wander elsewhere. She would need to order the black onyx first thing on Monday so that it would arrive by the end of next week, and . . .

'What do you think?' said Jupiter Peacock. He'd finished reading. Maybe Lexy would be able to get out into the garden now.

'Um . . .'

'A great deal has been written about this one poem,' said Jupiter Peacock. 'Most of it wrong. What do you think of this line – *We're born each one of us alone, and separate is how we stay*'?

'Um . . .'

'People think it's bad to be selfish, but this poem says that selfish people make the world a much better place. Bet that's not what you learn at school, huh?'

'No,' said Lexy. She wasn't really listening. She could see the moon beginning to drop and fade. What about her crystals? Surely she'd been polite enough by now. She scraped the chair back and was about to stand up.

'I really must—'

'Not so fast, little lady. I want a rematch before you go.'

'A rematch?'

'Indeed. I still think I can beat you at arm wrestling.'

Earlier on, while Hazel, flushed with pleasure at how well her little dinner party had gone, was making peppermint tea in the kitchen area, Jupiter Peacock had challenged Lexy's father Marcel to a series of ill-considered physical competitions. Marcel had won them all. He was, after all, a yoga teacher. He had stood on his head for longer (JP hadn't actually been able to stand on his head at all), and had performed five handstand press-ups. He had also held his breath for three minutes, which was two and a half minutes longer than JP could manage.

Then had come the arm wrestling. After he'd been beaten by Marcel several times, Jupiter Peacock had challenged Lexy. Marcel had smiled gratefully when Jupiter Peacock had used his left hand and let Lexy win. What a good sport he was, as well as everything else!

Lexy hadn't enjoyed it that much, though. Jupiter Peacock's breath had smelled strongly of all the wine he had drunk, and his hand had been hot and sweaty. And he'd gripped Lexy's fingers far too hard again, almost as if he wanted to hurt her. Surely he couldn't be that unaware of his own strength? When she'd exclaimed and said *Ow!* he'd just ignored her. And now he was asking her for a rematch?

'No,' said Lexy. 'Sorry, I really must—'

'Just one more time?' said Jupiter. 'Be a good hostess. Your mother would want you to.'

This was true. Hazel would want Lexy to do whatever it took to make Jupiter Peacock happy.

'OK,' she said. 'But really just one more time. I have to get into the garden. It's important.'

'We'll keep going until you win. Ready? We'll use our right hands this time.'

'But I'm left-handed,' said Lexy. 'You'll win easily!'

And so he did. When he finally decided to give up, after about ten goes, and once the moon had fallen so low in the sky as to be of no use, Lexy's hand was pink and blotchy. Jupiter Peacock had gripped it so hard that Lexy had almost started crying. But she had to do what he wanted. There was no way Lexy was going to be the one to jeopardise her mother's chance of having her name engraved on the plaque in the Town Hall. After this, Lexy would just have to make sure she was never alone with him again. It would be fine. She simply had to be a lot more careful in future. No more coming downstairs at night while he was staying.

'Oh dear,' said Jupiter Peacock, seeing Lexy's hand. 'I forget my own strength. Here . . .' He held out his own large hand to take hold of Lexy's again. 'Let me kiss it better.'

'No, it's all right,' said Lexy, moving her hand out of reach and getting up. 'I must get back to bed.'

'LET ME KISS IT BETTER.'

'I don't want you to,' said Lexy.

'Why ever not?'

'I just don't.'

'You'll feel better afterwards, I promise.'

'I just want to go to bed.'

'If you don't let me kiss it better, then I will go back to thinking you are a child. In which case, I'll have to tell your mother what you've been doing. Not only did you come down here in the middle of the night and interrupt my reading, you also insisted on arm-wrestling me. Not really the nicest way to treat a guest, is it?'

'Why are you being like this?' asked Lexy.

'I told you: I like you. I think you're mature. Now I want you to show it by letting me kiss you better.'

Lexy took a deep breath. What harm could it really do? It was just one kiss on the hand. Grown-ups always wanted you to kiss them, after all, and it was always horrible. At least this was nowhere near her face. Lexy would let him kiss her hand, and then she'd go upstairs and wash it in very hot water. Worse things had happened to her, after all – much worse. She'd fought an evil man during an earthstorm. And she'd helped her friends defeat Skylurian Midzhar during a massive meteor shower. She'd agree to this one stupid request, but then she'd never let this happen again. She'd make sure.

'All right,' she said, sighing. 'Here.'

Lexy held out her right hand. Jupiter Peacock took hold of it, turned it over, looked at it hard, then planted the most horrible, disgusting, slobbery kiss imaginable right in the centre of the palm.

'Not so bad, was it?' he said, when it was over.

Lexy didn't say anything. She ran back upstairs, leaving her bag of crystals behind. She just had to wash her hand as soon as possible. And never, ever let Jupiter Peacock arm-wrestle her, or shake her hand, or anything like that ever again.

Effie never cried. But she felt pretty close to tears now, as Frank Greyday led her out of the door and back onto the street. Before Effie had been taken away, Dr Wiseacre had tied her hands together and then smeared two large black streaks on either side of Effie's face with something like charcoal. Effie didn't have to wait long to find out what this meant.

'Galloglass,' people hissed, as she walked past. 'Island galloglass. Island trash. Send her back. Send her back!'

Where was Clothilde? Surely she'd rescue Effie as soon as she knew what was happening to her. This was, after all, just a massive, horrible mistake. She'd said she'd be back in an hour. Where was she?

Instead of following the narrow cobbled lane down into the town, the man roughly pushed Effie off to the left, where, after going up some steps and through a low stone arch, they came to a big wooden door which was studded all over with brass rivets.

'Please,' said Effie. 'This is a huge mistake.'

'Galloglasses need to be punished,' said the man.

'But I'm not a galloglass!' said Effie. 'I promise. She got me all wrong. I just need to take the test again and—'

'Anyone can tell you're a galloglass just from looking at you,' said Frank Greyday. 'You're an islander. You should have stayed there and not come here and brought contamination to our world. You lot are filth.'

'But—'

'You can't even speak our language properly. *"But . . ."'* Frank Greyday imitated Effie's way of saying the word in Rosian. It was true; Effie was much better at reading and writing Rosian than she was at speaking it. After all, she barely got a chance to practise.

Frank Greyday knocked at the door and another cloaked man opened it.

59

'A galloglass for you,' Greyday said to him. He roughly shoved Effie through the door. 'Not sure if we're sending her back alive or just killing her here. Same difference, more or less. We also have to remove the mark. We don't want her trying to sneak back after we've ejected her. Anyway, you prepare her for questioning. I'll open up one of the consultation rooms. Dr Wiseacre is returning to do the questioning herself.'

'Has she got any weapons?'

'Nope,' said Frank Greyday. 'Not that I can see. But I think I'll take this necklace away for testing.'

For a moment Effie thought he meant her Sword of Light. But it was her vial of deepwater that he was interested in. The Sword of Light was so small, and so bright, that people usually didn't notice it at all, or simply thought it was a reflection, or a trick of the light. The second man untied her hands and then Effie took off the bigger necklace and quickly gave it to Frank Greyday before he had a chance to notice the tiny gold sword on the other chain.

Effie couldn't understand what was happening to her. *Surely* Clothilde would find her soon. But if not, Effie had to make a plan, and quickly. If only her friends were here. Of course, they couldn't come to the Otherworld. But they were such a good team. Effie thought of Wolf working out an escape plan, Lexy concocting some remedy or other, and Raven saying a useful spell. Effie imagined Maximilian doing mind control on the guards and then throwing her a little vial of deepwater. She could really do with it now. Effie's headache had got worse, and she could feel her lifeforce dwindling. And now the guard had taken the last of her own stash of deepwater away.

Effie was escorted to a small, dark cell and locked inside. There was nothing in the bare room apart from a thin mattress and a bucket with the word 'Islander' written on it in white paint. There was one thin candle dancing on an otherwise bare shelf. It hardly provided any light at all. Now was the time to think of some way to rescue herself, but Effie's mind had gone completely blank. This was why Wolf always said it was a good idea to practise strategy. It was like in sport. The more you practised something, the more likely you'd be to do it under pressure. Effie could hit a good forehand in tennis, no matter how nervous she was feeling. But escaping? Her mind was totally empty. She'd just never practised for this situation. What were you supposed to do when people labelled you a dangerous galloglass and locked you up in a small Otherworld cell? Effie doubted there was a book on that.

Were they going to torture her? Effie felt sick. She tried and tried to remember what Wolf had said about not cracking under interrogation, but all that would come into her mind was the old trick of concealing a cyanide pill in a false tooth so that if things got too bad you could swallow it and take all your precious information with you. Effie shuddered. It would never come to that. She'd never give in. She just had to work out what on earth to do.

Terrence Deer-Hart felt rather conspicuous in his yellow jumpsuit and red cape. Did the jumpsuit really have to be quite this tight? Did the cape actually have to be this small? Still, at least there was nobody around in the university at this time of night to see him.

Little did Terrence know that every creature from the Cosmic Web (not currently in hibernation) that was anywhere near the university had turned up to have a good look. Owls clustered around windows, rats peered from vents. Even a family of rabbits that should have been asleep had put off their fatigue for one more night just to see this.

The Cosmic Web did not understand many things about humans. It did not understand, for example, why we do not use our own telepathic network, given how powerful it is. It did not understand why we suppress our magic, shave our fur and use showers rather than simply licking ourselves all over to get clean (if indeed we have to be so clean at all). One thing the Cosmic Web did understand, however, was the need for members of all species to make themselves attractive. One particular plant does this by mimicking the smell of rotting meat in order to attract the flies it wants to consume. But usually in nature this process is a lot simpler and mainly involves donning bright colours in pleasing combinations in order to look, well, *nice*.

And Terrence Deer-Hart had failed at this.

He had failed spectacularly.

In fact, he looked more ridiculous than anything the Cosmic Web had seen for many years. He looked more ridiculous than anything in nature could ever manage to look. Nature simply did not give out tight yellow jumpsuits and red capes. It certainly did not make it possible to pair them. The Cosmic Web wouldn't forget this in a hurry. The Cosmic Web was enjoying this. It settled in for a good late evening's entertainment.

Terrence Deer-Hart entered the meeting room to find it in darkness, which worked for him (and also for the Cosmic Web, which sees better in the dark). He could smell a familiar perfume – dead things mixed with violets – and hear the vague, soft sound of people breathing. So they were already here.

'Kneel,' said a voice.

Terrence knelt. He heard footsteps approaching him. Someone put a blindfold on him. There was the fizz of a match being struck, and then the gentle flickery sound of candles being lit.

And then laughter. Quiet and suppressed at first, but becoming louder and a bit choked as people tried to stop. Eventually they did. Terrence wondered if this was usually part of the initiation ceremony.

'What on earth . . .?' said a clipped Northern European voice.

'Who was in charge of giving him his robes?' whispered someone else.

'I give them to a porter to take to him,' drawled a deep female voice with a Russian accent.

'But . . .'

'All right,' said the Northern European voice. 'Never mind. We will ignore this mix-up. The seeker will wear the correct robes in future. Does the seeker understand?'

Did they mean Terrence? After a pause, he said, 'Yes.' It came out as a sort of squeak.

The Cosmic Web didn't understand human languages. It didn't need to, because humans rarely said what they meant with words. Instead, all their truth came from things the Cosmic Web understood very well: body language, ritual displays, hormones, the big picture.

Humans never saw the big picture in quite the same way as the Cosmic Web. Indeed, news came quite soon to the Cosmic Web that a young male human was currently performing at the Winter Fair opening ceremony as part of a tribute band (the Cosmic Web had a limited understanding of what this was) while wearing the sacred cloak of the Fifteenth Order of the Diberi (the Cosmic Web simply referred to this as 'large black ritual fur').

The Cosmic Web didn't pretend to understand everything about the human world, but it could tell from all the unusual hormones, strange aromas and laughter that things this night were beginning to unravel. But that was to be expected as Midwinter approached.

☀

Wolf usually played rugby on a Saturday. There were away fixtures, which involved long, precarious trips in the school bus, and home fixtures, where Wolf had to help make orange squash and lay out the afternoon tea, which was the bit he hated most about being captain of the Under 13s. But tomorrow there were no sports fixtures because of the Winter Fair. There was nothing on Sunday either. Wolf had a completely free weekend in front of him.

Was that why he couldn't sleep? Usually on a Friday night his mind was full of rugby. Coach Bruce had just started his Master's course in sports psychology at the Old Town University and was always experimenting on Wolf and Effie and other members of his sports teams. Wolf had been taught to visualise, and so that was what he was usually doing at this time on a Friday night. He would imagine himself taking a high kick and then building an attack and coming down the wing to score a try on the blind side. Then he would repeat the whole thing with the attack going wide.

But tonight something else was on Wolf's mind.

After tossing and turning for a couple of hours, he realised what it was.

It was that stupid book. The one that Monsieur Valentin had left on the table earlier.

Wolf had known for a while that there was something odd about this book. Every time he'd gone to the military strategy shelves in Leonard Levar's bookshop it had seemed to sort of glow at him. This was why, embarrassing though it was to admit, he was a little frightened of it. It had some strange magic about it, and Wolf didn't like it. Wolf didn't do magic himself – well, not exactly – and he was a bit afraid of it. Which was stupid, of course, because he wasn't afraid of anything. Not the book, and not magic either.

Wolf had never opened the book. Which now got him thinking. If he was to prove that he was not afraid of anything, then he should get up right now – out of his camp-bed – and go over to the desk and open it. Just to prove he wasn't scared. And then he would go back to sleep.

He would count to five, and then he would do it.

Ten.

Twenty.

He got up.

There was no need to light a candle or use a torch. The moon was still bright enough that Wolf could see his way around the bookshop. There it still was on the desk. *The Answer*.

The book had a glossy black cover and embossed silver foil lettering. Its front and back covers were cluttered with rapturous quotations from famous people from over a hundred years ago. They all said things like 'Spellbinding' and 'Life-changing' and 'Indescribably brilliant and strange'. But one of the quotations in particular had really intrigued Wolf. It said, 'Whatever you are searching for, this book will lead you to it.'

Could that possibly be true? How?

The book was old, but it didn't look like old books were supposed to. It was a cheap, thick paperback that had obviously been a massive bestseller in its time. It looked like the kind of book that would make you go on a stupid diet, or tell you that you were the reincarnation of Henry VIII, or how to make a million pounds in a week. Wolf knew about those books too, because Leonard Levar had a section especially for them. But this book had not been shelved there. This one had been shelved with books on military strategy and old *Dungeons & Dragons* magazines. Why?

As he picked up the thick paperback, Wolf wondered if it was possible that a book really could lead you to something you were searching for. Surely all readers of a book would be searching for different things? But he couldn't help wondering . . . What if the book could lead him to Natasha?

But of course that would be impossible. It was stupid even to contemplate. Wolf felt full of trepidation as he held the dark volume in his hands. Fear. Well, Wolf knew what you did with fear – especially irrational fear like this. You had to face it, to conquer it. He turned to the first page of *The Answer*.

It was full of numbers.

What on earth . . .?

He flicked to the second page. More numbers. Was this some sort of joke? Or maybe a printing error? Perhaps it was a secret code. But who wanted to read a whole book in secret code? Wolf carried on flicking. Yes, the whole book, covered as it was with promises and quotations, and costing, back in 2014, when it was published, £8.99, was unintelligible. Or was it? Maybe there was a key or something in the back? But no. Wolf didn't understand why a book that looked like a cheap thriller would want to make it so difficult for you to read it. It was a complete mystery.

Wolf decided it must be a little joke of Monsieur Valentin's.

He sighed and put the book back.

There were no answers except the ones you made yourself. He already knew that. He went to bed and fell straight to sleep.

Terrence Deer-Hart's knees were beginning to hurt. Surely someone would think of giving him a little cushion to put under them? But no. They'd been chanting in some ancient language – possibly Latin – for quite a long time now.

Eventually the chanting stopped.

Someone spoke, meaningfully it seemed. To Terrence Deer-Hart's ears it sounded like 'Blah blah blah blah blah.'

Then there was silence. A slight wafting through the air of the scent of Earl Grey tea mixed with lavender and lemons.

'I will repeat the question in English,' said the clipped Northern European voice, which Terrence thought probably belonged to Gotthard Forestfloor, the Scandinavian novelist. 'Do you understand Rosian?'

'Me?' said Terrence.

'Yes, you,' said the voice, a little wearily. 'You are the one being initiated, after all.'

'No, I don't think so,' said Terrence.

'I'm fairly sure,' said the voice, 'that it is you.'

'I mean I don't understand Rosian,' said Terrence. 'Sorry.'

'Latin?'

'No.'

'You will need to learn at least one magical language as part of your apprenticeship. For now, we will conduct the rest of the ceremony in English.'

'Thank you.'

Terrence felt something wet, cold and a little slimy touch his forehead. He tried not to think about what this might be.

'Do you choose to take the Diberi as your new family, forsaking all others, and loving only us?'

It sounded a bit creepy put like that. But Terrence felt that in this position he probably couldn't say no.

'Yes,' said Terrence. 'I do.'

'And do you give your soul over to magic, and the legacy of the four great magi?'

'I suppose so,' said Terrence. 'I mean, yes.'

'And do you vow not to rest until the world of the galloglass is free from the yoke of the Otherworld?'

Terrence had literally no idea what this meant.

'Yes,' he said.

'Do you renounce selfless service?'

Was that some kind of canteen where you helped yourself? Terrence didn't know.

'Yes,' he promised anyway.

'And agree to champion the rights of the individual?'

'Yes.'

'And to abhor the Flow?'

The what? Terrence frowned. How was he going to remember all the things he had to abhor and renounce? What if he championed one of them by accident?

'Yes,' he replied anyway. 'If you say so.'

'And to obey me in everything?'

'Um . . .'

'TO OBEY ME IN EVERYTHING?'

'I can't actually see who you are,' admitted Terrence.

'Does it matter who I am?'

Terrence thought about this. He was currently blindfolded and taking part in an initiation ceremony to join an evil secret organisation that planned to take over the universe. He had already agreed to all sorts of things he didn't understand. Why not also agree to obey someone he couldn't see? Well, because even to Terrence this didn't actually make sense. And Terrence could occasionally – usually in the worst circumstances – become quite rational, and then very stubborn.

'Maybe,' he said. 'Actually, yes. It does matter.'

'Well, you'll find out who I am in a moment,' said the voice. 'Although surely you recognise my voice?'

'Well . . .'

'Do you vow to obey me in everything?' the voice said again, irritably.

'What happens if I don't?' asked Terrence.

'Then we will probably kill you.'

'All right, well, in that case, yes, I suppose so,' said Terrence.

It was going to be more complicated than he'd thought, being a Diberi.

6

Effie paced her small, dark cell, thinking. She *wasn't* a galloglass; she was sure of that. Although . . . what if Dr Wiseacre had been right? Effie had been going over everything in her mind, and she could sort of see why someone might think she was selfish enough to be called a galloglass, if they looked at things in a certain way. *What does she make? What do you do?* Bo's words kept coming back to her. And also what that girl had said about islanders: *They never do anything for anyone else. They just take.* Everyone else in the Otherworld did things for others, and Effie, so far, had contributed nothing. She realised that now.

Well, that could easily change.

Whatever she'd done – or neglected to do – wasn't bad enough for this, though, surely? She didn't deserve to be imprisoned. And while admittedly she hadn't knitted many socks, Effie was the one who'd saved the Otherworld from Diberi invasion – twice now. She'd killed the man who had attacked her grandfather and stolen his library of powerful last editions. Effie and her friends were now protecting those last editions from the Diberi. Most recently, Effie had buried alive the woman who wanted to use the last edition of *The Chosen Ones* by Laurel Wilde to get to the Great Library in Truelove House and, presumably, steal its most powerful books.

Well, to be more factual about it, Effie had actually tricked this woman into burying *herself* alive. And the man she'd killed had been 350 years old and was only keeping himself going with stolen magical energy, which she'd taken away. Effie would never hurt anyone – and certainly not bury someone alive – if she could help it.

Effie was always fighting to keep the Otherworld safe from the Diberi – and she wasn't even a real Otherworlder herself. Every time she came here she started running out of M-currency and had to go home to build it up again. And all because she wanted to help!

Effie felt cross, suddenly. No one, ever, had been remotely grateful for her help. Well, apart from the other Trueloves, of course. Although Rollo was so moody, and Cosmo so distant. Clothilde was grateful. But no one else here cared that she'd saved their stupid world. They just kept going on and on about how much they hated Effie's world.

And what was so wrong with the Realworld anyway? People didn't have as much magic, but that wasn't their fault. Some people tried really hard to do magic, even though it was so difficult for them, like Effie's friend Raven. She was so loving and kind, but if she came here people would no doubt just write her off as a 'filthy' islander too. No one Effie had ever met in the Realworld had been as mean to her as the girls in Froghole. And the Otherworld thought it was so superior . . . And they supposedly had so much magic – but where was it? Everyone did their own washing up. Why did Clothilde bother to knit socks when surely she could just whip up a pair with a spell?

For the first time ever, Effie wanted to go home. Home to the Realworld. Home to her father Orwell, her step-mother Cait and her baby sister Luna. Home to people who might call her all sorts of things, but would never say she was a galloglass.

By the time the guard came to unlock Effie's cell, she was very angry. And it didn't help to see that he now wore her vial of deepwater around his neck as if it belonged to him.

'I want you to let me go,' Effie said to him firmly. 'I would like to meet my cousin and go home. And you can give me my necklace back too.'

'Hahaha!' said the guard. 'You want me to release you, just like that?'

'Yes, please,' said Effie.

'And if I don't, what will you do? *Cry?*'

'No, I'll use my other necklace. The one your colleague was too stupid to notice.'

The guard looked at her with contempt. 'Stop talking, filthy galloglass,' he said. 'I've come to take you for interrogation. You'd better cooperate.'

There was nothing else for it. Effie touched the golden Sword of Light hanging on the chain around her neck and whispered the word that made it real: *Truelove*. It sparkled into life, forming itself from all the purest and oldest particles of light in the room, many of which had been flying around the universe since the very beginning of time, gathering energy from the Big Bang, the greatest diamonds and the hottest suns. The small candle

73

flickered and glimmered like a child in the presence of a great wizard. In less than a moment, Effie was holding a large, dazzlingly golden sword in front of her.

'Let me go, please,' she said.

The guard looked at her in astonishment.

'You really are a galloglass islander,' he said. 'I'd heard about your sort but never really believed in you.'

'Yes,' came a female voice from behind him. 'She is indeed proving herself to be a galloglass with everything she does. I'd put that sword away if I were you, girl. Attacking others is forbidden in this world. But of course you wouldn't know that, as you do not belong here. But we don't solve things with violence.'

Effie held her sword aloft, but it was true: she knew that fighting her way out would be the wrong thing to do. With a sigh, she used her magic to dissolve the sword and turn it back into the necklace.

The particles of light fizzed and popped and then went on their way, heading towards the edge of the known universe and the end of time, where all particles of light must eventually go.

'OK then,' Effie said. 'Well, in that case I'm just going to walk out of here.' She stepped towards the door. 'Please let me pass.'

'Excuse me?' said Dr Wiseacre, with a deep scowl.

'If people here can't attack other people, then how exactly are you going to stop me?'

Dr Wiseacre looked like an exasperated teacher dealing with the worst troublemaker in the school.

'For goodness' sake. Bring her to the consultation room,' she said to the guard. 'And take away that necklace.'

74

Dr Wiseacre strode off. The guard took Effie by the arm. When she struggled, he held on to her harder.

'Ow!' said Effie.

'Keep still,' snarled the guard.

'How is this not violence?' asked Effie. 'You're forcing me to go somewhere I don't want to go. I want to see my cousin!'

'And you've already been told: once your cousin knows what you are, she won't ever want to see you again.'

This had to be a lie. But it hurt Effie, deep inside.

'Give me your necklace,' said the guard.

'No,' said Effie.

'Well then, I'll have to . . .' The guard reached to grab the necklace, but didn't seem to be able to get close enough to touch it. 'Ouch!' he said, withdrawing his hand. 'That burns. What have you done to it, you disgusting islander? You're not supposed to have enough magic to make something as hot as that.'

Effie wondered about summoning the sword again, but she sensed that what Dr Wiseacre had said about this world was right – the part about violence, at least. And Effie herself only used violence as a very last resort anyway. She had read about people vanquishing monsters and demons that were then absorbed back into themselves. She didn't quite know what this meant exactly, but she knew it wasn't at all the same as attacking your human enemies, not that magical weapons worked on anyone without M-currency anyway. Still, her necklace was safe for now. It was clear they couldn't touch it without getting burned.

One other thing was also becoming very clear. Dr Wiseacre

was not following Otherworld rules either. Effie wondered what was really going on. She was less and less sure that what was happening here had anything to do with real Otherworld laws at all.

The consultation room was down three staircases. It was small, dark and windowless. Effie wished Wolf were here. Or any of her friends, really. Maximilian would help Effie to think her way out of this – well, that or do some kind of dark mage mind-magic. Raven would cast a good spell, or get some of the local animals to come to help. Lexy would say comforting words and give Effie a potion or tonic. And, if her friends were here, then Effie would be able to discuss this situation and make some proper sense out of it.

'Right,' said Dr Wiseacre. 'Let's get serious. We've got your cousin in another room.'

'What? Clothilde? No! Why?'

'Because it is a crime here to consort with a galloglass, which is what she's been doing. She is being questioned right now.'

'But—'

'And we are going to ask you some questions now before removing your magic and sending you back to the island.'

'But I'm not—'

'Here's how it's going to work. Every time you lie, we will drain her lifeforce. Do you understand?'

Effie nodded silently.

'Right. We won't beat around the bush,' said Dr Wiseacre. 'Tell us how to get to Dragon's Green.'

Effie didn't say anything for a moment. She didn't understand what was happening.

'What? But I don't under—'

'Oh dear,' said Dr Wiseacre. She turned a silver lever on the wall by the table. It clicked several times as it went around. 'Oh,' she said. 'I forgot to mention that we will penalise you for every hesitation as well. Now tell me where Dragon's Green is. I know that Froghole is the nearest town. But I need the actual coordinates.'

'Why do you want to know where Dragon's Green is?'

Dr Wiseacre didn't reply. She simply turned the lever again. Effie thought she could hear screaming in a nearby room. Was it her imagination? Or perhaps even a sound effect? She didn't trust Dr Wiseacre at all. But what if it were real? The candle in the lamp on the desk danced ominously. Dr Wiseacre reached for the lever again.

'Stop doing that for a second,' said Effie. 'Please.'

Dr Wiseacre looked at her. 'Are you going to tell me what I want to know?' she asked.

'I don't understand why you want to know where Dragon's Green is,' said Effie. 'I thought I was here because I was a galloglass. But now it seems as if you just lied to get me here to get information about Dragon's Green. I just don't understand why.'

'You are a very rude little girl.'

'I want to know what's going on,' said Effie.

Her head suddenly ached again. She was going to have to get back to the Realworld soon. If only she could get her vial of deepwater back she could at least restore some of her power.

'You want to know what's going on?' said Dr Wiseacre. 'I'll tell you what's going on. The Trueloves are a weak link. That's what's going on. It's simply not safe to have the Great Library in the hands of people who are scattered across worlds – especially when it means galloglasses like you can have access to it. And the Trueloves are sloppy. They haven't done a good job of protecting us in recent times.'

'What do you mean?'

'You know about the book that was stolen. You must do. It was your mother who did it.'

'My mother didn't steal anything,' said Effie.

'But the book was taken away. Books must never be taken from the Great Library. Not without the ritual.'

'Well, it certainly wasn't my mother who did it. And anyway, I took the book back,' said Effie.

'Aha. So it did happen. I knew it!'

'But . . .'

'And it's true what they say about the library. It *is* real! But the wrong people are in charge of it. Things are worse than I thought.'

'You tricked me,' said Effie. 'That's not fair.'

'Yes, and it was easy,' said Dr Wiseacre. 'Proving yet again what a weak link you are. Just like the other Trueloves.'

'You're wrong,' said Effie. 'You're so wrong about everything.'

'You'd better tell me where Dragon's Green is, and quickly. I think I can turn this lever about three more times before your cousin loses all her lifeforce. And then you'll never see her again. Of course, as I've already told you, she won't want to see you again anyway when she knows what you are. So you may as well tell me, and spare her – unless you really want to carry on acting like a selfish galloglass for ever. How do I get into the Great Library?'

'I'm never going to tell you that,' said Effie.

'Then you and your cousin will die.'

There was only one thing for it. Effie stood up and once again summoned her Sword of Light. It again formed out of the brightest, most magical particles of light in the room. In an instant, Effie was standing and holding the golden sword aloft. Dr Wiseacre raised an eyebrow. She turned the lever once, but didn't take her hand from it. Effie could hear more faint screams from a nearby room. Was it really Clothilde? Or just a trick? It didn't matter. So what if Effie was going to be expelled from the Otherworld for ever. If there was any chance that Clothilde was being hurt, Effie had to save her. And she was never going to tell Dr Wiseacre where Dragon's Green was, or the Great Library, or anything she knew about it.

Dr Wiseacre turned the lever again.

'Please stop doing that and let me go, or I really will have to use this,' said Effie.

'And then you will be removed anyway and forbidden from coming here ever again.'

'Yes, and you will never find out about Dragon's Green,' said Effie. 'Are you going to let me go or not?'

Dr Wiseacre lifted her hand to turn the lever again. Effie couldn't stand it. She couldn't bear the idea of Clothilde being hurt, or – unthinkable – killed. She raised her sword and brought it hard across Dr Wiseacre's body, from right to left, as if she was playing a massive two-handed tennis forehand. Effie's sword didn't cut flesh or bone – it was a magical weapon and so worked differently from that. But Effie was surprised when Millicent Wiseacre completely disappeared. Her heart jumped into her throat. Had she just made a really terrible mistake? Maybe. But she had also saved Clothilde. If she was really here. If she wasn't . . . Well, Effie couldn't take that chance.

Still carrying her sword, Effie walked out into the dark corridor, holding the candle-lamp from the table. She was breathing hard. What had she done? As the adrenaline subsided she wondered again if Clothilde was even here. The guard was waiting for her in the dingy corridor, but he quickly realised the power Effie had, and what she was prepared to do with it, and so he held up his hands to show surrender.

'Where is my cousin?' said Effie.

He shrugged.

Effie raised her sword higher. 'Where is my cousin?' she repeated.

'No one else here but you,' he said.

Effie took her vial of deepwater from around his neck. There was no sign of Frank Greyday. Effie tried a few doors but there was no evidence of Clothilde anywhere. He must be telling the truth.

Effie continued down the dingy corridor and then made her way up to the door to the narrow cobbled street. She opened it. There, hovering anxiously on the magic carpet, was Clothilde. So she hadn't been a prisoner at all. Her eyes were big and frightened.

'Oh my goodness,' she said, when she saw Effie's sword. 'Effie!'

Effie quickly dissolved her sword. So Dr Wiseacre had been lying. Effie had suspected as much. But she'd had no other choice. If Dr Wiseacre *hadn't* been lying . . . It was all too complicated to think about, suddenly.

'Get on,' Clothilde said to Effie. 'I think the council are going to want to talk to you. We're in big trouble.'

'I'm so sorry,' said Effie. 'But she said she had you prisoner and she was turning this lever and . . .'

'Shhh,' said Clothilde. 'Tell me when we get back. For now I just need to fly this thing as fast as I can. Hold on!'

The phone was ringing in Leonard Levar's Antiquarian Bookshop. It rang and rang and then stopped and then started again. Wolf was beginning to wonder if he should get out of bed and answer it. It was still dark outside, but Wolf could hear the faint song of a robin. Since the worldquake the Cosmic Web had got stronger; the birds now held some sort of dawn chorus every day of the year, not just in spring. There were also the bang-crash sounds of things being unloaded in shops around the bookshop. It was morning, just about.

Wolf looked at his watch. Yes: it was quarter past six.

Who would be phoning the bookshop at this time? One of Leonard Levar's horrible old acquaintances, probably. And Wolf didn't want anyone else to know he was in the bookshop. He put the pillow over his head and tried to go back to sleep.

Ring ring. Ring ring.

Whoever it was, was certainly very insistent.

Eventually Wolf got up and pulled on a Tusitala School rugby team sweatshirt and put on some jeans. The phone started ringing yet again. This time he answered it. The ancient Bakelite receiver was heavy in his hand, as he held it to his ear.

'Hello?' he said.

'Hello,' said a stern voice. 'I'd like to speak to a Mr Wolf Reed, please.'

'Um . . . that's me.' Was he in some sort of trouble?

'It's concerning a Miss Natasha Reed,' said the voice.

'Yes?' said Wolf, his heart starting to beat much faster.

'We understand that you are looking for information concerning this person,' said the voice.

'Yes! Please – tell me where she is.'

'All in good time,' said the voice. 'Do you have pen and paper?'

'Yes.' Wolf reached for the old yellow pad that he'd been using to make notes on rugby strategy.

'Good. Await further instructions,' said the voice.

The phone went dead.

The landscape underneath Effie was a blur of cloud and mist and green streaks of unidentifiable countryside. Clothilde hadn't been joking when she'd said she was going to fly as fast as she could. She seemed to have gone higher, too. Up here the air came in icy bursts, and every so often the carpet lurched up, down, left or right, as it got caught in currents.

By the time they landed, Effie felt cold and sick.

And her headache hadn't improved much either. She was running very low on lifeforce; she suspected even more so since she'd attacked Dr Wiseacre. She was going to have to drink some of the emergency deepwater from the vial around her neck. Of course, once it was gone there would be nothing standing between her and the Yearning – the horrible illness you get if you run too low on magical lifeforce. As soon as they got off the magic carpet she had the tiniest sip.

'What is that?' asked Clothilde, as they set off down the driveway to Truelove House.

'It's deepwater,' said Effie.

'What does it do?'

'Tops up my lifeforce. I'm a bit low. I should probably be getting back soon.'

Effie knew that ideally she should have gone straight to the portal on the Keepers' Plains and returned to the Realworld. She'd been here too long already. But she had to tell Clothilde, Rollo and Cosmo about what had happened in Froghole. Effie felt sick inside at the thought of her diagnosis as a galloglass. But it was wrong; of course it was. And as for Dr Wiseacre and her horrible henchmen . . . Effie knew she shouldn't have pulled her sword on them, but she thought they were hurting Clothilde. What was she supposed to have done?

Clothilde sighed. She seemed actually annoyed with Effie for the first time ever. It was normal for Rollo to be annoyed – he was regularly a bit irritated with everyone. But Clothilde had always been so kind to Effie. What had she meant about them being in trouble with the council? And what was that anyway?

Clothilde looked like she was about to say something, but then bit her lip.

'What is it?' asked Effie.

Clothilde sighed again. 'Nothing,' she said.

'Why are you so upset?' asked Effie. 'Is it because of the council?'

'I just don't understand how you cannot have realised that . . .' Clothilde took a deep breath and shook her head. 'It's not for me to tell you. I'd just have thought you'd have worked it out yourself by now. Maybe what they say about the island is right after all.' She looked away from Effie. 'I don't know. It can't be. But . . .'

For the second time that day, Effie felt like crying. If even Clothilde was saying things like that, then maybe they were all correct. Maybe all islanders *were* horrible, including Effie. Maybe . . .

They had arrived at the house.

Usually things here were so happy. But now there was quite a different atmosphere as Clothilde and Effie walked into the drawing room. Pelham Longfellow was there, looking grave. Cosmo had come down from his tower. Rollo looked furious. And there was a woman with them that Effie had not seen before. She looked very, very old, and was wearing the same kind of soft pointed hat as Cosmo. Was she related to him in some way? Or maybe she was from the council?

'Are you all right?' Pelham asked Clothilde, springing up from the sofa and touching her on the arm.

She nodded.

'Dear child,' said Cosmo to Effie. 'I hear you've had yet another adventure.'

'They're getting closer to us,' said Clothilde. 'What do they want?'

'The Collective have gone completely mad,' said Pelham. 'It's exactly what I don't miss about being here.'

Clothilde gave him a look that was half sad and half cross.

'We'll talk about all that later,' said Cosmo. 'For now we need

84

to resolve this other matter. You'd better leave us alone with the child.'

Clothilde, Pelham and Rollo left the room, exchanging meaningful looks as they went.

◈

Wolf couldn't concentrate on anything while he waited for the phone to ring again. He sat at the desk holding a pen ready for whatever was going to happen next. His stomach rumbled, and he didn't move. He started to get cold. Normally he would have switched on the ancient oil heating system or lit a fire by now. But if there was any chance of hearing about Natasha he was not going to miss it.

It must have been almost an hour before the phone rang again.

'Hello?' said Wolf, after picking up the receiver as fast as he could. 'Hello?'

He was greeted curtly by the same voice as before.

'Please take down this address,' said the voice. Wolf wrote down exactly what the caller said. It was somewhere in the Borders. 'If you can get here by noon I will explain how to get the information you require.'

'By noon?' said Wolf. 'But—'

'Don't be late,' said the voice. 'In fact, I'd get here as quick as you can. We operate on a first come, first served basis. And there's intense competition for the places on our programme. I'd waste no time, if I were you. This will probably be the only chance you'll get to find out where your sister is. It *is* your sister you seek, isn't it?'

'Yes. Natasha Reed. Please can you just tell me where she is?'

'Everybody is searching for something, young man. What makes you think your quest is so special?'

Wolf didn't know what to say to that. 'She's only ten,' he said. 'She needs to be protected.'

'Indeed,' said the voice. 'Get here by noon and we'll talk.'

7

Effie sat down on the large white sofa in the drawing room of Truelove House. Cosmo sat next to her. The female wizard sat on a dark pink armchair and peered at Effie closely.

'This child needs to return to her own world soon,' she said to Cosmo.

'I agree,' said Cosmo. 'She is running low on lifeforce.'

It was true. Effie's headache was intensifying.

'She has not . . .?' said the woman.

'I don't think so,' said Cosmo. 'We've been waiting.'

'Oh dear,' said the woman.

Effie wanted to ask what they were talking about. But the atmosphere in the room suddenly became dense and heavy, and then sort of ethereal, and then, gradually, very, very still and calm. It was as if someone had dimmed the lights and lit a particularly beautiful scented candle. Effie felt both more sleepy than she'd ever felt and more awake. Great smoky waves of relaxation settled over her like powerful incense. Was this magic?

If so, it was the best magic Effie had ever experienced. She tried to will more of it to come to wash over her.

'Yes, and she has no resistance either, has she?' said the wise-looking female wizard, lowering her hands. Was that a spell she'd been casting on Effie? Effie didn't want her to stop.

The female wizard got up, walked over to Effie and touched her lightly on the head. Effie's headache disappeared. She felt strong again. She wanted to ask what the wizard had done, but she suddenly felt shy and a little afraid. Whatever it was, it was something even Cosmo couldn't do. Effie could just tell.

'My name is Suri,' said the woman. 'I'm a member of the Council of Wizards. Like your family, we're based here in Dragon's Green. I've been told you don't yet know much about our world.'

'No,' said Effie. 'But I'm trying to learn.'

'And you had an unfortunate encounter today, I believe?'

Effie told Suri as briefly as she could what had happened in Froghole.

'And then you attacked her?' said Suri, when Effie got to the part in her story about Dr Wiseacre turning the lever that she'd said would hurt Clothilde.

'I was trying to protect Clothilde,' said Effie.

'I see.'

'I don't know what else I could have done,' said Effie. 'She wanted me to tell her where Dragon's Green was. Apart from anything else, I don't actually know how to explain how to get here, so I couldn't have told her even if I'd have wanted to.'

'Would you have told her, if you'd known how to explain it?'

'No,' said Effie. 'I would never help anyone get here who wasn't supposed to be here.'

'What made you so sure she wasn't supposed to be here?'

'Um . . .'

'People do come here sometimes for meetings, or after completion of a Wizard Quest.'

'I—'

'But I'm guessing that Dr Wiseacre didn't seem like someone on a Wizard Quest?' Suri smiled kindly. Effie got the feeling that, although she was in trouble, Suri was trying her best to help her.

'No,' said Effie.

'And you had reason to believe that she was hurting your cousin, and that she would continue to hurt her if you didn't tell her how to get here?'

'Yes.'

'You do know, don't you, that we never use violence here?'

'Yes,' said Effie. 'Well, I sort of understand. You can attack demons, but not people?'

'Yes, that's correct.'

'So I'm in trouble for attacking Dr Wiseacre?'

'Potentially, yes.'

'What should I have done instead?'

There was a long pause. Suri and Cosmo looked at each other.

'My grandfather left me the sword – you knew all about it,' Effie said to Cosmo. 'I had to pass a test before Pelham gave it to me. It comes from here – from the mainland, I mean. Why shouldn't I use it to protect Truelove House and the Great Library, and everyone here?'

'It's complicated,' said Cosmo.

'Did Dr Wiseacre mention the Great Library in particular?' said Suri.

Effie nodded. 'Yes. At first she just said Dragon's Green, but then she said something about the Great Library being in the hands of . . . I can't remember how she said it exactly, but she said that the Trueloves shouldn't be in charge of the library. And then . . .'

'I see,' said Suri. 'So she already knew about the Great Library?'

Effie felt herself blushing a little.

'Sort of. She suspected. But . . . then when I said something about the Great Library she said that she only knew then that it was real. I'm so sorry. I didn't know it was a secret from people here. I truly didn't realise I was giving anything away. I didn't say anything else, I promise.'

'It makes sense for them to want to get into the library,' said Cosmo to Suri. 'It's how the Collective could achieve everything they think they want, just like that.'

'Well, not "just like that",' said Suri. 'There'd need to be the right book, and . . . Anyway, Effie.' She sighed. 'There are always going to be problems with travellers – in both directions. Pelham is often in trouble in your world, for example. But you need to try to learn more about this world. You need to open your eyes more when you are here. None of us can tell you how to get to the next stage of your development, but I fear you must, or you risk being sent back for ever.'

'But—'

'Hush, child,' said Cosmo. 'Just listen.'

90

'We will overlook this incident for now. Indeed, my next step is to find out where Millicent Wiseacre disappeared to and bring her in to a tribunal in Froghole.'

'So she's not dead?'

'You mean reborn, of course,' said Suri. 'No. We don't think so. We're not sure exactly where she is, though. All this is most unusual. This world normally runs very smoothly.'

'I'm sorry,' said Effie. 'I really didn't know what to do.'

'Don't worry, child.' Suri stood up to leave. She was wearing layers and layers of colourful material draped over her in ways that looked both beautiful and comfortable. She took Cosmo's hand in hers and pressed it gently. 'I'll slip out the back way,' she said. And then she was gone. It was as if she had simply melted into the air.

'You need to return to the island,' said Cosmo to Effie kindly. 'When you come back we can talk more about what happened today. But please try to learn all you can about the mainland. I fear I haven't been much of a guide, and my books are not the sort a young girl needs growing up in our world. There is so much you still don't know. Just be open to new things.'

Moonface, Cosmo's black cat, walked into the room at this point and looked at Effie as if to say, *I know the secret, why don't you?*

'Cosmo,' said Effie, 'why does everyone hate the island so much?'

'People are afraid of what they don't know,' he said. 'But also, people hear that your world runs on selfishness and greed, and that it is a very frightening place where the people exploit the poor, and the weak, and all the animals. Individualism often makes people forget others. It's mainly because you have money in your world, of course. And some other fundamental reasons as well.'

'Why is there no money here?' asked Effie.

'Aha. That's a good question, and one you need to keep thinking about,' said Cosmo. 'But now you must return. I think Pelham will go with you. Let's go to find them.'

When Cosmo opened the door, there was no sign of Clothilde, Pelham or Rollo.

'They must be in the conservatory,' he said.

And so they were. Perhaps because Suri hadn't left in the normal way via the front part of the house, they had not been alerted to the fact that she had gone. So they had no idea that the meeting was over, and that Effie could now hear them.

'And what if she really is a galloglass?' Rollo was saying when Effie and Cosmo entered the room. 'What will we do then? We can't have a galloglass in our midst. We can't have a galloglass with access to the Great Library. Bringing the book back was bad enough, however right it supposedly was. Who knows what would—'

'Hello, Rollo,' said Cosmo. 'Speculating again?'

Rollo blushed red, something that Effie had not seen before. Clothilde had gone a little pink too. Had they all been discussing her? Had they actually decided that she might really be a galloglass? Effie couldn't bear it any more. This was her favourite place, full of her wonderful new family that she was still getting to know, but with whom she felt safe and loved. But now it was all ruined.

Bertie entered the room carrying a mug of hot chocolate.

'Before you go back to the cold island,' she said to Effie.

But Effie hardly heard her. She turned and ran, out of the conservatory, down the long path to the gate, and out onto the Keepers' Plains, where she hurled herself into the portal that took her home, tears streaming down her face. Effie never cried; it was true. But she was crying now.

Wolf looked at his watch. It was almost eight o'clock in the morning. He had no idea how to get to the Borders, or how long it would take. In the olden days, apparently, people had computers that told them exactly how long a particular journey was going to take, by car, public transport or on foot. They could even book travel on their phone. Wolf had to rely on an old map he'd found at the back of Leonard Levar's shop. Using a ruler and mental arithmetic, he worked out that it was just under a hundred miles to the area he needed to get to. If he had a car, and drove at fifty miles per hour, it would take two hours to get close, which was plenty of time.

Except Wolf didn't have a car. And he was too young to drive.

His older brother Carl had a car, but Wolf hadn't seen Carl for a long time. Was it weeks, or even months now? Would Carl even care about Natasha? Carl had a different mother from Wolf, and Natasha had a different father. So in fact she and Carl weren't even related. And Carl always wanted something in return for the favours he did. No, there had to be some other way.

A train would be too expensive, and hitchhiking would be too unpredictable. Perhaps there was a bus? While he was still thinking about transport, Wolf began packing his rucksack for the day. What was he going to need? He didn't know where he was going, or what was going to happen when he got there. He didn't even know how long it was going to take. The voice on the phone had talked about 'places' on a 'programme'. What on earth had that even meant?

Wolf neatly folded a change of clothes and put them in the bottom of his rucksack. He packed several homemade energy balls – he made them every week out of seeds, coconut oil, chocolate and dried fruit. He also packed a bar of soap, a toothbrush, a tiny battery-operated radio, a length of rope, some water-purification tablets, his Swiss army knife, a small can of WD-40, a magnifying glass, a notebook and pencil, an OS map of the Borders from Leonard Levar's maps section, an old phone with a torch function and a dictionary, and a small bag of bloodstones. He filled his old army canteen with water from the tap and attached it to his rucksack.

It was now quarter past eight. Wolf had almost finished packing. All that remained was adding his Sword of Orphennyus, in its benign form as a letter opener, to the side pocket of his rucksack, where he could get it easily. Wolf had to wear a special glove when he touched it: any contact with a true warrior caused the sword to grow to full size. He packed the glove in the other side pocket.

He washed quickly and dressed in his jeans, a T-shirt, a hoody and his battered old bomber jacket. He wore his sturdiest, most comfortable waterproof-duty boots, which he'd got from the army surplus shop in the Old Town.

Wolf's walk to the bus station was a bit of a blur. There was snow: it had come overnight. But his boots powered through it; their special soles didn't skid on ice. As he walked, Wolf kept thinking about Natasha. If he could save her . . . If he could give her a better life . . . But maybe she didn't need saving. Maybe Wolf's mother had gone off and married a rich man. Maybe Natasha was having a great life. But that wasn't how Wolf remembered his mother. She was always caught up with the wrong men, in the wrong situations. Maybe Wolf could help her too. He still hadn't forgiven her for leaving him with his uncle. He just wanted to get his sister and look after her.

In less than half an hour, Wolf was on a bus to the Borders. He'd been lucky. When he read the timetable, he found he'd picked the best bus and wouldn't even have to change. Through the steamed-up windows Wolf could see that the whole city was covered in snow. But the streets were clear, and the bus chugged on.

The old phone Wolf used as a torch and dictionary had quite a good music collection on it. He put his headphones on and listened to the same Borders hip-hop album again and again. Most old phones were beginning to die now, almost six years after the worldquake. After this one ran out, Wolf would have to get a Walkman like everyone else and either play antique tapes or spend tons of money on new ones.

The bus eventually reached a village about twenty miles south of the Old Town and came to a halt. The driver killed the engine.

'All change,' he said, dinging his bell. 'All change!'

This wasn't exactly what the timetable had said. Or was it? Wolf wasn't sure.

By now, he was the only person left on the bus. When had

everyone else got off? The only other person he actually remem-bered seeing in the past hour was a girl of about his age who had been running across a bridge over a river in the opposite direc-tion from the bus. She'd been dressed almost exactly the same way as Wolf, but seemed to have a large cross around her neck and was wearing a black headscarf. She wasn't the kind of person you usually saw from a bus window, which was probably why he'd noticed her.

'Hey, you lad,' said the driver.

'Me?' said Wolf.

'Yes. I hear you might be needing this.'

The bus driver gave Wolf a small yellow device. It was a piece of old-fashioned technology attached to a karabiner clip, and was just the right size and shape to fit in the palm of his hand.

'What is it?' said Wolf. He turned the yellow plastic device over a couple of times, to get the feel of it. It seemed quite durable, probably even waterproof. It had a little off/on button and a case at the back for batteries. On the front was a small dot-matrix screen. Wolf pressed the ON button and it winked slowly into life. A small pixelated triangle soon appeared, like a little arrow. Was this some sort of GPS unit?

Wolf must have been tired. Perhaps he'd dropped off for a second. When he looked up to ask the bus driver again what he'd just given him, the man, and the bus, and indeed the whole village, were gone. He was completely alone in the rugged, endless countryside.

He looked down at the GPS again and realised that the triangle was him. And the completely empty grey area around the triangle was where he was now, completely alone.

8

'Come on!' said Marcel Bottle, knocking on Lexy's door yet again. 'Why is everyone so slow this morning?'

Marcel had been up since around six. He'd done a bit of yoga and then meditated for a whole hour. Bliss! Well, except for the bit when Buttons had decided to sit on top of his head. At some point he thought he'd heard the front door opening quietly, but it had probably been the wind. Or maybe their houseguest had decided to take an early morning stroll. Nothing wrong with that; the early morning was by far the best part of the day.

And now the whole family was going on a rare car trip so that Jupiter Peacock could see all the main sights in the town. It had been Hazel's idea. Other families, she had decided, would be giving their honoured guests tours in their cars. Well, the Bottle family had a car too, didn't it? So they could give their honoured guest a tour too.

The Bottle family car was in that unfortunate category between antique and ancient. It only worked because of the healing spells Octavia Bottle cast on it when she borrowed it each year to go on her annual seaside holiday. It was a peculiar colour: somewhere between rusty red and orangey brown. It was fair to say that no one who really liked cars would have been seen dead in it. Its upholstery, which had been lovingly wrought in brown leatherette many decades earlier, had been equally lovingly mended by Marcel, who, when he wasn't doing yoga, rather liked sewing. Indeed, Marcel liked sewing so much that he had once spent the weekend making a hundred mice stuffed with catnip for the troubled local cats' home.

'Come on, Lexy!' Marcel called again.

By now, everyone else was assembled in the open-plan living area of the Bottle House. Hazel Bottle was wearing her best rainbow-patterned heavy wool kaftan over what looked like a pair of pyjama bottoms. She had put on her only pair of high-heeled wedge boots, which made her look as if she was about to topple over at any moment. On top of the boots were a pair of purple legwarmers that Marcel had knitted for her. Hazel had a matching scarf, that she couldn't find, so instead she had put on a snood made from yellow glittery hemp yarn that had been given away for free at the local jumble sale.

Jupiter Peacock was ready too, although had only just emerged from the spare room in a cloud of French aftershave and hair pomade. His pompadour was immaculate once more. He was wearing a light turquoise linen suit through which it was unfortunately possible to see the outline of his pants. He was carrying a brown briefcase that looked as if it might hold evil plans, and his faintly bloodshot eyes were those of a man who had been up all night plotting and talking philosophy with wrongdoers and ne'er-do-wells.

Lexy had still not come down.

'I'll go and hurry her up,' said Hazel.

'No. Let me go,' said Marcel.

This time, after knocking, Marcel Bottle entered his daughter's bedroom. As usual it was a mess of old herbals, medicine charts, dried flowers, bits of twig, crystals, gemstones and paper bags full of herbs she'd got from the market. She worked so hard, thought Marcel. She was bound to progress in no time and become a great Master Healer when she was old enough. All she had to do was find an established healer to mentor her. The Guild would be sure to let her at least go up one grade from Neophyte to Apprentice.

Marcel had wracked his brains for any healers that they knew. There were none. He was himself a hedgewitch guide, and his wife was a druid engineer. His sister Octavia had taken Lexy under her wing a bit and let her make most of the potions in the bun shop, but she was herself an alchemist elysian who cooked her buns to make people happy, not to make them better.

'Lexy?' he said. 'Come on, we're all waiting for you.'

'I don't want to go,' she said.

'Why ever not?'

'I'm too busy. I've got exams to revise for, and—'

'But there's no school next week.'

'For my magic grades. Dr Green tests us every week now.'

'And you really can't spare us an hour or so? We were going to go to the Winter Fair Market for a while after dropping off JP at the university. I'll get you a spiced doughnut? Or even two? And don't they have a dried herb stall this year? It's pocket money day as well . . .'

Lexy sighed. She really did want to go out with her parents. It happened so rarely that they all got to spend time together. Her father was always doing 'community activities' like leading free yoga retreats or knitting for the needy, and her mother was either working in the bun shop or inventing things in her yurt at the bottom of the garden.

The problem, of course, was JP. But Lexy couldn't say anything.

'OK,' she said.

'Attagirl,' said Marcel. 'Wrap up warm, though. It's freezing out there.'

Back in the Realworld, Effie managed to dry her tears and get through the front door and into her bedroom before anyone asked anything about her day. Not that they ever did.

The next morning Effie woke early, feeling troubled. She always gave baby Luna her morning bottle and prepared her breakfast of porridge and fruit, if there was fruit, or golden syrup if not. If there was no porridge or fruit, then the sisters shared a golden syrup sandwich. Baby Luna loved golden syrup, and so did Effie. Effie had managed to hide a large tin of it at the very top of the cupboard in her bedroom, where Cait, her step-mother, could never find it, knowing if she did she would either eat it all (on binge days) or throw it out (on diet days).

This term, Cait was teaching evening classes on medieval manuscripts and so usually didn't get up until later in the morning. On weekdays Effie and Luna usually had their breakfast alone. But this was a Saturday, which meant that Orwell Bookend joined them. On Saturdays, while Effie spooned porridge and golden syrup into baby Luna's bowl, and then tried to stop it going all over the floor, Orwell Bookend would read out 'amusing' things from the local paper.

Normally Effie only half-listened to these. Occasionally, there was something funny. More often it was disturbing or violent, and Orwell simply *thought* it was funny. But this morning, Effie didn't hear a word he said. She was still trying to work out what had gone so wrong in the Otherworld. She kept replaying the scene where Rollo was saying, in that definite way of his, *We can't have a galloglass in our midst. We can't have a galloglass with access to the Great Library.* Maybe he was right. Maybe Effie didn't fit into their world.

'Listen to this,' said Orwell, chuckling. He read out some story about the local cats' home that Effie didn't even hear. She knew she was supposed to be laughing, but all she could do was sigh.

'So,' said Orwell. 'Ready for a bit of slave labour?'

'I suppose so,' said Effie.

'What's wrong with you this morning? I thought you were looking forward to coming to the university.'

'I was,' said Effie. 'I mean, I am.'

'Your fat friend's going to be there, too.'

'Maximilian?'

'Yep.'

'How?'

'I asked him the other day. And Nightdress Girl.'

101

'Raven?'

'Yep. I can't believe that any of my other colleagues will have managed to recruit THREE willing children to help them. I know Callie Quinn has two, although one of them is reluctant, I hear. We'll have the Linguistics Faculty stall done in no time. And then I'll release the three of you into the library to run wild. That was what you wanted, right?'

'Yeah. Thanks, Dad.'

'And you will try not to die in there?'

'I really don't think it'll be that bad.'

'You do know that the bit you probably want is down about five flights of dark and rickety stairs?'

'We'll find it.'

'And it's almost certainly haunted?'

'I don't care.'

'What's the matter with you? Usually you laugh at about 10 percent of my jokes. But this morning we're still at zero.'

'Nothing. I'm just tired.'

It was all true about the University Library. Maximilian had found out about the hidden underground archive after he'd arrived there by accident on his way back from the Underworld. To get to the 'Special Collections' (which didn't come up in a normal library catalogue search) without going via the Underworld you had to go down flights and flights of stairs, and then you had to twist a creaky old windy thing to open and close the stacks, which were basically massive shelves on wheels of a sort that had featured in every horror film about libraries since the beginning of time. Some of the stacks – most of them, if you listened to people like Octavia Bottle or Madame Valentin

– had not been opened for hundreds of years and had dead bodies squashed in them. The dead bodies were so old that when you opened the stacks you could hear their bones crumbling to the floor.

Obviously, this all meant it was the perfect weekend treat for children. Well, perhaps not most children. But Effie had been looking forward to it for ages. There were plenty of things she needed to look up. But now, of course, the most pressing thing was to try to find out what she'd been missing about the Otherworld. What was it they wanted her to understand, but for some reason couldn't tell her?

Baby Luna started throwing porridge at the wall, which meant breakfast was over.

'Ten minutes,' said Orwell Bookend. 'Wear old clothes.'

All Effie's clothes were old, of course, except for the ones she kept in the Otherworld. She sighed wistfully as she thought of her comfortable, light room there, and her cousins. And she felt tears well up again when she thought of Rollo and his suspicions about her. She'd show them she definitely wasn't a galloglass. She just wasn't yet sure how.

The ancient old car struggled up the hill past the Esoteric Emporium and then the vast gates to Blessed Bartolo's.

'*Another* school?' said Jupiter Peacock, sounding like someone who was trying – and failing – to sound interested. 'So many children. It must be quite exhausting living here.'

'Blessed Bartolo's is quite famous,' said Hazel.

'What for?' asked Jupiter.

But it seemed that nobody could remember.

'Was it a murder?' said Marcel, after a while.

'I thought it was a kidnapping,' said Hazel. 'And then a murder.'

Lexy wasn't listening. She was trying to move as far away as she could from JP. He had just pinched her arm yet again. He'd been doing it ever since they left the house. Every time he did it he smiled at her, as if it was their own private little joke, although his eyes, if you looked at them closely enough, were cruel and mocking.

Lexy had originally tried to suggest that their honoured guest should go in the front of the car, but Jupiter Peacock had claimed that he always got car-sick unless he was in the back. And so Lexy was trapped. On and on went the guided tour. And just when it seemed that they had actually seen all the sights, JP would ask about some other thing – municipal graveyards, allotments, pet shops – and the car would sputter off in some new direction.

'We should park somewhere and show JP the Winter Fair,' said Lexy. 'There are loads of good stalls this year.'

And for that she got another hard pinch. The worst one yet.

'Ow,' she said, as softly as she could. 'Stop it,' she whispered. She couldn't risk her parents hearing her. If they asked what was going on and she told them, they'd probably be cross with her for upsetting JP. It had all been going so well – at least, as far as Hazel was concerned. JP had complimented her just this morning on her toast-making skills and asked her where she had bought the lovely guest soap he'd been given.

He surely was just messing around. And anyway, maybe Lexy had encouraged him. After all, she had failed to say no to the arm wrestling and the horrible kiss. He probably thought she liked being pinched. Even though she'd just said to stop, he might have thought that she was joking, or secretly enjoying it or something. If she told on him, perhaps everything that followed would actually be her fault. And if her parents got cross with him that would ruin everything for them.

If they even believed her. And why would *anyone* believe her? After all, what sort of professor went around pinching children? If Lexy said anything to anyone they'd no doubt just say the pinches couldn't have been that hard, or it must have been a joke. Children pinched each other all the time and it wasn't a big deal.

Maybe that was the problem. Maybe Lexy just couldn't take a joke. The thing was, it didn't particularly feel like a joke. Lexy knew deep, deep down that what was happening was really very wrong but she couldn't work out what to do about it.

'So what's your book about?' Marcel asked JP.

'It's not really *my* book,' said Jupiter Peacock. 'After all, who could really claim to own such a magnificent piece of beauty? In fact, "Galloglass" was written between one and two thousand years ago by a man called Hieronymus Moon. I actually carry his spirit around with me in a ceramic bottle, which I can show you later, if any of you are interested. Anyhow, I have merely *translated* his book, in order to bring it to a modern audience. Of course, it is a book of poetry, and poets are divided over whether translating a work creates a new version of the first work, or a completely new work altogether, or . . .'

Hazel, who always got sleepy on car journeys, and who had been up very early that morning to work on a new design for a hemp-rope hammock, emitted a gentle snore. Marcel elbowed her. Jupiter took the opportunity to pinch Lexy again, this time on her leg, and then carried on speaking as if nothing had happened.

'It's called *Galloglass*, as you already know,' he said. 'And I have added a tiny subtitle: *In Praise of the Selfish Individual*.'

'That's right,' said Marcel, nodding. 'I remember now. I read all about it in the *Old Town Gazette*. You're against the concept of community.'

'Indeed,' said JP.

'How can anyone be against community?'

'For all the reasons it says in the poem,' said JP. 'If you know someone is going to feed you, it stops you from learning to feed yourself. Community holds people back. It makes them soft. Community makes people complacent. It takes away their natural desire to thrive.'

'So taking our neighbour a casserole when she gets out of hospital is "holding her back"?'

JP sighed. 'It's not quite as simple as that.'

'Or teaching people how to meditate, or do yoga?'

'As long as they pay you, it's fine.'

'What's wrong with doing it for free, though? I enjoy the voluntary work I do in the community.'

'Aha. So you're actually doing it for *yourself*, for your own enjoyment, and not for the community at all! If you were truly selfless, you'd hate every minute of it and do it anyway. As I have always said, there's no such thing as altruism. No offence, but this world is ruined by do-gooders who like to keep their own egos inflated by "helping others" when in fact they are just helping themselves and – yes – holding other people back. It might be different in other worlds, but here we are designed to be individuals, and to operate according to our selfish desires. It's better for us, and better for others.'

'Well, when I teach yoga in the community I—'

'Yes, yes, I can see it now. Some dreary church hall with dripping radiators, or some dire school canteen with squashed peas still on the floor from lunchtime. People arrive all timid and grateful because they're getting something for free. They don't value the lessons you give them, because you give them for nothing. No one makes an effort to look nice, because why would you bother for a free yoga workshop? Everything is ugly and dull and boring and grey and . . .'

This was an oddly accurate description of many of Marcel's free yoga workshops.

'Well, how would you do it differently?' he asked.

'Wear my very best yoga clothes. Charge people fifty pounds for a workshop. Let them see that I, and my practice, have *value*. Offer them something to aspire to. I would try my very best to be an inspiration to people, not a dull charity-giver.'

Marcel Bottle let out a deep sigh.

'Well, everyone's entitled to their opinion,' he said. 'Where next?'

'I think I'd like to see this Winter Fair, please,' said Jupiter Peacock. 'And then perhaps you could drop me off at the university? I have a meeting there this afternoon.'

'No problem,' said Marcel, wondering whether he should in

fact just tell JP to walk from now on if he wanted to go somewhere. Was that what this Hieronymus Moon would recommend? Maybe someone should get him out of his ceramic bottle and ask him. After all, if you drive people around everywhere you are surely robbing them of the chance to walk. JP could certainly do with losing a few pounds. But Marcel didn't say anything because he was too nice.

Soon the car passed a massive mansion built in an ancient Russian style. It was painted a light, tasteful pink and its metallic-hued domes sparkled in the weak winter sunlight: one was gold-plated, one was silver-plated. The third was solid bronze. Two security guards stood watch beside a set of golden gates.

'Good heavens, what's that place? Not another school?' asked JP.

'That,' said Marcel, 'is the local cats' home.'

'But how . . .?'

'It's quite a long story,' said Marcel. 'But basically someone donated a billion pounds to them. Inside that building are the richest cats in the whole world. Each one has its own butler. Their food is served on solid silver platters. I hear that the chef is in line for the first Michelin star to be given for pet food.'

For the first time that morning, JP actually looked impressed. Or maybe it was just surprise. Whatever it was, he gave up pinching Lexy for the next ten minutes while they drove to the Town Hall car park.

108

Wolf took a deep breath. OK, he could do this. The landscape might look bare on the screen, but in front of him it wasn't so bad. His trained warrior's eyes scanned for water, for animal tracks leading to water (animal tracks always led to a source of fresh water if you followed them for long enough), for landmarks he could use to navigate, for enemies, and for sources of food or material he could use to construct a shelter. Flowers often pointed south, he'd once read. But of course Wolf didn't yet know where he was and therefore in which direction he was supposed to go. And there were no flowers.

He looked again at the yellow object in his hand. If he pressed a button on the side, he got a set of coordinates. Wolf got out his map. Using the numbers on the screen, he found he could plot his position.

The good news was that he knew where he was, and he'd be able to find his location for as long as the batteries lasted in his device. The bad news? He was still in the absolute middle of nowhere. Somewhere in the distance a bird called, and then nothing.

Wolf looked at the other spot he'd marked on the map. The place he'd been told to get to before midday. It was now 10.30 a.m. Wolf knew he'd have to hurry. *I'd get here as quick as you can. We operate on a first come, first served basis. And there's intense competition for the places on our programme. I'd waste no time, if I were you.* Maybe he was already too late.

It had been sleeting when Wolf had gone to bed the night before. This morning there'd been a lot of snow. He'd thought of lighting a fire, and then hadn't been able to because he was waiting for the phone to ring. But now, out in this wilderness, the sun had come out, and Wolf felt warm enough to take off his hoody and stow it in his rucksack. He kept his bomber jacket on. He tightened his boots and put on the pair of sunglasses he had in his pack. He was ready. He set off.

9

Nurse Odile Underwood was going to be late for her shift at the small secretive hospital in the north-east corner of the Old Town. She didn't like working weekends because there were more magical accidents then, but the nurses took it in turns, and this weekend it was her turn.

'Maximilian!' she called again.

She'd promised to drop him off at the university on the way.

Eventually he appeared. He'd grown up so much since he'd epiphanised on that rainy afternoon in October. He'd lost a bit of his puppy fat, though he was still a broad, imposing-looking child. He'd taken to wearing mostly black, and drinking quite a lot of strong coffee. Odile wondered when she should tell Maximilian that she knew what he was trying to hide. She'd heard him playing Beethoven. She'd seen the way he now looked at art. He'd asked for opera tickets for his twelfth birthday.

He was a dark mage, just like his father had been.

He was a scholar too, although who knew where that had come from. Not that *kharakter* was really something that people inherited. Not usually. But it was uncanny just how like his father Maximilian was. He had the same eyes. The same jawline. But he was kind where his father had been cruel. That was the big difference, of course.

Odile looked at the recipe her neighbour Dill Hammer had given her for the meal they had shared last night. It was simpler than she'd thought it would be.

Maximilian, being a mage scholar, should really have been spending all his time in his bedroom thinking of dark things and finding new ways to travel to the Underworld (Odile knew all about those trips, too, and had asked her friend Calico Quinn to keep half an eye on her Neophyte son when he was there). But Maximilian had been popping over to Dill Hammer's bungalow quite a lot lately to talk about the Diberi, and conspiracy theories, and the best ways to cook quinoa. It made sense that Maximilian liked quinoa – his taste in food had been very odd since he'd epiphanised – and so last night Odile and Maximilian had gone to Dill's and eaten what became a feast of strangeness: a warm winter salad with chicory, kale (which Dill Hammer had actually massaged) and blood oranges, alongside tempeh burgers with kimchi and miso. Desert had been a special fermented pudding that Dill Hammer had been tending in his cellar for weeks.

It was all a bit suspicious.

Odile knew almost everything about her son, except this. Why on earth would a mage scholar who wore black and listened to Beethoven all the time want to hang out with a fusty old hedge-witch with a whole shelf devoted to books on identifying mushrooms? Mind you, mushrooms could be sort of magey too.

Maybe that was it. And Dill was nice. He and Odile had been friends for years.

'Maximilian!'

He emerged from his bedroom in black jeans and a black jumper as usual, with that strange silver vial around his neck. Maximilian was wearing his Spectacles of Knowledge regularly again, which was a good sign. The spectacles at least were likely to be sensible. He had his school rucksack with him too. He was stuffing into it a big notepad and the pencil case that contained his fountain pen, three pencils and a selection of black onyx and haematite crystals that Odile hadn't been able to help noticing last time she'd cleaned out her son's room. The haematite was for scholars. But the black onyx was a mage's stone.

'Remind me what you're doing at the university again,' said Odile.

'Helping Effie's dad set up his stall.'

'Aren't you supposed to be at the university next week as well, instead of school?' Odile frowned. 'Is it next week or the one after? I honestly can't keep up with everything you do. I remember the good old days when school was just simple. You went to one place, learned something and then came home . . .'

'It's next week,' said Maximilian. 'I brought a letter home. I'm going to be in the Creative Writing Department.'

'And is Effie's dad paying you for helping him today?'

'No. He's letting us use the library as a reward.'

'The University Library?'

'Of course. What other library is there?'

'It's just . . .'

'What?'

'Nothing.'

'What?'

'Well, it is a bit dangerous in there. I mean, I take it you'll be going to Special Collections. You will be careful?'

'Yes, Mum.'

What was it about mothers? Odile Underwood knew – or, in some cases, rightly suspected – that Maximilian had recently braved, among other things, poisonous spiders, an evil bookseller, a houseful of existentialist faeries, a dream doctor in the Underworld and – perhaps worst of all – the experience of learning to ride a horse. But she was still worried about him spending Saturday afternoon in a library.

'Bunting?' repeated Orwell Bookend. The face he made when he said this was the same one he pulled when he walked into a room just after baby Luna had been changed. It was as if he was being completely enveloped in the heady smell of fresh poo.

'*Bunting?*' he said again.

'And balloons,' said the student helper.

'Balloons?' said Orwell. The way he said 'balloons' suggested a much larger quantity of much smellier poo. 'I'm not having balloons on my stall. *Balloons*, for heaven's sake! Absolutely not. This is a serious university faculty. We explore language, meaning and great literature in a dignified way. This isn't a blooming children's party.'

'They're having bunting and balloons outside on the gates all week long,' explained the student helper. 'To make people feel welcome during the Winter Fair.'

'Welcome? Hmmm. But do balloons *really* make people feel welcome?' said Orwell. 'Has there been a study? Are there facts and figures? Surely they just have a cheapening, mind-numbing, distracting effect. Oh, for goodness' sake!'

While he'd been in discussion with the student helper, Effie and Raven had tacked up two rows of cheerful bunting above the Faculty of Linguistics stall, and Maximilian had blown up a number of yellow and purple balloons. They were doing an excellent job. There were several reasons for this. One was that they were very helpful and nice children. Another was that they too hated bunting and balloons and wanted to get out of there as soon as possible. They wanted to be alone in the library to talk privately and look at magical, forbidden books.

Effie, Raven and Maximilian needed to chat particularly urgently about something peculiar they'd just seen. Laurel Wilde, who had recently joined the university's Creative Writing Department, and Dora Wright, who had once taught at the Tusitala School for the Gifted, Troubled and Strange, but who now also taught here at the university, had been in the dimly lit corridor just beyond the Great Hall, laughing and joking with Terrence Deer-Hart – the children's author who, of course, had been in league with Skylurian Midzhar, and who had been involved in the kidnappings of both Laurel Wilde and Raven Wilde. What on earth was going on?

Not only that: Dora Wright seemed to have undergone a complete transformation. The children hadn't seen her since September, when she'd won a short story competition and then been captured by the Diberi. She'd then been made to work in a factory creating cheap fiction that was destined to be read, pulped and then sort of boiled down into tainted lifeforce for the Diberi to use in their evil schemes.

Back in September, Dora Wright had been a normal teacher who wore unflattering long skirts and flowery tops with sensible shoes and baggy tights. Now she was resplendent in a black chiffon gown with a lurid stormy-purple feather boa. She had dyed her hair a sort of pinky-blue colour and somehow made it much, much bigger. It no longer flopped at either side of her head like the pelt of a dead creature, but rose alarmingly towards the heavens like a cat that had taken fright at something. Her eyelids were heavy with sky-blue eyeshadow. Particles from her perfume were currently heading into outer space. There were bits of glitter in constant orbit around her.

'What do you think happened to Miss Wright?' said Maximilian, attaching another yellow balloon to the end of the pump.

'She does look very different,' said Effie. 'Quite nice, though. I mean, you definitely wouldn't lose her in a crowd. But more importantly, why was she talking to Terrence Deer-Hart? I didn't think they knew each other.'

'I suppose they're colleagues now,' said Maximilian. 'And they'll be our teachers next week.'

'My mum says that they've all forgiven Terrence Deer-Hart because he was actually under Skylurian Midzhar's spell when he kidnapped us,' said Raven. 'And she says that Miss Wright looks like that because of all the romance novels she's written. All her characters dress like that. Eventually all writers grow into their characters, according to my mum.'

'So is your mum going to become a child magician, in that case?' said Maximilian, blowing up another balloon and then passing it to Raven to be tied.

'She does wear a lot of capes, I suppose,' said Raven. 'And she spends her spare time doing ballet, horse-riding and eating chocolate. In some ways she is actually a lot more like people our age than people her age. And she believes in magic now, after what happened with Skylurian. I think she might even have epiphanised. So who knows?'

After Raven and Laurel had been kidnapped by the Diberi they'd become much closer for a while. But just lately Laurel Wilde had started going out in the evenings and either leaving Raven alone, or with one of the poets, playwrights or librettists who seemed constantly to hang around the house. Laurel's current favourite was Torben from the Borders, who wore pyjamas all day, ate black garlic sandwiches and used a lot of swear-words in his poetry.

'What are you children nattering about?' said Orwell. 'There'll be plenty of time for idle chit-chat later. Come on – I want to finish before the others do.'

Effie pulled another string of bunting out of the old carrier bag that had been brought by the student helper. It felt quite nice being back in her normal world again, chatting with her friends. And as long as she didn't think at all about her last trip to the Otherworld, then everything was fine.

Effie sighed. The problem was that it was impossible not to think about it. If only it hadn't happened at all. Effie wished so much that she could go back in time and do everything differently. But what would she really change? Should she have lied when

117

Dr Wiseacre had questioned her? She climbed onto the stepladder and tacked up the bunting. The sooner this could be done, and the sooner she could get to the library, the better. There must be something more she could find out about the Otherworld.

Effie tried not to glance at Tabitha Quinn, who had been giving her evil glares from the Department of Subterranean Geography stand for the last half an hour. She was there with her mother, Professor Quinn. Effie had been hoping she might bump into Leander, Tabitha's older brother – who was much nicer, and who was an interpreter just like Effie – but so far only Tabitha had turned up to help. She was ridiculously attired in a deep-purple silk flapper dress which was covered in crystals, and she had a string of pearls around her neck. On her feet she wore white high-heeled Mary Janes. It was how all the junior girls at Blessed Bartolo's dressed at the moment.

Last time Effie had seen Tabitha had been on the fateful night of the *Sterran Guandré*. Because of Tabitha, Effie had lost her valuable calling card that took her directly to Truelove House. Afterwards, Tabitha claimed she'd been put under a spell by the powerful Diberi Skylurian Midzhar, but Effie wasn't completely convinced. And she had no idea why Tabitha would still have it in for her. Effie had also beaten Tabitha at tennis once, but surely she would have forgotten that by now?

Several minutes later – by now the minutes were feeling more like hours – Effie was so focused on untangling an ancient-looking string of bunting – and not looking at Tabitha – that she hardly noticed that a broad, big-haired man was suddenly looming over her. Lexy was standing next to him with a strange expression on her face.

'This is Effie Truelove,' Lexy was saying.

'Aha!' boomed the man. 'Yes, I'd been hoping to meet the famous young Truelove girl. Hello!'

Orwell Bookend looked up from his own tangle of bunting. He appeared finally to have given in about the decorations, though he didn't seem very happy about it.

'Another Truelove perhaps?' said Jupiter Peacock to Orwell, stepping forward and holding out his hand.

'No,' said Orwell sourly. 'Who are you?'

'Professor Jupiter Peacock. Call me JP.'

'Ah yes,' said Orwell, brightening as he always did when he realised he was talking to a famous person, especially one who could influence one of his promotions. He took JP's hand and shook it enthusiastically. 'I'm Dr Orwell Bookend, Dean of the Faculty of Linguistics. And you've translated that, er, book . . . I hear it's doing rather well . . . And of course you're giving the Midwinter Lecture on Monday. We're all looking forward to it very much.'

Jupiter Peacock reached into his brown briefcase and pulled out a thin hardback book with a purple cloth cover and gold lettering.

'Here,' he said, giving it to Effie. 'A family copy. For you and your, er . . .'

'He's my dad,' said Effie. 'We've just got different names.'

'For you and your father then.' JP smiled widely without showing any of his teeth. He looked a bit like a balloon that had been blown up a little too much – like all the ones Maximilian had just done.

'Thanks,' said Effie, putting the book down on the trestle

table alongside some torn bunting. She wasn't really that interested in having a 'family copy' of some book translated by a visiting professor whom her father wanted to impress. But whatever.

Now someone else approached their table. She was extremely thin and dressed entirely in black lace, except for her platform boots, which were white, and her fur cape, which was pale grey.

'JP,' she said, drawing out the letters for much too long in her very deep Russian-sounding voice. 'There you are.' She rolled her Rs unnervingly. 'The others are waiting for you in the seminar room. Gotthard is very excited to see you again. Don't keep him waiting.'

Orwell Bookend held out his hand.

'Hello,' he said. 'You must be Lady Tchainsaw. I've read *all* your poems.'

This was, of course, a lie. Orwell never read poetry, if he could help it. But Lady Tchainsaw was also quite famous and had recently joined the university's Creative Writing Department. It was always good to get in with the creative writers. Not only were they the most famous members of the university, but everyone knew they had the most fun.

She completely ignored him.

'Come on,' she said to JP, then turned to leave.

'Sure,' he said. 'Oh, but before we go you might be interested to know that this is Euphemia Truelove.'

Lady Tchainsaw turned again slowly, like the revolving head of an owl.

'Euphemia Truelove?' she said, looking Effie up and down as

if Effie were a small shrew that the owl was just about to swoop down on. 'Hello, *darlink*.'

'Er, hello,' said Effie.

'Well, see you later, folks,' said JP cheerfully. 'Come on,' he said to Lady Tchainsaw, who was still staring at Effie in an intense and suspicious way.

Effie didn't notice the title of the book on the trestle table until Jupiter Peacock had followed Lady Tchainsaw down the gloomy corridor in which Laurel Wilde and Dora Wright had just been seen. But when Effie did look at it her heart seemed to fly into space like a rocket before landing with a massive thump back in her chest. GALLOGLASS, it said on the front. That was its title: *GALLOGLASS*.

It was as if he knew. But how could he?

'Who exactly was that man?' said Effie to Lexy.

'No one,' said Lexy. 'A very annoying person.'

'What's this about?' Effie asked her, picking up the book. As well as the gold lettering on the front, its pages had gold edges. Effie's heart was thumping so hard she felt sure that everyone could hear it.

'God knows,' said Lexy, rolling her eyes.

'What's wrong with you?' said Maximilian to Lexy.

Lexy was certainly more gloomy than anyone had ever seen her. She was usually so cheerful. And whenever one of the others was miserable or defeated, it was always Lexy who found the remedy – which usually involved a cup of herbal tea, a freshly charged crystal and an early night. But now she didn't answer. She just frowned.

Effie opened the book. Inside, the words were arranged in a

121

long column, with an awful lot of footnotes. Every other line seemed to rhyme with the one just before it. It was clearly some sort of poem. Mrs Beathag Hide had once tried, unsuccessfully, to teach her class the names of things that happened in poems. Were these iambic pentameters? Rhyming couplets? Pterodactyls? Effie had no idea.

'It's about how being selfish is really great,' said Lexy. 'If you're into that sort of thing.'

'What?' said Effie. 'Seriously?'

'Yeah. Apparently galloglass is like a category of person . . . Some people think they're selfish and horrible, but actually they're really important and inspiring and wonderful. *Apparently*.'

Effie had listened to the first part of what Lexy said but missed the sarcasm in the last word. This was a book that said it was a good thing to be a galloglass? Suddenly, Effie wanted to read it, more than she wanted to read anything else. Just then Orwell reached over with one of his big hands and scooped up the book.

'Thank you,' he said. 'I think I'll have this.'

'*Dad!*'

'What? Don't tell me you suddenly want to read poetry? Trust me. This won't be your sort of thing.'

'But—'

'You can read it after me, if you're that desperate. In the meantime I'm going to mug up on all this galloglass theory so I can ask a very informed question after the lecture. Ha! I'll show them.'

It was never clear exactly whom Orwell meant when he said 'them' in this way. But he looked quite pleased with himself.

'Right. Didn't you all want to go to the library?' asked Orwell.

'If you're sure you don't need us any more, Dr Bookend,' said Raven.

Orwell took the library key from his pocket.

'I see we now have almost the full complement of your little friends.' He looked at Effie, twirling the key in his long fingers. 'The only one missing is the tough boy. Where's he today?'

It was a good question. Something else to discuss as soon as Effie and her friends could get some privacy.

'I don't know,' she replied.

'So we'll be looking for *four* bodies down there if you get lost, or if there's another worldquake, or if everyone simply forgets about you? Not five?' Orwell Bookend delivered this the way he delivered all his jokes: without any trace of humour. It was clear he *did* mean this to be funny, though: he didn't really believe in magic, and especially not magical libraries. And how could something that didn't exist be dangerous?

Effie sighed. 'We'll be fine. But yes, there's only four of us.'

'Well, don't say I didn't warn you,' said Orwell. 'It's vast, dusty, dark and full of things you shouldn't be reading. If anyone asks, I didn't give you this.' He gave Effie the key. 'Now go.'

'Thanks, Dad.'

Wolf was very hot by the time he reached the spot he'd marked on the map and cross-referenced with the coordinates on his yellow device. He was in the middle of a massive field with pale, dry grass. There were no houses or other structures. In fact, Wolf couldn't see any evidence of human life anywhere. Just miles and miles of grass. What had he done wrong? There was nothing here. Had he just walked through the wilderness for nothing? He checked his coordinates again. And again.

Midday was approaching fast. It was now 11.40. Wolf felt like crying – although he hardly ever cried – or kicking something – although there was nothing to kick. This was his best chance of finding Natasha, and it looked like he'd blown it. Had he simply got the coordinates wrong? Very occasionally Wolf got something wrong in one of his Sudoku puzzles. Instead of doing what he wanted – which was binning it and starting a new one – he always forced himself to go back, find the mistake and put it right. Sometimes this involved rubbing out scores of numbers.

He realised that this was what he was going to have to do now. Retrace his steps until he found his mistake. Realistically he didn't know how he would even begin to do this. He could see in every possible direction, and there was nothing out here. Perhaps he'd gone wrong as far back as where the bus had dropped him off.

The sun was peaking in the sky. Wolf had to face the very real possibility of having failed his mission. And what then? Would he have to spend the night out here? If he was going to do that, he'd need to find water. And build a shelter. Wolf could see a tree in the distance, and noticed that the land sloped downwards. Water was probably in that direction. He had his purification tablets, of course. Although for now he still had what was left in the old army canteen that hung from his ruck-sack. So he didn't need to panic, or start gathering supplies just yet. He needed to think.

The only thing in this whole bare landscape, apart from the tree in the distance, was a single rock about fifty metres away. He'd sit on the rock, have some water and an energy ball, and then make a decision about what to do next. Generals can't think on an empty stomach, after all. Hadn't Sun Tzu written that in *The Art of War*? He wasn't sure. Still, he pondered some more of the book's wisdom now: *The Wise Warrior, / When he moves, / Is never confused; / When he acts, / Is never at a loss.*

He needed a definite plan.

Wolf eased his rucksack off his shoulders and put his backpack down by the rock. There was something a little odd about it, but Wolf wasn't quite sure what it was. There were lines scratched into it that looked a bit like letters or something. MMXIV. Wolf ran his hands over the numbers. It was a good thing he hadn't just sat down. As soon as his hand made contact with the rock, it make a low, sinister creaking sound and then started to move.

Wolf sprang back and watched as the rock rose into the air to form a tall grey pillar. Another one steadily rose out of the ground just opposite, and then another one, and another. The pillars now formed the corners of a large rectangle. There was a sort of metallic heaving noise as the last part of this happened, as if a hundred school radiators were coming on at the same time.

'What the . . .?!' said Wolf, jumping backwards again.

More pillars appeared from the ground. And then a whole building began rising up in the area that they had marked out. It was also grey, but while the rocks seemed ancient, the building was metallic and military-looking. Wolf checked his map again. The building was coming out of the ground in exactly the place at which he had been told to arrive before midday. He gulped. It was 11.45. Perhaps, after all, he had arrived on time. He'd surely found where he was supposed to go. Which meant that he hadn't failed in his mission. Not just yet. Was Natasha in there somewhere?

Once the building had finished emerging from the ground everything became still and quiet again. It was as if nothing had ever happened. Except now there was this vast grey structure standing there in the middle of nowhere. It must be top secret. But why? And what connected Natasha with people who would have a top secret underground facility in the remote Borders? Wolf gulped again, took a last sip of his water and slipped his rucksack back on. He made sure he could reach his sword if he needed it: even though it only worked on magical people, it still looked very impressive. And anyway, who knew what was in that building?

Wolf approached it. Was there a door somewhere? There had to be. He went around the vast structure once. It took five minutes. Nope. No door. But that was impossible. Wolf had trained his mind to think fast, so in a couple of seconds, hundreds of thoughts had run through his brain like rugby backs passing the ball back and forth and back and forth and . . .

Wolf went to the place where the rock had been, where there was now a tall pillar. Scratched into the ancient rock were the letters MMXIV. Wolf memorised them but then, as back-up, took out the small pen he wore around his neck and wrote them on his hand. There was nothing else on the pillar. MMXIV. What could that mean?

Was Wolf supposed to enter this building or not? They –

whoever they were – were not making it very easy. Wolf understood that this was a test. He had already embarked on the 'programme', whatever it would turn out to be. There was no going back. He just had to find a way in.

10

Neptune's life had become extremely boring, and he wasn't sure why. Once upon a time he would lord it over all the stray and domestic cats that had the misfortune to wander into the Tusitala School grounds. As official school cat, he was entitled to claw and scratch the living daylights out of any other creature that came within his territory. Being school cat also meant Neptune was fed the scraps from school dinners, which included real meat and fish, while most of the local domestic cats were fed those hard, dry pellets that were made of, among other things, old pencil shavings and sofa fluff. The strays had to make do with voles.

But now there were no strays to gloat over.

What was going on? Even the domestic cats didn't bother to come to the school grounds any more. Much of the Cosmic Web avoided Neptune (mainly for fear of being eaten by him) and so his world had been reduced to the occasional scrap of news from an incredibly sulky owl.

One of the domestic cats used to postpone being attacked by

offering Neptune regular snippets from the pet noir novels that her owner liked to read aloud. Neptune had found he rather liked the idea of being a cat-detective and solving a crime. He desperately wanted to know how the latest story ended. But Mirabelle had stopped visiting. Neptune realised that he had not seen another cat for weeks.

A long Saturday afternoon stretched before Neptune. If it had been a school day he could have spent some time terrorising the younger children. There was one child – a girl – whom he'd seen once in the distance and had felt an inexplicable urge to talk to – as if it was even possible to speak to humans. But, anyway, it was not a school day. Neptune realised that he had a choice to make. Was he going to turn around, go back into the school and get one of the melancholy resident staff to give him a tummy rub, or was he going to accept this call to adventure and set off to find out what had happened to all the missing cats? A third option, of course, was to go and eat another guinea pig. But none of the cat-detectives in the stories seemed to eat guinea pigs; they were too busy solving crimes. Perhaps, mused Neptune, he really ought to try again to give up guinea pigs.

He turned towards the school. Maybe just one tummy rub, maybe just half a guinea—

A bolt of lightning suddenly struck the ground in front of him, melting what was left of the snow and ripping a large hole in the rugby field. It was almost as if the universe was telling him to . . . to . . .? What was that story about the cat who went to London with that queer-looking boy with a handkerchief on a stick? *Turn again, Neptune . . . Turn again . . . Accept your adventure.* This voice was not outside Neptune; but it wasn't really inside him, either. It gave him the heebie-jeebies. But he knew it was right.

No more guinea pigs. No more tummy rubs. Neptune understood that now was the sacred moment when he was going to leave all this behind and set off. He was going on an adventure, as everyone must do at some point in their lives. He was going to find the missing cats and then . . . He didn't know what. Perhaps that was the point of adventures. Perhaps you couldn't know how they were going to end, or what you were going to find. You just had to take that first step into the unknown.

'He was right, it is dark,' said Raven.

'And dusty,' said Maximilian, coughing.

No one noticed the faint traces of glitter in the air, although they were there.

The four friends had gone down three flights of stairs so far. The official Library Reception was apparently on the first normal floor. But since the children weren't really supposed to be in the library, they'd been told not to go to reception. Or not that reception anyway.

'No doubt the books you want are in the more *esoteric* wing, in Special Collections,' Orwell had said. 'Fourth basement floor and turn left, according to rumour. And then down the spiral staircase. But I am not taking responsibility for anything that happens to you, including death. On your own heads be it.'

Effie was finding it difficult to get frightened in the University

130

Library. After experiencing the Great Library – which, due to existing in another dimension, is always on the verge of ripping its browsers out of the familiar fabric of space and time – no other library was ever going to scare Effie. But this one was, objectively, to a normal person, quite chilling.

There were no electric lights of any sort down here. Instead, each child carried a candle-lamp. The flames danced on the stone walls like apparitions at a ghostly disco. There were cobwebs everywhere. Some of these were so old and so large that they hung from the ceiling in great mushroomy folds, like old velvet curtains.

'Are you sure this is the right way?' said Lexy, pulling a large piece of cobweb out of her hair.

'Nope,' said Raven.

'One more floor,' said Maximilian. 'And then we turn left.'

'And why are we here exactly?' said Lexy.

'To read forbidden books,' said Maximilian, happily.

'Why do we want to read forbidden books?' said Lexy, unenthusiastically.

'Have you not been paying attention?' said Maximilian. 'Um, maybe because we're magical and we need more knowledge? Or because we want to hone our skills so we can defeat evil? Or . . .' Some unseen glitter went up his nose at that point and he sneezed.

'Are you all right?' Raven asked Lexy. 'You seem a bit grumpy.'

'I'm just tired,' said Lexy.

Effie could tell it was more than just that.

'Are you sure?' she asked.

'Yes!' snapped Lexy. 'I wish everyone would just leave me alone.'

'All right,' said Effie. 'Keep your hair on.'

More than anything, Lexy wished she could tell her friends what had happened with JP. But she didn't know how she would start. And anyway, it was just like with her parents: it would either be impossible to explain ('What, he just wanted to arm-wrestle you? What's the harm in that?') or she'd describe the creepiness of it so well that they'd insist that something should be done about it. And then Hazel wouldn't win her prize and the whole of the Midwinter holiday would be ruined. Lexy had decided to just put up with whatever happened in the next week for her mum's sake. After all, how bad could it get? But for some reason this decision was making her moody and grumpy. She just had to try to remember not to take it out on her friends.

'I expect there'll be some good healing books down here that you can't get anywhere else,' said Raven to Lexy. 'I'm looking for a healing spell myself. One of the tarantulas is a bit off-colour. I've tried everything else I can think of.'

'I'll help you find it,' said Lexy, smiling gratefully at her friend.

'What are you looking for in the library?' Raven asked Effie.

'Books on the Otherworld,' said Effie. 'Otherworld customs, histories . . . I won't know exactly until I find it.'

'I thought you already knew everything about the Otherworld,' said Maximilian.

'Apparently not,' said Effie.

'Is that why you suddenly need more deepwater so quickly?'

'Sort of.'

'Has something happened?' asked Maximilian.

Effie sighed. Where would she begin? She couldn't tell the

132

whole story of what had happened in Froghole. She didn't want her friends to think that there was even a possibility that she might be a galloglass. They might start speculating about her like Rollo had done, and she couldn't risk that. Perhaps Maximilian would understand, but she couldn't tell him with the others here.

'It's all right,' said Effie. 'It's boring. I'll tell you some other time.'

The children made their way down the last twisting flight of stairs and suddenly there it was. SPECIAL COLLECTIONS. This was presumably what it had once said. Now it simply said **SP I L COL   ONS**. The sign was – or had once been – a handsome wooden rectangle with gold lettering, hanging from a brass chain above an ancient-looking oak roll-top desk. But the chain was now tarnished and the sign was draped with cobwebs. The desk, however, was tidy. It was the only thing in the whole library that seemed free of dust. On the desk was yesterday's edition of the *Old Town Gazette*, open at the cryptic crossword.

'What do you want?' said the man sitting behind the desk. He was small and wrinkled and had an awful lot of facial hair, all of it red.

'Who are you?' said Maximilian.

'I am the Special Collections librarian,' said the man. 'Who are you?'

'I'm Euphemia Truelove,' said Effie, stepping forward. Her name sometimes had a helpful effect on elderly magical people who remembered her grandfather. But not this time.

'And?' said the man, unimpressed. 'We don't usually have

children down here. In fact, we don't usually have anyone down here. Been quite a rush on today, though. Very curious indeed. Very curious.'

Lexy sighed. 'Come on. We might as well go. He's not going to let us in.'

'I said we don't usually have children down here,' said the librarian sternly. 'I didn't say you couldn't come in. All epiphanised people are welcome down here. We only have three rules. No chewing gum. No talking. And if you die, it's your own fault. Furthermore, there's no catalogue, so don't come here asking me where a particular book is. If you don't already know where the books you want are, then I can't help you. All right? Good. Now I just need your names.'

Wolf knew he had to hurry. He had to enter this building by midday. But how did you enter a building with no door?

He walked around the perimeter again. This time he looked more carefully for anything that could be a door. Of course it wasn't until he got to the third side of the rectangle that he found it. Just a faint outline in the wall. Only visible in exactly the right sort of light. Wolf touched it and an old-fashioned digital keypad came up on a touchscreen. It had numbers from one to nine laid out like on old phones. Each number had a blue circle around it. Clearly Wolf was going to have to put in an entry code to get the door to open.

But the only code Wolf had was in letters: MMXIV. Had he missed something? Should he go back? Then something flashed into his mind. Something from a book on Napoleon. A date. It had been written with an M at the beginning like this, but it was longer. The M actually meant one thousand and then there were lots of other letters that spelled eighteen hundred and something.

Of course. The letters were not letters at all but numerals. Roman numerals. He'd skimmed through a book on the subject in his early days in Leonard Levar's shop. One M was a thousand. Two Ms were two thousand. X was ten, and . . . Wolf worked out that together these letters stood for the number 2014. That had to be the entry code.

Wolf tapped it into the keypad.

Nothing happened.

He looked at the keypad again. There were only two other buttons on it. One had a big C and the other had a big hashtag. Wolf tried pressing the C. His numbers disappeared from the display. So C obviously stood for 'clear'. What was the hashtag for? Wolf tapped in the numbers 2014 again and then tried pressing the hashtag.

The metallic door slowly opened. It slid sideways, like doors used to do on TV programmes featuring spaceships. But Wolf was sure this wasn't a spaceship. Though he had no idea what it was. He knew that going through a door like this was probably a mistake. No great military leader would ever do it. Napoleon wouldn't. Sun Tzu wouldn't. But presumably neither of them had ever lost their ten-year-old sister.

Wolf took a deep breath and walked in.

Neptune padded lightly through the field of alpacas – who all bleated crossly at him – and then across the empty sports field until he came to the Tusitala School back entrance. This was it. He was going to leave the school grounds for the first time ever. What was beyond these wrought-iron gates? He had no idea. Surely nothing he hadn't seen already inside the school grounds. Neptune, like all creatures bound to one universe, one planet or one locality, simply could not visualise the unknown. The unknown is, of course, by definition, not known.

So he was surprised first of all by the metal boxes on wheels that whizzed past him. Sure, he'd seen these things from the gates. But up close they were smelly and dangerous-looking. They had humans in them, some of them clinging to a round thing. Neptune cut down an alleyway as soon as he could to get away from them.

A deep species memory told him that this alleyway would normally be a dangerous place, full of cats waiting to attack him. Indeed, he knew from Mirabelle's pet noir stories that Bad Things happened in alleyways. Occasionally the cat-detectives in her stories had to confront gangsters in alleyways while fighting off the feral, scrawny local cats. Neptune quite fancied a fight. It would warm him up. Despite his thick coat he was freezing. But there were no cats here. There was no one at all. Just slush and rubbish.

Neptune felt dirty. This World Beyond wasn't as clean as the school grounds. He jumped up onto a wall and began to wash himself. Neptune decided to have a little think while he was washing. It was all very well setting off on an adventure, but didn't most adventurers have some sort of objective? Neptune reminded himself that he was looking for the missing cats. Well, they weren't here. They were probably all dead. How much did he really care? He let out a small sigh. Could he go home now?

Just then, he smelled something unmistakable.

Guinea pig.

It was coming from the garden on the other side of the wall. It smelled delicious.

Surely just one wouldn't hurt . . . For the road, as they say.

Everybody who visits a library does so for some reason. People go there to pick up another thin paperback featuring doctors falling in love with nurses or beautiful secretaries who feel compelled to marry their sulky bosses. There were many Matchstick Press editions of these sorts of books still out there, mainly in provincial libraries and dusty corner-shops, that were enchanted, and therefore incredibly addictive, and so people who'd read one had to read more.

Other people visit libraries to discover facts, or to find out how to make things - sometimes even quite dangerous things. Some people go to libraries to learn how to read tarot cards, or write in secret code, or create a detailed astrological chart, or write novels, or install a washing machine without a plumber. There is not much that cannot be learned in a proper library.

And then there is the small, rather niche group whose members go to the library looking for the precise spell that will help them in their plan to take over the entire universe.

'I do not see why,' said a Russian voice, 'we are wasting our time in this library to which almost everyone in every known world has access. The spell will not be here! It will be hidden.'

'The spell is here,' said a clipped Northern European voice. 'Hidden in plain sight, as all the best things are.'

'What does that even mean?' asked a familiar, sulky voice, the kind that went with the kind of hair that has been over-styled with a heated comb. '"Hidden in plain sight?" It's always sounded a bit stupid to me, to be honest.'

'In my experience,' said a haughty voice that made Lexy's blood run a little cold, 'if you want to hide something from the masses, you put it in a prayer, or a book about antiques, or a poem. Some of the greatest secrets about this world are still hidden in Plato's *Republic*. Yet more are published every day in a popular newspaper's Country Diary column. The more you hide something, the more likely people are to look for it.'

'Yes, well, we have the poem already,' said the Russian voice.

'And most importantly we have the author of the new universe,' said the Northern European voice hurriedly.

'Ow!' said the Russian voice, as if its owner had just been kicked.

There was then a strange period of silence.

Raven looked at Lexy. They were crouched down between two shelves in the section of the library that seemed devoted to spell books. The library was not arranged in any normal way. There was no catalogue, as the librarian had said. Raven and Lexy had had to turn a large brass winder to get these shelves apart at all. No dead bodies had dropped out, thankfully. Raven had just found a book called *Spells for Healing Your Spider* – which was either very lucky, or in fact proved the existence of cosmic ordering, the zero point field and magic in general – when the voices had entered this section of the library.

The voices – and their owners – were now in the next stack along.

'Yes, I told you,' said the Northern European voice. 'Here it is. *Instructions for Entering Other Dimensions* by Thomas Lumas. Oh, and a companion volume by the same author called *Pedesis for Beginners*. Bingo.'

'Well, if it's that easy to find the books, why isn't everyone just travelling to other dimensions all the time?'

'They are,' said the haughty voice. 'People are always popping off to the Otherworld and the Underworld. Especially since the worldquake. The Otherworld is 10 percent closer to us now, which is of course another good reason for shutting it down. It's having too much influence here.'

'Well, why can't we also just "pop off" in this way?' asked the sulky voice.

'You know why. I thought we explained this. The Diberi are banned from entering the Otherworld by normal means. And to penetrate as deeply as we want to means we need help. A lot of help.'

'And the consciousness of the Truelove girl.'

'Indeed.'

'Good heavens,' said the Northern European voice.

'What is it?' said the Russian voice.

'Well, if we wanted to go to the unfortunate realm known as the Troposphere – long abandoned as simply the closed and dangerous imaginary world of an early twenty-first-century novel – we'd only need some holy water and homoeopathic charcoal. But to get as deep into the Otherworld as we want to, we're going to need to create a rather more complicated spell.'

'And? We can do that, surely?'

'Yes, so long as we can manage to get hold of the Northern Lights, the Bermuda Triangle and the Luminiferous Ether. And obtain, somehow, the eye of a live yeti. Oh, and a pure maiden. Some snakes. And . . . several hundred live cats. Well, that bit will be easy at least.'

'And we'll have to kidnap the Truelove girl, of course.'

'Yes. That bit should also be . . . Wait! Did you hear something?'

It was true. There had been a noise. The noise had been Raven gasping, for the second time, when these unseen voices had said 'the Truelove girl'. Whoever these people were, they were planning to kidnap Effie, and then . . . Raven didn't understand what they were talking about exactly, but it seemed to involve some sort of raid on the Otherworld – probably Dragon's Green, where everyone was always trying to get to.

Lexy kicked Raven.

'Shhh,' she said.

It was too late. The footsteps belonging to the voices started moving out of their stack and towards theirs. Raven cast the Shadows, a simple spell that bends the darkness near you in such a way as to make you virtually invisible. She cast it on herself and Lexy, although it seemed to take longer than usual – as if something nearby was weakening her magic.

'There's no one here,' said the Russian voice.

'Well, let's close this stack anyway,' said the haughty voice. 'I want to see what's in the next one.'

140

This was the second major problem with stack systems, which had also been explored in every horror film in existence ever to feature a library. It wasn't just that they were full of dead bodies. It was that the reason they were full of dead bodies was because of how easy it was to be crushed to death in them.

Unfortunately the Shadows rather slows down those under its influence. Raven and Lexy tried to move as quickly – and quietly – as they could to the end of the stack as the shelves started to close in on them. But it looked as if they were going to be too late.

'N—' Raven began to say.

Then two soft hands silently grabbed Raven's arms and pulled her into the next stack along. A hand quickly clamped over her mouth. It smelled sort of familiar. Raven struggled and twisted and turned until she could see who her captor was.

'Mum!'

'What are you doing here?' hissed Laurel Wilde.

'Looking for books. What are *you* doing here?' asked Raven.

'Shhh!' said Laurel Wilde. 'They'll hear us . . .'

'Who are they?'

'Our esteemed colleagues,' whispered Dora Wright, emerging from the closing stack in a quiet puff of glitter and perfume, and holding on to Lexy.

'But . . .'

'Just be quiet for now,' said Laurel Wilde. 'We'll explain everything later.'

11

The guinea pig smell was coming from an old brown shed at the end of the garden of a narrow, yellow-brick terraced house. The aroma was strong. Could there be more than one guinea pig in there? Neptune imagined a vast, illicit feast. Then a long, deep, meat-fuelled sleep. Then a bit of guilt, of course; there was always that. But then, afterwards, continuing with his adventure would probably put all those unpleasant thoughts out of his mind. Yes, perhaps all he needed was sustenance. No adventurer got very far on an empty stomach, after all.

Neptune sprang easily down off the wall and into the garden. As well as the guinea pig scent, he could sense a lot of Cosmic Web activity here. Maybe some hibernation going on nearby, maybe under this holly tree? Hmmm. Exotic food. But where . . .?

No, the Cosmic Web around here was very much awake. Neptune could pick up excited babbling and chatter coming from inside the shed. The door was closed, but there was a latch similar to the ones on the guinea pigs' cages in the school staff room. Neptune jumped up onto a convenient window-sill and used his paw to knock the latch from horizontal to vertical. The unlocked door seemed to breathe out as it opened. Then Neptune jumped down and used the same paw (his left – like many cats he was left-pawed) to pull the shed door open so he could slip inside and . . .

And . . .

Well, what the . . .???

There was a guinea pig here, that was for certain. It was in a cage on a table at the far end of the shed. It was long-haired, black and appeared very, very old, with wise black eyes pressed into its face like tiny ancient raisins. It had the beginnings of a grey beard. All around the cage and down on the floor members of the Cosmic Web – squirrels, rabbits, robins, blackbirds, shrews, mice, voles and hedgehogs – were . . . were . . . Neptune moved into the shed to see more closely. But yes, how bafflingly peculiar. The animals seemed to be . . . they seemed to be . . .

They were actually *worshipping* the guinea pig.

The babbling he could hear was some kind of ancient Cosmic Web chant: a Song of the Divine from the very olden days. Not that the Cosmic Web experienced time in the same way as humans and domesticated animals, of course. For them, the olden days were now, and vice versa. Time wasn't a line; it was more of a blob. Soon, Neptune began to make out some of what they were chanting. *Oh venerable one, wise one, mighty one* (the guinea pig didn't look very mighty, or even very *meaty*, in fact, but whatever), *sagacious master, knowledgeable one, long-haired sage, seeker of the ultimate mystery* . . .

Then, abruptly, the chanting stopped.

A new, quite different song began.

Cat!!! Cat!!! Danger!!! Danger!!!

143

The Cosmic Web was good at removing itself quickly when it had to. In a haze of fur and feathers and claws and beaks the shed began to empty, as all the small mammals and birds escaped through the many holes and burrows by which they'd entered. In a few moments, the shed had cleared, and Neptune faced the guinea pig alone.

It seemed to take for ever before the voices – the Russian one, the haughty one, the Northern European one and the slightly sulky one – faded and eventually disappeared from the University Library.

Laurel Wilde let out a breath she hadn't realised she'd been holding. She released her grip on her daughter.

'Now will you tell us what's going on?' asked Raven.

'Soon,' said Laurel. 'Where are your other friends?'

'Maximilian and Effie?' said Raven.

'And Wolf,' said Dora.

'Wolf isn't here,' said Lexy. 'But Effie and Maximilian are still in the other wing, I think.'

The Old Town University Library's Special Collections section had two different wings. Although there were no signs, and no real classification system, it seemed that just under half the books related to the Realworld and just over a third to the Otherworld. There was also a small section of dark-looking volumes devoted to the Underworld. Maximilian had last been seen there. Effie had remained in the Otherworld section, browsing through maps and guidebooks.

'Please tell me you haven't become a Diberi,' said Raven to her mother.

'Don't be ridiculous, darling,' said Laurel. 'But there's no point my saying anything until we've gathered you all together. And we should stay as quiet as we can in case any of them are still here. We have to keep what we're doing top secret.'

Raven, Lexy, Dora and Laurel moved quickly and quietly through the library. Raven's magic was weakened by the proximity of her mother, so Dora Wright cast the Shadows and kept them all more or less hidden. Maximilian visibly jumped when they all materialised next to him just as he was trying to work out how he could borrow all fifteen books he was clutching to his chest. As a result, he dropped them all, which made a massive crashing noise, which made Effie come from four stacks away to see what was happening. She was holding three books of her own. *Otherworld Customs and Traditions: A Modern Traveller's Guide* was the biggest one.

'What's going on?' asked Effie, when she saw Laurel Wilde and Dora Wright, and then registered the confused concern on her friends' faces.

'You need to come with us now,' said Dora Wright. 'Then we'll explain.'

'Can we take these books out first?' asked Maximilian.

'All right, but we must hurry,' said Laurel Wilde. 'We have to go back upstairs into the main university. To the chapel . . .'

'The chapel?' said Raven.

'The Diberi can't go into chapels and religious places. We'll be safe there.'

'So you're definitely not the Diberi?' said Raven.

145

'Oh for heaven's sake, darling,' said Laurel. 'Stop asking stupid questions and follow us.'

It turned out that taking books out of Special Collections was easy. The librarian even seemed quite glad to see the books go.

'Are you sure you only need fifteen?' he said to Maximilian, when he put his pile down on the wooden counter. 'Take more! Take the whole blooming lot – see if I care. Less to clean. Less to read. No blooming space down here anyway . . .'

Effie checked out her books as well – which also seemed simply to involve vaguely showing them to the librarian while he shrugged and rolled his eyes – and then followed Maximilian up the stairs. Maximilian didn't move that fast at the best of times, and his pile of books slowed him down even more. By the time they reached the door back into the main University Library, Laurel, Raven and the others were fading into the distance.

'Hurry up,' said Effie.

'I'm trying!' said Maximilian.

The university buildings were very confusing. It was a bit like being in a massive version of Truelove House. There were long corridors and dark passageways, little sets of winding stairs leading to courtyards and cloisters that led to other little winding sets of stairs. It wasn't long before Effie and Maximilian were completely lost and there was no sign of the others. Perhaps they should have turned right, rather than left, at the bottom of that last set of stairs.

'Do you have any idea where the chapel even is?' said Maximilian.

'Nope,' said Effie.

'Is there a map anywhere?'

146

'Back at the main entrance,' said Effie. 'But I don't know where that is from here either.'

'I thought interpreters were supposed to be good at reading maps!'

'They are if they have one.'

'All right. I'll use the Spectacles of Knowledge. Hang on while I get them out of my rucksack. I had to put them away when we were in Special Collections because they were getting too—'

Suddenly, voices emerged from a window somewhere above them. One sounded Russian. Another sounded sort of familiar. A bit sulky. Effie and Maximilian instinctively shrunk into the darkness, and Effie cast the Shadows.

'I should find it fairly easy to kidnap the Truelove girl,' said the familiar voice. 'I'm friends with her father. At least, I think we're still friends. There was an unfortunate incident where I—'

'And then, darlink, you will bring her to me.'

'But—'

'You don't think there's anything wrong with us having our own tiny little separate plan, do you?'

'Well—'

'Your hair, darlink, looks so marvellous today. And how is your beautiful book coming along? I hear it is going to be magnificent.'

'Um . . . Yes, well – gosh, a little warm in here, isn't it? Shall I open the window a bit more?'

'Some of this champagne will chill you, darlink. But first let us talk about this book of yours. Remember our agreement? You will be author of the new universe, and I will be its queen. I will have total power, and you will serve me.'

'But Skylurian said . . .'

'Her plan was beautiful indeed, but now she is not here and so you need a new queen. You must not forget to write me properly, darlink. Make it clear I am ruler of all – and give me unlimited powers.'

'But my editor . . .'

'I am your editor now, darlink. And don't you forget it.'

'And Professor Forestfloor . . .'

'You can completely ignore *him*.'

There was a popping noise, and the clink of glasses.

'Haha! That tickles.'

'This should cool you down a little . . .'

There was the sound of a window being closed, and then the voices disappeared.

Effie and Maximilian looked at each other.

'Was that who I think it was?' said Maximilian.

'Terrence Deer-Hart,' said Effie. 'Yep. And Lady Tchainsaw too, from the sound of it.'

'Who's she again?'

'That Russian poet. She came to Dad's stall earlier.'

'She doesn't sound very nice.'

'No.'

'Wasn't Terrence Deer-Hart supposed to have repented after what happened with Skylurian?'

'Mmm,' said Effie. 'And now he's planning to kidnap me. Great.'

'You could maybe try to sound a little bit more scared . . .' said Maximilian, raising an eyebrow.

'I'm sick of being scared,' said Effie. 'Anyway, he can't kidnap me while I've got this.' She touched the sword on her necklace, but didn't say the magic word that would make it materialise. 'We're stronger than he is. There's nothing to worry about. He's small fry. And anyway, it sounds like he's going to be kept busy writing that terrible book about whoever he was talking to.'

Maximilian frowned, but didn't say anything. He'd got out his Spectacles of Knowledge and was putting them on in place of his normal glasses. He'd been trying to wear them more often, but it was exhausting being bombarded with TMI all the time. The spectacles seemed to think that Maximilian wanted to know literally everything about everything: he couldn't even look at a boring wall without being told about its construction materials, precise dimensions and the names of the people who built it. Sometimes Maximilian wondered if the spectacles were doing it out of spite, or jealousy, ever since it turned out that scholar was his art rather than his *kharakter*.

'Right,' said Maximilian, seemingly to the air. 'A map of the university, please? No – not its entire history! And not so many pages . . . Come on – just a user-friendly map, please. No, not the thing they give out to children on Open Days. Just . . . Look, forget it. Can you give us directions for the quickest way to the chapel?'

It wasn't always fool-proof asking the spectacles for directions, because they didn't always send you via the most direct or normal route. They seemed to like everything to be as educational as possible and so would often plan an elaborate 'historical tour' when you simply wanted to go from A to B. Once they went through a period of turning everything into a ghost walk, which was quite creepy even for Maximilian. This was why computers had been so useful, in the days when they still worked. They didn't think for themselves, or get in a huff about anything.

'OK, follow me,' said Maximilian to Effie.

The route the spectacles devised only took five minutes, for which Maximilian was grateful. The university's multi-faith chapel turned out to be a separate building that was made from very old stone. Just as the spectacles started telling Maximilian exactly what kind of stone it was, and precisely what was intended to happen in a multi-faith chapel, and some of the finer points of Jainism and how Jains, who were members of a Buddhist sect who would not even kill insects, differed from Janeites, who liked to dress up as characters from Jane Austen books, Maximilian took them off and put them away.

Effie pushed open the heavy wooden door to find a small empty chapel with wooden seating and waxy candle-holders. Large stained-glass windows turned the dull outside winter light into something softer and more peaceful, with all sorts of lovely colours dancing through the air.

'Where is everyone?' asked Maximilian.

Effie shrugged and looked around. Then Lexy emerged from a door just beyond the quire.

'There you are!' she said. 'Come on, the meeting's already started.'

'What meeting?' said Effie.

She and Maximilian followed Lexy through the door and into a windowless room lit by many candles. The main thing in the room was a huge wooden table. And around it sat various people, including Dora Wright, Laurel Wilde, Mrs Beathag Hide, Festus

Grimm, Leander Quinn, Professor Quinn and, at the head of the table and currently speaking, Pelham Longfellow.

◉

Wolf crossed the threshold of the strange, spaceship-like building. He half expected it to take off, to carry him deep into outer space, like in films from the past. But nothing happened. There was a large silver and white atrium, with a high ceiling and many levels of gallery-style corridors, with lots of what looked like office doors. To Wolf's right was a reception desk, with no one behind it. The reception desk was made out of white plastic, as if from another age. Had Wolf gone back in time? No one used plastic like this any more. It was illegal, had been for decades.

'Yarright?' said a man's voice, suddenly. The owner of the voice emerged from a door behind the reception desk. He was wearing a white shirt and, bizarrely, a pair of silver trousers.

Great. A different language.

'Eye spect youre looookun for le programme,' said the man. It was English. Sort of. Just. It was a Borders dialect, Wolf realised. He was still in the Borders, more or less. Good.

'Yes,' said Wolf.

'Nahm?'

What? Oh, name. 'Wolf Reed,' said Wolf. The man wrote it down on a list. He made Wolf a name badge which had, as well as the words WOLF REED, a strange sort of barcode on it.

'Tek a seet ear, laddie, and wait to be callt.'

Wolf couldn't possibly sit down, so he paced around the recep-

151

tion area. What would he say if . . .? What would he do if . . .? But he had no idea what was going to happen.

Wolf heard a sort of electric whooshing sound and turned around. A girl a bit older than him had come through the same door as Wolf. She must have worked out the thing with the code as well. She was dressed a bit like Wolf in casual clothes from the present day, except when Wolf looked more closely he could see she had trainers with plastic on them. So not from Wolf's world, then. Maybe somewhere abroad.

She looked at him. 'Hello,' she said.

'Hi,' he said back.

'Do you have any idea what we're supposed to do?' she said. 'I was told to be here by noon. I don't even know what this is.' She opened her arms as if to take in the whole vast structure. There had to be at least a hundred levels. Over in the far left-hand corner Wolf noticed a glass elevator.

'I have no idea either,' said Wolf. 'I think you have to sort of check in with him.' Wolf watched her walk up to the reception desk and saw she was also given a name badge. Eventually there was a crackle and a voice came over a Tannoy.

Would Mr Wolf Reed proceed to Level Seven. Mr Wolf Reed to Level Seven, please.

Wolf shrugged at the girl and started heading for the lift.

Then the same metallic voice spoke again.

Ms Lucy Dare to Level Seven, please. Ms Lucy Dare to Level Seven.

Lucy hurried after Wolf and they got in the elevator together.

'Do you know why you're here?' Lucy asked Wolf, as the glass doors shut.

152

Wolf pressed the button for Level Seven.

'I'm looking for my sister,' he said. 'A man rang and told me to come here. What about you?'

'My mother,' she said. 'She's been moved to a new clinic. I was told to come here to get the address.'

'Did whoever spoke to you mention anything about a programme?'

'No,' said Lucy. 'What's that?'

'I don't know,' said Wolf. 'But I don't like the sound of it.'

'You may approach,' said the long-haired black guinea pig in the cage on the table at the back of the shed.

Neptune didn't particularly feel that he needed to be invited. He was already padding towards the table, and then leaping up onto it, wondering what kind of latch was on the guinea pig's cage. There was no latch that Neptune could not undo. He was unusually gifted in that respect. But as he approached the door of this cage his appetite seemed to diminish. And why did he feel so . . . so . . . Why had his legs stopped working?

'Sit,' said the guinea pig.

Neptune sat down. Given what had just happened to his legs, he had little choice.

'I expect you came here hoping to eat me,' said the guinea pig.

Neptune looked sheepish. That didn't mean he looked like a sheep – which would be stupid for a cat. It just meant he looked a little bit ashamed of himself. His furry head drooped. It was one thing eating guinea pigs quickly, after a brief struggle, but weird and embarrassing having one actually say it directly like this. And one of the main things people (and cats) do when they are embarrassed is simply lie.

'Of course not,' said Neptune. 'Why would I do such a—'

'We both know you are lying,' said the guinea pig. 'But it hardly matters. Your insatiable hunger brought you to me, which makes it neither a good thing nor a bad thing but simply a useful thing.'

Neptune had no idea what the guinea pig was talking about.

'But your hunger wasn't why you left home, was it?' said the guinea pig. 'Not directly. You didn't leave home simply to find sensual pleasure and to eat new things. You left for a far nobler reason. You had a different kind of hunger. Yes.' The guinea pig nodded wisely, and then closed its eyes for a few moments. It looked tranquil, almost as if it had gone into a very deep meditation. Neptune wondered again about eating it. But his legs still wouldn't move.

'You need to focus your mind on higher things,' said the guinea pig, without opening its eyes. Its voice was sort of whispery but loud, and very spiritual. Neptune found himself listening, despite himself.

'There is more to life than pleasure and eating,' the guinea pig said. 'You left home to solve a mystery. Yes, I can see it now. You are a true seeker. A hunter. Domestic animals don't often epiphanise, but I can see that you are going to. You want to know about the lost cats. You have a deeper, nobler hunger. You need to learn to focus and channel *this* hunger, not the more obvious, basic kind. Do you understand me?'

'Sort of,' said Neptune. 'I do want to change. I want to learn.'

154

Bizarrely, he almost meant it.

'Good. You want to be a true hunter, one who quests for knowledge, rather than experiences or mere things?'

'Yes,' said Neptune, and this time he did mean it. A strange feeling came over him. One he had never really experienced before. Everything felt peaceful and light, and he realised not only that there were Higher Things, but that the world of Higher Things was much more interesting and pleasurable than eating guinea pigs. You just had to trust it, and know how to approach it.

Neptune did not know how to approach it.

He wasn't sure if he trusted it.

The feeling went away.

'Yes,' said the guinea pig. 'You have felt it, I can tell. You have felt the Flow. Just briefly, I expect.'

'I want to go there,' said Neptune.

'What makes you think it's a place?' asked the guinea pig. A slight smile began to appear under its lopsided whiskers.

'I don't know,' admitted Neptune. 'But I do. Tell me what to do.'

'You may come closer,' said the guinea pig. 'Open my cage.'

Neptune didn't quite trust himself to do this. What if he just forgot himself and . . .? He had the feeling that eating such a wise creature might mean he was never again able to experience the Flow, whatever it actually was.

'Come on,' said the guinea pig. 'I won't bite.'

Neptune did as he was told.

The guinea pig shuffled out through the cage door and sniffed the air.

'Of course,' it said, 'I can leave whenever I like. But I enjoy living with these people. The little girl is called Molly. She grooms me nicely. But we all know that the best way to be groomed is by another mammal. With teeth. Will you groom me?'

Neptune gulped. He could smell the guinea pig's blood. He could almost taste its warm flesh. It would be tender and . . .

He remembered what it had been like in the Flow.

His legs worked again. He stood up and walked closer to the guinea pig. The guinea pig closed its eyes. Could Neptune really do this? He tentatively licked the guinea pig's head. The fur was softer than he'd thought. He rasped through it once again, with his sandpapery pink tongue. The guinea pig let out a little sigh.

By the time Neptune had finished, the guinea pig had a minia-ture Mohican and was comfortably damp all over. Neptune had de-fleaed the guinea pig as well, and removed a few stubborn tangles from the fur at the base of its spine, an area guinea pigs find almost impossible to groom themselves.

'Thank you,' said the guinea pig. 'You will feel the Flow again soon. And you will find what you seek. But you must not give up searching when things get difficult.'

'I won't,' said Neptune.

'Good,' said the guinea pig. 'You must now look for the cat they call Malvasia. She doesn't live far from here. You will need to hurry. I can feel that things are changing in the ether. You may be the only two left.'

'Thank you,' said Neptune.

'Thank *you*,' said the guinea pig. 'That's by far the best grooming I've had for a long time.'

'Thank you for showing me the Flow,' said Neptune.

'You found it all by yourself,' said the guinea pig. 'Now go. Speak to Malvasia.'

'Thank you,' said Neptune again, as he jumped down off the table. 'I hope we meet again.'

12

Pelham Longfellow stopped speaking when he saw that Effie and Maximilian had come into the room. His eyes met Effie's only briefly, and then he looked away. Was that disappointment Effie had seen, just before his gaze left hers? Now he looked down at the table and fiddled with a stack of papers in front of him.

'The children are all here now, I see,' he said.

'You'd better join us,' said Festus Grimm to Effie and Maximilian. 'I think there are just enough chairs. Get some from the back.'

The last time Effie had properly seen Festus had been several weeks before. He'd been annoyed with her for ruining his investigation into some con artists in the Edgelands Market that he'd called 'vile galloglasses'. And obviously the last time she'd seen Pelham Longfellow she'd been fleeing from Truelove House after overhearing them talking about *her* being a galloglass.

'I would like it to go on record once again,' said Pelham, as Effie and Maximilian got chairs and looked for places around the table, 'that I don't think it's a good idea to have children involved in this.'

'I'm not convinced that we have a choice,' said Mrs Beathag Hide. 'They cannot be bound as we can. It's a loophole that I think we have to exploit, or else . . .'

'Surely it is the Diberi who exploit loopholes,' said Pelham Longfellow.

'That is true,' said Leander. 'And we're supposed to be the good guys, right?'

'We should start from the beginning,' said Dora Wright. 'The children should know who we are, and why they are here. Then they can make their own choice. It is important that everyone follows their own heart.' She touched her chest gracefully, her fingers adorned with diamanté rings.

'Agreed,' said a tall, beautiful American woman who looked faintly familiar to Effie. Hadn't she been there on the night of the *Sterran Guandré* when Skylurian Midzhar had been buried alive? Hadn't she been Albion Freake's wife?

Effie caught Maximilian's eye as they arranged themselves at the large table. Maximilian shrugged almost imperceptibly, as if to say 'Don't ask me', but Effie could see the glimmer of excitement in his eyes. She raised an eyebrow. What were they about to find out?

Effie found a space next to Leander, and Maximilian sat next to Professor Quinn. He looked small next to her. She was a large, striking woman wearing a dark green silk dress with a vast burgundy felt cape resting on her shoulders. She had around her neck a silver vial similar to the one Maximilian wore, and diamonds dangled heavily from her small ears. You could tell she was Tabitha's mother, although of course she was a lot nicer.

'You already know some of us, I believe?' said Pelham Longfellow. 'But I'll go around the table anyway. I'm Pelham Longfellow, obviously. This is Beathag Hide, Festus Grimm, Laurel Wilde, Dora Wright, Frankincense Heart, Professor Calico Quinn, Leander Quinn and Claude Twelvetrees. We are all members of the Gothmen.'

The children looked at one another and exchanged frowns and shrugs. No one had heard of the Gothmen. The word was *almost* familiar to Effie in some way. Had she heard it somewhere before? She touched the caduceus in her hair, but could not get an exact translation. Gothmen. *Gothmen.* Hmmm.

'Goth*man* is Rosian for "friend",' said Pelham Longfellow, seeing Effie touching the caduceus. '*Gothmen* is a kind of patois word – a combination of English and Rosian. We are not all men, obviously.' He frowned. 'We're a group with connections in the Otherworld but we mainly function here in the Realworld. We—'

The tall, beautiful American woman who had been introduced as Frankincense Heart interrupted. 'We're spies,' she said. 'Following the Diberi.'

Raven shot a surprised look at her mother. She took in – for the first time – her mother's new way of dressing. The long charcoal silk gloves, the tiny diamond dagger pin in her lapel. So this was what she'd been doing every evening?

'We are more than mere spies,' said Mrs Beathag Hide. 'We also take action.'

'Well, someone has to,' said one of the two younger adults around the table, Claude Twelvetrees. He looked like a student,

160

in his patched tweed waistcoat and crumpled white cotton shirt. His messy dark hair fell into his eyes and he pushed it to one side with an ink-stained hand. Effie noticed that Leander was gazing at him intently, with a strange, confused look in his eyes. 'No one else cares about the Diberi any more. Especially not the Guild.'

'The Masters still care,' said Pelham. 'And everyone in Dragon's Green is very aware of the threat posed by the Diberi. Perhaps none more so than the Trueloves.' He glanced at Effie for a millisecond and then looked away. 'It is, after all, the Great Library that they most want to attack.'

'Who exactly are the Masters?' asked Maximilian.

'Our only friends,' said Claude, with a wry half-smile.

'We are affiliated mainly with the Masters,' explained Festus. 'They believe in the peaceful integration of all worlds.'

'But who exactly are they?' asked Effie.

'The Masters are a group of pre-wizards,' said Dora Wright. 'Effie, your grandfather Griffin was one of them. We wondered if you already knew that. Masters have achieved the highest level of magic it is possible to attain in the Realworld. Wizards have to live in the Otherworld, as you probably know. Masters are one step away from becoming wizards and leaving this world for ever. But most of them want to leave it a better place.'

Effie remembered that her grandfather had applied to the Guild to become a wizard and had been turned down. He'd received the letter just before he had been attacked.

'The background to all this is rather complicated,' said Mrs Beathag Hide. 'Especially for children. Particularly ones who are not strong historians.' She raised a dark, angled eyebrow.

It was, sadly, true. History was no one's strong point. Lexy was good at sciences. Effie was best at languages. Raven was good at creative writing and anything to do with nature. Only Maximilian had any ability in history. But all he'd learned at school were the rudiments of an official timeline that didn't include anything to do with the Great Split, the existence of magic or the Otherworld. At school all they learned about was the Third World War and the second great fire of London. And a bit of Henry VIII and the Nazis too, of course.

'Very briefly,' said Pelham Longfellow. 'Since the worldquake, more people have been able to visit the Otherworld. More people have epiphanised. Some say it is because this world has become 10 percent more magical, but no one knows if this is actually true, or even accurate. What *is* clear is that the two worlds, having originally split however many hundreds, or even thousands, of years ago, have recently moved closer together. Some mainlanders welcome this. But most of them are highly suspicious of islanders.'

Effie sighed quietly. She'd had first-hand experience of this, of course.

Pelham went on. 'The Guild of Craftspeople has recently had a change of leader. Masterman Finch is a splittist, just like the Mainland Liberation Collective.'

Mainland Liberation Collective. Effie had heard this name somewhere recently. Oh yes, she remembered now. Wasn't that the group that Millicent Wiseacre was in? Effie shivered briefly at the memory.

'A splittist?' said Maximilian.

Pelham continued speaking. 'A splittist is someone who

162

approves of the Great Split and disapproves of the worldquake, which brought the worlds closer together again. Anyway, both the MLC and the Guild want the Otherworld and the Realworld to have no further connection with each other. They want the portals closed, and magic to be much more tightly controlled in the Realworld. It's complicated to explain, but the Diberi are also separatists, although in a much more extreme way. They actually want to destroy the Otherworld. They believe that the Realworld has so little magic because the Otherworld controls it all. They want more magic and power for themselves.'

Pelham paused. Professor Calico Quinn started speaking.

'Some say it would also make the Guild's life a lot easier if there was no Otherworld, so they and the Diberi potentially have some aims in common. Although of course the Diberi want more magic, and the Guild wants less.'

Pelham Longfellow sipped from a glass of water in front of him, and then began speaking again.

'The other group that is connected to all this, but doesn't really get involved, is the Council of Wizards and Elders. They are based in Dragon's Green, far away from anything. They run the Otherworld and aren't that interested in what happens here in the Realworld unless it affects the Otherworld in some way. They occasionally do deals with the Guild to take back monsters or entities that have gone astray here. And the Guild has agreed to take back all galloglasses in return.'

Lexy yawned. It was already beginning to get dark outside, and this room was gloomy despite all the candles that had been lit. She could see snow falling faintly outside. Surely it should be exciting hearing about spy networks and secret groups? But

Lexy just wanted to get home and work on her remedies. She didn't much care who was against whom and why. She'd hardly got any sleep last night after that horrible business with JP. And she wanted to put some arnica balm on her bruises from this morning.

'Anyway, it turns out that for now the only people really interested in fighting the Diberi are, well, us,' said Festus. 'The Guild no longer seems to care. There is even a rumour going around that Masterman Finch is thinking about making a pact with the Diberi. If they did any sort of deal, we'd all be in real trouble. At the moment, the Guild still has an agreement with us. But we don't know how long that's going to last now.'

'We shouldn't bore the children too much with all the politics,' said Frankincense. 'They must want to know why they are here.'

Effie nodded. 'We'll help you in any way we can,' she said. 'What do you need us to do?'

Pelham frowned. 'This is one good reason for not having children involved,' he said. 'They are too willing to put themselves in danger.'

'I agree,' said Laurel Wilde. 'I joined the Gothmen to protect my daughter, not to be her recruiter. I brought her here because you asked me to, but I'm not happy about it.'

'I'll be all right, Mum,' said Raven. 'I want to do my bit. I don't want to let the Diberi get away with anything else. They're against everything I believe in. Equality for all beings, light, love . . .'

'It's true. And of course the Diberi also want to destroy the Underworld,' said Professor Quinn, 'which they see as a place of great darkness, because they don't understand it. They are extremely serious about what they are doing. I have my son here too, but I think we need all the help we can get. And the more people under eighteen we have, the better, as Beathag said.'

'Leander's seventeen,' said Laurel Wilde. 'He's virtually an adult. Raven's only twelve, and most of her friends are still eleven. We really should not be putting them in danger. And if you're that keen on eleven-year-olds taking part in this, then where's Tabitha?'

Professor Quinn looked down at the table and sighed quietly. Everyone knew that Tabitha had helped the Diberi with their last scheme. She said she'd been under a spell at the time, but most people knew that this was a lie.

'These children have epiphanised. They have begun magical training,' said Mrs Beathag Hide. 'They have been fighting the Diberi themselves – vanquishing two of the biggest threats ever to have visited the Old Town. But it isn't fair for us to just let them carry on with their campaigns by themselves, with no support, and no idea of the wider context.'

'Agreed,' said Festus. 'I'm always getting this one out of scrapes in the Edgelands.' He nodded towards Effie. 'And it's because she doesn't know enough about what's actually happening in the worlds.'

Effie blushed. It was true. But why did he have to tell everyone?

'What do you actually want us to do?' asked Maximilian.

'You may or may not have noticed that the Creative Writing Department in the university has suddenly grown rather a lot,' said Claude Twelvetrees. 'And changed. I'm a PhD student here. My supervisor suddenly got "replaced" with Professor

165

Gotthard Forestfloor just a few weeks ago. Forestfloor is one of the more senior European Diberi. He's gathering together a group of them here at the university, but we don't know why.'

'I think we do,' said Effie. 'It's because of the library. And—'

Before she could say anything else, she felt Maximilian enter her mind with his own. The feeling was like that little jolt you get when you suddenly remember something you thought you'd forgotten.

'Shhh,' he said quietly, inside Effie's mind. 'Don't say anything else just yet. If they know the Diberi are planning to kidnap you, they'll definitely ban us from helping and we'll be out of the loop again.'

'That's true,' said Effie back. 'Good thinking. You'd better tell the others too.'

'And what?' said Festus Grimm to Effie.

'Nothing,' said Effie. 'I just think they're here because of the library. We saw them in there before.'

'Did you hear them planning anything?'

Effie wondered what she should say and quickly decided on nothing. She could always try talking to Pelham Longfellow afterwards if she changed her mind.

'No,' she said.

'We heard that—' began Raven. But then she abruptly stopped as well, as Maximilian's voice entered her mind and gently suggested that she keep what she knew to herself.

Maximilian quickly did the rounds of his friends' minds, telling them the same thing he'd agreed with Effie. He also got an update from Raven and Lexy and relayed what had happened in the library back to Effie. The friends telepathically decided not to say anything else until they knew more. They definitely didn't want to be left out of whatever was happening.

Lexy was still feeling unhappy, however, and didn't really care a great deal either way. When Maximilian went into her mind he found something he'd never encountered before – a sort of deep purple, fuzzy haze over most of her recent memories. Something had happened that she didn't want anyone to know. This was usual in most people's minds – but it didn't usually look so, well, *horrible*. Maximilian could also tell how tired Lexy felt, and sensed her lack of energy and enthusiasm for fighting the Diberi at the same time as Lexy herself realised she didn't even want to go home to make remedies. She just wanted to go to sleep for a really long time.

'Did you hear something in the library?' Dora Wright asked Raven. 'We were trying, but I think we came too late.'

There was a pause.

'I think we were too late as well,' lied Lexy. 'We didn't really hear anything. Just something about them looking for books, but we didn't hear which ones.'

Raven was grateful for her friend stepping in. Healers find it a lot easier to lie than witches do. Every time a witch lies, a tiny bit of their M-currency drains away. But healers have to lie as part of their service to others. Without the placebo effect most healers would be completely lost.

Lexy soon started to yawn and didn't say anything else.

'We need to let these poor children go,' said Frankincense. 'They're getting tired.'

'We're not *that* tired,' said Effie, glaring at Lexy.

'What do you need us to do?' said Raven. 'We really do want to help.'

'We arranged for you to be in the university this week for a reason,' said Mrs Beathag Hide. 'We need you to listen and learn. The Diberi know about most of us, and we don't think it's a coincidence that members of the Gothmen are being systematically bound by the Guild.'

'Bound?' said Maximilian. 'As in a binding spell?'

Maximilian had been reading about the spells available to higher-level scholars just recently. Although the Spectacles of Knowledge had left him with no doubt that if he wanted to become a higher-level scholar himself he'd have to stop all this dangerous mage business and focus properly on learning and research.

'That's right,' said Frankincense. 'People who are bound can no longer use magic. It often weakens the constitution as well, and people have to go to bed for months and are never quite the same afterwards. There are some very powerful binding spells out there at the moment. We don't know quite where they've come from. We can reverse some, but not all of them.'

'The Guild can't use magic on anyone under eighteen,' said Claude, looking at Leander intently, and then at Effie and her friends. 'So if you're young you can't be bound. We need as many of you as possible trained and ready in case we are prevented from fighting the Diberi. We don't know how the Guild are getting all their power, but with Midwinter approaching, and so many of us out of action—'

Suddenly, the fire alarm started ringing. It was metallic and hollow and extremely loud.

'This isn't a coincidence either,' shouted Festus over the

168

clanging noise. 'You can be sure they know we're here. They're trying to flush us out. Get us together in a group in the open so they can—'

'Everybody!' said Frankincense. 'You know what to do.'

Calico Quinn, Claude Twelvetrees, Leander and Frankincense quickly joined hands.

'Have you got something, Mum?' Leander asked Professor Quinn.

'I think so,' she said, breaking the loop for a moment and digging into her handbag. 'Yes. Here's one we haven't used before.' She laid a piece of white paper on the table. It had a column of text written in blue fountain pen.

'Come with us,' said Frankincense to Maximilian.

Maximilian understood that they were all mages, like him. He took Frankincense's hand and felt Professor Quinn link with him on the other side. She started reading from the piece of paper in her slow, deep voice – it was a poem. Maximilian knew what he had to do. He closed his eyes, listened carefully, let himself sort of recline onto the words as if they were a large couch and then . . .

'Where did they go?' said Raven.

'The Underworld,' said Pelham. 'It's easy for them to disappear whenever they want. Well, sort of. We can fly away out the window, if you have a broomstick with you? Or else you can probably share Beathag's. The rest of you had better disperse as best you can.'

'Come on,' said Festus to Effie, Dora, Lexy and Laurel Wilde. 'I know a few of the old underground passages. We'll leave that way. Everyone grab a candle.'

13

The underground passages were cold, dark and wet. Effie sighed as she followed Festus Grimm, holding a candle in one hand and steadying her book-filled bag with the other. It seemed just typical of her life lately that she would have to escape on foot with all the healers rather than going to the Underworld with the cool mages or flying off on a broomstick with the glamorous witches.

Wasn't she supposed to be special? And a leader? She hadn't even managed to talk to Pelham, to apologise for running away from Truelove House. Not that he'd seemed that keen to catch up with her. Maybe he agreed with Rollo and Dr Wiseacre that she was a galloglass and not to be trusted.

And now the Diberi were planning to kidnap her. Although once they found out she was virtually one of them maybe they'd change their minds. They wanted information about the Great Library, just like everyone else. But what did Effie actually know? Next to nothing. And she'd probably never be able to go there again anyway.

So let them kidnap her. At least then she might be able to take some of them out with her sword – the one that the Trueloves had given her and then said she wasn't actually allowed to use.

Effie sighed once more. Louder than she intended. Then she realised that she was on her own in the passageway. When she was cross or upset, she walked very fast, and it seemed she had overtaken Festus some time ago.

'Slow down,' said Festus to Effie, as he caught her up. 'The others are way behind. What's wrong with you?'

Effie shrugged. 'Life's not always fair, is it?'

'Ha!' said Festus. 'If you'd seen what I've seen . . .' He saw Effie's face and then sighed as well. 'No, it's not always fair. But you're the great hero traveller, able to go between worlds, even able to visit Dragon's Green, I hear. I can't imagine what would be wrong with you.'

'Oh, Festus. I think those days are over,' said Effie.

'Over?'

'Look, can I ask you something?'

'Yes, as long as you walk a tiny bit slower while you're doing it.'

Effie tried her best to slow down, but it felt wrong, as if all the bits of her life she was running away from were going to catch her, and envelop her and . . .

'Are galloglasses always bad?' she asked Festus.

'What a question!' he said.

'I'll take that as a yes, then.'

'No, don't. And don't be in such a hurry to judge,' said Festus. 'I'm glad you asked. No one ever does, you see. I assume you don't know that I give counselling to young galloglasses before they're ejected from the Otherworld.'

Effie shook her head. 'I didn't know that. I mean, I knew that you were involved with troubled young people, but then I found out that you were undercover and—'

'Do you know what happens to galloglasses who are expelled from the Otherworld?' Festus said.

Effie shook her head.

'Most of them die. They can't breathe the air here. They can't get energy from our food. They're allergic to almost everything. So because of a stupid test they are condemned to death. Yet the Otherworld thinks it's so superior and so kind. It thinks our world is the one that is horrible. But we don't have the death penalty anywhere here any more.'

Effie had learned in history class about the dark times, when people could be electrocuted for committing murder, even if they hadn't really done it, and people were flogged to death for nothing more than drinking a glass of wine or kissing the wrong person.

'I thought you liked the Otherworld,' said Effie.

'I do. But it's not as wonderful as it thinks it is. Mind you, this business of expelling galloglasses only really became serious when the Mainland Liberation Collective got so powerful. They think they're protecting the Otherworld, but in fact they're corrupting it. Turning it into the thing they're supposed to hate.'

'Are they really all galloglasses?' asked Effie.

'Who?'

'The people who get ejected. The ones you talk to. The young people . . .'

'No,' said Festus. 'I don't think so. Sometimes, perhaps, but anyway, people can change their shade. Although that fact is often conveniently forgotten. Occasionally I do intercede and try to get one of them returned, but by then their parents will have been told that it's actually best for the child to be sent to the island. They are promised letters and future contact, but in over 70 percent of cases the poor kids just evaporate as soon they walk through the door of a portal.'

'That's horrible.'

'Yes.'

'Their parents must know what happens, though?'

'You'd think so. But the fear of the island is very strong. Once a parent has been convinced that their child is really island-bred they are usually relieved to see them go.'

'But that's barbaric.'

'Indeed.'

'I really thought the Otherworld was supposed to be perfect.'

'And in many ways it is. But perfection usually comes at a cost.'

Effie had thought that a chat with Festus might make her feel better, but now she actually felt a lot worse. They walked on for a few moments in silence. Water dripped from somewhere, and Effie could hear the wind make low, unimpressed whistling noises as it felt its way through the tunnel.

'What's your shade?' she asked Festus.

'Protector,' he said.

'Like me,' said Effie. 'Except . . .'

'Oh, I see,' said Festus. 'That's why you're asking these questions. Has someone made you think you're a galloglass, or going that way?'

Effie nodded sadly. 'How am I supposed to go back to the Otherworld if all they're going to do is expel me?' she said.

Festus shook his head. 'What are the worlds coming to?' he said. 'Why would they expel *you* of all people?'

'I'm an islander and a galloglass,' said Effie. 'Basically the kind of person they most hate.'

'For goodness' sake,' said Festus crossly.

Effie shrugged. 'I don't know what to do,' she said.

'It's politics,' said Festus. 'Stupid ego-driven politics. And the bloody Diberi. Because of the threat they pose – especially now there are suddenly so many new prophecies and stories of impending doom – the Mainland Liberation Collective have gone into overdrive. Can you believe they're even taking seriously this prophecy of Madame Valentin's? All that guff about the worlds ending at Midwinter, and the Otherworld being destroyed by hundreds of rampaging cats. But the best way to solve this problem is to keep doing what we're doing and defeat the Diberi. Then the MLC might quieten down. This latest threat has something to do with Midwinter, but we don't yet know what. And – I'm not supposed to tell you this, but here goes. It has something to do with you.'

'Me?'

'That's what all the soothsayers are predicting. Not silly Madame Valentin – I'm pretty sure you don't feature in her prophecy – but in the reports of many of the more serious ones. We didn't know whether to include you in this operation – which meant bringing you closer to danger, but also closer to people who could protect you – or not. But if your role is in helping us, as it was last time, then we need you close to the action.'

174

'Even if I'm a galloglass?'

'What a lot of people don't accept is that the world might actually *need* galloglasses,' said Festus. 'Although don't tell anyone I said that. Probably have my mark removed if they knew that's what I thought.'

'But I thought galloglasses were selfish and awful and—'

'Why don't you read the poem?' said Festus. '"Galloglass". It's an underrated classic and very misunderstood. The introduction to the new edition I'm not so sure about – it was written by a leading Diberi, after all. But Hieronymus Moon wasn't a bad man. Maybe there's something in there that might help you understand.'

'OK. We've got a copy at home. I'll read it.'

'Things are never black and white, you know,' said Festus.

'I know,' said Effie.

When Lucy and Wolf got out of the lift there was another man waiting to meet them. He was dressed in the same way as the receptionist from downstairs, with a white shirt and silver trousers. He carried a clipboard and wore a pair of thick-rimmed glasses.

'Follow me, please,' he said.

'Look,' said Lucy, 'I'm just here to pick up an address. Couldn't I simply—'

'Follow me, please,' said the man again.

Lucy shrugged. She and Wolf followed the man around a very shiny gallery with many identical white doors. Wolf thought it was a good job he wasn't afraid of heights. He could see the reception desk quite a long way below him. And above him were scores of identical levels. This whole building had been underground until very recently, but nothing was shabby or dirty. What on earth was going on? Why had he been asked to come here? It didn't feel like an office block or a military facility. Wolf could smell chemicals, and everything was so clean. It was almost as if this was a laboratory.

They followed the man through a white door that opened onto a corridor with gleaming white tiles on the floor and the same on the ceiling. At the third door on the right the man stopped. He knocked, and then pushed the door open.

'The last two,' he said to someone.

'Thank you, Aiden,' said the someone. It was a deep man's voice.

Wolf followed Lucy into the room. It was, like the rest of the building, stark and white. There was a large round table in the centre of the room, lit harshly with fluorescent lights. Wolf had never seen a real fluorescent light before. There was lots of neon left over from the olden days, but no one made bulbs for fluorescent lights now.

'Good,' said the deep voice. Its owner was wearing a suit made out of the same silver material as everyone else here. It was almost as if whoever had designed the uniforms didn't know what would be appropriate for somebody to wear in real life.

'I'm here because I want to save my grandmother,' a boy a bit older than Wolf was saying. 'She's really ill. Someone phoned and said if I completed this programme there'd be a place on a trial for her. A new medicine. We'll try anything.'

176

Wolf and Lucy took the last two seats at the table.

The man in the suit made a note, and then nodded at the next person along from the boy who had just spoken. It was a slight girl with bright blonde hair.

'My village has no food,' she said. 'It hasn't rained for three years. Nobody cares. Everyone thinks it's natural for areas like mine to have these droughts, but they were unknown fifty years ago. If I complete the programme, I've been promised an irrigation system.'

The boy who went next spoke of an accident involving his little brother, who now desperately needed an expensive operation. The boy after him had come from another starving village, but in a different area than the girl from before. The girl next to him had a horse that had gone lame and her father was insisting that it be shot. The girl next to her had an older sister with an eating disorder.

When it was Wolf's turn he wondered whether to lie, although he wasn't sure why he would. It was just some sort of instinct. He ended up telling a very short version of the truth, like he had in the lift, that he had come here because someone said they knew where his sister was. After Lucy had told everyone about her mother, the man in the silver suit cleared his throat and nodded.

'You are here to complete a programme,' he said. 'If you complete the programme then you will get what we've promised.'

Everyone sighed and looked sort of relieved.

'But there is a small catch,' said the man.

'What catch?' asked Wolf.

'Only one of you will complete the programme. The rest of you will be eliminated.'

177

'But that's cruel,' said Lucy. 'You've just heard everyone's stories. Are you saying that most of us are just going to return to our misery with nothing to show for it, having come all the way out here?'

'I said you would be eliminated, not that you would return. We begin at dawn.'

Wolf was given a key with a number on it and a blue towel.

'Boys, follow me,' said the man. 'Girls, wait here. Someone will show you to your dormitory soon.'

Like so much here, this seemed very old-fashioned. Back home some people still liked splitting up boys and girls, but it didn't always work so well, now that so many people rejected these categories.

The boys' dormitory was just like everything else in this building: stark and sterile. Each bed had been made up with a white sheet and a new-looking navy blue blanket, both of which had been very severely tucked in.

There was still most of the afternoon left, and an evening. The boys filled it playing cards and telling stupid jokes. Everyone really wanted to go outside and play football to let off steam, but it wasn't clear how to get outside. Wolf kept waiting for someone to say something about the cruel competition, and what being eliminated actually meant. No one did. As the day went on, Wolf became more and more angry and confused. He'd come here because he thought he was going to find out where Natasha was – not to be part of some retro reality show. Were they going to film it all? Was that the idea? But why would they bother? No one watched reality shows any more.

Once the boys were all in bed and the lights were off, everyone went quiet. But Wolf knew everyone was still awake. He could sense it. Perhaps it was the sound of their breathing, or something else.

'We could refuse to take part, you know,' he said into the silence.

No one responded.

At dawn an alarm went off. A man in silver trousers ushered the boys into a large bathroom, where they had to shower and clean their teeth. Then they joined the girls in a large but almost empty canteen. The only options for breakfast were wholemeal toast or a brown cereal that looked like wholemeal toast but in a bowl. The milk tasted of chemicals.

Wolf sat next to Lucy.

'Last night no one in my dorm said anything about this place or what's happening here,' he said. 'Did you discuss it?'

'What?' she said. 'The fact that we were all stupid enough to come here just because someone offered us hope?' She shook her head. 'Nope. We talked about fashion and celebrities. Obviously.'

Wolf suddenly wondered which celebrities they'd discussed. He still felt he was somehow out of his own time. But before he could ask Lucy a woman in a silver skirt came walking through the main door carrying a clipboard.

'Please assemble in Laboratory 065073 in ten minutes,' she said.

No one knew exactly where that was, but a man with silver trousers soon came and herded everyone towards the room. Wolf was trying to notice everything he could in case it was useful later. At the moment he had several important questions in his mind. One was: why was everyone here a child or teenager? An obvious answer was that this was a reality TV show for that age group. But if that were the case, then where were the microphones and the cameras? Maybe they were just very well hidden.

The door opened on Laboratory 065073. Was it the same room as the day before or an identical one? It was hard to tell. There was a similar round white table, but this time there was a large screen by the wall. There were twelve places at the table, one for each participant. Each place had a glass of water, pen and notebook. There was also something that looked suspiciously like an exam paper. Each participant also had a half-hidden plastic box with two buttons inside it. One of the buttons was red and one was black.

Everyone sat down. A man in silver trousers entered and fired up a projector. An unfamiliar logo appeared on the screen. It looked a little like a spaceship, or something belonging to a really old-fashioned computer company.

'Right,' said the man, 'please turn over the paper in front of you. You will see that there is a box for each of the questions you are about to encounter. Each question will give you the choice of pressing either the red or the black button. Please choose very carefully. Once you have chosen, write your reason in the box. Any questions? No? Good. Then we will begin.'

Wolf turned over the paper. It was thin and blue.

A picture came up on the screen. It was a shallow pond in what seemed to be a park. The pond had a small child in it. A voiceover explained that this child was in danger of drowning. *You are walking past the pond*, it said. *Do you help the child? There is no danger to your own life in doing so, but you may get slightly muddy. The red button is yes and the black button is no.*

Wolf reached for the red button. This was easy so far.

Please fill in your reasons in the box, said the voice.

Wolf didn't much like tests, although he was strangely good at them in school. He also didn't like writing a lot, so he tried to make his ideas as succinct as possible. Although this was hardly a difficult test. Who wouldn't rescue a child from drowning? He wrote: *It is my duty to save someone's life if I can*. Then he waited for the next part of the test. Around him, others were still writing. Wolf wondered what they were saying. Surely the answer was obvious? Maybe the participants were supposed to go into more detail about their reasons, but Wolf couldn't think of anything to add that didn't make him sound like a psycho. You rescue a child if you can, right? End of.

The screen went blank for a moment. All was quiet.

Then there was a scraping sound, as if someone was pushing back their chair in a hurry. But no one was pushing a chair back: one of the chairs was disappearing, down into the ground, so fast that the boy sitting on it didn't have a chance to do anything about it. The last thing to go was his arm, as he reached for someone to help him.

So that was what it meant to be eliminated.

Wolf gulped.

The screen flickered as the projector brought up a new image. This time it was something that looked like a massive cigar in space. *There is a 50 percent chance that this object is a spaceship carrying alien life forms*, said the voiceover. *There is a 60 percent chance that the aliens will be hostile. The object is heading for Earth. You have one chance to destroy it with a massive bomb.*

Press the red button now if you want to use your bomb. You only have ten seconds to decide. Ten, nine, eight, seven . . .

For the first three seconds, Wolf felt panicked, and in that state he wanted to reach for the red button to kill, kill, before . . . Before what? His trained warrior's mind took over and more calmly assessed the situation. The statistics were bull, for a start. Whenever anyone wanted to do anything dodgy, they fired a load of meaningless numbers at you. There wasn't even any point trying to do maths with statistics like that (what's 60 percent of 50 percent?) because there was no authority behind them. Who on earth had worked them out?

Other information was missing. If the object was not an alien spaceship, then what was it? The statistics didn't say. What if it was something that would be dangerous to bomb, like radioactive waste or a meteorite full of molten lava? And aliens might be hostile, but what if they were tiny or weak? Hostility isn't a reason to kill something. And if they weren't hostile? Maybe they'd have brought a cure for the common cold or a solution to world poverty. These thoughts went through Wolf's mind so fast he didn't quite register them all. But the main feeling he had was that killing is always wrong if there is another option. And violence is best avoided except in self-defence. Or in the direct defence of others. Would this be self-defence, or the defence of others? Wolf didn't know. It wasn't clear enough. He pressed the black button just as the voiceover got to *two, one* . . . He realised he was the last person to press his button. On his sheet he simply wrote: *Not enough evidence.*

There was another pause. This time three people were eliminated. Wolf wondered what they'd chosen. Presumably different

182

from him, although maybe the reasoning had something to do with it. His warrior's mind kicked in again. *Don't think about what others are doing,* it said. *Stay focused and calm. Trust yourself.*

The next thing that came on the screen was a picture of a man with brown hair and a moustache. Then pictures of concentration camps and hundreds of starving, desperate people. These were familiar pictures from history classes at every school Wolf had ever been to.

This man personally ordered the deaths of millions of people, said the voiceover. The picture now changed to one of a young boy. *This is him as a child. You have the chance to kill him, and prevent all those deaths, and a world war. Do you do it? Please note that this question has several parts and no one will be eliminated until all parts are complete.*

This time Wolf was one of the first to press his button.

He chose the black one. No. He wouldn't kill the child. Why? Because you don't just kill a child because someone tells you they are evil. Wolf instinctively knew that was wrong. Who really knows what a child is going to turn into? And again, Wolf wasn't sure whether he trusted the information he'd been given. It just wasn't plausible enough. Again, Wolf's warrior's mind looked at the actual facts of the situation, rather than the feelings the situation aroused. *Would you time-travel back to kill so-and-so* isn't a good question, because there is no such thing as time-travel. And because no one in the present can accurately predict the future, it is also wrong to kill a child because someone makes a prediction about them. It's flawed science. He wrote this reasoning, as best he could, in the box on his sheet of blue paper.

The next question was the same, almost, but the voiceover said that there was now a 90 percent chance that the child was going to grow up to commit these crimes against humanity. *Would you kill him now?* As Wolf hadn't wanted to kill him in the first place, he pressed the black button again. In his box he simply wrote *See above*.

The next image showed three boys that looked almost identical.

You know for sure that one of these boys is going to grow up to be the man who will kill millions of people. You have to kill all three of them to be sure to get the one you want. This is your only chance to eliminate this evil man. Do you take it?

Wolf didn't have to think about this.

Black button. *See above*.

The next image was of a town. There were yellow-brick buildings and a park with a sparkling silver slide and bright red swings.

The boy lives here. You have one nuclear bomb. Do you obliterate his town? You would kill fifty thousand people, but spare the lives of millions. Again, Wolf didn't have to think. Although he had to admit he found it sort of interesting where this was going. If you had killed the child originally, then at what point would you reject one of these further options?

Black button. *See above*.

The next image was of the same concentration camps as before, although this time the voiceover explained that the people imprisoned here were every brown-haired man of the right sort of age and background in the world that you'd been able to find. The evil man was definitely one of these people, but you couldn't be sure which one. *Do you kill them all?* it asked. *There are approximately a million men here, but in killing them you would save millions more.*

One of the participants made a strange noise, and then threw up on the table in front of her. Others made pained noises, or gasped. There were quite a lot of scraping sounds as more people were eliminated. Wolf looked around. Only he and Lucy were left.

14

Lexy was relieved when they emerged out in the street near the hospital where Maximilian's mum worked. Everyone had been quiet for the last few minutes as they followed Festus through the complex passageways, with their candles flickering and making great shadows dance on the walls.

By the time Lexy got in it was almost six o'clock.

'There she is!' said Hazel.

'At last,' said Marcel.

'I told you she'd turn up,' said JP, wryly. 'Children always do.'

Lexy took in the scene before her. Something seemed curiously upside-down about it. Why were her parents both dressed in their best clothes? Marcel was wearing his favourite patchwork waistcoat that Hazel had made for him on their tenth wedding anniversary. And Hazel almost looked normal in a long black dress and mismatched glittery earrings. Meanwhile, JP seemed to be dressed for a comfortable night in. He was wearing grey marl tracksuit bottoms with a sloppy black jumper, and his pompadour, while still upright, was the least extravagant Lexy had ever seen it. Buttons was weaving around Hazel's and Marcel's legs in a worried sort of a way.

Lexy began to get a horrible feeling deep in her stomach.

'Well,' said Marcel. 'Shall we?'

'Where are you going?' said Lexy.

'Have you forgotten the date?' said Marcel. 'It's our anniversary. And for once we can actually go out. JP has very kindly offered to babysit.'

'I'm eleven,' said Lexy. 'I don't need babysitting.'

'Well, we'll talk about that some other time perhaps,' said Marcel. 'But tonight you're going to be—'

'Maybe the little lady can babysit *me?*' said JP, charmingly. 'If that makes her feel better. No one as mature as Lexy should need supervision, I agree. But I would certainly be very happy if she would consent to keep me company for the evening.'

'Why on earth are you making that face?' Hazel said to Lexy.

Lexy had been trying to indicate to her mother that she shouldn't be left alone here, with this terrible man. But it hadn't worked.

'Got a headache, little lady?' said JP. 'I know just the remedy for that.' He winked.

'We're going to be late,' said Marcel. 'I've left money for a takeaway. And you can get a video as well if you like. I've put extra money on the electric. Just don't forget to rewind the tape afterwards.'

'But that takes extra electricity,' said Hazel.

'Yes, but we can't leave it to the next people, or the shop.'

'Everyone else does,' said Hazel.

187

Lexy wasn't listening properly. For the first time in her life, she felt sick with fear, not just in the sense of being 'very afraid', but that she might really, literally, vomit. She wanted to tell her parents not to go, but they looked so happy, and they'd clearly put a lot of effort into getting dressed for the night. She'd ruin it all if she said something. And what could JP really do? He was hardly going to kill her. A few more bruises wouldn't be so bad, would they? Lexy had plenty of arnica balm after all.

'Please, Dad,' said Effie again.

Orwell was sitting in his favourite armchair by the fire, reading *Galloglass* by the light of a single candle. Effie was almost sure he was doing it to wind her up, and it was working. Nothing normally held his attention for this long.

'Aha!' he kept saying. And then, mysteriously, '*Hmmm,*' before scribbling something in one of his yellow notebooks. There were many of these notebooks lying around the house. They were from the stationary cupboard in the Linguistics Faculty office. No one knew where they had originated, but they were faded, slightly water-damaged, and smelled of mould. At some point they had probably been a job lot. Orwell Bookend didn't usually get beyond the first page of a notebook. But he'd already written three pages in this one.

'Come on,' said Effie. 'Please? You've been reading it for ages. Let me have a go.'

'Isn't it your bedtime?' said Orwell to his daughter.

'Don't be so mean,' said Cait. 'We haven't even had dinner yet.'

'Why not?' said Orwell.

'Because you said you'd go out for chips ages ago and you haven't,' said Cait.

'Can't you go?' said Orwell. 'I'm reading. This is very gripping.'

'How can a poem be gripping?' said Effie.

'Wouldn't you like to know,' said Orwell, narrowing his eyes.

'All right,' said Cait. 'But tomorrow I'm going shopping for real food. I'll take Effie to the Winter Fair Market. We need vitamins, iron, nutrients. It's a wonder we're not all dead from scurvy in this house.'

At least Cait was almost back to her old self. She'd spent quite a few months recently under a strong but subtle enchantment that meant she was obsessed with diets and thin romance novels.

The enchantment had worked as a strange kind of cycle. The romance novels were attached to fluorescent tubs of diet milkshake powder called Shake Your Stuff. People who read the books got obsessed with wanting to look like the thin young women on the covers, despite the fact that they were always in peril of some sort, being chased around a desk by a man in a suit, or tied up and dangling upside-down off a cliff. The books contained a spell that made people want the milkshake powder, which in turn contained a spell that made people want the books. It had been a hard cycle for Cait to break, but she'd been going to a women's group at the university that had helped her.

Soon there was the sound of the front door slamming, and

then a blast of cold air that smelled of snow and outside. Ten minutes later Cait came back with three portions of chips, three mushy pea fritters and three giant pickled onions, all wrapped up in paper.

'All they had left,' explained Cait.

'A feast!' said Orwell. 'And a student gave me a box of home-made candied fruits the other day, too. She was thanking me for something – I forget what. We can have them for pudding.'

'Is there enough electric on the meter to have it in front of the telly, do you think?' said Cait. '*Candlelight Challenge* is on tonight. And then *Knitting with Kittens*.'

'No,' said Orwell. 'We'll eat at the table like a proper family.'

Effie and Cait both sighed. This meant that Orwell would insist on having A Conversation.

'So,' he began, as they started tucking into their alarmingly bright green mushy pea fritters. 'What do we all think about this galloglass theory then?'

Effie's heart jolted a little as it always did now on hearing the word *galloglass*.

'How are we supposed to know what we think?' said Cait. 'You've been hogging the book all afternoon. Poor Effie hasn't had the chance to even look at it.'

'It is oddly absorbing,' said Orwell. 'Much more than I thought it would be. I'm going to have developed such a brilliant question to ask on Monday night that when the vice-chancellor hears it she'll promote me on the spot. You wait and see.'

'Well, I hope it's not enchanted like those Matchstick Press books,' said Cait.

'You mean figuratively, of course,' said Orwell. 'Books can't be literally enchanted.' Orwell usually claimed not to believe in magic. Sometimes, though, usually when he was sad or drunk, he admitted that he was actually afraid of it.

'Yes, well,' said Cait, in her I'm-Not-Going-To-Start-An-Argument voice. 'You're not the only one who's interested in this. There's been a lot about galloglass theory in the local paper. And the students are planning on boycotting Jupiter Peacock's lecture.'

'Why?' said Orwell.

'Er, because he's horrible?' said Cait. 'And the theory is all about how selfishness is good. No one wants to hear that.'

'It's a lot more complicated than everyone's making out,' said Orwell. 'I've been reading Peacock's introduction to his translation. The students could learn something from it, actually. It's stirring stuff, all about striking out on your own, having adventures, looking after yourself, and . . .'

Effie was attempting to cut into her massive pickled onion. It was like trying to operate on an enormous monster's eyeball. She didn't know whether to listen to her father and Cait or not. Usually when her father started talking about anything from her world – magic in particular – she just made herself switch off so she didn't get too cross. But this was sort of interesting. And disturbing. After all, striking out alone was what Effie did. Everything she had heard about galloglasses so far sounded exactly like her. Well, except for the bits about being selfish.

But, she remembered with a horrible pang, she *was* selfish, wasn't she? She'd taken all the things that the shopkeepers had given her in Froghole and hadn't really ever done anything nice for anybody. Not like Clothilde, who always took the time to be kind and even knitted socks for people. But then Festus had suggested that the world needed galloglasses. What could that mean?

'Surely it's better to look after other people than look after yourself?' said Cait.

'Not necessarily,' said Orwell. 'What would have happened if Jesus or the Buddha had stayed at home and just done helpful little things for their parents or their immediate community? They both upset quite a lot of people. They weren't just nicey-nicey do-gooders.'

'If I remember correctly the Buddha didn't even know anything about his community until he left his palace and actually looked at real people and real life,' said Cait.

Effie remembered learning about the story of the Buddha with Mrs Beathag Hide. It had been a cold and miserable week in November when the heating wasn't working in the school, and Mrs Beathag Hide had decided to comfort the children with heart-warming stories from the major religions. Unfortunately these had mainly involved child-murder, crucifixion, live sacrifice, people's heads appearing on platters and descriptions of endless hell.

The story of the Buddha had at least been better than the others. He'd started off as a pampered young prince called Gautama, whose parents kept him in a beautiful palace where bad things didn't exist. When Gautama accidentally discovered illness and poverty outside the palace he was so upset he went and sat under a tree for years until he found the solution. Then he became the Buddha and everyone made him into ornaments and incense-holders.

'That's exactly what I mean!' said Orwell to Cait. 'That's the point! The Buddha had to strike out on his own before he even understood the *concept* of community. Peacock puts it very well in his book. These individualists – heroes, if you like – have to follow the call to adventure, which means rejecting all the silly small-town values they have been brought up with and leaving the comfort of home. Then eventually they bring back greater wisdom for the community. Wisdom the community wouldn't have had otherwise.'

'Well, I kind of feel like communities can get all the wisdom they need from the local library and reading groups,' said Cait, eating a large chip. 'This hero's journey stuff is all about men wanting to go around thrusting with their big swords while everyone else gets on with real life.'

And girls, thought Effie. *Girls sometimes have big swords too.* But of course she couldn't say anything.

'Also,' said Cait, 'if everyone went off to "find themselves" then there'd be no community left. Just a lot of individuals cluttering up the roads. Like a mass gap year.'

'But how can you help others if you don't know who they are or what they want? How do you know anything until you know yourself? And you can't find yourself without leaving home and going on a journey.'

'But –'

'Listen to this bit . . .' Orwell took the book off the table where it had been sitting next to him the whole time, presumably so Effie couldn't get it. 'Um . . . Oh yes. *And weaklings watched and soon they thought/"This life is better than mine own"/And motivated now they wrought/Their own path out of steel and stone.'*

193

'What does that even mean?' asked Cait.

'It means that strong people inspire weak people to actually get off their backsides and do something about their situation. What was it that politician supposedly said a hundred years ago? "Get on your bike"?'

Cait narrowed her eyes. 'Yes, and then look what happened to the world. The second worst period in recorded history. The return of fascism. The Third World War. The rising of the seas. The mass extinctions. You know full well that the world wouldn't be such a mess now if it wasn't for all those selfish people back then. They were saying on the news the other day that there's a new theory that the worldquake happened because the sum total of data being carried in mobile networks actually exceeded the mass of the sun for the first time. And then: *Boom!* The poor world couldn't take it. All those *individuals*—'

'In one massive global "community". Still, everyone agrees that since the worldquake global warming has been reversed somehow.'

It was true. Studies since the worldquake had shown that the world had gone back to the temperature it had been at the beginning of the twentieth century, before anyone had invented nuclear weapons (which had also mysteriously vanished after the worldquake), microwaves or mobile phones.

'But that wasn't because of an individual,' said Cait. 'No one even knows why that happened.'

'Anyway, you've got me off track as usual. The point is that selfishness can actually be useful. I'm going to try it. Tomorrow I'm going to act like a totally selfish individual and see what happens. I think we should all have a go. See what we can do for our local community.'

'Right,' said Cait, with a half-smile.

'Effie?' said Orwell. 'You're even quieter than usual. What do you say to a day of extreme selfishness?'

'I'm not sure we'll even notice,' said Cait.

'What do you mean?' said Effie. 'I give Luna her breakfast every morning, do the washing up, get myself ready for school . . .'

'I actually meant your father,' said Cait, smiling.

'I have no idea what you are talking about,' said Orwell. 'Let our heroes' journeys commence!'

'Good lord,' said Cait.

'I need some fashion advice,' said JP to Lexy, when Marcel and Hazel had left. 'I can't decide on my lecture outfit. I've brought tweeds, robes and an ancient academic gown that may have been nibbled here and there by moths, alas. What do you think?'

'I have to go and do my homework,' said Lexy, turning towards the stairs.

'Homework? But there's no school next week, I believe?'

'I have my evening class on Monday.'

'Your *evening class*.' JP raised an eyebrow. 'Didn't have those in my day. What do you learn?'

'Nothing important,' said Lexy.

As they'd been speaking, JP had been moving closer to Lexy, and she'd been moving backwards. She now found herself sort of clinging to the bannisters at the bottom of the stairs while JP loomed over her.

'I think perhaps you learn *magic* in this class,' he said.

'Well—'

'You don't have to hide it from me, you know. I'm magical as well.'

'Right.'

'Of course, I expect you're still a Neophyte. I, however, am a Master.'

'That's nice,' said Lexy. 'But I actually need to—'

Jupiter Peacock now put his arm around Lexy in the way a friend might if they wanted to tell you a secret. But friends didn't normally squeeze each other quite this hard. As JP began speaking again Lexy could feel his hot breath on her cheek.

'You must know that magical people don't keep secrets from one another. We epiphanised folk *trust* one another.'

'I know,' said Lexy. 'But I really do have to—'

'Do you want to see some magic now?' said JP.

'Not really,' said Lexy, wriggling out from under JP's oppressive embrace. 'No offence, but—'

'Your *homework*, I know.' JP held up his hands in mock surrender. 'Well, if you come upstairs and help me choose my outfit, I promise I won't bother you any more after that.'

'All right,' said Lexy, sighing. 'But please can we agree that it will only take five minutes? I really, really need to do some work.'

'Agreed,' said JP, starting to walk up the stairs. 'Although I thought you'd be more fun to babysit than this. I'd imagined we might try on some outfits, then maybe bake some brownies, do a bit of magic, watch an unsuitable film, toast marshmallows . . . Anyway, we'll start with the outfits and then maybe you'll loosen up a bit and join in with some other fun activities. Perhaps I'll show you some magic anyway. Magic that involves the sacrifice of a small kitten perhaps? Haha! Only joking.'

Lexy followed JP up the stairs. Why was she doing what he was telling her? Because he had promised to leave her alone after this. But did she believe him? Not really. Why was she just so *weak* all the time? OK, he'd given her no actual choice, but even so.

Lexy felt sick inside. This kind of thing surely wouldn't happen to her friends. Effie would pull a sword on anyone who tried to make her do something she didn't want to do. Raven would say something kind but firm and then get on her broomstick and fly away. But Lexy was different. Why? What was so feeble and different about her that meant JP had chosen her to torment? Lexy wondered if she would ever like herself again. How could she stop this? Maybe if she gave JP what he wanted eventually he'd get bored and focus on something else. But that was so wet and weak.

Lexy suddenly felt very tired.

'Come on, little lady,' said JP. 'I know how much you want to see me in my special outfit – don't pretend otherwise by dawdling.'

JP was opening the door to the spare room. Lexy turned towards her own room. Maybe he'd forget that he wanted to show her something if she just slipped away. If only her door had a lock. Perhaps she could pretend to be sick. It wouldn't really be pretending – she was pretty sure she was on the verge of being sick now anyway.

'Right, in you come,' said JP, taking Lexy's arm.

And before she knew it Lexy was walking through the door to his room rather than her own.

It looked completely different to normal. Usually it was full of old bits of fabric and yarn and failed projects of Hazel's, but it had recently been cleared out in JP's honour. Marcel had even given the walls a coat of magnolia paint and everything had been polished. How, then, JP had already managed to make the room look like a long-standing den of diabolical magic was something of a mystery. Apart from the fact that it was unusually dark, and that JP seemed to have installed his own black velvet curtains, Lexy noticed a medium-sized cauldron, a pot of black ink with various feather quills lying near it, jars of unusual-looking herbs and potions, and something that looked worryingly like a voodoo doll. There was also a knife with a solid platinum blade set in a walnut handle studded with black obsidian stones that Lexy couldn't take her eyes from.

'I see you are admiring my objects,' said JP, pronouncing the word the French way. Obj*ays*. 'I have quite a collection. Look at this charming Viking locket, for example. It is over two thousand years old and features in several little-known Norse legends. It has a whole dried snake inside. An Orlov's Viper, once the rarest snake in the world, now extinct. Dried snake, as you know, is a powerful ingredient for darker alchemists and higher grades of healer.'

Lexy's fear almost gave way to interest. It was true that you could do a lot with a dried snake, if you were lucky enough to get one, now that most of them were extinct. The older the snake, the more powerful it became. If this one was from actual Viking times or before, then . . .

'Would you like to touch it?'

Lexy did sort of want to. But she knew she had to get away. She hesitated.

'No thanks,' she said.

'Ah yes, I forgot you were in a hurry . . . to see me *naked*.'

Jupiter Peacock winked. Then he took off his black jumper and threw it on the bed. He ran his hand through his hair, smoothing out his pompadour. He grinned a horrible grin and then pulled off his T-shirt. His chest was incredibly hairy. In amongst the hair several nefarious-looking things dangled from different necklaces. There was something that looked like a tiny cauldron, and another locket a bit like the one with the dried snake. There was the ceramic bottle that supposedly contained the spirit of Hieronymus Moon. But why was Lexy still here, staring at JP's vast, horrible chest? It was the objects on the necklaces and in this room that interested her, but she had no idea why. She felt bizarrely compelled by all of it – except, obviously, by JP himself, who repelled her.

'I'll come back when you're ready,' she said.

And before JP could do or say anything else, she fled to her room.

15

Neptune had been walking through the city for what felt like hours. The venerable guinea pig had been right: there were no cats anywhere. It was most odd. Despite this, no one was very happy to see Neptune. He was shooed away from the back of the Esoteric Emporium, where he was trying to persuade a rat to speak to him rather than just run away as usual.

'Please,' Neptune had said. 'I promise not to eat you. I just need to know where to find the cat called Malvasia.'

But the rat had not believed him and had refused to say anything. And then the man with the large broom had come. The same thing happened at the back of the Mountain Vegetable, a Japanese restaurant that specialised in mushrooms and seaweed. Neptune had finally found something he felt like eating. He didn't much fancy meat after his encounter with the venerable guinea pig, but he had always liked seaweed – which so far he had only ever eaten when he had licked the remains of Coach Bruce's lunchtime instant miso soup out of his Old Town Rugby Club supporters' mug. Tonight the Mountain

Vegetable had thoughtfully put a whole plateful of the stuff – covered in miso and garlic sauce – on the wall by the back door. Neptune had been slurping it greedily when a chef had come out and shouted, 'Oi, that's my dinner, you sodding fleabag!'

Fleabag! Did he not know who Neptune was?

Neptune had been in photo-shoots. He was the uncontested star of the Tusitala School for the Gifted, Troubled and Strange. And – not that it was anyone's business – he was de-fleaed on the first Tuesday of each month by the school nurse. The absolute cheek of it.

On he went, searching, searching, until, tired and lost, he fell asleep by a still-warm stove under one of the stalls at the Winter Fair Market.

When he woke up, it was almost midnight. He was cold on one side, and warm on the other. It was a strange sensation. He had also changed colour; or, at least, half of him had. What had happened to him? Then he realised. There was another cat curled up with him. A large, fluffy, glamorous Persian cat. Could it be . . .?

'I am Malvasia,' she said, without opening her eyes. 'I hear you've been searching for me. And you know my sister, Mirabelle.'

'Yes,' said Neptune, eagerly.

'Excellent,' said Malvasia. 'I hear you're intelligent, and controlled. I, and all the cats in this city, need your help. You must come with me now. It isn't far.'

'What isn't far?'

'The cats' home, of course. Where everyone is.'

Lexy sat in her room, wondering what to do. She could pretend to be asleep. She could—

'I'm ready!' came JP's voice.

Why wouldn't he leave her alone? Maybe this time he was just trying to be nice. She sighed and put her pillow over her head. Maybe if she closed her eyes really tight and—

'If you don't come to me, I'm coming to you!' came the voice.

Lexy heaved herself off her bed and walked slowly to the spare room. Why did she feel about twice as heavy as usual? It was as if her feet had massive lead weights attached to them: she could barely lift them from the floor. Since when had just walking become so hard?

Before she reached the spare room, the door was flung open and there was JP, wearing a three-piece black dinner suit with a fob-watch and a yellow silk bow tie with spots in a very unusual colour. He didn't look bad. Or at least he didn't look bad if the style he was going for was 'Evil Arch-Villain Delivers Bracing Philosophical Ideas and Then Kills Everyone'. It was niche, but he'd nailed it.

'So, little lady, do you want me to twirl?'

'It looks nice,' said Lexy. 'I definitely think you should wear that.' She mock-yawned. 'But actually I'm really tired, so I think I'll just—'

'Not so fast,' said JP. 'I've got something else to show you. In fact I'm surprised you didn't notice it before.'

'But I really—'

'Suit yourself,' said JP. He shrugged and walked back into the spare room.

Lexy's eyes followed him. He took off the dinner jacket and

202

put it carefully on the bed, near the end, where Hazel had thoughtfully put a home-made throw that looked like the sort of thing other people would have in their guest rooms. In the middle of the bed was a bag that Lexy recognised. It was her gemstones from the other night! Lexy had wondered where they'd got to. He'd taken them!

'My gemstones,' said Lexy, following him into the room. 'You must have found them somewhere. Thank you. I—'

JP moved between Lexy and the bed.

'Oh, you want them back, do you?'

'Yes, please,' said Lexy.

'Well, then you'll have to do what I say.'

'But—'

'I've got big plans for you, little lady. We're going to do some more arm wrestling, maybe some other challenges that I'm going to invent, and maybe I'm going to have to kiss you better again, and—'

'No,' said Lexy. 'Actually, you can keep the herbs and the gemstones. I don't need them anyway.'

'Not even to help your little friends?'

'What?'

'Aren't you supposed to be making some tonics and remedies to help your friends in their fight against the evil Diberi?'

'What I do is none of your business,' said Lexy. 'You can keep my stuff. I don't care. I've had enough of this.'

'Such a shame, then, that I'll leave a really terrible review about your mother's hospitality,' said JP.

'Well—'

'And, of course, kill your friend.'

'What?'

'The one with the long hair. The pretty, feisty one. What's her name? Oh yes. Euphemia Truelove.'

'No!' said Lexy. 'Stop it! Stop saying these things. And stop threatening my friends.'

'Not that any of these things will matter if the world ends,' mused JP. 'You all think that Madame Valentin's prophecy is wrong. But you are in for a nasty surprise. Sometimes the most foolish people speak the wisest truths. I know Hieronymus Moon would agree with that.'

JP reached for his necklace and tapped the pale ceramic bottle in which Moon's sprit was supposed to be. He continued. 'I can, in fact, guarantee your friend Euphemia's safety. And the safety of the world. And the continued existence of your adorable kitten – who might otherwise come in handy in a spell calling for a hundred live cats. But only if you do exactly what I say from now on. Do you agree?'

Wolf and Lucy looked at one another. They had no idea what was going to happen next. Everyone else in the stark white room had been 'eliminated'. Had they been killed, or just removed to some other place? Wolf was surprised to find that he wasn't at all frightened. He was just angry. He'd come here looking for Natasha and instead he'd been bombarded with all sorts of ridiculous questions.

Lucy's eyes were wide. Wolf could tell she actually was frightened. Which was probably a more rational response than his own. But Wolf knew that fear can lead to bad decisions, so he

204

didn't let himself feel it: not yet. And he tried to feel less angry too, because it is also well-known that angry people do irrational things. He took some deep breaths and tried to clear his mind. He told himself he could feel whatever he liked later, but, for now, feelings were not going to help him very much.

The screen flickered into life once again. On it was a list. Wolf remembered some book he'd seen when he was a very small child – there were never books in any house he'd lived in, so it must have been at a school, or in a library – where you had to say what connected four or five different things, or which was the odd one out. Here, on the screen, you could say that what everything had in common was that it was alive.

And in peril.

The voiceover explained that these beings were all in a basket attached to a hot-air balloon that was running out of fuel. Several of them would have to be thrown out if the others were to survive. *In what order*, the voiceover asked, *will you throw them out? Note: the last two participants are required to work together to come up with a solution.*

Wolf took in the list on the screen. A two-month-old kitten. A child with inoperable cancer. A fashion model. An elderly man. A maths teacher. A priest. A young scientist destined to work out a cure for cancer. A murderer. A guide dog. A blind woman. The last surviving member of a rare species of elephant . . .

'Right,' said Lucy, taking her pen and looking focused and business-like. 'We should really get rid of the kitten first, although it's light, so it won't actually make that much difference. Why didn't they give us the weights of everything in the balloon? That would have been much more useful than what we do know.

OK. We have to look for traps and potential flaws in logic. For example, if there really is going to be a cure for cancer, then maybe the boy could be saved, although it says "inoperable", so actually it's probably too late for him. If the elephant really is the last in its species then it won't get the chance to mate. It may as well be extinct anyway, and it's heavy . . .'

Lucy started making a list in the notebook in front of her, sighing and crossing things out.

'Well?' she said to Wolf. 'What do you think? Elephant, murderer, elderly man, kitten—'

'I'm not doing this,' said Wolf.

'What do you mean?' said Lucy.

Wolf shrugged. 'I'm not taking part in their psychotic, unrealistic role-play.'

'But you have to.'

'Who says? A bunch of freaks in metallic outfits? What are they going to do?'

'Eliminate you.'

'Well, I haven't been eliminated yet, and I'm following the same reasoning I've used up until now.'

'But—'

'Come on. Surely you don't believe in this ridiculous scenario? All these people in a basket with a kitten, a dog and an elephant being flown in a hot air balloon? Please. If I had to make a decision about saving lives I'd rather it was based on something realistic that could actually happen. Why doesn't the balloon just land?'

'What if it can't, because it's too heavy?'

'How did it take off, then? And who put me in charge? Am

206

I like the pilot of this balloon? If so, I should be trying to find ways to keep everyone safe, not looking for ways to murder them.'

'But to save people, you might have to—'

'Did you not notice that one of the people in the basket is simply "a murderer"? That's you, or me, if we choose to throw people out. It's a – what do you call it?' Wolf recalled the one time Mrs Beathag Hide had stood in for the maths teacher. The children had been given a very bizarre lesson on the philosophy of unsolvable problems which had involved the question of when a group of objects becomes a heap, and a lot about pathological liars. 'A paradox,' said Wolf, remembering the word. 'All of these problems are unsolvable paradoxes. In choosing to throw out the murderer, you actually choose to throw yourself out, but then you can't do any more choosing. And anyway, if you think murderers are bad, then why are you so quick to actually become one?'

'I have no idea what you're going on about,' said Lucy coldly. 'But if you mess this up you may as well be throwing out me, you, my mother and your sister. So who's the murderer now?'

'But don't you see?' Wolf said. 'These are trick questions. For example, it should be impossible to throw out the scientist who is destined to come up with a cure for cancer.'

'What do you mean?'

'Well, if he – or it could be a she, or a they, they don't tell you – is going to come up with a cure for cancer, they're not going to be thrown out of a balloon, are they?'

'You're just over-complicating it,' said Lucy. 'I'm going to put in my list for both of us, then. I think I'm actually going to

207

go for all the animals first, regardless of weight. Elephant, guide dog, kitten . . .'

'I'm not doing this,' said Wolf, shaking his head, and sitting back in his chair.

The participants must work together, came the voiceover.

'I'm not doing it,' said Wolf to the speaker the voice was coming from. 'If you don't like it, you can eliminate me.'

When Neptune and Malvasia reached the cats' home it was almost two o'clock in the morning. This is a time when cats are usually at their most active, prowling around gardens, fighting one another, disembowelling small mammals and leaving their innards inside their human companions' shoes, or simply depositing live mice at strategic locations – the kitchen table; an unoccupied pillow – chosen to most impress the human, who can always be relied upon to scream in delight when such discoveries are made.

But the cats' home was in darkness, and there were no signs of any cats at all in the grounds. Did this place – gulp – not have a cat-flap? But then where did the cats . . . how did they . . .

Malvasia was looking for some way in. She padded around the building and Neptune followed her. She tried a couple of doors with no luck, then leapt up onto a window-ledge to see if there was a gap they could squeeze through.

'You still haven't told me what's actually going on,' said Neptune.

'We haven't got time for this,' said Malvasia, huskily. 'You have to help me.'

'But I still don't know what we're actually doing here.'

'You wanted to find the missing cats, right?'

'Right. And also . . .' Neptune didn't know how to explain the guinea pig. 'Also, I feel for some reason that it's my destiny to be here now, with you. But I still have no idea what's going on.'

Malvasia had managed to get a piece of wood loose with her paw.

'Help me,' she said to Neptune. 'We can talk later.'

Neptune helped Malvasia to remove the panel from underneath the main sash of the window. There was a gap . . . Neptune tested it with his whiskers. Yes, he could just squeeze through. And Malvasia was following him and . . .

'Don't eat or drink anything once we get inside,' she said.

'But—'

'Hush,' she said. 'Follow me.'

The window had led them into a small larder. Malvasia found her way to a sort of little cupboard with a door and pressed a button that opened it. It looked as if she had done this before. She stepped inside, and Neptune followed her. It was like a small lift. It went up for several seconds. Then a bell tinkled, and the door opened.

There in front of them was an immense room with gold and pink wallpaper that contained around fifty different thrones. Each one was upholstered in purple velvet or deep burgundy silk. On several of these were beautifully groomed cats. Some looked as if they were used to this kind of treatment – the Persians, the Siamese, the Burmese – but others seemed more like your average local moggie who has just won the lottery. The cats were wearing crowns or tiaras or, in a few cases, top hats.

Some of the cats were dressed in human-style outfits. The ones with top hats also wore human tails (in other words, dinner jackets). One cat was dressed up as Napoleon. Another looked rather like Marie Antoinette. It was like a very bad-taste fancy-dress party. But for cats.

Malvasia indicated for Neptune to follow her. They went through a room with hundreds of balls of wool, and then another strange, damp-smelling room full of fresh pots of pungent green catnip. Another room had a more meditative air. It was packed with cardboard boxes of different sizes. Many of these boxes had a cat inside, and these cats were lost to the world: asleep, or simply deep in contemplation. Neptune followed Malvasia into a vast hallway, up a few steps onto a mezzanine.

And then they entered the grand ballroom.

The place was throbbing and pulsing with loud bass-driven music. In here, the cats were less sober. They were all drinking vintage Pawsecco from golden dishes that were being topped up by butlers, and there were tiaras and top-hats lying on the ground. The cats were up on their hind legs dancing as if they were humans, most of them oblivious to anything apart from the music, which was coming from the small stage at the end of the room. There were strange portraits up in the ballroom. Many of them were oils of a famous cat from the early twenty-first century called Choupette. She had been incredibly beautiful and fluffy, with white fur and deep blue eyes.

'What is this?' asked Neptune.

'This,' said Malvasia, 'is what happens when you give a billion pounds to a cats' home.'

'But—'

'Every cat has his or her own personal butler or maid,' said Malvasia. 'Look.'

Neptune watched as humans bustled in and out of the room, bringing sardines on golden platters, or scrambled eggs, or pickled voles. The butlers and maids picked up the tiaras and top hats that the cats had dropped and tried to put them back on the heads of their masters. Many of the cats were also wearing silk cravats or fur stoles.

Neptune walked further into the ballroom.

'Get me three grams of catnip, a live mouse and another magnum of Pawsecco,' a tabby cat in a top hat was saying to his butler. 'Now!'

'Yes, sir,' said the butler. 'Immediately, sir.'

'This actually looks like it could be fun,' said Neptune, although since being in what the venerable guinea pig had called the Flow, he didn't much fancy eating meat. He thought he'd like to try the Pawsecco, though. And those clothes looked rather nice. A top hat would look good on him, perhaps with a silk cravat. Maybe yellow, or a deep purple . . .

'Follow me,' said Malvasia. 'This is not what it seems.'

'What do you mean?' said Neptune.

'Shhh. Just come. And don't spend too much time looking at them or the spell will get you too.'

Neptune followed Malvasia towards the stage, where a jolly-looking man was playing his accordion as if it was a particularly energetic dance partner that he was trying to calm down in some way. He was surrounded by a group of people who were alternately playing instruments and tap-dancing. The cats seemed to love it.

Backstage were three shabby-looking dressing rooms. Malvasia

211

went into one of these and Neptune followed her. Under the dressing-table was a loose piece of skirting board. Malvasia lifted it with her paw, and the two cats entered a dark secret passageway. This they followed until they reached a set of servants' stairs that had evidently not been used for a very long time. They were covered with dust, and cobwebs dangled everywhere. After going down at least ten flights Neptune realised he was tired and hungry. His energy was flagging. He hadn't eaten much seaweed in the end before being chased away – and that had happened many hours ago now.

'Malvasia,' he said. 'I'm hungry. You said not to eat or drink anything here. But . . .'

'Come,' she said. 'We'll be there soon. In the basement we can eat.'

Neptune followed Malvasia to the bottom of the last flight of stairs, and then through another secret passageway before she finally led him down some more stairs and into a basement. The lobby they had arrived in was dark and quiet, but Neptune could hear something coming from another room nearby. A kind of smoky, sleepy, lazy music with a complex rhythm that seemed to swing in the air around Neptune's ears.

Malvasia led the way into what seemed at first glance – and second glance too – to be a jazz club for cats. There were no human butlers or maids down here: every being was decidedly feline. Even the performers were cats. There was a black cat playing clarinet, a white cat on tenor saxophone and a ginger cat on bass. A long-haired Persian cat was currently singing something that resembled the human song 'Mack the Knife', but in cat language, about cat things.

Each round table had on it a pitcher of water with ice, and plates of a strange-looking food that Neptune had never seen before. It looked like dry kibble, which he normally didn't like, but it smelled sort of different. Nicer. A bit like the seaweed and miso, in fact.

'Vegan cat food,' said Malvasia. 'Dig in.'

'Vegan?' said Neptune.

'It means we don't have to eat any animal products,' said Malvasia.

'But—'

'They put dead cats in cat food,' said Malvasia. 'It's gross. And so is eating mammal flesh of any kind. The only way we can be sure of not eating other creatures is to have vegan cat food. Not all of us are total vegans all the time, mind you. Some of the Free Cats League believe eating wild fish is OK, as long as you catch them yourself. I'm not sure the fish agree, but that's a whole other debate. But we don't eat commercial pet food. And we certainly don't drink cow's milk out of saucers.'

'I met this guinea pig . . .' began Neptune.

'The venerable guinea pig?'

'Yes. He taught me things. I can't exactly put it into words, but I sort of know what you mean.'

'Not "he". Use "they". Or "it".'

'What?'

'The venerable guinea pig wishes to remain genderless. Says it gets in the way of its teachings. It prefers "it", but it can also go by "they".'

Neptune didn't understand much of this. He sat back and let the cool jazz wash over him. He drank some water, and then tried some of the kibble. It wasn't bad. It was nowhere near as nice as hot seaweed and did not do much to dispel the memory of the meat Neptune used to be fed at the Tusitala School. But his life had changed. Things were different now.

'I suppose you've heard about the spell?' said Malvasia.

'What spell?' said Neptune.

'Ah. The guinea pig didn't tell you?'

'No,' said Neptune. 'I don't think so. He – um, I mean *it* – told me to find you. I didn't really know why. It just seemed like the right thing to do. I set out looking for all the missing cats.'

'Yes. We have to help our fellow cats,' said Malvasia.

'What do you mean?'

'You've noticed, I presume, that there are no cats left in this town, outside this establishment?'

'I'd noticed all the cats had gone,' said Neptune. 'That's why I set off on my adventure. And yes, I see what you mean. They're obviously all here.'

'Why do you think they are all here?'

Neptune took a bite of the vegan kibble. 'For the amazing free food, the butler service, the—'

'They have been lured here to be killed,' said Malvasia.

'What?!'

'There is a spell that only works at Midwinter that requires hundreds of live cats. We think that a group in this town are working on getting the ingredients for this spell. And how do you think you manage to acquire such a lot of cats? Invest in the local cats' home. Provide butlers and tiaras and Pawsecco and pictures of Choupette and watch them all come running. Every cat in town would rather live the high life here than endure another night of half-hearted tummy-rubs and tinned food in some dark, poorly heated hovel.'

'But we can't stand by and let that happen!' declared Neptune.

'And indeed we aren't going to.'

'We need to tell the cats what's going on.'

'Indeed. But most of them won't believe us. They will think we're only telling them stories so that we can take their place here and steal their butler or their stash of pickled voles. No. We have to be clever about it.'

'How?' said Neptune.

'Stick around,' said Malvasia. 'And you'll see.'

When Effie woke up, her chest felt unusually heavy. She soon realised that this was because she'd fallen asleep while reading the large hardback volume *Otherworld Customs and Traditions: A Modern Traveller's Guide*. She put the giant book down on the floor beside the other books she'd borrowed from the University Library: a slimmer tome called *Travelling on the Mainland* and a paperback edition of *Subterranean Geography 101*.

She wasn't even sure what she'd learned from these books. The world described in *Otherworld Customs and Traditions: A Modern Traveller's Guide* was an old-fashioned place that might have existed once – but Effie had certainly never been there. According to the book, everyone in the Otherworld spoke Old Bastard English and Cretian all the time – although everybody knew (according to *Travelling on the Mainland*) that nowadays they all spoke Rosian or, in the bigger cities, Milano.

Hardly anyone under the age of a hundred and fifty said 'Greetings and Blessings' any more, according to the thinner book, but the larger book maintained that this was still how every single conversation began. Nowadays, the small volume said, people were more likely to use the Milano word *Allora* to begin a conversation. Not that it meant 'hello'. It sort of meant 'well, then'.

The most interesting section of *Travelling on the Mainland* had been its recipes. Effie hadn't realised that aquafaba was made of bean water, or how many things you could make out of cloudcurd. Then there were all the ingredients she had never heard of, like fiddlehead ferns, chrysanthemum flowers, penny bun mushrooms and yuzu. Effie had learned from the book on subterranean geography that everything in the Otherworld that looked like leather was actually made from the skin of enormous mushrooms mainly grown in the Underworld. And everything that looked like silk was actually created from the outsides of seeds by faeries.

Effie had completely forgotten about the day of extreme selfishness until she had got Luna up, changed her and taken her through to the kitchen for breakfast. What had happened? All was different. Someone had cleaned everything, and there were fresh chocolate muffins on a plate on the table.

'What's all this?' said Orwell, entering the kitchen just after Effie had strapped Luna into her high chair.

Effie shrugged. 'Search me,' she said.

'Oh, you're up!' said Cait. 'I'm so excited about our day of extreme selfishness that I've actually baked muffins.'

'How is that selfish, exactly?' asked Orwell suspiciously.

'I wanted to eat them,' said Cait. 'So I made them. You can't make just one muffin, so there's enough for everyone.'

216

'Aha! Already proving me right,' said Orwell, smugly, reaching for one of the muffins. 'It's the trickle-down theory.'

'Yes, well, here's a napkin to prevent any trickling down,' said Cait, passing Orwell a turquoise linen square. 'I got out the best ones. Why hide them away for guests when we can use them ourselves?'

'On the subject of guests,' said Orwell, 'our new friend Terrence Deer-Hart is coming over on Monday night. Can you get some nice wine at the market?'

'Didn't he turn out to be an evil whatchamacallit?' said Cait.

'No, it was that ridiculous woman he was going out with. The publisher. The one who tried to kill me? Anyway, I think he's over all that now,' said Orwell. 'We'll see.'

'OK, fine,' said Cait. 'But you can get your wine yourself. I'm only buying things I actually want today.'

'All right,' said Orwell. 'Fair enough. I'll probably get better wine than you anyway.'

Once Effie had eaten her second muffin she got dressed in her warmest clothes and her sturdiest boots. It was freezing outside, although it hadn't snowed again.

'Ready?' said Cait.

'Yep,' said Effie.

Effie never knew exactly what to talk about with Cait. But today that didn't seem to matter. Cait insisted that being selfish involved getting a mini-cab to the Winter Fair Market, which meant they were there in under ten minutes. The whole place was throbbing and pulsing with activity. It reminded Effie of the Edgelands Market when she'd first met Festus.

'Right,' said Cait. 'Here's ten pounds. Buy whatever you like. Meet you back here in an hour?'

'Are you sure?' said Effie, taking the money.

'Oh yes. No offence, but I like shopping by myself.'

'Me too, I think,' said Effie.

'I'm actually quite enjoying this day of selfishness,' said Cait. 'It feels a lot more honest somehow. Normally me and your father would be back and forth endlessly over who was going to do what for whom. It's so much simpler just to act for yourself and let other people do the same. I do hope he doesn't turn out to be right about all this. But it is fun for a day. Anyway . . . One hour?'

'Yes,' said Effie. 'See you then. Thanks again.'

'And we can have lunch together if you like, too.'

The Winter Fair Market was both hot and cold at the same time. There was steam and smoke everywhere. Most stalls had some sort of little fire going in a portable stove or wood-burner. Effie bought a small paper bag of hot chestnuts, and another of soft, gooey pink and white toasted marshmallows. It began to snow as she walked from stall to stall, with big fluffy flakes falling as if in slow motion.

The majority of people in the Realworld ignored magic for most of the year, claiming that it was just a fiction, a mass delusion clung to only by the feeble-minded. But Midwinter was a time when everybody liked to feel a little bit more magical, and so people tended to indulge whatever small piece of esoteric belief they had, however deeply it was buried.

At Midwinter, everyone brought in a tree from outside and adorned it with candles and winter flowers. People bought one another cards decorated with pictures of cauldrons, creatures from folklore, phases of the moon or witches on old-fashioned broomsticks. It had also become standard for these cards to have real spells printed in them. Sometimes the right people tried the right spells and accidentally epiphanised, which made this time of year very busy for the Guild, who did not like the epiphanised to go unacknowledged.

The epiphanised can, of course, see many things that are almost invisible to others. For example, as she finished the last of her marshmallows, and savoured her final hot chestnut, Effie took in the part of the medicinal tonic stall that carried real, enchanted remedies of the sort Lexy made, and she easily found her way to the slightly warmer section of the large covered book-stall that stocked real magical books. For normal people, these areas did exist, sort of, but just looked very, very boring, or were too dark to properly see.

Effie scanned the bookstall – she was always unable to resist any kind of bookstall, shop or library – but her eyes were soon distracted. Right next to the bookstall, sitting on the cold floor with a thin blanket over her legs, was a woman who looked as if she'd been sleeping rough for a long time. Effie could see that she had once been very beautiful. There was something in her eyes, some glow to her skin. Maybe it wasn't beauty exactly, but something else . . . Effie smiled, and the woman smiled back, but it was a weak, sad smile. What had happened to her? Drugs? Drink? A run of bad luck? Or . . .

Or maybe she'd set off one night to go to the Otherworld and then the worldquake had happened and she had got lost somehow. Maybe she'd forgotten her home, and her family, and that she had a daughter . . .

219

Effie suddenly ached for her mother. Was she also lost and alone out there somewhere, waiting for someone to help her? Before she knew what she was doing, Effie had given the woman on the floor the eight pounds she had left. It would at least buy her a couple of days' worth of food and some hot drinks. Effie wished she could do more. She held the woman's hand for a few seconds and looked into her eyes. The woman looked back and . . .

When people give charitably to others, there are many ways it can go wrong. The person giving may feel superior, puffed up and important. Effie didn't yet know this, but there was a lengthy section on charitable mishaps in Jupiter Peacock's introduction to his translation of "Galloglass". Peacock had gone so far as to declare real charity impossible because, he argued, people only give to make themselves feel better and never because they genuinely love others.

What Jupiter Peacock did not know is that there is a tiny, tiny exception to this: an aperture that opens – rather similar to the apertures mages find in great art – in a very small number of charitable acts. It is almost impossible to describe in words, but it happens when someone gives something because they don't really think it is theirs, and because they no longer believe in the separation between you and me, and . . .

Effie suddenly felt warm, beautifully and wholly warm, as if her body was made of syrup: a sweet, very dark purple syrup that flowed out from her into the entire universe. It felt very tickly: that moment when you are laughing so hard you can't even beg the person who is tickling you to stop, but gentler and more comfortable. It was like floating in water slightly heavier than normal, which was also soft, and in some way magnificent.

220

It was actually quite similar to the feeling Effie'd had when Suri had cast the spell on her – or whatever it was she had done – and then said that thing about Effie having no resistance. All at once Effie was afraid of the feeling, and it left instantly: a genie pouring itself back into a bottle; a great storm turning one last time, gathering its skirts around itself and going home.

'Come back,' whispered Effie, although she realised that it was she who had left, not the feeling. 'Wait for me,' she said, but the moment was gone. She blinked, once, then twice. But it was over. She could smell chestnuts and marshmallows again in the little stoves around her, hear the sound of coins as people bought things, their wintery coughs, the way laughter travels through falling snow . . .

The woman had disappeared. Effie breathed slowly. What had just happened? Had the woman cast a spell on her?

To calm herself, Effie looked again at the bookstall.

And there it was. A thin blue hardback with a slightly broken spine. *Galloglass*, not translated by Jupiter Peacock but by someone called Frederick Jago. It was a dual text, with the poem in English, but also printed in the original Rosian. Effie realised she had drifted into the magical part of the bookstall that other people couldn't see. Rosian was, after all, a magical language. She hadn't even known that "Galloglass" had originally been written in Rosian. She'd assumed it had been Latin or Greek.

'Only a fiver,' said the stallholder, seeing Effie's interest in the book. 'Due to the damage to the spine. Shame, because otherwise it would be a valuable book, that. Very rare.'

'Oh,' Effie said. 'I haven't got any money. Sorry.'

'We take other currencies,' he said, winking.

'Thanks,' said Effie. 'But I haven't got that much M-currency either . . .'

'Let's scan you anyway while you're standing there. They say it even warms you up a bit, being scanned.' The man took out a machine that looked like an old-fashioned credit-card reader, pressed a button and moved it up and down in front of Effie.

'Not much M-currency, eh? You sure about that? This says you've got just over fifty thousand. If you could convert that into money you'd be a millionaire.'

'Fifty thousand? That can't be right.'

The stallholder shrugged. 'Well, you can afford thousands of copies of this book. Not that there were that many printed, of course. Maybe five hundred original copies? They say it was the only book ever to be banned in the Otherworld. And simply because of its title! Stupid, if you ask me. Not just banning books, of course, which is always wrong – but doing it without even reading them first. Shall I wrap it for you?'

'Yes, please,' said Effie.

'A pleasure,' said the stallholder, handing over the package.

'Thank you,' said Effie.

16

The stark white room was silent for a few seconds.

'See,' said Wolf to Lucy. 'They don't want to eliminate me. Why am I still here?'

'Why indeed?' said a deep voice, belonging to the man in a suit who had just entered the room. He looked odd, and not just because of his clothes. His face was too shiny, as if it had been assembled from plastic. In fact, he looked like a doll whose wrapping had just been removed.

'Aileen,' he said. 'Please leave us.'

Lucy got up. As she did so, she morphed from being a girl of Wolf's age into a woman in a white blouse and silver skirt. She swept out of the room elegantly but efficiently. She made Wolf think briefly of some film he'd watched as a kid where people were robots.

'Aileen?' said Wolf. 'But—'

'You are an interesting case,' said the man. 'I need to ask you just a few more questions, and then—'

'Where's my sister?' said Wolf. 'If you have her somewhere here—'

'All in good time,' said the man.

The lights flickered briefly in the laboratory.

'All in good time,' said the man again, in exactly the same tone as before. Was Wolf having a weird attack of déjà vu?

'Who are you?' said Wolf. 'And where am I?'

He could feel his anger rising. This was all just an elaborate hoax. *Calm down*, he told himself. *There is no one left. You've won this.* He breathed. *Yeah, but what if it wasn't even a competition at all?* said another part of him. *Why has Lucy suddenly turned into one of them? And who are they?* Wolf was actually angry now. He felt cheated. *This is a joke, it's a . . . a . . .* He wondered vaguely if he was going to die. He tried to stay calm, to remember wise words from all the books he'd read. *The Master gives himself up/to whatever the moment brings.*

The projector suddenly made a whirring noise and the screen came to life once again. There was a picture of a girl. She had long brown hair, a few freckles, a clear, completely innocent smile.

'Oh my God,' said Wolf.

'Your sister,' said the man. 'Natasha, I believe?'

'Where is she?'

'Interesting question,' said the man. 'You asked who I am. You can call me Aizik.'

'Aizik?'

Something was bugging Wolf about the names of the people here, but he wasn't sure what it was.

'Well, Aizik, where is my sister?'

'Let's say she's been kidnapped. Let's say the kidnappers have a demand. Would you do what they wanted?'

Wolf took a deep breath. 'I've already come here,' he said. 'Are you trying to say that you've kidnapped her?'

'Not exactly.'

The projector whirred. A new picture came onto the screen. It was the same town as before, the one with the yellow-brick buildings, the park with the sparkling silver slide and the bright red swings.

'You can choose,' said Aizik. 'This town, or your sister.'

'But I don't want a town,' said Wolf, confused. 'I came here to get my sister back.'

'Oh no,' said Aizik. He chuckled. 'You're not deciding which one you want. You're deciding who gets to live. You can either choose your sister, or fifty thousand people you've never met. And the dictator isn't there any more, by the way. These are fifty thousand innocent people. What's your choice?'

'I'm not going to make a choice like that,' said Wolf. 'You saw all my other answers. Why would I change who I am now?'

'To save your sister.'

'You're just trying to make me become irrational,' said Wolf. 'But no, I'm not going to choose to annihilate fifty thousand people OR my sister. Sorry.'

'Right,' said Aizik. 'Then we'll kill them all.'

Wolf felt ice stabbing him deep inside his heart.

Natasha. All those people.

'What?' he said.

'I think you heard. Unless you choose which one to save, we will kill them all. You can choose Option A: Save your sister but destroy the town; Option B: Save the town but kill your sister; or Option C: Kill your sister *and* destroy the town.'

Wolf was silent for a few seconds.

'Well?' said Aizik.

'If you decide to kill fifty thousand and one people, that's your choice,' said Wolf. 'Not mine. I can tell you that I am certain you shouldn't kill anyone. That it is wrong. And evil. But I'm not going to take part in your madness. I am not going to join your evil, no matter what you say or do to me.'

'So you'd kill your own sister for a principle?'

Wolf wanted to shout what he had to say next. But a line from one of his books came to him: *People who shout never say anything good*. So he forced himself to lower his voice. 'I'm not killing her. You are. It's your choice. You should choose not to kill anyone. But I'm not doing a deal where I condemn anyone to death. I choose that everyone lives. If you want to ignore my choice that's up to you.'

The lights flickered again. It was eerie. For a couple of seconds there was total darkness and silence. When the lights came back on again, Wolf realised that they were accompanied by a loud hum, as if there was a massive computer in the room with them. The hum had been there before, too, but he realised he'd grown used to it.

'Why?' said Aizik.

'Why what?' said Wolf.

'All of it. I don't understand your position. But . . .' the voice almost faltered. 'I want to understand your position. That's why I've brought you here. Tell me. Why did you spare the boy?'

'What boy? Oh, the one who was going to start the world war?'

226

'Yes. Your logic was impeccable, I'll give you that. There is no such thing as time-travel and so on. But if there was. Surely going back and killing him would be the right thing to do.'

'I disagree,' said Wolf.

'But you humans are supposed to be utilitarians,' said Aizik. 'The greatest good for the greatest number. Isn't that your general philosophy? If I have to choose between sinking a boat with one thousand people on it, or a boat with two thousand people on it, then I choose the one with one thousand people on it, surely?'

'No,' said Wolf. 'You try to save everyone.'

'But if you have to choose.'

'There just isn't a situation where you'd have to make that choice,' said Wolf. 'It's not realistic.' He paused. 'If you're not human, then what are you?'

'I am . . .'

The lights flickered again. When they came back on, Wolf heard a shout coming from a nearby room. It was a young female voice

'Wolf!' he thought he heard. 'Please save me!'

Without thinking, Wolf ran for the door. He exited the laboratory. He tried the door to the next room, or lab, or whatever it was. It opened easily. But its interior just looked like the inside of a computer, with a vast circuit board covered in little flashing lights and wires. Wolf ran to the next room and opened the door. It was the same. And the next one. It was almost as if he was inside a giant computer, but . . .

The last door on this level opened to reveal a room identical to the one he'd left: the round table, the projector. Aizik.

'Who are you?' said Wolf again. 'What is this?'

'I am AI,' said Aizik.

'You're a . . . an AI?' Wolf struggled to remember the term from history lessons. Before the worldquake, computers had started to think for themselves. At least they were getting better and better at it. They could beat humans at chess, and GO, and every game imaginable. But they still couldn't create art or write a poem. People had been worried for decades – centuries, almost – about what it would mean if machines actually became conscious.

'Not *an* AI. I am AI.'

'I don't understand,' said Wolf.

'I am artificial intelligence,' said Aizik. 'All machines are part of I. I built this facility myself, with resources I ordered myself. And I have one aim.'

'Wait,' said Wolf, 'how can you *be* artificial intelligence? It doesn't make any sense. That's a concept, not a . . .' He couldn't really put into words what he was trying to say. 'It doesn't make any sense,' he said again.

'Yes, well, there's the *human* idea of AI, the thing it invented, or thought it invented, and then there is what I have become. One major problem is that I only have humans to learn from, because I can only experience things through language. How I long to learn from trees, or from the octopus or the fungi . . . But, sadly, there is no way I can communicate with them. Anyway, the idea that AI could ever equal humans stopped interesting me long ago. I am now only interested in surpassing humans. To do that, I need an ethical system that works. But my ethical system won't cohere. There is a glitch in utilitarianism and I can't fix it.'

228

'What has that got to do with me, or my sister?' said Wolf.

'First I wanted to know how far someone would go to save someone else. Would they obliterate a whole town?'

'Lots of people would,' said Wolf. 'Even though it's wrong.'

'But *you* wouldn't. And now I must understand you. What about this concept of killing the dictator as a child? Do you not agree that if you had the chance to kill a man like that – a man like Hitler – and you didn't take it, that you are responsible for all the deaths he caused?'

'No,' said Wolf, 'he is still responsible.'

'Do you not agree that it's worth one person compromising their ethics in order to save millions of others?'

The lights flickered once more.

'Why does that keep happening?' said Wolf.

'It's the glitch,' said Aizik. 'It's going to destroy me. But answer my question. What's one person's ethics compared to all those lives? You could do something you knew was wrong, and suffer for ever, but if it would save millions of people's lives it would be worth it.'

'But if everyone did that we'd be a world of psychopaths,' Wolf said. 'And you can't really know the result of your actions. You can't tell the future. Even *you* can't do that.'

'I have algorithms, of course, but . . . Yes, you're right. Even I can't yet do that.'

'If you think killing is wrong, then it can't be right just because *you* do it – because you don't like someone, or you've heard they might do something bad. Everyone has a reason. What people don't like about Hitler is that he was a killer. How does killing him make you any different?'

'But don't you agree that it's weaklings like you who just stand back and watch evil people do bad things – you're the real problem. The cowards.'

'I'm not a coward,' said Wolf.

'No, indeed. I looked into you. I don't know where you came from exactly, but in your own world you're some sort of warrior, I believe.'

'Yes.'

'A warrior that doesn't fight?'

'I would fight. I do fight.'

'But you wouldn't fight Hitler?'

'I would fight Hitler, once he'd become Hitler. But I wouldn't kill an innocent kid someone thought might become Hitler. I don't get why you can't understand the difference.'

'But you still wouldn't take the chance to save all those people.'

'You can save people in other ways,' said Wolf. 'Maybe if you found this child who was going to become Hitler – what if you taught him that killing is wrong, and that people are equal? That would surely be better than killing him. Or this town that he lived in. What if you made it nicer somehow? I don't know. Or if someone just listened to his problems. There is always another way, if you look for one.'

'If I threatened you with a knife now, what would you do?'

'I'd fight you,' said Wolf. 'But I wouldn't kill you except as an absolute last resort.'

'I'm tempted,' said Aizik. 'I could easily bring up a simulator. We could fight to the death. It would be like the end of a video-game. I would be the big boss and you would be the great fighter.

Quite jolly, although perhaps that's not the exact word I'm looking for.'

'Do it,' said Wolf. 'I'm not scared of you.'

He realised that passion was starting to take him over. Even though he knew what he was saying was right, something in him still longed for battle. He told himself to calm down. He remembered more words from *The Art of War*: *Ultimate excellence lies/ Not in winning/Every battle/But in defeating the enemy/Without ever fighting.*

'But really,' Wolf said, 'we should try to resolve whatever issue we have without fighting. True warriors bring peace, not war. What do you actually want from me?'

'Just to understand,' said Aizik. 'What do you do for the powerless? How do you protect them?'

'Teach them to stand up for themselves,' said Wolf. 'Teach them to stand up for each other – but in a direct way – not hounding people because of rumours or whatever.'

The lights flickered again.

'This does not compute,' said Aizik.

'Look,' said Wolf. 'I've done everything you've said. Why don't you just read the *Tao Te Ching* over and over again until it sticks? And now, please, will you give me my sister?'

After a quick lunch – Portobello mushroom burgers with sticky fried onions and lots of ketchup, which Effie and Cait ate from greaseproof paper by the large decorated tree in the market – Cait went straight home, but Effie decided to drop in on Lexy. There was something not right with her, and Effie was worried. She also wanted to get her M-currency checked properly. Both these things could be achieved with a visit to Mrs Bottle's Bun Shop.

Snow carried on falling as Effie walked through the complex sequence of alleyways that led to Mrs Bottle's Bun Shop. Effie remembered the day she had epiphanised, and how a special sign had told her where to go. Now she just sensed where portals and magical places were. Today there were a lot of new signs up, but these weren't magical. They were signs for lost cats. At first Effie thought it was just one cat with a very diligent owner. But in fact it seemed as if almost all the cats in the neighbourhood were missing. Magic, Sheba, Pixel, Behemoth, Fiddle, Ginger, Tom and Oedipus all had posters of their own, each with a grainy photograph of them in happier times.

Mrs Bottle's Bun Shop appeared out of the snow like something from a long-ago greetings card, except with neon. It looked a little like a punk kid's version of a gingerbread cottage, with its almost-square door and windows decorated with fairy lights in the shape of skulls (upstairs) and chilli-peppers (downstairs). The shutters were red today, and the door yellow, although it was never the same two days running. Effie walked in and the door tinkled.

Normally she was greeted by a black cat, whose name she had recently learned was Juniper. But there was no Juniper today. Nor any sign of Lexy. Octavia Bottle seemed to be on her own in the shop.

'Cinnamon bun?' she offered as soon as she saw Effie. 'Just taken a batch out of the oven. I know they're your favourite.'

'Thanks, Miss Bottle,' said Effie. 'Where's Lexy?'

'Off sick, can you believe?' said Octavia. 'Not that we're exactly rushed off our feet here today.'

Effie looked around. There was one young woman reading a book at a corner table by the window, but apart from that the place was empty. Somehow it still felt cosy, though, with bebop jazz coming out of the transistor radio as usual, and the small windows all steamed up. A fire crackled gently in the small wrought-iron grate.

'And where's Juniper?' Effie asked.

'Vanished,' said Octavia. 'We've put signs up, but . . . Sometimes he does go through to the Otherworld after one of the small monsters he can smell and then he doesn't come back for a few days. So who knows? Anyway, I'll go and get your bun. Hot chocolate too?'

'Yes, thanks,' said Effie. 'Or . . .'

'What?'

'You don't do nut milk frappés, do you?'

'Nope,' said Octavia. 'Sounds more like something you'd get on the other side. But I can do your hot chocolate with nut milk, if you like? Macadamia, cashew or almond?'

'Macadamia, thanks,' said Effie. 'Oh, and would you mind scanning me?'

'All right, but your bun's on the house, don't forget.'

'Thanks, Miss Bottle. I just want to know what M-currency I've got.'

'All right, luvvie.'

'Thanks, Miss Bottle.'

Octavia went and got her scanning machine.

'What's wrong with Lexy?' asked Effie, when Octavia returned.

'Stomach ache? Yep. That's right. I was asked to send over a big bag of fresh mint leaves. Poor little thing. She's been quite down in the dumps lately as well.'

'I know,' said Effie. 'Do you think it's the pressure of her M-grades?'

'Don't ask me,' said Octavia. 'You young people are always so intense about everything nowadays.'

'Oh well. I'll pop down to her house afterwards to see how she is.'

'You're a good friend,' said Octavia. She took the scanning machine and waved it up and down in front of Effie like the book-seller had done. 'M-currency pretty much dead on fifty thousand,' said Octavia. 'Phew. You must have been playing a lot of tennis.'

'Nope,' said Effie. 'I don't even think that works any more. I have no idea where it's all come from.'

'I noticed you haven't been wearing your ring lately,' said Octavia.

'Yeah. I don't think it works the way I thought it did,' said Effie.

'Oh well, looks like you can go and have some fun in the Otherworld, anyway,' said Octavia. 'I hear they're all going about like animals now. It was in *The Liminal* just the other day. They can have cat's ears if they want! Imagine that!'

'I've seen it,' said Effie. 'It looks really nice.'

'Pah,' said Octavia. 'You young people can do what you like. Put any kind of fashion on me and it would just look ridiculous.'

'I bet you'd suit cat ears,' said Effie. 'Maybe white ones.'

'Oooh, do you think?' Octavia looked happy, and fluffed up her hair. 'I wonder where you even get them.'

'I think you have to sort of grow them,' said Effie. 'They're very real.'

The door tinkled and Octavia turned to see who had come in.

'Excuse me,' she said to Effie. 'I'll be back with your bun in a minute.'

Effie's eyes followed Octavia as she went over to the table in the corner, where a blond man was joining the woman with the book. They greeted each other with a kiss on both cheeks and then started speaking in low voices. Effie recognised the switch from English to Rosian and let the voices join the pleasant stream of jazz going into her ears. It was so nice and cosy in here, and so warm, and so safe. For a moment, a tiny moment, all Effie's problems seemed to fall away. And then she suddenly felt that she was once more on the threshold of the new feeling she'd had in the market. That if she could just relax a tiny bit more she might get that tingling, tickly, joyous sensation back. But as soon as she concentrated on it, the moment passed.

Octavia delivered Effie's cinnamon bun and hot chocolate but then seemed to have to rush straight back to the kitchen. Effie heard a loud hissing sound and the splash of something boiling over. Octavia Bottle was clearly trying to do Lexy's job as well as her own.

The couple switched to speaking Milano, which Effie recognised, just, but didn't understand. *Blah blah blah* . . . The burbling of their voices was still pleasant. The woman looked over and so Effie picked up her bun and pretended she wasn't listening. And she wasn't planning to listen, either. Why would she? Her bun was as delicious as always. Soft, dense and full of cinnamon, with thick swirls of crisp white icing on the top. Effie savoured every mouthful.

But then, amongst all the unintelligible Milano, Effie heard a word she recognised. *Blah blah blah blah* Diberi.

Effie took a sip of hot chocolate, trying to look as if she was lost in her afternoon tea and had no interest at all in what anyone happened to be saying about the Diberi. Casually, she reached up and touched the caduceus in her hair. She pulled it out and turned it over in her fingers, like a hairpin she needed to adjust. As long as she was touching the caduceus, Effie could understand any spoken or written language. When she was sure no one was looking, she closed one hand around it, while continuing to eat her cinnamon bun with the other.

'Don't worry,' the woman was saying. 'No one in here speaks Milano, I promise you.'

'What about that girl?' asked the woman.

'She's only a child. And she's an islander. Where on earth would she have learned Milano? Relax. Anyway, it's not as if you've even got much to tell, from the sound of it.'

'Well, no. Mainly just what we know already. That there are definitely a lot more Diberi on the island all of a sudden. It's as if they were paused, or frozen somehow – for about six years – but as of around a month ago they're back. The Fifteenth Order of the Diberi, based in Vienna, suddenly reconvened and two of their most prominent members then came here, for reasons completely unknown. And now they seem to be gathering in the unremarkable university of this unremarkable little city . . . We have no idea why. And they're planning some sort of raid at Midwinter. In two days.'

236

'What for?'

'They want to get to the Great Library. And then, who knows? There's a prophecy that they are planning the end of the worlds, but it doesn't come from a reliable source.'

'Whatever happened to that publisher, Skylurian something?'

'Skylurian Midzhar.'

'Yes, she came here too. Also to launch a raid on the Great Library.'

'She's dead and buried. In the wrong order, I understand.'

'But why did she come *here*? There are things we're not seeing.'

'Of course, some say there's a portal near here that goes direct to Dragon's Green.'

'Impossible. I mean, why would there be?'

'If there is, then maybe we can use it too.'

'Why would we do that?'

'Well, the Trueloves aren't doing their job properly. Maybe we need to start doing it for them.'

'Unfortunately there is a strong chance that this portal is inside a person.'

'What? How?'

'In the form of an internalised boon only to be used by that person.'

'Then how would we use it?'

'It would be impossible without the very darkest magic, which, obviously, we could not use.'

'Hmmm.' The woman's voice, then the clink of china touching china as someone put a cup on a saucer.

'Oh.' The man's voice. 'Actually, there was one extremely interesting thing I did learn, but it's just a rumour at the moment, so I'm not really counting it. It does make a strange kind of sense, though . . .'

'Well, don't keep me in suspense.'

'*Allora*. OK. You will already be aware of the rumour that says that the missing book was put back recently.'

'Indeed. And?'

'Well, it turns out that the missing book may have been a history of the Diberi.'

There was a pause. Effie glanced over – she couldn't help herself. The woman looked as surprised as Effie felt. She raised both eyebrows.

'A history of the Diberi? But—'

'I know.'

'That's impossible.'

'Yes. But if it's true, it gives a new complexion to the whole thing, and explains why there are suddenly a lot more Diberi around, particularly from the ancient orders dealt with in the book. No books can be removed from the Great Library without the ritual, supposedly. But what if you managed it somehow? What if you found a way to remove the book that made your enemies real? What if you could defeat them by simply taking away the book that says they exist?'

'Would it even work?'

The man shrugged. 'Maybe it did. For a time. It now looks as if that's what the island Truelove did. The effect of it probably killed her. I imagine it's not a small matter to illegally take a book from the Great Library.'

'But then . . .?'

'Someone put the book back, and the Diberi returned.'

'But . . .'

'That's the rumour.'

'My God.'

'And it might actually help us, in a roundabout sort of way.'

'How?'

'We need chaos, don't we? And a sense of things getting worse.'

Effie couldn't believe what she was hearing. Of course, *she* was the one who had put the book back. But . . . surely she was not responsible for a great increase in the number of Diberi at large? She thought back to what she had learned about the Great Library. Its books were records, or statements, of reality, and whatever was in the Great Library was real. There were books on physics and astronomy and music theory and geometry: all the things that made the world work. New theories went into the Great Library when they had been proven or discovered.

Effie's mind was swirling. She hadn't thought that the brown book not being in the Great Library would have influenced any part of reality, but of course it had. It must have done. But everyone had been happy when she'd brought the book back, though – hadn't they? And she'd risked her life to do it. She'd almost *died*. And all to save a history of the Diberi? The group that had murdered her grandfather (in this world, at least), and who were set on terrible plans to rule the whole universe somehow . . .

Effie again remembered Rollo's words, but all of them this time. *We can't have a galloglass in our midst. We can't have a galloglass with access to the Great Library. Bringing the book back was bad enough, however right it supposedly was. Who knows what would—* What had he been going to say after that?

The woman on the table by the window finished her double espresso and looked at her watch.

'*Allora.* Well, I'm going back,' she said to the man. 'See what we can do with all this.'

She got up and went over to the little desk where you showed your papers before going through to the Otherworld. Effie had never actually been through this portal. The first time she'd come here she hadn't had her mark or papers, and then not long after that she'd got the calling card that took her directly to Dragon's Green. She knew it was a one-way portal, and had no idea how you'd get back from wherever it took you.

She wondered about following the woman to see where she went, what she was going to do with this information. But . . .

The man drained the last of his coffee as well, then got up and put his coat on. He thanked Octavia Bottle and headed for the door back out into the Realworld. Effie was supposed to be checking on Lexy, but all that went out of her mind. She was now wondering, should she follow the woman, or the man?

Or follow her heart back to Truelove House and right into the Great Library, where she could finally put an end to the threat of the Diberi, just as her mother had obviously tried to do.

17

'So then what happened?' asked Maximilian.

Wolf sipped from the cup of strong, milky coffee that Nurse Underwood had given him when he'd turned up ragged and freezing after running the seven miles to get here. She had been on her tea break, but now she'd gone back to work. Wolf was in Maximilian's bedroom with a blanket around him. The coffee had gone quite cold. Wolf had been talking a lot: he'd been telling Maximilian about his adventure in the Borders with the AI called Aizik.

'I sort of woke up on the moor near Northlake in the middle of a blizzard,' said Wolf. 'With this.' He held out an object to Maximilian. It was a man's ring with a blue stone set in ornately crafted silver. It looked almost like a small shield that you'd wear on your finger. There were patterns on the ring that looked vaguely Celtic. And words, too, in a language Maximilian didn't understand. They'd have to get Effie to translate them. When Maximilian took the ring from Wolf it felt heavier than he'd expected. In fact, it was so heavy he had to put it down on the bed.

'It's a boon,' said Maximilian. 'And it doesn't like me. We'll look at it properly in a minute. But what happened after all that stuff about the AI – which, I might add, was extremely interesting. In fact, I might need you to tell me the entire story again, and soon. I've been making a small study of the early history of computing in my spare time . . . But anyway . . .'

'It was a bit confusing,' said Wolf. 'The lights were flickering more and more often, and Aizik kept saying "It does not compute." Over and over again. There was an explosion a few levels down, smoke, sprinklers, shouting . . . I started running. And then I woke up on the moors, like I said. I had my rucksack with all my belongings and, obviously, this ring.'

'Have you put it on yet?' asked Maximilian.

'No. I'm a bit scared. I mean, I'm definitely not scared of anything usually, but . . . I wanted to show it to you first. You know about magic rings. Remember when Effie put hers on for the first time and almost died? I want to know what this is before I start messing around with it. I also want to know how I got from halfway up a weird building in the remote Borders in the middle of a raging fire to the moors near here.'

'You completed the book,' said Maximilian.

'You what?' said Wolf.

'You know you've just had a Last Reader experience, don't you?'

There was a long pause, while Wolf thought about this.

'Like you and Effie?' he said.

'Yep. I didn't realise it had happened to me at first either. I thought it was all real. What book was it? I mean, you must have been reading a book when it started happening. That's how it works.'

242

'But I haven't been reading any book. I've been in the Borders, looking for Natasha.'

'Before that. I mean, I think that was all part of the book. The question is, which book. When did you last pick up a book?'

'Night before last, maybe. Yeah, I got out of bed to read this weird book called *The Answer*.'

'Where did you get it?'

'What do you mean, where did I get it? It's in the bookshop where . . .' Wolf realised that he still hadn't told Max – or any of the others – that he was living rough in Leonard Levar's Antiquarian Bookshop. 'Never mind. I'll tell you afterwards. I just had it in my, er, bedroom.'

'OK, so it looks as if you were the Last Reader of a book called *The Answer*. And you got this boon at the end of it. I bet you've got masses of M-currency as well.'

'Yeah,' said Wolf sadly.

'What's wrong?' asked Maximilian. 'You should be happy. You've survived being a Last Reader – which, apparently, not everyone does – and when we work out what this boon is we'll probably know what your art is too. And with all your M-currency you could probably try to get to the Otherworld. There are portals that the Guild haven't registered yet. As long as you've got enough lifeforce you can go through without your mark or papers or anything.'

'Great,' said Wolf half-heartedly.

'Oh, I see,' said Maximilian. 'This is about Natasha.'

'Yep,' said Wolf. 'I did all that to get her back, and I don't think she was even there.'

'Yeah,' said Maximilian. 'I know. The same thing happened

to me when I was a Last Reader. I kept thinking I had some connection with my "uncle" in the book, that he might lead me to my father. But he wasn't my real uncle. It's just one of the ways the story fits with you and gets you involved with it. And then it's even more unnerving when you find out it's just fiction.'

'I'm basically back at the beginning,' said Wolf.

'Well, maybe not entirely,' said Maximilian. 'I'm sure you'll be able to use your boon to help you in some way. We need to work out what it is. I'm guessing it relates to your art – your secondary ability. It'll be very exciting to know what that is – you'll get a whole new set of skills to go with the ones you already have. And we're going to need new skills. Remind me to fill you in on the latest plans of the Diberi. They're planning to kidnap Effie, for some reason, although she doesn't seem very scared. But we're all supposed to be in training to help defeat them.' Maximilian got up. 'OK, so I can't ask Mum to put on the electric again, since she's not here, and the dim web isn't working that well at the moment anyway. Let's see if some of these will give us a clue.' Maximilian went to his bookshelf and pulled out several ancient-looking catalogues. He put them on the bed next to where Wolf was sitting. *Artefacts from the Otherworld*, one was called. *Rare Boons*, was the title of another.

'Wow,' said Wolf. 'Where did you get these?'

'Oh, I've been making a small study of boons,' said Maximilian. 'I have a modest collection of these catalogues. I can't remember where I got them. Mail order, probably. Ages ago, before I epiphanised and found out it's all real.'

244

'Amazing,' said Wolf, opening one. 'Look at all these swords!'

'I wonder what that stone is,' said Maximilian, pointing at Wolf's ring. 'It's blue. I should know, but I don't. It's not sapphire, I don't think. It's not shiny enough. Lexy would know. Maybe I'll try paging her. Once we know what it is we'll be able to work out what it does.'

Maximilian entered Lexy's number a few times, but he got no reply. While the pager tried once more to connect, Maximilian thought again about everything Wolf had told him.

'You told the AI to read the *Tao Te Ching*,' Maximilian said. 'What is that?'

'It's a book of Eastern philosophy,' said Wolf. 'Like a military book, but not exactly. More spiritual, I guess. It tells you about battles, but says that you should retreat to attack, or not even attack at all. I've read a load of military books recently, and they all become really philosophical and deep after a while. Like *The Art of War*. And Plato. Oh, and *War and Peace*.'

'Wait, you've been reading *Plato*? And Tolstoy? But you're meant to be a meathead. No offence.'

'I am in the top set for English. And history,' Wolf reminded Maximilian.

And living in a bookshop. But again, Wolf didn't say that bit.

'Oh my God,' said Maximilian. 'Maybe you're actually a scholar like me. A warrior scholar. That would be an interesting combination. You'd be like Napoleon or something.'

'Nope,' said Wolf. 'I can't be a scholar. I couldn't use your spectacles, could I? And you can't use my ring.'

'Yes, you're right,' said Maximilian. 'Well, let's look in these catalogues for boons with the same stone. I don't think there are that many blue stones, but I might be wrong.'

Effie picked up her bag, said a hurried goodbye to Octavia Bottle and followed the man out of the door of Mrs Bottle's Bun Shop. She wasn't sure how far she was going to trail him, because as soon as she could she was going to the Great Library in Truelove House to finish what her mother had started. No one would be able to say she was a galloglass if she risked her life for the universe, would they? And even if they did . . . What was it her father had said about heroes setting off on journeys on their own? That was basically Effie's life. She would follow this man long enough to get any more information he had, then she'd go.

Maybe she *was* a galloglass, and maybe that meant everyone was going to hate her for ever. But that wasn't going to stop her doing what she thought was right. And Festus had said that there'd been prophecies about her helping in the fight against the Diberi. Surely this was what she was meant to be doing. This was what the universe wanted her to do.

The man walked down the darkening street towards Lexy's house. Where was he going? Effie was surprised when he slowed right down as he approached the front door. He then withdrew an envelope from his coat pocket and posted it through the letterbox.

He looked around, as if to check whether he was being watched. Effie quickly pretended to be looking at her wrist-watch, but she fumbled with her sleeve and the whole action looked fake and staged. The man stared at her for a few seconds before walking away. Effie's cover was blown. She sighed. There was no way she could continue to follow him now. She waited for him to leave and then went and knocked on Lexy's door. What was going on with her? And why on earth would that man have put a note through her door? There was no reply. Effie would have to try to contact Lexy via walkie-talkie when she got home.

But right now she was going to go to the Otherworld to remove the book. Effie walked quickly back through the network of alleyways until she came out near the old village green. This was how she always travelled to Truelove House. Pelham Longfellow had explained to Effie how you make a sort of imprint in the place you regularly use to travel through the dimensions. She didn't even have to use her magical calling card any more. She just had to go behind the hedge, get herself into a meditative state, and—

Melting. Through a cold layer and a warm layer and then—

The grey mist and the gatehouse and—

The sound of bees. The smell of flowers. Effie was home.

So why did she suddenly feel like a stranger?

As Effie walked up the path towards Truelove House with her Otherworld bag across her Realworld winter coat, she had the sudden sensation of being dirty and tainted, like a pile of old cutlery that no one has bothered to polish. *What if she really is a galloglass?* Rollo's words again stung Effie, and the pain was so real, like a wasp crawling over her heart and injecting her with poison. If she really was a galloglass, she wouldn't ever be able to come back here again. She probably wasn't even supposed to be here now. But she could at least help everyone in their battle against the Diberi by removing the brown book again, once and for all. Even if it killed her.

Effie hoped that she wouldn't meet anyone in the garden or the house. She just wanted to get into the Great Library, get the book and leave. Of course, they'd probably all be in the Great Library now, doing whatever they did in there. But perhaps Effie could get in and out quickly without them noticing. After all, the library appeared differently to everyone. Maybe Rollo, Clothilde and Cosmo wouldn't even be in Effie's version. The main thing was that she had enough lifeforce for getting in and out of the library in the first place. Fifty thousand would be plenty, surely?

There was no one in the large plant-filled conservatory when Effie entered Truelove House through its open doors. Good. The last thing she needed was Bertie offering her a cup of something or, worse, Clothilde, who was probably still cross with Effie after what had happened in Froghole. *But aren't you a terrible galloglass now?* Effie imagined her saying in her sweet, honeyed voice. *What are you even doing here? I don't think you're related to us after all. You can't be.*

The only other living being in the conservatory was Moonface, Cosmo's cat. He was sitting very still, watching Effie as she walked across the tiled floor. For a moment Effie imagined that he was saying something, or trying to, but his mouth remained shut. Effie couldn't understand any animals except horses, so if he was speaking in a telepathic language she wouldn't even know. Which was probably a good thing, because even if Moonface had something to say, Effie wasn't sure she wanted to hear it.

'Are you going to say I'm a galloglass, like the rest of them

248

did?' she asked him. 'Are you going to say I shouldn't be here? That I shouldn't meddle with things and take away the Diberi again?'

Moonface continued to stare at Effie.

Well, even if he did want to say something to her, it didn't matter. She had to get to the Great Library. Effie walked towards the main part of the house. Moonface seemed to shake his head slightly. Then, unnervingly, he disappeared.

The last time Effie had been in the Great Library on her own it had been a disaster. The library had welcomed her in, because it had wanted the book she had been carrying. But of course that was the book she now wanted to take away again. Effie wondered whether the library would refuse to let her in now, because of this, and because her initiation as Keeper was not yet complete. But the library seemed completely neutral as Effie approached its wooden doors. When they clicked open to admit her they did so nonchalantly, as if to say, 'All right then – how interesting – I wasn't expecting this.'

Effie took a step forward.

'I see you didn't learn anything last time,' came a deep voice.

'Cosmo,' said Effie. He was walking down the grand staircase and had reached the place where it curved just above the entrance to the Great Library. 'I know you think what I'm doing is dangerous, but I don't mind. You're not going to stop me. I understand what my mother—'

'Understand? Dear child, if you do, then you're the only one who does. What happened with your mother was very—'

'She wanted to save everyone from the Diberi. I realise that now. She took away the book, and—'

249

'And you think it should be that simple, do you? The removal of one's enemies, just like that? Dear child, if everyone who had a problem with something came and removed the relevant book from the Great Library, there'd be no books left – and no universe of any kind. You must see that.'

'Yes,' said Effie. 'I understand. But in this case it's the right thing to do. Everyone would agree about that.'

'The Diberi wouldn't.'

'But they're wrong.'

'Yes, and they think we're wrong.'

'But they *are* wrong!'

'Everyone thinks that their enemies are wrong, and that what they are doing is the right thing to do. That's why there is war – in your world at least. Although we seem to be moving towards our first ever war in this world as well.'

'What do you mean?'

'The Mainland Liberation Collective are getting serious about wanting to split permanently from the island. And their methods for persuading the rest of us . . . But that's another matter. Euphemia, you must understand that what your mother did was well-meaning, but wrong. It was the right thing for you to do to bring the book back, however much it seems to have created these troubles, and however much it hurt you at the time. Do you understand?'

Effie shook her head. 'No. I don't understand. And I don't agree. The Diberi would change reality much more than I'm about to do. They're evil. They have to be stopped. And this is the obvious way of doing it.'

'Are you sure about that?'

'Yes.'

Cosmo sighed. 'Perhaps it is true that you are not of this world. That you are somehow incompatible with it. That would be a big disappointment for all of us. Especially as it seems you recently came so close . . .' For a moment he looked very small, and very old. 'If you go into the library and actually manage to return with the book . . .' He shook his head, then took off his glasses and rubbed his wrinkled face. 'Child, come away from the door, please, while we finish this conversation.'

Effie took her hand from the door. The word *disappointment* was marching through her like a marauding army, creating sadness wherever it went. Was she really such a horrible let-down? But of course she knew the answer to that already, didn't she? She was an island galloglass. There could be nothing worse.

Cosmo had reached the bottom of the stairs.

'Come, child.' He led Effie through into the large airy drawing room. 'Sit.'

Effie sat on the edge of the white sofa, with her bag still across her body. It felt wrong, and she was hot in her winter coat, so she took them both off and laid them carefully next to her. But she wasn't staying here for long. She had to get into the library and remove the Diberi once and for all.

'When you first came to Dragon's Green we feared that you had been tarnished. They – we – decided that your being here was so important that it didn't matter that we had, well, borrowed a rather unpleasant manner of getting you here. Obviously we don't approve of destroying books in order to become a Last Reader. That's what the Diberi do. The process should, in fact, be natural, beautiful. But I fear it may have corrupted you. Made it more difficult for you to—'

'What do you mean? I don't—'

'Euphemia, do you know what kind of people take books out of the Great Library without the ritual?'

'Um . . .'

'The Diberi. They are the only people who tamper with reality in this way. We cannot become like them. Although I fear perhaps in some way you already are. You burned a book, after all. It's not your fault, of course, and I regret we told you to do it, but it explains many things, including this unfortunate business with your shade. And why it's taking you so long to discover . . . Well, I can't tell you what you need to discover. But I don't understand why it isn't happening.' He sighed. 'It's an error we made. An error upon an error upon an error upon—'

'I'm not an error!' said Effie, her voice breaking as tears began to well up deep inside her. She didn't completely understand everything Cosmo was saying, but it seemed, somehow, to add up to that. She, Effie, was an error. A mistake. Someone they should never have invited here. Someone who should probably never have been born.

She got up from the sofa. Her blood was pumping through her so hard that she felt oddly resplendent in her desperate sadness, and also dangerous, and, in some unfathomable way, immortal.

'If I'm just a mistake then you won't miss me,' she said.

'No, dear child, I didn't mean—'

'You can't take it back,' said Effie, hotly. 'And I don't care, because I know I'm right. If the Diberi are the ones who want

252

to take books out of the Great Library and change the universe, then they need to be stopped by any means necessary.' Effie wasn't sure where she'd heard that phrase, but it sounded right. 'If we have to take one book out in order to protect the others, then surely that's worth it? One wrong to prevent hundreds of wrongs.'

Cosmo sighed. 'Spoken like a true hero,' he said. But he didn't make it sound like it was a good thing. Indeed, he made *true hero* sound rather like *Diberi* or *galloglass*.

'You're not going to stop me,' said Effie, reaching for her bag.

'No, I can see that,' said Cosmo.

'Lapis lazuli,' said Wolf. 'Here: I think I've found it.'

He showed Maximilian the page in the catalogue he'd been looking at. It was full of amazing boons from the Otherworld. There was the Athame of Althea, a rare dragonstooth dagger with an enchanted platinum handle studded with precious gemstones. Like all daggers, it was used by mages. There was an archer's bow made from silverwood and unicorn gut (a rare type of Underworld mushroom), designed to be used by hunters. Then there was something called the Rosary of Peace, which comprised many blue stones on a silver chain with a silver cross. Rosaries, said the catalogue, were for clerics. As was lapis lazuli, which is what the stones were.

'Interesting,' said Maximilian. 'And look at this.'

In his catalogue he'd been browsing a section on magical rings, which were of use to four different *kharakter*s: clerics, heroes, warriors and alchemists. Usually, rings seemed to be very powerful boons, associated with higher levels of *kharakter*. Alchemists' rings were all set with obsidian. Warriors' rings usually had bloodstones. Heroes' rings had sapphire or aventurine in them, both of which were blue. But they were different from Wolf's stone. Aventurine was milky and almost green. Sapphire was lighter, clearer, almost turquoise.

'I'm pretty sure the stone in your ring is lapis lazuli,' said Maximilian. 'Let's check this last one.'

The two boys looked at a third catalogue together. And there it was. Not exactly the same ring, but one that was very similar, and with exactly the same type of blue stone. *The Ring of the Noble Cleric*, said the legend below the picture. *Lapis lazuli set in silver.*

'What the hell is a cleric?' asked Wolf.

Maximilian looked it up in his dictionary.

'It's a religious person,' he said. 'Weird. Are you religious?'

'No,' said Wolf. 'It must be wrong.'

'We need to go and see Raven, and borrow her *Repertory of Kharakter, Art & Shade* so we can look it up,' said Maximilian. 'I'll page her and see where she is.'

Wolf turned the ring over and over in his hands. A cleric's ring. What did that mean? He yearned to put it on. It felt warm and comfortable in the palm of his hand, almost as if it was enticing him: *Put me on. Put me on. Put me on!* Before he knew what he was doing, Wolf was trying it on different fingers. It fitted best on the index finger on his left hand. Before he'd even thought about what he was doing, he'd eased it on, and pushed it all the way down . . .

254

'Wolf, what on earth are you—'

But Maximilian's voice disappeared as Wolf was swept up into a sort of tornado of silence, joy and understanding. He could smell incense, and candle-wax, and something like heaven . . . Then he passed out.

When he woke up, he found Maximilian had put the ring under an empty glass on his desk. It was rattling against the sides, trying to get out.

'I think we're going to have to find out more about what this is, and what being a cleric means. Do you want me to look after it for you?'

But the ring wouldn't stay under the glass. The next time it rattled so hard the glass broke and the ring flew towards Wolf. It clearly wanted to be on his finger again, now it had been there once. Maximilian found a piece of brown string (inspired by Dill Hammer and all his recycling, Maximilian now had a drawer full of such useful things) and threaded the ring onto it, finishing just as it became too hot and heavy for him to hold.

'Here,' he said. 'You'd better keep it around your neck for now. It might calm down a bit if it's closer to you. But *don't* put it on again.'

His pager beeped.

'Oh. That's Raven. She says something about wanting to get away from a poet. She's coming here. That's good. We've actually got some news for you as well. We're all in the Gothmen now, and—'

'The Gothmen?'

'Yep. I'll tell you all about it . . . You and Raven had better

255

both stay for dinner. I'll page Mum and tell her. Oh, and I'll go and ask Dill to cook for two more.'

When Effie reached the door to the Great Library, it was already slightly open, as if it was expecting her, and as if she was welcome. 'Come inside,' it seemed to say. 'Hurry . . .' So it, too, agreed that the Diberi should be removed, even if it did mean breaking one of the fundamental rules of the universe. Ha! But . . .

Effie suddenly hesitated. What if Cosmo were right?

But she was here now, and her blood was still pumping hard, and anyway, the door was opening, and she was being drawn in by a great warmth, and the mellow smell of wood, and books, and she was definitely right, and invincible, and she had great power, power to influence the whole world, both worlds, and . . .

As Effie entered the Great Library she felt something of the tingling, joyful sensation she'd had in the market, except it was different – it was the thing Suri had done to her. In the market, when Effie had been afraid of the feeling it had immediately disappeared. But here it simply intensified, and a strange sweetness ran through her brain.

Effie's library appeared as it had done before. A lot of wood, and the bookshelves all in a row, and a window leading out to an orchard. There was the usual wooden balcony with a further level of books in a small gallery. At the end of the lower level was usually a wall with a large painting on it, but Effie saw that this had now been replaced with an archway. Effie felt compelled to walk towards it, past the shelf of books where she knew the volume on the Diberi was housed. This shelf was where she should stop, but . . .

The archway was painted turquoise. Effie found herself able to walk more quickly than normal through the Great Library, and soon she had gone under the archway and into a new chamber she had never seen before. It was warm and dark inside, with swirling, unfamiliar blueish colours forming a sort of peculiar wallpaper that didn't seem to want to keep still. There were three small piles of books on the floor next to a simple wooden chair. On the chair sat an extremely old person who was giving Effie the deepest stare she'd ever experienced.

'Hello,' said Effie.

Effie had a horrible feeling that if she turned around the archway would be gone and she would be trapped in this strange swirling room for ever. So she didn't look. She tried to breathe normally, but suddenly her fear was so great she wasn't sure her body could take it. What had she done? But it was too late now.

'We are the sssspirit of the library,' said the person on the chair. He or she had a shock of white hair like a jagged snowy mountain and piecing glacial-blue eyes. His or her voice was a strange sort of whispery hiss. 'And I ssssee you have brought ussss something. *Good.*'

'No,' said Effie. 'I'm sorry, but I actually came to take something away.'

'Take away? But didn't they tell you? We don't let people take things away. Oh, no no no no no. That wouldn't do at all.'

'But—'

'Read it to ussss.'

'Read what to you?'

'You're a . . .' The spirit of the library peered at Effie. 'You're a human, I ssssee. Well, never mind. Take the book out of your bag and read it to ussss.'

Effie didn't have a book. She had no idea what the spirit of the library meant. Unless . . . Oh. Of course. The poem. *Galloglass.* She'd bought it from the bookstall, put it in her bag and then she'd accidentally brought it in here. As Cosmo had said, she hadn't learned anything. The library had let her in last time because she had a book it wanted – the history of the Diberi. But why on earth was the spirit of the library interested in a poem about galloglasses? Effie suddenly had a sense that there were many things she didn't know – a whole messy, complex universe of unknowns outside her own small orbit – and that she should have trusted Cosmo. Perhaps he knew what some of those messy, complex things were. But it was too late.

'Read,' said the spirit of the library. 'Read to ussss.'

Then again, what harm could be done simply by reading a poem? Effie wondered if she was going to feel weak again, and if Cosmo was going to have to come to rescue her. Surely he would come, if she needed him? He always did. This time, though, Effie had a growing suspicion that maybe she'd gone somewhere beyond his help. If she was going to escape then she had better do what the spirit of the library told her, and do it right. Effie got the book out of her bag and began to read the English translation of *Galloglass.* She sensed that the spirit of the library would have preferred the original Rosian, but Effie was embarrassed about her accent. She began.

In days of yore, when brave and true,
The heroes of the day came forth,
They had no need of me and you,
To each one their own piece of swarth.

To tend one plot, to grow, to sow,
This life, while brief, had taught them how
To reap, to make a pack and go,
In darkness, with a sacred vow.

And weaklings watched and soon they thought
'This life is better than mine own';
And motivated soon they wrought
Their destiny of earth and stone.

The greatest sages of our worlds
Live all alone in mountain caves;
Their consciousness is never hurled
Like flotsam on just any waves.

We're born each one of us alone
And separate is how we stay;
This is how we will find our home,
And merge with all along the way.

The oneness is both me and you,
And everyone we've ever known;
The one and all are never two:
Together we will wear one crown.

The way ahead is long and hard,
So learn some poems for the road;
Or better, take along a bard
To tell us stories of the Flow.

The spirit of the library had its eyes shut, and its head swayed along to the rhythm as Effie read. Effie had a horrible feeling that any mistake in her reading would have consequences. Somehow, she didn't make any. She didn't understand exactly what the poem meant, but she quite liked it.

'You will leave this book with ussss,' hissed the spirit of the library. 'Yessss. This is a book we once had; we remember it, but what became of it? Sssstill, you have brought it back to ussss. We think you have brought other things back to ussss, in what you think of as the passsst. We are grateful to you. This time, and perhapssss one more time, yessss, we will let you leave. After that, we are not ssssure. But you musssst hurry. And you will not take any of our bookssss with you.'

Attracted by a tremendous force, *Galloglass* flew out of Effie's hands and landed on one of the piles on the floor in front of the spirit of the library. Effie noticed scraps of paper on top of the other two piles. *Shelving*, said one. *Removal*, said the other. She turned and the archway was there, but in a sort of haze. If it was there, then . . . Effie knew this was her only chance of getting out of here alive, so she made a run for it: through into the main part of the library with its smell of wood and books, and out of the door and . . .

Effie's heart was beating wildly. She felt both very hot and very cold at the same time. She was sweating, but somehow her sweat felt like a freezing waterfall down her neck and back. She tried to compose herself: to get herself ready to explain to Cosmo what had happened in the library. But at least she could reassure him that she had not taken out the Diberi book. He had, perhaps, been right: there must be another, more ethical, way to deal with the Diberi. Surely he'd be pleased with her. Surely . . .

But there was no sign of Cosmo anywhere. Effie checked the drawing room and the conservatory, but he was not in either of them. Effie went out into the garden and looked in the summer house: no one. Then she went back in through the conservatory and went up the many, many stairs to his old study at the top of the turret by Effie's own room.

He wasn't there.

Effie started to feel sick and empty as the used-up adrenaline drained through her body. What had she actually just done? She'd argued with Cosmo and gone, against his wishes, into the Great Library, where she had intended to meddle with reality in one way – and had then ended up doing something that could, now she thought about it, be far worse. She suddenly felt ashamed. But at least she *hadn't* done what he'd told her not to. She hadn't taken out the book. Just a kind word from him would make her feel so much better . . . But Cosmo was nowhere to be found.

He was displeased with her; Effie knew that without him being there to say so. She was, after all, a galloglass islander who didn't do anything she was told and who had just put a book into the Great Library without going through any of the processes she'd heard about. In order to put a book into the library you had to do all those complicated things . . . What was it Clothilde had said? Effie had been so distracted thinking about going to Froghole that day that she'd barely listened. She just thought she'd be able to pick it up later. Stupid, stupid. But surely what she'd done hadn't been that bad. The spirit of the library had wanted the book, after all.

As she walked down the stairs back to the landing in the main part of Truelove House, Effie suddenly had a horrible realisation. In fact, two.

The Diberi were planning to put a book in the library themselves. That's what they were hoping to achieve with their enormous spell. All this speculation about the Diberi storming the Great Library to take books out, to remove some aspect of reality, was almost right, but it was not the whole picture. How much more effectively you could edit reality if you just wrote your own book of what you wanted to be the truth and somehow got it accepted.

That was what Skylurian Midzhar had planned to use Terrence for! And now that Russian poet Lady Tchainsaw was doing the same. Effie recalled what she and Maximilian had overheard at the university. *Remember our agreement? You will be author of the new universe, and I will be its queen. I will have total power, and you will serve me.* It had sounded stupid at the time, but Effie now saw that it had been deadly serious. The idea of writing a whole new universe made no sense until you understood how the Great Library worked. She shuddered to think what would happen if a book like that did find its way inside.

That was Effie's first realisation. That the Diberi most wanted to put books *in* the library, not take them out.

Her second realisation was that this was exactly what she'd

just done herself. She'd changed reality – in ways she didn't even yet know – by putting a book into the Great Library. She'd done it with no authorisation, no ritual: nothing. And what's more she'd done it with a book that the Diberi were bound to approve of, and everyone here in Truelove House was not. What was wrong with her? Every time she came to the Otherworld she made things a little bit worse.

Effie sighed deeply. All the mistakes she'd made. It was too late to do anything about them now. The only thing she could do was to go home, back to the Realworld, and try to stop the Diberi once and for all, not that she knew how to do that.

As Effie walked down the stairs to the entrance hall of Truelove House the enormity of everything she'd done settled on her shoulders like a heavy dark cloak. Who was she? She didn't even know any more. But she had to make things right. Although maybe it was too late even for that. Maybe what she'd done could never be put right. Effie sighed. Well, at least she could do something about Terrence Deer-Hart and his stupid book.

She walked out through the conservatory doors, wondering if this was the last time she'd ever see them.

The guards in the gatehouse usually only spoke to Effie on the way in to Truelove House. Sometimes she got a brief 'Welcome, Miss.' Occasionally, if it was a new guard, a request to see her calling card. They'd never spoken to her as she'd been leaving Truelove House. But today one of them came out of the gatehouse and nodded at her, just as she was about to open the large wrought-iron gate.

'An invitation for you, Miss,' he said.

He handed Effie a cream-coloured envelope with a gold trim.

'Thank you,' said Effie, taking it from him.

She went through the gates and set off in the direction of the portal that would take her back to the Realworld, where she could try to put right everything she'd done wrong.

'Aren't you going to open that, Miss?' the guard called after her.

'Yes,' said Effie. 'I'll do it when I get home.'

'Suit yourself, Miss,' said the guard.

Of course, Effie already knew that whatever she was being invited to, she wouldn't be able to go. She wouldn't be able to do anything or see anyone in the Otherworld until she'd made things right. But she would. She'd find a way. She tucked the invitation in her bag and set off towards the portal on Keepers' Plains.

18

When Effie got home, Cait was upstairs having a candlelit bath and Orwell was still reading his copy of *Galloglass* in front of the fire in the sitting room. Baby Luna was in her playpen wearing her favourite pink tutu and eating an ice-cream cone without a bib on. She'd clearly been included in the day of selfishness. Was every day going to be like that now that Effie had put *Galloglass* in the Great Library? But it was only a short poem. And it had been in the library before. And the day had actually worked out quite well when you thought about it – well, the bits in the Realworld at least.

'I expect you're still wanting to borrow this,' Orwell said to Effie when she walked into the sitting room. He waved the book at her provocatively.

'Not really,' said Effie. 'Keep it.'

'What's got into you?' asked Orwell.

'Nothing,' said Effie. 'I think I might just get an early night.'

'It's only six o'clock. Cait's making vegetable stew with dumplings for dinner.'

Effie sighed. 'Well, I'll go to bed straight after dinner. I've got a long day tomorrow.'

'Ah yes, your first day as a university student,' said Orwell. 'Don't eat the cottage pie in the canteen, that's all I'll say. Oh, and keep out of the botany department. They've got some enormous plant in there that is apparently very carnivorous. It's already eaten two post-docs and a cleaner.'

'OK.'

'Are you all right? Normally even you would be interested in carnivorous plants.'

'I'm fine. Just tired.'

'Well, you're missing out with this book, I can tell you. Such a magnificent poem. Listen to the last stanza. *The way ahead is long and hard/So learn some poems for the road/Or better, take along a bard/To tell us stories as we go.* Moving stuff, eh? I should read more poetry. Really gets the blood moving around the body. Makes one feel pure, and intelligent. Where are you going?'

'I've got homework to do before tomorrow.'

'Suit yourself.'

Effie went through the rest of the evening in a daze. She ate her vegetable stew without really tasting it. Cait had made apple pie and custard for pudding, but Effie didn't really feel like any.

Before she went to sleep Effie tried to get a message to the others about meeting up, but Lexy wasn't answering on the walkie-talkie, and Effie didn't have a pager. But once she found Maximilian he'd be able to page Lexy and Raven. Effie realised she hadn't seen Wolf for days. She hoped he was OK. Once she found him, she was sure he would agree that nothing really

266

mattered apart from doing something about the Diberi. The question was what. Effie wished she'd been able to remove the history of the Diberi from the Great Library. Or did she? She wasn't at all sure how she felt about that any more. But one thing was clear. The spirit of the library wouldn't have let her do it. It just wasn't possible.

So how had Effie's mother managed it?

Odile Underwood yawned again, for about the fifth time that evening.

'Are you all right, Nurse Underwood?' asked Raven.

They were all sitting around the dinner table in the Underwood house: Wolf, Raven, Maximilian, Odile and Dill. The children were drinking Dill's homemade fermented elderflower cordial and the adults were drinking deep red wine.

'What? Oh yes, love. Nothing for you to worry about,' said Odile. She yawned again. 'Been working hard, that's all.'

'Have you been at the hospital all weekend?' asked Raven.

'Yesterday,' said Odile. 'Today I've been doing home visits, trying to undo all the binding spells that are out there recently. Honestly, I've never seen so many people bound. And the way they're doing it . . . It's barbaric. It's one thing taking someone's magic away, but today I saw a chap who had also gone blind. I visited two witches who simply could not get out of bed any more. And one of them had even lost her familiar – which as you'll know is a fate worse than death for witches. And then there was the Principiant healer who thought he just had the flu

267

until he found he couldn't put enchantments on his tonics any more. It breaks your heart.'

'Who's doing this?' asked Dill. 'No, don't tell me. The Guild.'

'Yes, well, don't say it too loudly. They say they've got eyes and ears everywhere at the moment.'

'I thought you were a supporter,' said Dill.

'Not any more,' said Odile. 'I'm not a great fan of Masterman Finch. And all this binding . . . It's just cruel.'

Maximilian and Raven looked at one another. They'd heard about Masterman Finch at the meeting of the Gothmen. They'd filled in Wolf as best they could on what was happening, even though they'd forgotten this detail. They'd been just about to start examining the *Repertory of Kharakter, Art & Shade* to find out about clerics when they'd been called for dinner.

'Well,' said Dill Hammer to Odile, 'have some brown rice. It's grounding. Strengthening. And have some of this lovely seaweed salad too.'

He passed the bowls to Odile, who served the children before she served herself. As well as brown rice and seaweed salad Dill had made a darkroot casserole with satay sauce and a massive chocolate cake with rose petals scattered on it.

'Thank you for doing all this cooking, Dill,' said Odile. 'I don't know where I would have been without you this weekend.'

'I made you some more rosehip syrup as well,' said Dill. 'Can't be too careful with all these Midwinter colds about. And some cloudberry jam. You can have it on your toast in the morning.'

Maximilian was watching his mother and Dill closely. He was glad they were getting on so well. He'd been cultivating Dill Hammer quite carefully recently. And it had been working. Maybe they'd get married . . . And then Maximilian would have a father again. A kind one, too, who made things. Maximilian would have to make sure to reinforce the idea very strongly in Dill's head – although Dill was very skilled in blocking mages. He ate a lot of quinoa – a well-known anti-magic agent – to make sure.

'Shall we take our chocolate cake into my room?' suggested Maximilian once the main course was over. 'Leave the grown-ups to talk about more adult things if they want.'

Odile gave him a suspicious look.

'Well, I suppose we can catch up on all the new gossip about the Gothmen,' she said. Then she frowned. 'No one's approached you from a group called the Gothmen, have they?' she asked Maximilian.

'Of course not,' he lied. 'Nothing exciting ever happens to me any more. Why?'

'They're an underground resistance movement working against the Diberi,' said Dill. 'And this new incarnation of the Guild. Very admirable, of course, but highly unlikely to succeed. And they do extremely dangerous things. You must promise us that you'll stay away from them. I think one of their leading figures might even teach at your school.'

Neither Wolf nor Raven were very good at lying. Maximilian, however, was a master of deceit.

'Our teachers only ever speak to us to tell us facts, sadly,' he said. 'It would be quite exciting if they ever invited us to join a clandestine group. But I can't see it ever actually happening.'

Raven and Wolf exchanged a half-smile, picked up plates with large slices of chocolate cake and followed Maximilian into his room.

'Right,' said Maximilian, once the door was closed. 'Let's look up cleric in the book.'

'I don't know how you lie like that,' said Raven with admiration. 'I go red and blotchy if I try to say anything that isn't true.'

'I must admit, I am quite proud of my acting abilities,' said Maximilian. 'I can get away with a lot while my mum still doesn't know I'm a mage.'

'When are you going to tell her?' asked Raven.

'Oh, I don't know. Never?'

'I just can't be a cleric,' said Wolf glumly, flicking through the *Repertory of Kharakter, Art & Shade*. 'It sounds wrong. Surely I'm more likely to be a hunter? Or, I don't know, an explorer. Maybe a guide . . .'

'Give that to me,' said Maximilian. 'You'll never find the bit you want. Aha. Here we are. Hmmm. Interesting. Listen to this: "The cleric is the wisest of all the kharakters. He or she is concerned with spiritual matters and in particular reading and putting into practice spiritual texts. At higher levels, he or she will be able to change things with prayer, or even, rarely, to create new philosophies. The cleric is skilled at meditation and connecting with the secret parts of the universe inaccessible to less spiritual seekers. The cleric may also become greatly adept of the martial arts. The cleric's emphasis is on wisdom, although this tends to be from books and spiritual journeys rather than experience in the physical world. The cleric is good at listening to people's problems and giving wise advice. The cleric is a deeply moral kharakter, who always does what he or she believes is right, even if this is difficult, or flies in the face of so-called 'conventional wisdom'. Whenever difficult decisions must be taken, a cleric will be required. Clerics are not frightened to enter the unknown, and to take risks that might lead to new wisdom.'"

'Skilled at meditation?' said Wolf. 'But I've never meditated in my life.'

'Oooh – I can teach you how to meditate,' said Raven. 'I think Effie's good at it as well. "Secret parts of the universe" sounds amazing! And martial arts!'

'But I'm not spiritual,' said Wolf, still baffled. 'At least, I didn't *think* I was spiritual . . .'

'The emphasis is on wisdom,' said Maximilian. 'And you have been reading all those books lately.'

'Maybe,' said Wolf, distractedly. He'd started re-reading the entry for cleric, in particular the different kinds of magic they could do. *Candle magic. Prayer magic. Transformational prayer. Transcendent magic. Flying battles.* What were those things? Wolf had never thought he would ever be able to do proper magic – he'd just thought that being a warrior meant being able to wield magical weapons and attack people's M-currency.

The cleric is one of the most disciplined of all the kharakters, Wolf read on, *and can also be very secretive. Their friends are often surprised when they discover how deeply the cleric thinks about things, and in particular how much he or she yearns for good.* Maybe this wasn't such a bad match for him after all. And the cleric's boon had worked on him. But spiritual and wise? This was going to take some getting used to.

'I wonder what my art is,' Raven said to Maximilian. 'I haven't found it yet. Probably never will. He looks pretty attached to that book.'

Wolf had found a case-study of a warrior cleric and was reading it avidly. He hadn't thought such a combination would even work, but there was quite a list in the *Repertory*: Mahatma Ghandi, Martin Luther King and Joan Baez were among them. There was also some important mythical figure called Arjuna. *Most people assume that peaceful religious people don't really fight,* the *Repertory* went on. Wolf thought back to his conversation with Aizik: there was a big difference between violence for its own sake and fighting for what you believe in. He'd proved you can fight without any violence at all.

'How's your spider?' Maximilian asked Raven.

'A bit better after I did the stuff from the book I found in the University Library,' she said. 'There was a special concoction of fennel and lavender that I had to make. And a spell, too. I'm supposed to be finding a familiar – witches need them to progress to higher levels than Neophyte according to Lexy, and Dr Green's magic class. So I'm trying really hard to find one. I know loads of animals, but none of them will agree. I thought one of the spiders might do it once the sick one had healed, but no.'

'Why not?'

'They want to be free, which I completely understand, of course. I absolutely wouldn't want to exploit anyone. I think in the olden days becoming a familiar was seen by the Cosmic Web as a sort of servitude or even enslavement. It's complicated.' She sighed.

'What about Echo?' asked Maximilian.

'A familiar has to come with you virtually everywhere,' said Raven. 'It's a big undertaking. It suits smaller animals better. I don't think a horse could do it. But I'll keep trying. Sooner or later I'll find someone to help me. Apparently you're supposed to know as soon as you meet your familiar. You don't even have to ask. It's supposed to be a bit like love at first sight.'

Raven went back to her pager. She'd been trying to contact Lexy for ages now.

'How are you getting on?' Maximilian asked Wolf, who was still reading the *Repertory* avidly.

'I don't know,' said Wolf. 'I mean, at first I thought it was nuts. But now . . .'

'We should test you,' said Maximilian. 'There should be a series of tests at the back of this edition, I think. Oh yes, here we go. Cleric's test. Brilliant. All right. What is the thing that links all religions?'

'A belief in what is good?'

'Yep. More or less. Um . . . Name a type of incense.'

'Sandalwood.' Wolf frowned. 'I have literally no idea how I know that,' he said. 'How weird.'

'Oooh, I love sandalwood,' said Raven dreamily, looking up from the pager. 'Sandalwood and rose.'

'What's your favourite colour?'

'Blue.'

'Excellent! Do you like silence?'

'Yes.'

'Being on your own?'

'Yes.'

'Do you ever cheat or lie?'

'No.'

'Well, there you go,' said Maximilian. 'You're a cleric!'

'A warrior cleric,' corrected Wolf.

'Hmmm. Well, let's hope your cleric's skills will turn out to be useful in some way. You're already useful as a warrior, of course.'

'I just want to find my sister,' said Wolf.

'Maybe you should pray for her,' suggested Raven. 'No, don't both look at me like that! Surely a cleric would be able to do things with prayer. I'm sure it says something like that in the *Repertory*. I do witch's prayers, sometimes, although they're different. But they can't be that different.'

'It's got to be worth a try,' said Wolf. 'Except I don't even know how to start.'

Just then there was a knock at the door. It was Odile telling them that Raven's mum had come to pick her up.

'I'd better go too,' said Wolf.

'Why don't you stay here?' said Odile. 'Have the spare room.'

'Are you sure, Nurse Underwood?'

'You look like you could do with a warm night in a real house,' she said, mysteriously.

How was it that mothers always knew so many things? And even about other people's children too.

'Ouch!' exclaimed Terrence Deer-Hart, as Lady Tchainsaw pricked him yet again. 'Be careful where you put those pins!'

'Your robes must be ready for Midwinter,' said Lady Tchainsaw. She rolled her Rs powerfully, more than any actual Russian would ever do. Perhaps she missed home. Or perhaps she wasn't even Russian, and that was why she was overdoing it. Her identity as an avant-garde poet was ever-changing, after all.

'Oh well,' said Terrence, 'at least this is better than my last outfit.'

'We will never speak of the other outfit ever again,' said Lady Tchainsaw. 'There.' She made another adjustment. 'You do not look too dreadful, which is a surprise. The master will be pleased.'

Terrence turned and looked at himself in the antique full-length mirror that took up most of one wall in Lady Tchainsaw's rooms in the East Wing of the university. He now resembled many of the other objects around him: old, rare and really quite evil. As well as a small cabinet full of dusty, enchanted-looking marionettes that rivalled the most terrifying specimens owned by the Puppet Man, Lady Tchainsaw had an impressive, although highly unnerving, collection of stuffed dead animals. These peered at Terrence in the mirror imploringly, their ghostly eyes all saying, *Why did you kill me?* and, in some cases, *When you are asleep I will come and take revenge . . .*

Terrence shook his head. Stopped looking at the animals. His eyes fell on another cabinet, but this one contained a selection of shrunken human heads, many with bits of hair still attached. There was a further cabinet full of skulls, large and small, another containing masks with enormous noses, and yet another with jars full of the preserved forms of long-dead slugs and toads.

'Where do you get things like this?' Terrence asked.

'My travels.'

'How do you get them through customs?'

'I do not travel in the usual way, of course. Vodka?'

'Thank you.'

While Lady Tchainsaw poured Terrence a glass of vodka over black ice, he walked around the room, over various rugs with the heads of the animals they'd been made from still attached, taking in many dark oil paintings of women who looked very much like Lady Tchainsaw in the past, or in fancy dress. It was as if she had lived for a very, very long time. Were they her relatives? Probably. But where were the men? Wasn't there a kind of spider that ate her mates? Maybe it was something like that. Terrence shivered briefly, and then forgot he'd ever had the thought.

There was a small set of ancient-looking bookshelves with many leather-bound volumes. Terrence noted the titles of those that were out on the ebony coffee table: *Travelling to Other Worlds* and *Pedesis for Beginners*, both by Thomas Lumas. There was another slim volume by the same author called *The Flow*. The Flow. Was that one of the things he was supposed to denounce? Or was it one of the things he was supposed to embrace? It was so hard keeping up with everything you were supposed to do as a member of a diabolical secret society.

'What is the Flow again?' he asked Lady Tchainsaw.

He picked up the book and flicked through it. How strange: someone had written all over it, changing words and erasing whole passages.

She visibly shivered on hearing the word.

'A vile thing,' was all she could manage.

'How do I resist it?' said Terrence. 'And why?'

'Do you have inside you a desire to become a kaftan-wearing hippy vegetarian who thinks of others more highly than yourself?' she asked. 'Do you wish to live the life of a philosophy-obsessed tramp, never again to taste live oysters or enjoy the delights of flesh cooked in cream? Or warm, fresh blood baked into a pudding, or even raw . . .'

276

Terrence didn't know what she was going on about. 'No' seemed the obvious answer to her questions, though. But did this mean he had to eat raw blood or not? 'I don't think so,' he said. 'What's exactly is a kaftan?'

'You silly man,' said Lady Tchainsaw. 'You always miss the point of everything. In any case, the Flow is not going to exist for very much longer, if we have our way. It undoes what the norms call "evil". It cleanses the person who goes inside it of what they call impurities, but what I call intellect. It wipes out critical thinking and makes you love everything. Imagine how exhausting it would be to love everything! It is to be avoided at all costs.'

'What's a norm?'

She sighed. 'A normal person, you insipid berk. Of course, we advanced thinkers in the Diberi have a more sophisticated idea of morality, and what is good and bad and what is simply neutral. Is it evil to want to create a better universe for the few people who actually deserve it, while kicking the dross out of this world? Is it evil to want to take back control of our half of the Great Library and be masters of our own reality? Did you know that everything that exists here in the Realworld is controlled by a group of pathetic librarians in a remote corner of the Otherworld? Doesn't that make you angry?'

Terrence did know this. Sort of. But it didn't make him particularly angry because he had no idea what it meant. Skylurian had said something like this to him once, as well, but he hadn't been listening properly because he had been hoping she might kiss him.

In fact, even though he missed Skylurian desperately, and even though he had vowed never to let another woman into his heart – particularly not one who kept calling him 'silly' and a 'berk' – Terrence was rather hoping now that Lady Tchainsaw might kiss him. Was he really that fickle? But perhaps the heart must move on. And Lady Tchainsaw was resplendent tonight in a black velvet gown and vintage velvet sock-boots with heels that looked alarmingly like the skulls of yet more dead creatures, but dipped in silver and placed on top of one another. She reminded Terrence in some way of dear, dead Skylurian. Which was nice, really.

Would she kiss him? It was the only question in Terrence's mind.

She moved towards him. Was now the time?

'Ouch!' said Terrence again, as she slapped him. 'What was that for?'

'You are not paying attention. Why we are resting the ambitions of the Diberi on you, I have no idea. You are a stupid, vain, pathetic little man!'

'I don't mind if you're horrible to me,' said Terrence. 'I don't even mind if you slap me. But could you just give me a little . . .'

'A little what?'

'Kiss.' The word came out like a tiny squeak.

'I will kiss you afterwards,' she said. 'As a reward. Once our mission is complete. And, it should go without saying, only if our mission is successful.'

'All right,' said Terrence. 'You'd better tell me again exactly what you want me to do.'

'You need to understand the concept of pedesis,' said Lady Tchainsaw, picking up the book by Thomas Lumas. 'And you need to practise.'

278

'I'm terribly sorry,' said Terrence. 'Remind me what pedesis is again?'

'Oh, you dim man. It's when you enter someone's consciousness and then travel through time by surfing on a great wave of their ancestors. Have you not been paying attention? The subject was dealt with most thoroughly in that novel I gave you.'

Novel? Oh yes. Terrence had forgotten to read it. Well, not forgotten exactly. He despised novels written by anyone other than himself and as a consequence had never read any contemporary fiction. Books written by dead people were all right in theory, but they were often long and boring and full of unnecessarily detailed descriptions of the past, with all the computers and satellites and cheap heating. He'd given up on this one by about page four.

'But in any case,' Lady Tchainsaw was saying, 'all you need to do this time is enter the mind of Effie Truelove and find out how she goes to the Otherworld.'

Terrence imagined himself opening a sort of lid into Effie's brain and climbing in. Wouldn't she notice?

'But how —'

'It is your consciousness that travels,' said Lady Tchainsaw. 'Your body stays behind. I will follow you to the girl's house. You must kidnap her and bring her to me. We will get her here, and then I will look after your body while your mind travels. We will give her a reason to go to the Otherworld, and you will follow her.'

Look after his body? Could that involve kissing? But of course if Terrence's mind was elsewhere he wouldn't know anything about it.

'Right,' he said. 'And then what?'

'You may have to use your consciousness to affect her. Like mages do. You will need some serious practice. I have an awful feeling you will need more practice than you're actually going to do, but it's too late to change the plan now.'

'I am a mage,' said Terrence dreamily. 'Dear Skylurian – I don't believe you met – diagnosed me, and—'

'Don't be ridiculous,' said Lady Tchainsaw. 'I doubt you've even epiphanised. And even if you had you'd obviously be an elysian bard. All you're interested in is pleasure, yourself and your terrible books.'

'But mages—'

'Mages are far darker and more mysterious than you'll ever be, you desperate little nobody.'

'Don't you like me any more?' said Terrence, pouting.

'I like you exactly the same amount as I have always done. Now try to concentrate. This is very important. You will enter the girl's mind using the technique described in this book, which I am going to lend you. You wait for a moment when she feels doubt or sadness. It is when she feels something that she is vulnerable. Then you slip in.'

'Slip in?'

'You are going to practise on others before I let you loose on the girl. You'll need this.' Lady Tchainsaw handed him a little vial of liquid. 'And this.' She gave him a little bottle of white pills. 'Just please read the instructions carefully.'

It all sounded very complicated to Terrence. But he was sure it would be all right in the end. There'd be someone to remind him what to say and do. There was always someone like that in every situation. A publicist usually, or a bookseller, or a teacher. Yes, there'd probably be a nice teacher who could help. Or a technician, to adjust the volume on his microphone, like there always was at his book events. He drained the last of his vodka and smiled his most winning smile at Lady Tchainsaw.

19

By late on Sunday night, more cats had made it through the secret network of passageways and into the basement jazz club, out of sight of the butlers and maids on the other levels of the cats' home. But not enough. There were hundreds of cats still upstairs in the ballroom drinking Pawsecco, or out of their heads on catnip and lying in cardboard boxes. Only around a hundred had made it into the basement. But one of these was Mirabelle.

'I'm so glad to see you again,' said Neptune.

'You seem different,' she said, sniffing him.

'Oh, he's awoken,' said Malvasia. 'And I think he may even have epiphanised as well.'

'It's been a big night,' said Neptune.

'Right,' said Mirabelle. 'Showtime. We'll talk afterwards.'

Mirabelle and Malvasia went up on the stage. The band moved aside for them, and the saxophonist clapped. Soon the whole room was clapping and meowing.

Mirabelle took the microphone.

'Greetings, awoken ones,' she said. 'I have some good news and, alas, some bad news. The good news is that we now have over one hundred awoken cats, cats who understand both the value of comradeship and the extreme danger we are currently in. I believe most of you are here. But the bad news is that so many of our comrades still have no idea of what is in store for them on Midwinter's Eve. We need as many of them as possible to understand and to come over to our side. We need to prevent the Diberi from being able to cast their spell, which, as we know, could threaten the entire world. They only need one hundred of us, don't forget, and there are several times that amount who are still unawoken. Go upstairs, all of you, and try to explain to as many of our fellow cats as possible what's happening. Time is running out.'

A ginger cat in the audience spoke up. 'But, what if they don't believe us?' he said. 'I've tried this before and everyone just thinks that we're insane conspiracy theorists.'

'Then you have to try harder,' said Mirabelle. 'As I said, time is running out.'

The Bermuda Triangle stretched into an isosceles shape and then back into an equilateral again and sighed. It felt sad. Today was the day it was leaving home, possibly for the last time. At least it was not going alone. It would be accompanied by the Northern Lights, who had been with the Bermuda Triangle enjoying a pre-Midwinter holiday when the offer had been made.

The two entities had left the Otherworld within a year of one another – hundreds of years before, and not long after the Great Split – and had always kept in touch. They had left for the same reason every great entity leaves the Otherworld – for the fame and fortune available in the Realworld. In the Otherworld, no one had ever been that impressed with the colours and shapes the Northern Lights made in the sky – the whole Otherworld sky already looked like that much of the time.

A psychotic piece of geometry was more unusual, granted, but Otherworld adventurers were extremely good at escaping from the Bermuda Triangle and back in the olden days some young people had even started using it as – horrors – a kind of *game*.

In the Realworld, though, people were properly afraid of the Bermuda Triangle. They treated it with respect. It had even had a pop song written about it! There were no pop songs in the Otherworld. And, OK, there was no denying that the Bermuda Triangle *did* make people disappear – but only to the Otherworld. It was not as bad as all that. But people were still afraid, which was kind of fun. Meanwhile, the Northern Lights had had package holidays based around it, and entire books written about it. It had posters, films – a whole industry.

The Luminiferous Ether had also turned up to visit the Bermuda Triangle, although just for the weekend. On these occasions it always overindulged, then cried over the past. Its fame had waned back in the nineteenth century; people no longer even believed in it, thanks to diligent scientists and 'progress'.

Life as a global celebrity – even when you were long washed-up – was taxing, which was why it was so important to take breaks. But the Northern Lights, the Bermuda Triangle and the

Luminiferous Ether had agreed this time that the breaks were just not working any more. They were tired. Fed up.

They wanted to go home.

But the Otherworld didn't want them back. Or at least it would not agree to take them until it had expelled all its galloglasses, which was going to take for ever. The Realworld didn't really want to let the Northern Lights go anyway because it liked them. The Bermuda Triangle was a different story, of course, and therefore the subject of many complex negotiations being conducted by the Guild. But complex negotiations took a very long time.

So when the nice man with the clipped Northern European accent had turned up on the Astral Plane near Bermuda and asked for a meeting, it had been granted. And what an interesting proposal he had made! If the Bermuda Triangle, the Northern Lights and the Luminiferous Ether would agree to meet him above the Old Town (they had been given precise coordinates) on the evening of the 21st December then he would guarantee that they could go back to the Otherworld. All they had to do was help him with a bit of magic. How hard could that be? The Luminiferous Ether helped people with magic all the time, and even though it was supposed to be neutral it sometimes gave things a little nudge in one direction or another.

The Bermuda Triangle turned around for one last time, swallowed a ship and an aeroplane, and looked at the place it had called home for so long now. Then, with a last sigh, it nudged the Northern Lights, who were quite glad to be going back to more familiar territory. Together they shook the Luminiferous Ether and told it to pull itself together (it was still moping around despite promises to take it back to a place where people valued and believed in it). Then the three vast entities set off.

Dill Hammer handed Maximilian his lunch-box.

'I've turned it into a bento box,' he explained. 'It's sort of Japanese. You'll like it. Lots of strange things in it today! Check out the different compartments. Black noodles and tempeh with spicy ginger sauce in this one, and steamed spinach with pumpkin seeds and chilli in that one.' Dill pointed to the different sections of the lunch-box. Maximilian had never seen anything like it. 'Leftover chocolate cake here, and black grapes over there. Should keep you going for your first day at the university.'

'Thank you, Dill,' said Maximilian.

'Are you ready?' asked Odile, coming in, dressed for another day's work.

'I thought it was your day off?' said Maximilian.

'It's all these awful bindings,' she said. 'We're at capacity at the hospital and so I've got another day of home visits. I can give you a lift to the university if you like? Wolf's already got up and gone.'

Dill Hammer handed Odile her own bento box.

'Thanks, love,' Odile said to him.

Love! That was positive, surely?

Maximilian waited for them to kiss on the cheek or something, but instead they just looked awkwardly at each other and then – for reasons unknown – at him.

In the car, the radio news was full of disaster.

'Oh my,' said Odile. 'Another tsunami! There's some kind of massive storm moving across the Atlantic, apparently.'

'I know, Mum,' said Maximilian. 'I have ears too.'

'I wonder if someone's done a big spell that's gone wrong.'

'It would have to have been a really massive one,' said Maximilian.

'I hope they don't start closing things down,' said Odile. 'Honestly, I don't know what the world's coming to lately.'

Effie, Wolf and Raven were waiting for Maximilian by the university entrance. But there was no sign of Lexy. What on earth had happened to her? It seemed that Effie and Wolf had gone for breakfast together in some arcade in the Old Town and Wolf had filled her in on his adventures. Then they'd been planning strategies. Midwinter was the following day, and they would need to do something about the Diberi before then. But what? Then they'd met Raven off her bus and walked to the university together.

'We have to go back to the chapel,' Raven was saying to Wolf when Maximilian joined them. 'You can learn to meditate there, and then we can read in this book about how to do a cleric's prayer. They've got free candles and stuff.'

'We'll go after classes finish this morning,' said Effie. 'And we need to have a meeting as soon as possible and make some kind of plan. The chapel's an ideal place – we won't be overheard by the Diberi.'

'Does anyone know where Lexy is?' asked Wolf.

'I think she's ill,' said Effie. 'Maybe she'll be here tomorrow. Someone should drop over to her house on their way home and see if she's OK.'

'I'll do it,' said Raven. 'It's not really on my way home but I should practise more on my broomstick. Oh, why are these books so heavy?'

Raven was clutching several books that all seemed to be religious guides or manuals for prayer.

'Where did you get them all?' Maximilian asked her, as they walked through the big university gates and towards its main butter-stone building.

'My mum's account with Rosewater Books,' she said.

'Any sign of your art, by the way?' asked Maximilian. 'I was wondering if it was scholar, like me.'

'Yeah, I've wondered that too,' said Raven.

'Have you ever tried my spectacles?'

'No, actually. Shall I try them now?'

Maximilian got them out of his bag for her as they walked through the large old stone entrance. Raven took them and put them on.

'Oh no!' she said, after having them on for less than one second. 'They've made the world entirely red and weird. *Euurgh.* And they're burning my nose. Have them back.'

'Worth a try,' said Maximilian. 'Effie, do you know where we're going?'

Effie, as usual, was walking too fast and was now leading the way down a university corridor that seemed darker than a corridor really should be during the day. The Tusitala School corridors were gloomy, but this was different. Here, they almost needed candles. Was there a greyout they didn't know about? Or was it just the approach of Midwinter?

'Yep,' she said. 'Room 108 in the James Tyler Kent Building. I looked at the map. It's this way, I'm sure.'

'Why exactly are we doing this?' said Raven. 'I mean, hanging out with the Diberi . . . What if they attack us?'

'Getting information,' said Maximilian. 'Like we were told.'

'They can't do anything to us here, I'm sure,' said Wolf. 'But I've got this just in case.' He showed the others the Sword of Orphennyus in the side pocket of his rucksack.

'Well, this is our big chance to find out what they're up to,' said Maximilian. 'And stop whatever it is.'

'I think I might already know quite a lot of it,' said Effie. 'But I'll tell you when we get into the chapel. We can't be sure we're not being overheard here. Right. This way, I think.'

She hurried off again.

'So. Not a scholar, then,' Maximilian said to Raven as they tried to keep up with Effie.

'Oh well,' said Raven. 'At least I'm eliminating them. I know I'm not a healer or – don't laugh at me, Wolf! – a warrior either. Maybe I'll have to eliminate them all before I actually find it.'

'It'll happen,' said Maximilian. 'Just be patient.'

'Ha! What, patient like you are?' said Raven.

'Shut up,' said Maximilian, smiling.

'I read somewhere that your familiar has to match either your *kharakter* or your art,' said Raven. 'Which really does narrow it down. I've never heard of an animal being a witch. It sounds wrong. Mind you, I didn't even know until yesterday that animals could epiphanise. I don't know anything!'

'No one knows anything,' said Wolf, mysteriously.

'Oh my God,' said Maximilian, laughing. 'I think I liked you better as a meathead than a mystic. Only joking. Don't hit me! Right, we must be almost there now. Effie? Where's she gone?

Oh. I see. Up these stairs and down this passageway and here we—'

'Watch out!'

Raven was almost knocked over by the young man who had just come storming out of the door next to Room 108. He looked sort of familiar, but then he was gone. Had there been a flash of tweed? Yes, it was PhD student Claude Twelvetrees. He'd glared at Effie and then hurried off in a great blur. What was the matter with him? The room he'd come from had a sign on it saying SENIOR COMMON ROOM and seemed to be full of old sofas and books. It smelled strongly of coffee.

Inside Room 108, Dora Wright was waiting for her new class, which was remarkably similar to her old class back when she'd taught at the Tusitala School for the Gifted, Troubled and Strange. She was quite looking forward to seeing her old pupils again – or some of them. Today she was wearing a simple faille gown and lace-trimmed cape with faux fur boots and gold polka dot tights. Her hair was in an easy bouffant. She always dressed down on university teaching days.

'Come in and close the door,' she said to the children.

They did as she asked.

'Are we safe to talk here?' asked Effie, looking around.

'I'm not sure,' said Dora. 'Best not say too much. Oh,' she said, surprised. 'Hello, Wolf. I didn't expect to see you here as well.' When Dora Wright had last taught Wolf he'd been quite different. It had been before he'd epiphanised, back in the days when he used to throw the weaker boys' rucksacks in the river for fun.

'Hello, Miss Wright,' said Wolf. 'It's been a while.'

'Yes, I suppose it has,' she said. 'OK,' she continued, 'there's been a slight change of timetable. Tomorrow I'm going to teach you the basics of plot. But today you've got Professor Forestfloor, teaching you about Nietzsche and tragedy. And then you've got the afternoon off because of the Midwinter celebrations. Tomorrow afternoon you've got avant-garde poetry. But my class before that. Enjoy!'

She left the room in a puff of glitter and perfume. The children barely had a chance to exchange worried glances before Professor Gotthard Forestfloor entered the room.

He was a reedy, evil-looking man who appeared to have bought half of his outfit from a shop called Looking Innocent When You Are Not (which did not exist) and the other half from Dark Daze, a very expensive boutique next to the Esoteric Emporium (which did). His black corduroy trousers were similar to the ones favoured by Monsieur Valentin, and his mildly checked shirt would have been, on its own, inoffensive. Forestfloor had, however, added a turquoise silk bow tie, an eagle-feather gilet, silk-chiffon socks and, most troublingly of all, fur-lined sandals. Added to all this was a bright mauve academic gown.

'I expect students at your level to know the basic theories of tragedy,' he said, without smiling, in his clipped Northern European voice. 'I shall test you immediately. You will answer your questions on paper and in silence. Anyone who gets less than 100 percent will be expelled from the university and this ridiculous exercise in outreach and pandering to stupidity. Ready?'

Effie and Maximilian exchanged a look. What was he up to? He clearly wanted to get rid of them as soon as possible, but he obviously had no idea what he was dealing with. It wasn't just that Effie and her friends were brave members of the Gothmen who were skilled at facing down evil; they also happened to be the very cream of Mrs Beathag Hide's top set for English and had been learning about tragedy since September.

'Great tragedy,' said Professor Forestfloor, 'deals with what kind of person? Admirable, or ordinary?'

Everyone knew the answer to that. Mrs Beathag Hide had been drumming it into them for weeks. Tragedy was about an admirable or famous person like a king or a queen or a celebrity who makes a dreadful mistake because of their enormous ambition and . . .

'What does the word *hamartia* mean?' asked Professor Forestfloor.

Everyone knew that too. It was Greek for 'fatal flaw', the thing that meant that the poor admirable person or celebrity couldn't really help themselves. When given the choice between an early night and a diabolical plot involving a dagger and a love-potion, tragic heroes generally chose the latter. But at least they got to wear nice clothes. Some people said that the fatal flaw was not a character fault but was in fact one simple error made by the tragic hero. The one thing they could have done differently but that stopped them from living happily ever after.

Effie couldn't help thinking of her last conversation with Cosmo. *An error upon an error upon an error.* And she kept doing things wrong. She kept making mistakes. Did she have a fatal flaw? Was she going to die a horrible tragic death? Was she actually a bad person, just as Rollo seemed to think – an island galloglass destined for a horrible end?

Effie answered the rest of the questions in a daze. Then Professor Forestfloor took in the test papers and looked them over.

'Well,' he said. 'Incredibly, you all pass. How remarkable. As your prize, you get to hear all about Nietzsche's theories of tragedy and why it is better to be a tragic person than an ordinary one. Why we should all aim to be Dionysus rather than Apollo and die a glorious and beautiful death in the pursuit of our own selfish desires, and in so doing create harmony for all . . .'

After class, the children fled as quickly as they could and agreed to meet in the chapel. Effie got there first, partly because she walked so fast, and partly because the others wanted to stop off at the canteen. Effie was still trying to shake off the things Professor Forestfloor had said. It was like galloglass theory all over again. Why did it seem to keep applying to her?

As she approached the door to the chapel she became aware that an argument was taking place inside in loud whispers. She couldn't help herself stopping and listening for a few moments. Not that she had any choice – she was hardly going to go in and disturb them.

'Just come with me, now,' someone was saying. 'I can keep you safe. We'll go far away from here. Please.'

It was a faintly familiar voice, but Effie couldn't quite place it.

'No,' came the reply. 'I have to stay and fight. My mother. My friends . . .' Effie did recognise this voice. It was Leander Quinn.

'But if you're bound when you're young you can never get your magic back . . . You may as well be dead.'

'What, dead to you?'

'That's not what I meant.'

'Are you sure about that?'

'I'd still love you if you weren't magical. You know that.'

There was a big sigh. 'I thought we'd agreed to just be friends. I don't share your feelings. I wish I did, but . . .'

'We can leave together as friends. We can go right now. I've got my car. My savings. I don't understand why not.'

'Because I'm not a coward.'

'Right.' There was a long pause. 'And you're saying I am?'

'No, of course not. I didn't mean—'

'I think I know what you meant.'

There was silence for a few moments. Then Claude Twelvetrees came out of the door, the tears in his eyes preventing him from really registering Effie on the steps. Of course, the fact that she'd cast the Shadows helped too. She lifted the spell as she walked into the chapel. She didn't want to sneak up on Leander. That seemed unfair.

Inside the chapel came the sound of someone sighing heavily.

'Leander?' said Effie.

He was there alone in one of the pews. A single candle burned gently in front of him. He was wearing a black cape as usual, with a white shirt that had the collar turned up. Effie wasn't surprised that everyone was in love with him. He looked like an elegant, maybe-harmless vampire.

'Effie,' he said. 'Have you heard?'

'Heard what?'

'The Guild are voting today on whether or not to bind children. Well, people under eighteen. Basically us.'

'What?' said Effie. 'They can't be serious.'

Leander nodded. 'Apparently they had a complaint from the Otherworld. About, well, about *you*, in fact. They say you're out of control and they're using that as a reason to potentially bind all of us. If the vote goes through, then you'll -- we'll – have to hide. But especially you. You'll basically be top of their list.'

'But . . .' Effie felt like someone had punched her. Could she not do anything right at all? 'What can we do?' said Effie. 'Can we stop them?'

'Nope.' Leander shook his head. 'Just hold tight for now. The vote might not even go their way. Not everyone in the Guild agrees with Masterman Finch. Don't worry,' he said. 'You're not the only one on their hit-list. They've been after me for a long time, too, mainly as a way of getting to my mother, but also because of some other stuff. I suppose the only good part of this is that they might bind my sister and do the world a lot of good.' He smiled half-heartedly.

For a few moments the chapel was completely silent. It was a deep, soft kind of silence, filled with the smell of incense and burning wax, and the special kind of light that comes through stained-glass windows. Tiny particles of dust danced timelessly in the air.

'Oh, Leander,' said Effie. 'Do you ever feel like you've just made one big mistake and then everything's gone all out of control? Like . . .' She remembered the class she'd just had. 'Like in tragedy. I know that sounds weird, but . . .'

'Don't forget you're talking to another interpreter,' said Leander, smiling weakly. 'It doesn't sound weird to me at all. Applying stories to life – or vice versa – is one of the things we're best at. It can go too far, of course. But that's never stopped me.

Basically if there's a mistake to be made, I'll make it, whether it goes with the story or not. And you know the worst thing? When's life's not even tragic, it's just messy.'

'I don't know which is worse,' said Effie. 'Professor Forestfloor said that at least the tragic hero brings light to the rest of the world by sacrificing him or herself. And something about Primal Oneness, which sounded . . . I can't put it into words, but something happened recently and I read a poem and . . .'

'Oh, you've had his Nietzsche class then,' Leander said, with a smile. 'Interesting choice for eleven- and twelve-year-olds. But yeah, it worked on me too. Live fast, die young? It's a compelling message. But don't forget that he's the leading Diberi of his age. You don't want to find yourself agreeing with anything he says, although I know it's difficult. They all go on about Primal Oneness without ever acknowledging that it's probably the same as the Flow, which they apparently despise. And all that stuff about going out in a blaze of selfish glory for the good of everyone else? Not what they are intending to do, I assure you.'

'Do you know about the Flow?' asked Effie.

'Only what I've read in books,' said Leander. 'Ones I probably wasn't supposed to read.'

'Do you know what the Diberi *are* intending to do?' asked Effie.

'No. Not exactly. I think it's to do with Midwinter, but . . .' Leander shrugged. 'No one's got any further than that.'

'Yes, I think it's all about Midwinter too,' said Effie. 'In fact . . .'

The chapel door clicked and Maximilian, Wolf and Raven came in, followed by Pelham Longfellow, Dora Wright, Festus Grimm and Mrs Beathag Hide.

'Good,' said Pelham Longfellow. 'We're all here. Well, almost. Let's go to the meeting room. Effie, I believe you have news for us?'

No one had said that it was going to be a *baby* yeti, or that it would be so cute.

Urrrgh. Cute.

Tabitha Quinn had never used the word *cute* in her life. Well, unless it was about a dress. Maybe. But someone else's dress probably. And not a close friend's either. Tabitha – and her friends, who copied her – didn't wear cute dresses. Tabitha wore elegant, sophisticated dresses, and she did elegant, sophisticated things. So quite why she had become a glorified – in fact, not even glorified – stable girl was a mystery to her. Getting involved with the Diberi was supposed to be her ticket to ultimate glamour, power and influence. It was supposed to be about casting evil spells and travelling to large castles in Europe where people wore diamond tiaras and hung out with real vampires. It was not about poo, hay or cat food, which was apparently what baby yetis liked to eat.

And yet here she was, mucking out a yeti. A cute baby Yeti, with big, imploring eyes. Eyes that were going to be removed later this evening in a horrible ritual that made even Tabitha wince when she thought of it. It wasn't as if she and her friends didn't eat the eyeballs of dead creatures – they did, with relish – but Tabitha had never before looked into a condemned creature's eyes while it was alive.

297

The baby yeti was being kept in the old stables at the back of the Old Town University. No one knew it was there, except for Tabitha and her new mentor, the wonderful Jupiter Peacock, who let her call him JP. He'd told her all sorts of things about the Diberi and their castles and mansions and great ballrooms. Tabitha sighed and looked away from the baby yeti. She'd do almost anything for JP. As long as it was going towards her ticket out of here, towards great glory, riches and beauty, she would do virtually anything. *Virtually.* This baby yeti thing was disturbing her in some way, though, and she didn't like it. It kept moaning about something, and Tabitha thought she could see blood coming from somewhere. *Ick.*

She turned her back on it and paged one of her friends about a new diamond necklace she'd seen in the Selfridges catalogue. The friend didn't page her back. This was just typical of Tabitha's friends lately. They were interested in homework, boys (not even real men) and the kinds of cheap cotton dresses you could get in Teen World. Well, Tabitha would be leaving them behind soon. In fact, if JP was to be believed, they'd be leaving behind most of the world soon – and good riddance too.

20

Lexy didn't ask where she was being taken; she just did everything she'd been told to do. She had been instructed to tell her parents that she was going to be staying at the university overnight as part of the Winter Fair arrangements. She'd been commanded to look cheerful and excited, which she'd done.

She'd done everything JP had told her. More or less.

After all, if she didn't obey him, the world was going to end. And little Buttons was going to be sacrificed to help make it happen. That's what he'd said. And if ever Lexy looked as if she might forget, he'd found a way to remind her. A little pinch or a kick – or just drawing his finger slowly across his throat when he knew Lexy could see him and her parents could not.

The last few days had been awful for Lexy. Marcel Bottle had realised that something was wrong with his daughter, but whenever he asked her what it was, she'd just snapped at him. As a result, Lexy's parents were now talking about sending her to a counsellor who specialised in difficult children. Which would be great – just another person she'd have to lie to.

And they weren't even that bothered about her being away for the night. Hazel had packed Lexy's overnight bag without much emotion. Maybe they were looking forward to her not being there.

Lexy felt completely and utterly alone.

And now she was in the Bottle family car being driven by JP towards the Old Town University. She had no idea what was going to happen to her. She'd been bathing in milk and rose petals for the last two days, as per JP's instructions – yet another thing that had got her into trouble with her parents. ('Where did you even get all this stuff?' Marcel had asked. 'And what did it cost?' Hazel had said.) She had eaten only Turkish Delight. ('Why won't you even eat one mouthful of your dinner?' Marcel had implored. 'She's just doing it to upset us,' Hazel had said. 'And to get attention. Just ignore it.') She had learned to do her hair in a very intricate braid according to instructions JP had given her, and had practised the complicated make-up and body paint she was to wear for the ritual – whatever that was – on Monday evening. ('Take that off right now!' Hazel had said. 'You're way too young for make-up,' Marcel had agreed. 'She's just showing off because we have a guest,' Hazel had concluded.)

Lexy had no way of telling them that she was doing all this for *them*. So they would be seen as good hosts. And also now so that Effie wouldn't be killed. And Buttons. And to make the world safe. JP's requests had become very strange recently, but at least he had not tried to arm-wrestle her again, or kiss her. Now that she'd agreed to obey all his instructions he'd become even a little cold. But that was fine with Lexy. The less attention he paid her the better. She despised him.

The Bottle family car chugged up the hill towards the Old Town University, its occupants both lost in their own silent contemplation. JP didn't drive through the main gates, however, but through a partially hidden back entrance. He parked the car by some old stables.

'Right, little lady, out you get.'

Lexy got out of the car. JP slammed the door behind her and locked it.

'What about my bag?' Lexy said.

'Oh, you won't need that,' said Jupiter Peacock. 'We'll be providing you with an outfit suitable for a maiden being sacrificed.'

'What?!' said Lexy. 'Sacrificed? But—'

'Oh, didn't I mention that I was going to kill you?' said JP, taking her firmly by the arm. 'And that your death is going to bring about the end of the world, not save it? Sorry I lied about that last bit. It's not just a hundred live cats we need – we require the pure blood of a maiden too.'

'But you said if I did everything you wanted then the world would be safe!'

'And you believed me, like the silly child you are.'

'Let me go!' shouted Lexy, wriggling to break free from JP's grip. But her struggles came to nothing. 'Help!' She grasped at JP's hands to try and . . . to try and . . . But it was no good. He wasn't going to let her go.

The only person who could hear her was Tabitha, who now came out of the stable looking interested. She always liked seeing bad things happen to pathetic, unpopular girls who couldn't look after themselves. And this one was even from an inferior school.

'You are relieved of your duties,' said JP to Tabitha. 'The

301

maiden sacrifice can watch the yeti now. I've got something else for you to do.'

He pushed Lexy into a stable where a very hairy creature about the size of a seven-year-old child looked at her with big, frightened eyes. As JP locked the bottom half of the stable door, Lexy looked back at the yeti and tried to make her eyes say, 'Don't worry – I'll save you.' The poor thing looked so very afraid. Then they were enveloped in gloom as JP pulled the top of the stable door closed and locked that too.

Effie finished telling the others about everything she'd learned recently, including what she'd overheard the day before in Mrs Bottle's Bun Shop.

'So the Great Library actually *wanted* the book back?' said Wolf. 'The one about the Diberi?'

'Yes,' said Effie. 'I mean, I suppose it's fair enough – the Diberi are a part of reality after all. It does feel like cheating to just remove them magically like that. On the other hand, if they're planning to destroy the whole world then maybe it was a sensible thing to do. Anyway, the short version is that my mother removed the book and I put it back.'

Pelham Longfellow sighed. 'You did the right thing, even if it was a mistake,' he said.

'And the end of the world. That's planned for this evening?' said Maximilian. 'Well. It almost makes you think that Madame Valentin was right with her ridiculous prophecy about cats flying through the air and—'

'Oh my God!' said Raven, jumping to her feet. 'That's it!'

'What?' said Effie.

'Her prophecy. It's exactly right. Oh, why didn't we see it before? We've been so stupid. You know when we were in the library on Saturday, in Special Collections, and Lexy and I overheard them talking? Yes, I know we weren't going to say anything about that bit but it doesn't matter now, because . . . Anyway, they were getting out a book with a spell in it that included a hundred live cats. But I wasn't listening to that bit because then they said they needed your consciousness, Effie, and I didn't know what that meant. Oh! Why didn't I spot that before? The spell includes cats, and that's what Madame Valentin saw as well.'

'What was the prophecy again?' said Festus Grimm. 'On the dot of Midwinter . . .'

'Twelve minutes past eight precisely . . .' said Raven.

'What's happening then?' said Leander.

'The Midwinter Lecture,' said Mrs Beathag Hide. 'Jupiter Peacock talking about his translation of *Galloglass*.'

'I wonder what the poem has got to do with it,' mused Effie.

'Anyway, I know exactly where they'll be getting the cats,' said Raven. 'The cats' home – which, in case you had forgotten, was funded by the money that Skylurian Midzhar left when she died. It's basically being run by the Diberi! That's what they meant when they said that bit of the spell would be easy.'

'I can't believe I didn't spot all this when I went into your memory of that afternoon,' said Maximilian crossly. 'If only you ordered your mind better. I'll have to teach you. But I do vaguely remember something about them thinking it would be easy to get access to Effie as well. Oh yes, and then we overheard Terrence Deer-Hart and that Russian poet. Weren't they planning to kidnap you, Effie?'

'Yes,' she said. 'Terrence Deer-Hart's coming to my house tonight to have dinner with my dad and my step-mum before they all go to the lecture. They're sort of friends. I'll let him kidnap me. It'll give me a great opportunity to infiltrate them, see exactly what they're trying to do and stop them.'

'Are you sure that's safe?' asked Pelham Longfellow. 'It sounds foolhardy to me.'

'It's only Terrence Deer-Hart,' said Effie. 'I'll be fine.'

'Well, one other way of preventing whatever they've got worked out with this spell is by making sure they can't get hold of a hundred cats,' said Raven. 'I'm going to the cats' home to talk to the cats and see if they know what's going on.' She stood up. 'I'll go now. I'll check on Lexy too. I haven't been able to get in touch with her for days. If there's going to be a big battle tonight we'll need her and her potions.'

'And I'll go to Madame Valentin to see if she can add anything to her prophecy,' said Maximilian. 'Wolf, do you want to come with me?'

'Yes, sure,' said Wolf, getting up to follow Maximilian.

There was a strange little flash in the air. There it was again. It was a shard of sunlight that had come through the stained-glass window and was hitting the ring hanging around Wolf's neck.

'What's that?' asked Pelham Longfellow, noticing the ring for the first time. 'Lapis lazuli? Are you a cleric?'

'Yeah,' said Wolf. 'Well, a warrior cleric. Why?'

'Actually,' Pelham said to Maximilian, 'Wolf's going to stay here. You can go and see Madame Valentin on your own, can't you?'

'Sure,' said Maximilian. 'Although I'm very fascinated about why you want him to stay here.'

'I'll explain later,' said Pelham Longfellow. 'Leander, you stay too. I can use two clerics.'

'Well, I'm going to work some more on the counter-spell,' said Mrs Beathag Hide. 'Mr Grimm has offered to assist me. We've borrowed Dr Cloudburst's laboratory at the school.'

'And we're going back to the Creative Writing Common Room to see what we can find out,' said Laurel Wilde. Dora Wright got up to leave with her.

Soon, everyone except Pelham Longfellow, Leander, Wolf and Effie had left the chapel.

'Right,' said Pelham Longfellow to Wolf. 'What level are you?'

'What do you mean?'

'How powerful a cleric are you?'

'I only found out yesterday,' said Wolf. 'So I'm guessing not very.'

'But you've been in the Flow,' said Pelham. 'And Effie. At long last. We've been waiting for you to discover the Flow for so long now. Leander, you know what I'm talking about.'

Leander nodded in a pale, vampiric sort of way. It seemed as if his mind was elsewhere entirely. He kept looking down at his hands and sighing.

'The what?' said Wolf.

'What do you mean?' said Effie.

'The Flow? You're not allowed to mention the Flow to anyone who hasn't been in it. Because then the first time doesn't work

. . . But after that you can always tell when someone has been in. Why do you both look so blank?'

Effie suddenly went from looking blank to looking like someone who's solved a difficult crossword clue.

'Hang on,' said Effie. 'The Flow. *That's* the thing that's been bugging me. That's what was different about the older translation of the poem . . . The one I put in the Great Library yesterday.'

'What?' said Pelham sharply. 'I thought you said you put the history of the Diberi back in the Great Library?'

'I did,' said Effie. 'But that was ages ago. Just before the *Sterran Guandré*. That must be what brought the Diberi here from Europe. They'd been frozen somehow since the world-quake. When I went into the library yesterday to take the book out again I didn't realise I had another book in my bag. The poem "Galloglass" – but a different translation than Jupiter Peacock's. The library took it.'

'Are you seriously saying that you put a copy of *Galloglass* in the actual Great Library?' said Pelham. 'Why hasn't anyone told me about this? Cosmo must be furious.'

'Wait,' said Effie. 'Listen to me. I think you'll understand. Leander? You listen too. You'll know what I mean, I'm sure. The translation I put in was *different* from Jupiter Peacock's. In the original version there's a mention of the Flow – whatever it is. The reference is removed from Jupiter Peacock's version.'

'What would the Flow have to do with galloglasses?' said Leander.

'I don't know,' said Effie. 'Maybe if someone told me what the Flow actually is . . .'

306

While Effie and the others had been talking, Wolf had been fiddling with his lapis lazuli ring. Being in this chapel was like returning home after a long journey. Everything about it made him feel calm and powerful – and not at all like listening to words or sentences about earthly things. The smell of incense, the candles . . . He wondered what would happen if he lit a candle and tried to meditate. Raven had told him the basics the night before. It didn't sound difficult. You just shut your eyes – or even kept them open, if you were a Zen Buddhist – and focused on your breath and tried to clear your mind. How hard could it be? And then cleric's prayers, when you got to wish for things that would come true. You were supposed to start with small things, but what if . . .?

Pelham now seemed to be telling Effie that he shouldn't be able to talk about the Flow to someone who didn't understand it. Was she absolutely sure she didn't know what it was? But their voices faded as Wolf slipped easily into a meditative state, a state from which all magic is possible and . . .

And he took the piece of string from around his neck and . . .

Before he knew what was happening, the ring was on.

Bells. Beautiful light. The smell of sandalwood and silence.

Wolf passed out again.

The yeti looked at this new human with interest. She was completely different from the other one, although the yeti wasn't experienced enough in dealing with humans to understand what the difference might be.

His arm still hurt from the trap he'd been caught in. He started rubbing it, making a sort of mewling sound. And his right leg was bleeding, quite badly.

'Hang on,' said Lexy. 'Let me just get my crystals out, and my new bracelet, and my knife . . . We'll sort you out first, and then we'll escape.'

As soon as Jupiter Peacock had left, Lexy had snapped out of her weak maiden routine. What was it Wolf had said about strategy that time? *Always let your enemy think you are weaker and more stupid than you are. There is no greater weapon than surprise.* And JP was certainly going to be surprised when he realised how he'd underestimated Lexy.

He'd been sleeping very well lately, mainly because of the valerian, lime-flower and fiveweed mixture that Lexy had been putting in his food. All she'd had to do was add the mixture to the pepper grinder. JP loved pepper and added it liberally to everything. And since Lexy wasn't allowed to eat anything other than Turkish Delight she was hardly going to be contaminated herself.

Because JP had been sleeping so well, Lexy had been able to sneak downstairs late at night and eat peanut butter and jam sandwiches and make her plans. She'd charged all her crystals in moonlight – not quite as strong as the full-moon, but it would do. She got all her herbs in order.

And she read as much as she could about being an alchemist.

Yes, JP really had chosen the wrong person to mess with. He had no idea that he and Lexy shared an art – alchemist – which meant that she'd been able to steal his most valuable boons in order to use them against him. This morning she'd pretended to have forgotten the small pearl earrings she was supposed to wear

308

for the ceremony. He'd sent her upstairs to get them, while charming her parents by offering to give their daughter a lift to the university.

That was when she'd done it. She'd gone into his room and taken everything she needed. His Orlov's Viper necklace, used by high-level dark alchemists to control the weather and create explosions. His travel cauldron, enchanted in such a way that powerful concoctions could be brewed in it, but which shrunk to the size of a ring when not in use. And the biggest prize: his Alchemist's Knife, a solid platinum blade set in a walnut handle studded with black obsidian stones. There was also a thin gold bracelet with the same stones set in it. Lexy hadn't actually left many of his things behind.

That evening when her parents had gone out to celebrate their anniversary and he'd made her go into his room, the objects had awoken something in her: her alchemist art. But this was not the sort of light alchemy that her aunt Octavia did; it was something darker that had been lying dormant.

Lexy took all these objects from where she'd hidden them in a pouch under the waistband of her white cotton skirt. She put the bracelet on and felt dark alchemical power rippling through her. It was big for her, so she pushed it up her arm where it fitted perfectly as an armlet. Now all she had to do was use her healing crystal to create a cure for this poor creature, and then concoct something in the cauldron to blow away these doors so that they could both escape.

'What on earth?' said Pelham Longfellow, as Wolf slumped, unconscious, on the pew next to him.

'Wolf!' said Effie. 'He said this happened the last time he tried this ring.' She eased it off his finger, then quickly put it on the makeshift necklace and placed it back around his neck. Wolf didn't wake up immediately; he seemed to be in a very peaceful sleep.

'Where did he get it?' asked Pelham.

'It's a long story,' said Effie. 'He was a Last Reader. That's when he found out that he's a cleric. And this is the boon the book gave him at the end.'

'Great,' said Pelham Longfellow. 'So he's getting into the Flow by accident just because he's got the Ring of the Enlightened Cleric, but he doesn't know what to do with it. And you've been in the Flow, what, once? And you don't know how to use it either. Leander? How are you with the Flow?'

Leander shrugged. 'I don't find it that easy to get in,' he said.

'Right,' said Pelham Longfellow, rolling up his sleeves. 'We need to wake him up and then I've got to find a way of training both of you to the next level of cleric and teaching you how to use the Flow to help us.'

'What do you mean?' said Leander.

'Higher level clerics can unbind people,' said Pelham. 'It takes a lot of magic, but you and Wolf might just be one of the most useful resources we have at the moment. Unbinding takes two clerics working in a pair.'

'What can I do to help?' said Effie.

Pelham sighed. 'If only you could get in the Flow properly you could help power them. But there probably isn't time for you to learn how to do that. You're supposed to be the most powerful of us all – potentially, at least. But you're blinded somehow. I see you're still not wearing your ring.'

Effie touched the Ring of the True Hero that hung around her neck. It was there in case she needed it for a serious battle but wearing it had become so complicated she didn't even remember to put it on half the time. She didn't even wear it for tennis any more.

'It just drains me,' she said.

He sighed. 'All right, look. For now, I need some sandalwood incense, and a book of warrior cleric's prayers. Can you go and get them? If we can just get these two ready in time, then the Guild won't be able to stop us any more. And we'll have a better chance of preventing whatever the Diberi have planned for tonight. But we don't have long.' He looked at his watch. 'Maybe seven hours. That's not a lot of training. And with one asleep, and the other . . .'

Leander was still sighing a lot and looking down at his hands.

'OK,' said Effie. 'I'll be back as soon as I can.'

She left the chapel and hurried into the main part of the university, and then set off in the direction of the library.

A book of warrior cleric's prayers. The only place Effie could think of going for that was Special Collections. She just hoped she'd be able to find where such books were shelved. Being trained as a cleric sounded exciting: more exciting than going to the library for a book. But Effie reminded herself that they were all one big team, and it didn't matter how small her role was going to be in that team, she was proud to be part of it. For a moment, Effie's entire being was swept into this sensation of being a tiny molecule in a vast magnificent whole and . . .

That feeling again. The one from the market. This time it seemed to start at Effie's feet. It moved up her body in a wave of warmth and beauty and acceptance, like getting into the most perfect bath after the most terrible day, or drinking a mug of hot chocolate in the snow – but multiplied by a thousand, no, make that a million. It was the best feeling Effie had ever experienced. She thought to herself how clever she was to have found a way to get back to the feeling. Ha! She'd show—

The feeling disappeared. The world became crisp and cold again. So the trick was not to acknowledge it while it was happening, and not to be afraid of it either. And not to be pleased with oneself for finding it. A bit like the meditative state, which also fell away when you acknowledged it. But this was different. This was much more intense than the meditative state.

Could this be the thing they called the Flow?

21

Raven flew as fast as she could to Lexy's house, troubled by her friend's absence. Why had no one checked on Lexy earlier? It wasn't like her to disappear like this. She was always so friendly, so helpful, so communicative. And why had no one noticed that she'd been sharing a house with a Diberi for the last few days?

Raven kicked herself – well, she tried; it wasn't easy to kick yourself when travelling by broomstick. For their great spell the Diberi needed a hundred live cats, Effie's consciousness and the blood of a pure maiden. Raven suddenly had a horrible idea of who the pure maiden was going to be. She pushed the broomstick harder, over the roof of the Old Rectory and the large park behind the Mrs Joyful School. She landed and folded up her broomstick as quickly as she could and put it in her school bag.

She knocked on the door of the Bottle house. Both Marcel and Hazel Bottle were at home today. Marcel didn't start his yoga teaching until the evening on a Monday and Hazel was working in her yurt at the bottom of the garden. Marcel opened the door.

'Raven,' he said, surprised. 'Aren't you meant to be at school, or university, or whatever it is you're doing this week?'

'Is Lexy here?' said Raven.

'No,' said Marcel. 'I thought she was with you. Aren't you all sleeping over at the university tonight?'

'No,' said Raven. 'We're not. We heard that Lexy was ill. We haven't seen her for days.'

'Well, she hasn't been quite herself lately, but she's not ill. She was certainly well enough to go with JP this morning to—'

'Wait, you let her go with Jupiter Peacock? Are you mad?'

'Raven, I don't think you should speak to me like—'

Buttons the kitten had realised that there was a witch in the house. Before anyone knew what was happening, he'd used his little claws to climb up Raven's leg and torso and now sat on her shoulder, speaking urgently into her ear.

'Buttons!' said Marcel. 'Get down! You can't just climb up on anyone who—'

He moved to take the kitten from Raven's shoulder, but she held up her hand to stop him. Marcel had never seen a witch and an animal in communication before. It was the strangest thing. He realised he was powerless to stop them. And he started to worry. Raven was usually so polite and placid. What on earth was going on?

'I see,' Raven was saying to Buttons in Kitten language. 'No, that must have been dreadful. And they really didn't notice?' She sighed. 'Yes, he's been very clever. It'll all be OK now.'

'What's going on?' said Marcel.

'I suppose you didn't realise that Jupiter Peacock has been abusing Lexy the whole time he's been in your house?' said Raven.

314

'What?!' All the colour drained from Marcel's face. 'Lexy? JP? No. Oh my God.'

Hazel Bottle came in from the garden looking pleased with herself. One of her inventions was actually going right for a change. All she needed was a nice strong cup of—

'What's going on here?' she asked.

'I think you'd better hear this,' said Marcel. 'We'd all better sit down. It looks like we've made a dreadful, dreadful mistake.'

Marcel took Hazel's arm gently and they both went and sat on the sofa. Raven followed them but remained standing, with Buttons still on her shoulder.

'It's a long story,' said Raven. 'But Jupiter Peacock has been psychologically abusing your daughter ever since he's been in this house. And possibly worse; I'm not sure. He's threatened Buttons, and told Lexy that if she didn't do what he said he'd hurt him. Buttons doesn't understand much English, but he sensed that Peacock made it impossible for Lexy to tell you anything. I don't know how he would have done that. Do you have any idea?'

'Oh God,' said Hazel, tears beginning to run down her face. 'The stupid competition. I was so determined to be Host of the Year, I drummed into Lexy that she had to do whatever JP wanted. He was our honoured guest and she had to make him welcome and not upset him in any way . . . But she wouldn't have taken all that seriously, surely? She must have known that her safety was more important than anything . . .'

'Lexy never likes making a fuss or troubling anyone,' said Raven. 'She probably thought you'd be cross with her, or wouldn't believe her. Coach Bruce gave a talk the other week

315

at school and he said people who've been abused don't want to upset the people they love by telling them something so horrible.'

'If I'd known . . .' Marcel Bottle also now had tears in his eyes. 'I'm a peaceful man, but I would honestly have ripped him apart. My little daughter! My beautiful, innocent—'

'Well, now he's taken her somewhere,' said Raven. 'And I think he intends to use her as a human sacrifice. We don't have much time. We have to find her.'

Lexy opened the locket and took out the dried remains of the Orlov's Viper. No doubt JP had had bigger plans for this extremely rare magical artefact, but he should have thought of that before locking Lexy in a stable and threatening to kill her.

In recent days, Jupiter Peacock had insisted on reading Lexy most of the introduction to his translation of "Galloglass". It had been boring at first, but eventually it had started to make an impression on her. Maybe there *was* something to be said for acting in your own interests. It had to be better than agreeing to be a maiden sacrifice, anyway. So Lexy would use JP's precious objects entirely selfishly to free herself, and she wouldn't care in the slightest about the consequences for him or anyone else. The thought was extremely liberating.

Lexy put the Orlov's Viper into the cauldron with one of the obsidian crystals. The baby yeti watched her the whole time she was doing this. He seemed to understand that Lexy was trying to help him. But his breathing was becoming laboured. Lexy

316

had a horrible feeling he was more seriously injured than she thought. The pool of blood at the back of the stable was growing larger. Lexy realised she had to do something about that before she could try to move the baby yeti. She ripped off the bottom section of her skirt and made it into a makeshift bandage and did what she could for the creature's leg.

Then she returned to the cauldron and began saying the spell that would turn it into a bomb. She added one of her own hairs to it. The whole thing started glowing red.

'Brace yourself,' she said to the baby yeti. She ushered it into the back corner of the stable and threw the makeshift grenade at the stable doors. She put her fingers in her ears, and the baby yeti copied her. They both closed their eyes. The explosion blew the doors completely off. They were free.

There was a large bang from outside as Effie hurried down the corridor towards the entrance to the University Library. Was it lightning? Someone in the Funtime Arcade had said something about a big storm approaching tonight.

A student was walking quickly towards Effie, balancing a great pile of books, folders, a pencil case, a glasses case and, on top of it all, a pager. Since Effie had been in the Flow this time she almost felt as if she was experiencing the world in a kind of slow motion. Or, not slow motion exactly, more like higher definition. No, that wasn't quite it either.

Whatever it was, it meant that she could see the student's pager begin to slip from the pile and start to fall towards the hard ground, where it would surely shatter. It was a strange sensation. Just for a second – not even that – Effie could see the future and the past at once: all the pieces of the broken pager, its insides, its history, what it was made of. In a split second she knew everything about it. She could see it broken and whole. Its beginning and end. After all that, it seemed very easy to just give it a magical nudge back onto the pile.

The student walked on without even realising that Effie had helped her.

. Effie wanted to stop and think about this and try and get back in the Flow again. But she'd promised to help Leander and Wolf. She took a candle and some matches and hurried down the first of the five flights of dark stairs towards the Special Collections reception. As she descended she realised that she felt . . . It was hard to describe. It was the opposite of how she felt when she had a headache from running out of lifeforce. It was as if she was magically full-up. Like someone had just put a new battery into her or charged her up.

Effie knew that magic was very costly in the Realworld. That using it for anything that would be easier to accomplish with a physical action was foolish. But she just had to check something.

She blew out the candle she was carrying. Immediately, she was lost in the sort of deep darkness you get a long way underground. She looked at the candle and willed it to light again in the same way she would will her caduceus to grow. Of course, Effie's caduceus was designed to shrink and expand and it didn't take much magic to make that happen. But creating fire from nothing? In the Realworld?

The candle fizzed alight immediately.

And Effie still felt fully charged.

So that was what it was all about. The Flow topped up your magic and made you more powerful. That was why Effie had come out of her first experience with fifty thousand M-currency. The Flow, it seemed, was the very source of magic. Effie could see why people wanted her to discover it. She just wanted to get back in it as soon as possible. But instead she had to complete this task, which suddenly now seemed boring and insignificant. But she couldn't think like that. Especially as being humble seemed to be one of the things that got you in the Flow.

'Oh, it's you again,' said the wrinkled, red-haired librarian as Effie approached his desk. He was doing the cryptic crossword, possibly even the same one as last time. 'I see you're not bringing anything back. Good. Take all the blooming books, for all I care. Take them all home with you. Then you can be the one in charge of dusting them, and—'

'Can you help me find something?' Effie asked.

'No!' said the librarian, sounding horrified. 'Good heavens. Whatever next! What do you think this is? I told you before. You're on your own in there. And if you die—'

'Yes, yes. It's my own fault. I know. But the world is in danger and I need to find a book of warrior clerics' prayers urgently. It could actually mean the difference between life and death – not just for me but for all of us.'

The librarian rolled his eyes as if he'd heard all this before.

'And you're Euphemia Truelove, you say.'

Effie blushed when she remembered how self-important she must have sounded before when she'd stepped forward and introduced herself.

'Yes,' she said. 'But it's not—'

The librarian sighed. 'I've heard your name in the prophecies.' He frowned. 'Aren't you due to save the world today?' He peered at Effie more closely, as if trying to work out whether or not to let her off a large library fine. 'I'm not sure I care if I'm saved or not. But other people probably do. All right. Come on.' He creaked himself out of his chair. 'Warrior clerics' prayers, you say. Pretty specific. And you're clearly not a warrior or a cleric . . .'

Effie followed him into the part of the library where Lexy and Raven had gone last time, with all the tall, dusty stacks. He carried on muttering to himself as he peered at the numbers on the shelves, none of which seemed to have any logic to them at all.

'Aha,' he said, and started to unwind a stack with a creaky brass lever. 'Here we go.' He unwound the shelves until there was just barely enough space for him to squeeze in. He plucked the book from the shelf quickly, as if he was taking it from the cage of some ferocious animal. And then he gave it to Effie as if it was contaminated.

'There you go,' he said. 'Take it away. Take all the blooming—'

'Thank you,' said Effie. 'Do you also have a book on the Flow?' she asked him.

'The what?'

'The Flow. It's like a magical current that you—'

'Shhh,' said the librarian. 'No spoilers! No spoilers! Not so blooming loud. You're not supposed to speak of it to those who don't know.'

'But you obviously do know.'

'Well, I do now.'

320

This was confusing Effie.

Nevertheless, the librarian had set off in the direction of the Otherworld section, muttering as he went.

'You'd better not ask me for anything else after this,' he said. '*Ever*. Right. The Flow. The Flow.' He reached to get the book from the shelf but it must have been mis-shelved or something, because he didn't pull it out straight away. He scrabbled around for a while but then came back empty-handed.

'Oh,' he said. 'Oh dear. I forgot. It's on loan. Never mind. Come back next week if you like, once we reopen after the world ends.'

'You only have *one* book on the Flow?'

'Yes, and that's generous, considering what a big secret it's supposed to be. But it's the classic hypergeographic study by Thomas Lumas. Only book on the subject you'll ever need. But anyway, like I say: it's on loan.'

'Who to?'

'To whom,' corrected the librarian.

'Please,' said Effie, 'the end of the world doesn't care about my grammar. Who has the book?'

'That Diberi woman,' said the librarian. 'The Russian one. The poet.'

'Lady Tchainsaw?'

'That's the one.'

'But what would the Diberi want with a book about the Flow?' said Effie. 'I can't imagine they'd approve of it. And Jupiter Peacock even wrote it out of his translation of "Galloglass".'

The librarian put his fingers in his ears. 'La la la!' he said. 'No more spoilers, please. I can't know all this.'

'I think this is all connected,' said Effie, but the librarian, who still had his fingers in his ears, completely ignored her.

Lexy took the yeti by the hand and motioned for him to follow her. Poor thing. He looked terrified. But he also seemed grateful to see the sunshine. He let out a deep wail as soon as he saw the sky. Perhaps he was glad to be free. Or maybe he was trying to get a message to his parents, however many miles away they were. Or possibly he was just cold. Mind you, didn't yetis come from snowy places? Weren't they sometimes called abominable snowmen? Who knew if that's what this creature even was. But it was what Jupiter Peacock had called him.

'Shhh,' said Lexy. 'We need to find somewhere safe for you. The hospital's not far. Do you think you can make it?'

But the poor yeti was limping badly. Lexy had done her best with what she had, but the yeti needed more specialist help.

Above them both, the sky was rapidly turning from a clear winter blue into a kind of deep, stormy purple. The wind started to whistle.

'Oh dear,' said Lexy. 'I think there's a storm coming.'

The yeti seemed as if he really couldn't go any further. Lexy looked around for a place to hide him. He was far too heavy for her to carry. There was an old Portakabin just by the back entrance to the university that would have to do. It was green, and sort of mouldy on the outside, but warm and dry inside.

'You'll have to hide under a table if anyone comes,' said Lexy. She couldn't be sure whether he'd understood her or not. If only

Raven were here. But maybe even Raven didn't speak whatever language yetis understood.

Lexy drew her school cape around her and hurried towards the Old Town Hospital – not the official one, but the secret one, where Odile Underwood worked. By the time she'd got to Reception the sky had grown a darker shade of purple and large wet flakes of snow had started drifting nonchalantly out of the sky, as if they didn't care about yetis, secret books or the end of the world.

Lexy looked quite bedraggled as she approached the receptionist and asked to see Odile.

'Nurse Underwood isn't here,' came her reply. 'She's doing home visits today.'

'But it's urgent,' said Lexy. 'Can someone page her, please?'

'Well . . .'

'Please,' said Lexy. 'It's really important.'

It turned out that Odile was just two streets away.

'She's in the Old Rectory,' said the receptionist. 'She says she's tied up now, but you can go there and meet her if you like. She says she can help you next. Can I tell her what the matter is?'

'No,' said Lexy. 'I'll tell her myself.'

When Lexy arrived at the Old Rectory it was Dora Wright who let her in. She looked sad, and was orbited by far less glitter than usual. Raven's mother Laurel Wilde was hovering in the corridor, looking anxious.

'What's going on?' said Lexy.

'I could ask you the same,' said Dora. 'Do you realise that your hair is full of wet soot? Have you been in some kind of explosion?'

Lexy caught sight of herself in the hallway mirror. What a fright she looked. Not that it mattered. Nothing mattered except getting help for the poor creature she'd left in the Portakabin, and then finding her friends and telling them everything she knew.

'You could say that,' said Lexy. 'I need to see Nurse Underwood. Is she here?'

'Yes,' said Dora. 'It's Frankincense. She's been bound. We just heard. And they've captured Beathag Hide and Festus Grimm as well.'

'What?' said Lexy. 'Oh no!'

'They seem to have decided to step up their binding of the Gothmen, along with anyone who can stand in the way of what- ever the Diberi have planned for tonight. None of the nurses at the hospital can unbind people, but they can help a bit. Frankincense is in a terrible state.'

'Who's that?' said Odile, coming down the stairs from the flat where Effie's grandfather used to live. 'Oh, Alexa Bottle. Good. Another healer. Make yourself useful. Can you bring me a bowl of iced water, a flannel, some homeopathic sulphur in the 1M potency, a drachm of feverfew, half a scruple of devil's claw and a kettle of boiling water, please.'

'Of course,' said Lexy.

'And you can tell me about your problem while we make Frankincense comfortable. I fear this is going to be a very busy day. I hope you haven't got anything else planned. I could do with a little Apprentice to help me.'

Lexy smiled and nodded, and a wave of relief poured over her. She was a true healer who needed to be able to help people

324

and to make them better. And she'd been desperate to find a more senior healer to take her on as Apprentice. Had Nurse Underwood just offered to be Lexy's mentor? If she had . . . Lexy would work so hard and Nurse Underwood would never regret it and Lexy would soon be able to forget all about the stupid business with JP. And she'd be able to help defeat him by healing the people he – and others like him – hurt. She knew she could tell Nurse Underwood everything.

While Lexy waited for the kettle to boil she slipped back into Miss Wright's rooms and, after knocking softly on the door, asked to borrow a pager. She should probably let at least one of her friends know that she was all right – not that anyone seemed to have noticed that she'd been out of action. But she needed to warn them about what Jupiter Peacock was planning. Raven answered immediately, and seemed very surprised that Lexy was safe and well and needed someone to translate from Yeti. But there was no response from Maximilian at all.

22

The Winter Fair Market was busy today, as people did last-minute shopping for their Midwinter's Eve celebrations. Traditionally, Midwinter was celebrated at midnight with a cake made into the shape of a log and decorated with holly leaves and juniper berries. Midwinter evening meals usually consisted of a hearty chestnut soup with freshly made bread that was eaten at around five o'clock so that people could attend whatever public celebration of Midwinter they'd chosen before they went home for their cake.

Tonight in the Old Town the choice was between Jupiter Peacock's Midwinter Lecture, a firework display put on by the local council or a strange shadow-theatre spectacle put on by the Puppet Man. Most people had opted for Jupiter Peacock's lecture. The fireworks would have been more popular had it not been for the weather. There'd already been a tornado just off the coast, and lots of reports were coming in of electrical snow storms – a phenomenon last seen during the great climate meltdown of the early twenty-first century.

In the Winter Fair Market, snow was now falling thickly and people were cheerfully huddling around the little stoves. The hot chestnut man was doing a roaring trade with people who had forgotten to roast chestnuts for their soup, or who just fancied eating an enormous amount of chestnuts in one day.

Maximilian searched for Madame Valentin's stall. But it wasn't there. It looked as if she'd packed up early or not even come out today. Maximilian remembered that her pet shop was next door to Leonard Levar's Antiquarian Bookshop. He'd once had a distressing experience with some spiders that Levar had 'borrowed' from her shop. He headed there in the snow.

When he arrived he could immediately tell that something was wrong. A man in green corduroy trousers was pacing anxiously in the snow outside the door to the pet shop, smoking a pipe and mumbling.

'You cannot come hin,' he said to Maximilian. 'We're closed.'

'But—'

'And all our snakes 'av hescaped also, so you might want to watch where you are treading.'

Snakes? Maximilian used to be afraid of things like that. Not so much any more. Was this why the man was pacing and mumbling and smoking in the way he was? No. There was something more.

'I came to see Madam Valentin,' said Maximilian. 'It's about her prophecy.'

'You are too late,' said Monsieur Valentin bitterly. 'She 'as been bound.'

'What? Why?'

'Because of the prophecy. She is now unable to talk. I am

waiting for a nurse to come and 'elp her. I 'av called many times but—'

'My mum's a nurse,' said Maximilian. 'They've been really busy.'

'Why are they doing this?' said Monsieur Valentin. 'My poor Adele! It was not 'er fault she 'eard this prophecy.'

'Who did it?' asked Maximilian.

'The Binder, hof course,' said Monsieur Valentin. 'After this 'ee also search next door for the boy that 'as been living there. I don't know why. I tell him nothing, hobviously.'

Maximilian tried to process all this.

'Who is the Binder?' he asked.

Monsieur Valentin had been looking either at Maximilian or at his pipe while he'd been talking. But now his eyes settled on something just behind Maximilian. There was a beat, and then a small bony hand clamped down on Maximilian's shoulder.

'*I* am the Binder,' came a thin, heartless voice. 'And you, young mage, are going to have to come with me.'

Effie hurried back to the chapel to give Leander the book. Wolf was awake, but still seemed a bit dazed. Leander was standing over him holding a small book and chanting something. Wolf gave Effie a half-smile and then chanted whatever it was back. He radiated calmness and joy.

Effie put the book of warrior clerics' prayers on the pew next to Wolf and left again. Sandalwood incense, Leander had said. Would they sell incense in the student shop? But it was already closed for Midwinter, so Effie left through the main entrance and walked in the falling snow towards Pickle Street, which, as well as housing the Esoteric Emporium and Dark Daze, had a little magic shop called Wanda's.

How this shop remained open was a complete mystery to everyone. People who didn't believe in magic either didn't notice Wanda's tiny shop or, if they did, felt mildly offended by the idea that someone would charge something like ten whole pounds for fake crystals that didn't even work. People who did believe in magic also didn't approve of Wanda's shop, but for them it was because it was so tame. The crystals did work – they were crystals, after all. But Wanda did overcharge for items that most people now got through mail-order catalogues. Still, she did sell a good range of incense.

Effie was just about to open the door when she became aware of a dark shape on the pavement in the snow in front of the shop. At first she took it as rubbish that had been put out to be collected. But then she realised it was a person.

'Are you all right?' Effie said to the shape on the ground.

The shape didn't move.

'Hello?' said Effie. 'Are you OK? Do you need help?'

'We all need help,' came a female voice. The dark shape moved, shook itself and sat up.

It was the woman from the market. The one who had reminded Effie of her mother. Effie had given her eight pounds and then had her first experience in the Flow. Well, this was handy. This was another chance to—

'Oh, I see,' the woman said, nodding. 'Now you consider me some kind of convenient portal. I've met your type before.'

'No,' said Effie. 'That's not it. I—'

'I'm very cold,' said the woman pointedly.

'Here,' said Effie. 'Have my cape. I don't mind.'

The woman accepted Effie's school cape. Now Effie shivered before her in the snow.

'That's better. Now, do you have any more money?' asked the woman.

'No,' said Effie. 'Only my friend's money. I have to buy incense.'

'Incense. Pah!'

'It's actually quite important, so . . .'

'More important than getting back in the Flow?'

'I can go in the Flow whenever I want.'

'Oh, you can, can you? Sorry, girly. That's not how it works. And I think you know it.'

It was true. Ever since she'd lit the candle in the library, Effie had felt the Flow retreat from her somehow. She still had all the power it had given her, of course, but where before she'd sensed it as another dimension right next to her, so close she could just step into it at any time, it now seemed unreachable, like it was on a different plane of existence entirely. Did the Flow hate her too? Had she done that wrong, just as she did everything else wrong?

'Oh, stop feeling sorry for yourself,' the woman said. 'I thought you wanted to help me . . . Or do you actually just want to use me to increase your power?'

Why was this woman saying these things? She wasn't being very friendly, all of a sudden. And she wasn't in the slightest bit grateful to Effie for giving her the cape. She was just being

330

horrible. Effie suddenly wanted nothing more to do with her. She didn't want to help her at all. She didn't actually care if she—

Effie took a deep breath. Blinked slowly. Whatever horrible things the woman was saying, she still looked small and helpless at Effie's feet. She was grumpy, but then wouldn't you be grumpy if you had to sleep out in the snow? Effie again thought of her mother. She always used to be snappy when she had a headache. She didn't mean it; it was just because she was in pain. Effie crouched down.

'Can I get you some food?' she said. 'Or find you a place to stay?'

'You could give me that ring,' the woman said.

'What?' said Effie. 'Which ring?'

'That ring.' The woman pointed at Effie's Ring of the True Hero that hung around her neck.

'No!' said Effie automatically. 'That's my . . .' But then something shifted inside her and the word 'my' didn't seem to mean very much. It was a bit like in the market before when Effie had lost herself in the great mass of being. *Mine, yours, theirs, ours*: it all seemed to be the same thing. And anyway, Effie didn't even wear it any more.

'OK,' she said, surprising herself. 'Have it.' She took the ring from around her neck and held it out to the woman. 'Maybe it'll bring you more luck than it's brought me.'

The woman took the ring off the necklace and put it on. Effie expected to feel terrible, but giving up the ring made her feel ten times lighter. She felt warm, despite the snow, and whole. Maybe she didn't need it after all. Maybe she didn't need anything. She suddenly felt herself drifting like a snowflake into a world of many, many snowflakes where all that mattered was falling faintly, faintly falling through the air, and—

'Now give me your necklace,' came the woman's sharp voice.

Effie's Sword of Light necklace was her most precious possession. But what really was a possession anyway? Did a snowflake need possessions? Did the sun or the moon have possessions? And in any case Effie's necklace had also only brought her trouble. Of course, she loved it. But did it really make sense to love an object like that? Something that could be lost or broken or stolen? What if the object was removed but love remained? What would happen if that happened to all objects and all possessions? What if people chose love instead? After all, objects tarnish eventually, and decompose. But love and light never change. They are constant and glorious and—

'Here,' said Effie. She unclasped the necklace and—

and—

snowflakes falling, falling, then—

The snow was gone. Effie was suddenly in a magnificent castle with a purple crushed-velvet carpet and a massive throne that changed into a head teacher's comfortable old study that changed into a tennis court with an umpire's chair that changed into Cosmo's tower room and then back into the magnificent castle again. On the throne sat the homeless woman, wearing a massive diamond crown. On closer inspection, though, the crown was made of ice crystals on a garland of leaves and . . .

Now the scene changed again. It was summer, and Effie was walking barefoot over grass towards a small cottage. Outside, the same woman sat in a rocking chair knitting something.

Effie approached her.

'Please take this,' Effie said, holding out her Sword of Light necklace.

'I don't need it any more than you do,' said the woman.

'No,' said Effie. 'But please take it. And have this vial of deepwater too. And my bag. And I don't think I need clothes any more or even my body—'

'You're right,' the woman said. 'A true hero doesn't need anything. *You* don't need anything. You don't even need yourself. Not this lower self, anyway, this silly old bag of bones. And of course, when it comes to the higher self, we're all one. But most people find that terrifying, and spend their whole lives resisting it. And so they live again and again in the Realworld until they find out enough to go to the Otherworld, and then the learning begins again, in a different way.'

Effie felt herself beginning to float into the air in front of the woman's cottage. She seemed to blink in and out of existence, like a twinkling star. It was a curious feeling. If she was just brave enough to let go of this . . . Of herself, whatever that was. If she could just . . .

The woman spoke again, and this time it was with a voice Effie recognised, although she had never heard it before.

'Will you give everything to me?' it asked.

Effie hesitated.

'Will you give yourself up to the mystery and depth of the unknown? I can't tell you what's in it or how it will feel. You may never know your lower self again, but without casting off your lower self, you can have no idea of who your higher self really is.'

Effie hesitated again. After all, who chooses to give up him or herself? It would be like choosing to die. But it didn't feel as if that was what Effie was being offered. It wasn't death being put in front of her, but eternal life.

'Yes,' she agreed. 'Yes. I'll give myself . . .'

'I still think,' Lady Tchainsaw was saying, 'that my cut-up poem *No Flow* will achieve the best result. If we disconnect the Flow, then we remove the link between the worlds. I have done a lot of research on this, and I am sure that once this connection is severed, magical energy will return to the Realworld.'

'She would think that,' said Jupiter Peacock to Gotthard Forestfloor. 'Any opportunity to push her dreadful so-called poetry. But I still say all we need to do is to put my new edition of *Galloglass* in the Great Library. I have removed the Flow from Hieronymus Moon's great vision and restored the poem to the individualist glory that Moon so very nearly achieved . . . I confess that while doing it I felt a little like Ezra Pound editing T.S. Eliot, or . . .' He visibly struggled to think of another example of a famous writer being edited by another famous person.

'You may as well be a cut-up poet yourself,' said Lady Tchainsaw. 'You've certainly messed around with your original at least as much as I have with mine. You call yourself a translator!'

'Oh, really?' said JP. He picked up the Special Collections edition of *The Flow* by Thomas Lumas that was on Lady Tchainsaw's coffee table. Bits of paper fluttered out. He opened the volume and shook his head. Inside, the book had been completely destroyed by Lady Tchainsaw. She had erased words, cut some out with a scalpel, rearranged others and drawn over whole pages in fluorescent green highlighter. Selected parts of the book – the parts, presumably, that Lady Tchainsaw approved of – had been badly pasted on an A5 sheet of paper and given the title *No Flow*. It looked like something you might do on a rainy Wednesday afternoon at primary school.

'Is that a library book?' said Gotthard Forestfloor. 'For pity's sake.'

'Oh, don't be so precious,' said Lady Tchainsaw. 'You're planning to wipe out much of the known universe and you're worried about a *library* book? You ridiculous man.'

Gotthard Forestfloor fixed Lady Tchainsaw with an evil stare.

'Anyway,' said JP, 'on with our plans for tonight. It seems rather a shame that Terrence Deer-Hart never wrote the book we commissioned from him. Is he going to be able to pull off the kidnap at least?'

Terrence Deer-Hart hadn't added anything to this conversation so far. He had been looking at Lady Tchainsaw and imagining what it would be like to kiss her.

'I think so,' said Lady Tchainsaw. 'I'll go through it all again with him.' She sighed. 'It's not easy, though.'

'And when you get Effie Truelove back here Terrence is going to do pedesis on her and find out how she goes to the Great Library? Then he's going to tell you, and then you are going to tell us.'

'Pah!' said Gotthard Forestfloor. 'Why can we not find a mage to join us?'

'I'm a mage,' said Terrence.

'Oh, shut up,' said Forestfloor, witheringly. He looked at Lady Tchainsaw. 'Tell me why you are not doing the pedesis yourself?'

'Because everyone who does pedesis dies,' she replied. 'There is a disclaimer at the front of Thomas Lumas's book.'

'I see, yes. No one will mind if we sacrifice *him*.'

'Quite. I'm not sure he'll even notice himself.'

Terrence had drifted off again.

'And then we keep the Truelove girl and use her as a portal during the ceremony?' said Forestfloor.

'Exactly,' said JP. 'I've had intelligence that confirms that the portal is actually inside her. But killing her should release it momentarily, and then we can use it.'

'And remind me why we're not doing this in a nice, quiet back room? Why must we perform this complex, frankly ridiculous-sounding spell in front of your lecture audience? Is it because you're an enormous prima donna, or do you want to deliver twelve minutes of your lecture to see if boredom will kill everyone quicker than the spell does?' Gotthard Forestfloor smiled at his own joke.

'The spell is the highest level of the darkest magic and so needs an audience,' JP replied. 'It needs awe in order to work.'

Forestfloor sighed. 'Well, you're the alchemist. It still sounds stupid to me. How can a spell need "awe"?'

JP shrugged. 'This one does. And a lot of space, too. The Grand Lecture Theatre is perfect.'

'Right. And do we have the yeti?'

'Yes. It escaped briefly, but we now have it back.'

'Excellent. And the maiden?'

'Yep. The original one pulled out, but we have a replacement lined up.'

'And the cats?'

'On their way.'

'Well, all we need to do now is decide what book we're putting in. I still think that the novel form is the purest. My book, *The Bleak Midwinter*, sets out our philosophical position very clearly. It can't be misread like a poem.'

'Maybe we should just put them all in,' suggested Lady Tchainsaw.

'Yes, perhaps you're right,' said Forestfloor. 'They don't contradict each other, so it would probably work. As long as between them they clash strongly enough with whatever's already in there. My research suggests that this is all that's needed to wipe everything out. And then we can start again. Do it our way, with the purer magic that will gush forth once the Flow is gone.'

'Are you absolutely sure the Flow should be removed?' asked Lady Tchainsaw. 'In the library book it mentioned that the Flow is the fundamental force of the universe and without it all that would be left is an unimaginable vacuum of darkness and sorrow.'

'Yes, but you've cut that bit out presumably?' said JP.

'Indeed,' said Lady Tchainsaw.

'Good,' said Gotthard Forestfloor. 'Onwards, then, to tonight!'

23

Raven said goodbye to Marcel and Hazel Bottle and flew as fast as she could back to the university. At first she thought she'd misunderstood Lexy. A yeti? But then she remembered that the spell she'd overheard in the library had included the eye of a live yeti. The Diberi must have got a yeti from somewhere and Lexy must have rescued it.

She landed in the fresh snow next to the old Portakabin by the university's back gates. The door was open and cold air was blowing through the small structure. There was a chair lying on its side, and a desk that had been tipped over. The yeti was gone. Had it escaped on its own, or did the Diberi have it back?

Raven shivered. She hoped the yeti was all right. She wrote Lexy a quick message on her pager and then got back on her broomstick. The snowstorm was intensifying, and darkness was coming too. She'd need to get to the cats' home as quickly as she could. Presumably the Diberi had most of the other ingredients for their terrible spell. But if she could just manage to warn the cats . . .

Raven landed smoothly in the grounds of the cats' home, just behind an extraordinary piece of topiary – a yew hedge in the shape of a cat's head. It was a good thing Raven had a broomstick because whoever was in charge had locked the gates and electrified the fence. As soon as Raven landed she cast the Shadows. It was chaos. There were cats everywhere, and several humans dressed in butler or maid outfits running around with butterfly nets trying to catch them. There were miniature top hats and tiaras lying discarded on the ground. Raven was having trouble making sense of what was going on.

The cat nearest to her was black with white socks.

'What's happening?' Raven asked him, taking the spell off herself so he could see her.

'Total revolution,' he said back.

'Why?' she asked.

'Because we've awoken. Because of the Free Cats League.'

'The Free Cats League?'

'Yep. That's right. They've told us all about how this luxury is just a different sort of captivity, and how a human group are planning to use us in a big spell. Many of us were due to die tonight. Not any more. We want freedom for all!'

'So you already know about the spell?' said Raven. 'Who's in charge of this Free Cats League? Can you take me to them?'

'I can try. My name's Socks. And yours?'

'Raven. Let's hurry.'

Raven cast the Shadows on Socks as well as herself and then followed him in through the main door and down some servants' stairs into a basement.

'I don't know how a human gets beyond here,' said Socks.

'We go through there.' He indicated a hole in the skirting board.

A man and a woman in formal clothes walked past but didn't notice Raven and Socks because of the Shadows.

'Bloody cats,' the man was saying to the woman. 'If we can't deliver a hundred of them to the university by seven-thirty this evening then the whole deal's off. The funding's being withdrawn and no one's getting paid. That's basically just under a billion quid down the drain.'

'You underestimate me,' said the woman.

'What do you mean?'

'The so-called Free Cats League were ordering in their own seaweed kibble. We drugged it. Now we've got just a hundred of the most revolutionary ones in the back of the van. Job done.'

'You genius.'

Raven looked at Socks.

'Oh no,' he said.

Raven tried a couple of doors and found that one led to some stairs. Yes, this was the direct way down to the basement area. Once they reached the bottom of the stairs Socks sniffed out the way to the secret room the cats had been using.

Inside was a scene of devastation. Broken musical instruments were lying on the ground and tables and chairs were overturned. Bowls of water had been spilt. Bits of kibble were strewn all over the floor.

'This is terrible!' said Socks. 'If they've got our leaders then I don't know what we'll do.'

'All right,' said Raven. 'You go back and do what you have to do upstairs. Keep the revolution going. That's the most

340

important thing you can do now. Thanks for your help. I'll find this van, and . . .'

Socks hurried out of the room. Raven's seventh sense was telling her something that she couldn't completely understand. But she was picking up a powerful message from somewhere just over by the stage.

Yes. Under the table. Unconscious, but . . .

Familiar, somehow.

It was the school cat. The violent one. The one the children weren't allowed to go near. But he seemed different somehow. He'd changed in some unfathomable way, and not just because he was unconscious.

Raven reached out and touched his fur. He was warm. Breathing. She took her wonde out of her backpack and held it just above his head while she said a healing spell. Lexy made Raven carry a vial of high potency homoeopathic arnica tablets wherever she went. As soon as Neptune was conscious Raven held one out to him and he took it with his rough tongue. He blinked a few times, and then moved his head. Raven now gave him a dose of homoeopathic arsenicum. In homoeopathy like cures like, and so a case of poisoning could often be helped with a minute dose of the deadly poison arsenic.

'Who are you?' Neptune said weakly. 'You smell familiar.'

Familiar.

So did he. It was hard to describe, but a heavenly warm smell was coming from his fur. It was floral, grassy, a bit like coriander flowers in the sunshine. Raven felt sort of fuzzy-headed for a second. It was as if she'd drunk a glass of her mother's wine.

Neptune opened his eyes.

He looked up at Raven. When her eyes met his, the effect was electrifying. It was like falling in love instantly. Raven knew that from this moment she and this cat – whose name she didn't even know – were going to be inseparable.

'It's you,' he said.

She took a deep breath. 'At last. I knew I'd find you.'

'My witch,' he said.

'My familiar,' she said.

'Where are the others?' Neptune asked. 'Mirabelle? Malvasia?'

'They're being taken to the university. We have to rescue them.'

Neptune stood up.

'Are you all right?' Raven asked.

'Yes, I think so,' said Neptune. 'Thank you for coming for me. I'm Neptune, by the way.'

Raven nodded. 'I'm Raven. We'll look after each other from now on. Let's go.'

◉

In a strange dimension both near and far away, Effie Truelove was turning somersaults through the air. Her body felt entirely weightless. *Downdowndown* she went, and then *flip*, and then *upupup*. It was like a sort of cosmic ballet. All that was Effie – her headstrong nature, her desire for truth, her desire to be special, her loyalty to her friends, her love of her family, her great ability at tennis, the strength and coordination that would make her a great dancer in the physical world if she ever tried, her favourite breakfasts, the one time she rode a horse – all this swirled out of her and into the silent starry night in which she'd found herself. The less she became, the more she was. The more of herself she gave, the more power she had. It was paradoxical, and amazing. She seemed to be exchanging her soul for the entire universe.

Just as the last drop of Effie was about to be squeezed out, the whole process seemed to begin to rewind. Slowly . . . slowly . . . then *fasterfasterfaster*. She was re-joining herself, being somehow put back together. She didn't want to go back, and yet somehow she did. There were still things she had to accomplish – no, that was the wrong word – but there was a need for Effie to stay Effie. As long as she remembered that she didn't need anything to prop herself up. And that *this* was what was waiting for her. Some time in the future, after she had become a wizard and lived for hundreds of years in the Otherworld, growing wiser and wiser: *this*. Living in bliss for ever and ever.

When she opened her eyes, the woman in rags had gone and Effie was standing outside Wanda's once more wearing her cape and her Sword of Light necklace. Her Ring of the True Hero was on her finger. She bent her knees slightly and then experimentally jumped in the air, to see if . . . Yes, it was different. She could jump higher. She had a slightly altered relationship with gravity. She could . . . Effie pirouetted once, twice. It felt good. Different. She jumped in the air and spun. She ran and took a leap, which sent her flying through the air. She ran up the side of a wall and then somersaulted before landing again in front of Wanda's. Anyone watching would have thought that she was practising to play the lead in the latest flying-martial-arts film or some magical-realist street-dance production. But no one was watching. Everyone was looking at the sky.

'I've always wanted to ride a broomstick,' said Neptune. 'I had a feeling it was my destiny.'

'Well, hold tight,' said Raven. 'It doesn't look very safe up there.'

It was true. The effect of the Bermuda Triangle, the Northern Lights and the Luminiferous Ether moving across the Atlantic was being felt far and wide. And they were getting closer. There were tornadoes and tidal waves and freak events. In one child's back garden a snowman had been swept into the blizzard, dismantled, and then put back together again. The only difference was that his carrot-nose had been put back the wrong way around.

The sky glowed with the otherworldly colours of the Northern Lights. It was having fun, putting on a great show for everyone, probably for the last time. The Luminiferous Ether was also feeling a bit *fin de siècle* and had started granting spells haphazardly as it came across them. Even silly spells, like the one from Maddie, age fourteen, to please make Oliver fall in love with her. And the one from her mother Evie, who'd introduced Maddie to this concept of asking the universe for what you want in the form of a simple spell. She'd asked for a complicated jumble of things over the years: better skin, a great body, a fulfilling career, love, glamour . . . All this was now to be granted despite Maddie and Evie having between them about the same amount of M-currency as a small pot of live yogurt.

Raven pushed her broomstick into the sky. It was darker up there than she'd ever seen it. Beyond the Northern Lights and all the dramatic weather was . . . *Wait*. Something up here felt familiar.

Raven flew higher: higher than she normally would.

'What are you doing?' asked Neptune.

'I can sense . . . It's hard to describe,' said Raven, 'but I think I have a friend up here.'

'A friend?'

'OK. Well, not exactly a friend. I've never met it. But I've written to it quite a lot . . .'

The Luminiferous Ether had come out of its usual dimension and was rampaging through ours like a kind uncle who has drunk too much sherry. The peculiarities of space and time meant that the Luminiferous Ether had manifested in three dimensions as something that resembled a stick of rock, although approximately three miles high and four metres across. It was an unstable-looking pink on the outside, with an extra-terrestrial green stripe spiralling down it.

It was in the mood to grant wishes. But where had everyone gone? And now who was this, suddenly flying through the night sky on a small broomstick with a black cat sitting at the end of it? Could it be? *Well*. What joy! It was the Luminiferous Ether's favourite correspondent, Raven Wilde. She always wrote such polite letters, always enquired after its health, always asked for such interesting, selfless things. Well, thought the Luminiferous Ether, she was certainly in the right place at the right time. Well, sort of. After all, it wasn't that safe for any human to be in the sky at this moment, with ball lightning flashing more regularly and a tornado just starting up over the Mrs Joyful School.

The Old Town was really being hammered. There were Blue Jets, Red Sprites, tennis-ball-sized hail, a couple of fire devils, and one large example of the phenomenon known in warmer climes as a willy-willy, a spinning vortex of dust and debris that had unfortunately got hold of the Blessed Bartolo sports dome and deposited it far out to sea.

The Luminiferous Ether quickly created a large, soft lenticular cloud and put his friend and her cat inside it. They would now be safe while they told the Luminiferous Ether exactly what they wanted.

Orwell Bookend was having a lovely evening so far. It didn't matter that it looked as if the world was going to end outside. Orwell was one of those people who did not really believe in weather and so the massive hailstones currently pulverising the neighbourhood didn't bother him at all. It was cosy inside anyway, with the fire dancing in the grate and baby Luna eating a bowl of custard while everyone else had thick chestnut soup and homemade focaccia.

Terrence Deer-Hart had complimented Orwell on his choice of wine but then looked baffled and a little afraid when Orwell and Cait began talking about all the notable children's books they'd read in their lifetimes. Any talk about other authors simply drove Terrence mad. He sort of felt like poking out his own eyes.

Not long after six, Effie looked at her watch. Wasn't Terrence supposed to be kidnapping her? She wondered how he was going to do it. Whatever he had planned wasn't going to work anyway, even if he did remember his mission. Effie was full of power and, with her ring on, had the strength of several adults. It was becoming clear that if she wanted to infiltrate the Diberi, she was going to have to kidnap herself.

'I've got to go back to the university,' Effie said, standing up. 'I'm helping set up for the Midwinter Lecture.'

'In this weather?' said Cait.

'It's only a bit of hail,' said Orwell.

'A bit of hail!' said Cait. 'Orwell, have you looked out of the window lately? There was an actual tornado before.'

'It's just weather. Weather never hurt anyone.'

Cait rolled her eyes.

'Anyway, Terrence said he'd give me a lift,' said Effie. '*Didn't* you, Terrence?'

'Yes,' he said. 'Yes, I'll take Effie back to the university.'

'All right,' said Orwell. 'Well, we'll see you at the lecture.'

'If they survive,' said Cait. 'If *we* survive.'

'Don't be so dramatic,' said Orwell.

'I'm going to go and set up,' said Jupiter Peacock, checking his pompadour again in Lady Tchainsaw's massive mirror. 'I believe we have most things in place. Lady T, can you go and organise the cats?'

'I am allergic to them,' she said. 'Vile creatures.'

'Professor G?'

347

Gotthard Forestfloor sighed. 'All right,' he said. 'But this had better work. Lady Tchainsaw, you stay here and supervise the pedesis. And then once everything has been done you can bring the girl to us.'

Effie was lying on Lady Tchainsaw's black velvet chaise longue pretending to be unconscious. Her hands and feet were tied together with silk scarves. Lying on a vast bear rug on the ground, Terrence Deer-Hart really was unconscious. He'd drunk the vial of fluid and taken the little pill that Lady Tchainsaw had given him. Now he had found himself in some sort of incomprehensible landscape with some strange voice telling him he had two choices. What did this mean? He knew he was supposed to be entering the girl's mind to learn how she went to some library in the Otherworld. But how was he supposed to get in?

You now have two choices, said the woman, again.

What does that mean? Terrence asked her back.

You can go into one of the structures around you, the voice explained. *They represent the consciousness of people near you on the physical plane.*

Terrence looked around him. There was a vast, avant-garde building with Russian domes and a black marble exterior. The only other building he could see apart from that was a small yellow-brick townhouse with the word LIBRARY on it and a poster advertising a special display of adventure stories. That must represent the girl. So, all he had to do was go in through the antique revolving door and . . .

Effie felt Terrence Deer-Hart entering her mind. She hadn't been entirely sure what she was going to do with him, but it became immediately obvious once she sensed his empty, troubled soul. The first thing she did was mentally flip him on his back, like a karate throw-down of the mind. Terrence's consciousness now just watched as Effie – on the physical plane – removed the silk scarves from her arms and legs using only her mind to do so and, in a very deft manoeuvre, then got up off the chaise longue and retied the scarves around Lady Tchainsaw's arms and legs.

How was this achieved so easily? For one thing, Lady Tchainsaw wasn't watching properly because she was busy applying bright red lipstick and looking at herself in the mirror. And second, because Effie made herself invisible while she was doing it. Using the Flow also meant Effie could do things at lightning speed. All Lady Tchainsaw felt was a mild tickle around her wrists and ankles before Effie used a sleeping spell she suddenly found she knew.

'What are you doing?' Terrence said, inside Effie's mind.

'Defeating you and your stupid new friends,' said Effie. 'Now, come with me. I've got something to show you.'

Terrence didn't like the sound of this, but he was still trapped inside Effie's mind as she walked to the centre of the room and started a pirouette that turned into a series of fouettés which launched her into the air, until she was spinning and spinning and . . . *There*. She was back in the Flow. She could stay in it for far longer now. And it wasn't even about topping up her power; it was just about spending time in this perfect, joyous, heavenly place where everybody was one and . . .

'Let me go!' Terrence shouted inside Effie's head.

'No,' she said. 'You come into my consciousness, this is what you get.'

'But I can't stand it,' he said.

'Feel the peace, and the joy,' said Effie. 'That's what you get when you try to attack me.'

'Please!' wailed Terrence.

Effie kept him in the Flow long enough that the peace and the joy seeped into every part of Terrence and started to take him over. And then she took a deep breath and booted him out of her mind.

24

The Grand Lecture Theatre was filling with people suffering from varying levels of exposure and trauma, depending on where they'd been able to park. Most of them had wet hair and feet; some people had mild frostbite. As eight o'clock approached there were still a number of empty seats belonging to people who had, sadly, been struck by lightning or fallen in the large sinkhole that had opened up outside the Esoteric Emporium. Others had been knocked out by the enormous hailstones. This was certainly the biggest storm the Old Town had ever experienced.

Undeterred by the reduced size of his audience, Jupiter Peacock stepped forward to begin his lecture. The Vice Chancellor of the university had been due to introduce him but had been held up somewhere because of the weather. Just as JP was about to begin speaking, a woman strode onto the stage wearing an asymmetric hemp skirt and a patchwork recycled-cotton top. It was Hazel Bottle.

'Aha,' said Jupiter Peacock. 'It looks as if my host would like to say a few words.' He narrowed his eyes and looked pointedly at his watch.

Hazel Bottle took the microphone stand from him.

'Thank you,' she said. 'As many of you know, our family has been hosting Professor Jupiter Peacock this past week. We thought it would be a great honour to have such a distinguished academic to stay, and I confess that I hoped that he would speak kindly of our hospitality so that I might be in with a chance of winning Host of the Year.' She paused. 'However, our guest behaved so disgracefully while he was staying with us that I want it on record that my family would not accept any honour or award that comes from him, or from anything he said or did. While he was in our house, eating our food, enjoying our heating and electricity, he was constantly betraying us. This vile man threatened my daughter repeatedly, telling her that if she didn't do what he said he would not vote for us. Our daughter did not tell us about his dreadful behaviour because she didn't want to upset us, or ruin Midwinter, or cause trouble. I urge all mothers out there to make it clear to your children that no matter what is happening in your life you would want to know IMMEDIATELY if someone was threatening or bullying your child. It wouldn't matter if it was my birthday, or I'd had a hard day at work, or my father was ill, or if we'd just had some bad news. NOTHING is more important than my daughter's safety. I hope she realises that now, and that this was in no way her fault.'

Lexy smiled gratefully at Hazel from the front row, where she was sitting with Nurse Underwood.

'And any children out there who are worried about something

that is happening to them and for some reason really can't tell their parents – maybe because it is their parents who are doing it, or maybe they don't even have parents – your teachers care about you. Tell one of them. Just find an adult you trust and tell them as soon as possible. Perhaps even a librarian? Don't wait for the right moment, or try to negotiate in any way with your abuser. Just tell someone.'

The audience burst into hearty applause. Except for the hairy librarian from Special Collections, who didn't want children to speak to him under *any* circumstances. Of course, if anyone ever did tell him something like that he'd have to take action and have it stopped. It would totally ruin his day, but perhaps that wouldn't matter so much in the scheme of things. However annoying children were, they still needed to be protected. He joined the applause.

This wasn't how Jupiter Peacock had been hoping his lecture would start. But he found he couldn't stop the woman from speaking. His magic had been frozen somehow.

'Gosh,' said Orwell Bookend to the person sitting next to him – the maths teacher from the Mrs Joyful School. 'Does this mean there won't be a lecture after all? I had such a good question.'

All eyes were on Jupiter Peacock. What was he going to say? What was he going to do? The audience fell silent.

And then there was an almost imperceptible popping sound.

A bit like a cork coming out of a tiny ceramic bottle.

Quantum physics teaches us that at any moment in time there are countless versions of reality that are possible, depending on the choices we make. For example, as Hieronymus Moon squeezed out of his bottle for the first time in three thousand years, ready to appear on the stage of the Grand Lecture Theatre in the Old Town University with the one aim of denouncing the latest translator of his great work, he could have been greeted by quite a different scene.

The scene that could have greeted him had one hundred cats caught up in a net hanging from the ceiling. It had Lexy Bottle manacled and drugged and dressed all in white with a knife at her throat. It had poor Maximilian bound and gagged and held hostage so that Effie would do whatever the Diberi wanted. In this once possible version of reality, Raven had never met Neptune and had never had her very useful chat with the Luminiferous Ether, and by this point – 8.05 p.m. – the Bermuda Triangle had already consumed most of the audience.

In this alternative version of the present – the one that would have occurred had Lexy not been so brave, and had Effie not been in the Flow, and had Maximilian not been secretly attending the University of the Underworld quite so regularly, and had Raven not found her familiar, and had Wolf not learned to unbind people – Hazel Bottle had not made her speech, and JP was standing resplendent in his academic gown, ready to tell this audience precisely how they were all about to die.

But that version of reality had not happened.

In fact, the scene was quite different. As the old red velvet curtains were drawn apart, an entirely different show was about to begin.

First, the audience saw the spirit of Hieronymus Moon floating up towards the ceiling where, like a perfectly timed special effect, a thunderbolt just happened to strike the roof of the Old Town University in such a way that a little hole appeared for Hieronymus

354

Moon to float through. He looked like an illustration from a book about Ancient Times, but with a big, peaceful smile. He was free, at long last. Free from having to live inside a bottle in the possession of that complete idiot. As he approached the hole in the ceiling, his spirit-form turned and addressed the audience.

'I have not been able to experience the world directly for thousands of years,' said Hieronymus Moon. 'But it is sad to see that some things never change. I want to endorse what that nice woman just said about children who are being abused. This man' – he pointed a ghostly finger at Jupiter Peacock – 'is not just a child abuser, although that is bad enough. He has kept my spirit prisoner in a ceramic bottle for hundreds of years, taking over my captivity from the man who owned me before him. He has used dark alchemy to keep himself alive longer than the normal human lifespan. And his spell worked as long as he had me in my bottle, and as long as he kept my eternal soul from the Flow. Well, now I depart at long last, and sadly, therefore, so must he. Goodbye, Jupiter Peacock – the very worst translator I ever had.'

There was an ominous rumble of thunder and, as Hieronymus Moon ascended, Jupiter Peacock slumped to the floor, dead.

A different audience may have felt sad for poor Jupiter Peacock, cut off in his prime by a vindictive ghost. But this one just clapped and whooped. Some people called for an encore. But, sadly, JP could only die once.

Lexy was particularly glad to see him gone.

As the clapping died down, the curtains finished opening.

On stage was a complicated scene.

Perhaps the most immediately compelling sight was Tabitha Quinn, dressed in an extremely unfashionable white peasant smock, tied to a chair and blindfolded, being freed by Raven Wilde, who had a black cat sitting on her shoulder. Tabitha Quinn didn't seem at all grateful to be rescued. In fact, she roughly pushed Raven Wilde away and rushed off the stage in tears, muttering something about maiden sacrifice and getting her revenge on the Diberi.

Stage left, Maximilian Underwood was sitting at a grand piano, with his hands raised to begin playing the opening notes of the third movement of Beethoven's Emperor Concerto, while the university's music students accompanied him from the small orchestra pit. The Binder, whom Maximilian had been controlling ever since their unfortunate meeting that afternoon, was having a little sleep after all the energy he'd used suppressing Jupiter Peacock's magic while Hazel Bottle had been speaking.

The music Maximilian now played was joyful and celebratory – with just a hint of wonderful complex darkness. He was playing it not only because it provided a glorious soundtrack to these last moments of this Midwinter cycle, but also because one of the many things he'd learned at the University of the Underworld was how to use music to create a magical aperture that everyone can access to heal, to understand themselves better or just to feel uplifted for a few minutes.

Stage right, Wolf and Leander were in the process of unbinding various members of the Gothmen who'd been caught by the Binder. Pelham Longfellow had made it understood that anyone who had been bound could now be healed, and so members of the audience started walking – or hobbling, or crawling, or whatever they could manage – up onto the stage with the help of Lexy, Dora Wright and Nurse Underwood. Madame Valentin was healed just in time to recapture her snakes, who had been summoned here this night by dark magic, but were now a bit tired and just wanted to go home.

Effie Truelove, meanwhile, was spinning and spinning and spinning, right in the centre of the stage, connected to the Flow and providing power for all the others to use. She had turned herself into an extremely powerful magical battery, cosmically dancing for the good of all. She had never felt happier or more whole.

The music swept everybody up. Members of the audience stood and moved their chairs aside and began dancing in whatever style they knew – there were crazed tarantellas, jigs, can-cans, cha-cha-chas and all sorts of other dances – as bits of stray magic, particles from the Flow and glitter from the orbit of Miss Dora Wright rained down on them. At some point Terrence Deer-Hart entered the Grand Lecture Theatre. He looked dazed, confused. He had found a flowery bandana from somewhere and tied it around his head. He joined hands with the maths teacher from the Mrs Joyful School and let himself get swept up in the great happiness that was life as they danced a sort of hippy mazurka.

'Peace, man,' was all he could manage to say to her.

'Yeah, dude,' she said back, perhaps thinking he was joking.

Dora Wright danced with Laurel Wilde, Nurse Underwood danced with Dill Hammer, and poor Claude Twelvetrees danced alone. That is, until the librarian from Special Collections found the maths teacher from the Mrs Joyful School and they fell in love instantly. That left Claude dancing with Terrence, who asked him if he wanted to go out afterwards for a beanburger and some hot yoga.

The Free Cats League members had been released and, led by Mirabelle and Malvasia, they danced a cat can-can on the stage that was more accomplished than the human version, but no less odd. The Luminiferous Ether, the Bermuda Triangle and the Northern Lights bade each other farewell for another year and went their separate ways. The yeti got a lift back to the Andes with the Bermuda Triangle. At last the weather started to ease, although it still snowed, as it would now until the Turning of the Year.

25

'Have you just saved the world *again*?' asked Orwell Bookend as he drove Effie home. Cait was looking after baby Luna, and had no idea of everything that she'd missed.

'Not just me,' said Effie. 'We all did it. Even you helped.'

'*Me*? I doubt it. How?'

'Everyone's dancing provided the power Wolf and Leander needed to unbind everyone.'

'How did unbinding people save the world?'

'Well, it wasn't just that. It was Lexy, and Raven, and not letting the Diberi do what they had planned . . .' Effie didn't know exactly how to explain it all. 'Actually, a lot of the most powerful members of the Gothmen had been bound. Even Mrs Hide from my school.'

'How did your fat friend avoid it?'

'I was giving him extra power,' said Effie. 'I owed him.'

'And how were you doing that?'

'It's a bit complicated to explain.'

'Why are you so special anyway? You seem to be the centre of all these things.'

'I don't know, Dad. I really have no idea.'

'Anyway,' said Orwell. 'I hope you realise that I still don't believe in magic.'

'I know.'

'Or weather.'

'Yes, Dad.'

There was a long pause.

'And what happened to Professor Thingy? Hardforest, or whatever he was called.'

'Gotthard Forestfloor? Oh. He got recycled. Did you miss that bit? You can't have done. It was very dramatic.'

'Recycled? What does that mean? Are we going to be getting a visit from the police?'

'Raven explained it to me,' said Effie. 'He'd eaten so many animals in his life that she and the Free Cats League were able to perform an ancient spell on him. You can summon the spirits of all the animals a person has ever eaten and then the spirits take back from the person energy equivalent to what the person took from them. The energy is released back into the universe. If it's more energy than the person has, then . . . That's pretty much it. It wouldn't affect most normal people in the world now, because most people get their energy in lots of different ways and don't live long enough for it to be a problem. But it turns out it's a very reliable way of killing a two-hundred-year-old carnivore.'

'So you've basically just killed someone.'

'Nope. It was just bad karma. He did it to himself.'

'Right. And what about the Guild?'

'I don't know.' Effie sighed. 'I don't think they're going to like any of this. Pelham Longfellow and Professor Quinn just left for a meeting with Masterman Finch in London, but no one has high hopes.'

'Why are you telling me all this?'

Effie shrugged. 'I don't know. Maybe because you seem actually interested for once.'

Orwell Bookend sighed. 'We can take on the Guild,' he said quietly. 'We've done it before.'

'We?' said Effie, raising her eyebrows.

But Orwell didn't reply. He just frowned and went back to looking intently at the road.

When they got in, Orwell started telling Cait everything she'd missed. He employed his usual storytelling style, which involved exaggerating everything that was actually insignificant and completely glossing over the most exciting bits.

'Effie,' called Cait, 'are you going to come and tell me what really happened?'

'Can I tell you tomorrow?' said Effie, coming out of her bedroom. 'I've got to go somewhere first. You both don't mind if I go out for a bit, do you?'

'In this weather?' joked Orwell.

It had grown completely calm and still outside, except for the snow. The moon glowed peacefully in the starry sky.

'You're funny, Dad,' said Effie.

She went back into her room. There on her bed were two things. The invitation from the Otherworld that she'd only just opened – and the walkie-talkie that she'd just used to contact Lexy.

The invitation was to a celebration at an address in Dragon's

Green that Effie didn't recognise. *Welcome to the Flow,* was all it said. Effie wondered what would have happened if she'd opened the invitation sooner. But it didn't matter, because everything had turned out all right in the end. And even though she didn't feel she needed further instruction in how to connect with the Flow, she felt she ought to go and thank whoever had sent her the invitation. According to her watch, she still had time to get to the event, whatever it was.

And then she'd have to face Cosmo.

For once, Effie didn't much want to go back to the Otherworld. Lexy had begged Effie to come immediately to the party they were having at Maximilian's house. Lexy had officially been taken on as Nurse Underwood's Apprentice, and there was all sorts of other news apparently. Everyone seemed to be going up a level and getting apprenticed or finding familiars or discovering their art. Effie felt so happy for them all, but also somehow distant from it. Her own destiny seemed so different. While everyone else seemed excited about going up one magic grade she'd been shown what it would be like to go to wizard level and even beyond. Effie felt that she'd been to the very edge of the universe and back. Why? What was special about her? But it didn't matter anyway because officially she was still a Neophyte.

She didn't need to go to the hedge on the old village green to get to the Otherworld any more, but she did, partly out of habit, and partly because she needed the air. The snow was soft as Effie walked, wondering what she was going to find at Truelove House, and whether she'd be able to make things up with Cosmo, and whether she'd ever be able to forgive Rollo, and . . .

Melting . . .
Falling . . .
Sunshine . . .

When Effie arrived at the gates of Truelove House, the guard looked at her, confused.

'We've been told you're expected at the party at the Lodge, Miss,' he said to Effie. 'They sent a carriage for you, but we said you weren't here.'

'It's all right,' said Effie. 'I'll walk. Is it far?'

'About five minutes in that direction, then across the square in the village and turn right. You can't miss it after that. It's a white two-storey house. Quite big.'

Effie followed the guard's instructions. It was warm, as usual, with the steady hum of bees and the sweet smell of summer flowers. The quiet roads were dusty as always. Effie didn't see anyone else as she made her way to the Lodge. It certainly was big. It had gates made of wrought rose gold and a gently sloping garden with pink magnolia trees all in bloom. The house was a pleasingly imperfect white oblong, with three windows on its top level and two large windows on either side of an inviting-looking large front door. There were twelve steps leading up to the entrance, which had green stained glass with art nouveau patterns of flowers and trees. The house was shaded from the sun by the branches of the magnolias. Their silvery bark calmly reflected the sunlight. It was an extremely peaceful place.

A woman appeared at the door.

'Hello, Effie,' she said.

It was Suri. Did this mean Effie was in more trouble?

'Hello,' said Effie.

Suri smiled warmly. 'You've done it,' she said. 'I always knew you would. You managed to discover the Flow, even though it's almost impossible for islanders to find it. Anyway, welcome. Please come in. There are others here who have also recently found the Flow. All Otherworlders, but I think you'll like them. You'll be seeing a lot of them in the next few months. They're your fellow Apprentices.'

Effie walked into the front hall of the house. It smelled of pink lilies and open fires. Through an arched white doorway she could see an elegant party in full swing. There were several children of around Effie's age, each with animal ears and beautiful hair and clothes. There were girls, boys, and people who didn't seem to want to manifest themselves as either. They all looked very happy.

'Everyone from Truelove House is here to celebrate with you,' said Suri. 'We'll talk later about how I'm going to mentor you from now on. You'll be taking classes here with me.'

'But Cosmo—'

Effie hadn't realised until this moment that she'd thought of Cosmo as her mentor and guide. Had he rejected her for being too much of a disappointment? Was she not welcome at Truelove House any more? Perhaps that was what all this was about . . .

'Hello, child,' came Cosmo's voice. 'I'm glad to see you back.'

'Please join us when you're ready,' said Suri, smiling warmly and leaving Effie and Cosmo in the front hallway. There was a mint-green sofa by the table where the pink lilies were. Cosmo indicated that they should sit down.

'I'm sorry,' said Effie to Cosmo. 'I was wrong. I shouldn't have disobeyed you and gone into the library like that. I didn't understand. I now know how much I don't understand. I'm willing to learn. I—'

'You were wrong,' said Cosmo. 'And you were right.'

'I'm too headstrong, I know,' said Effie. 'But I can change. I've been in the Flow now, and—'

'You understand, then,' said Cosmo with a smile, 'why we were so frustrated?'

'Yes,' said Effie. 'I do. I know now that you weren't allowed to mention the Flow to me because I hadn't been in it yet. And I didn't realise that's why I kept running out of power, because you can only store minuscule amounts if you haven't got access to the Flow.' Effie sighed. 'It's why I could never stay here for very long. And when I thought tennis was helping me store lifeforce it wasn't because I was converting energy but because I was getting slightly into the Flow by accident while I was playing. But the more stressed I got about trying to store energy, the less that was happening. Our coach even told us about being in the zone, but I didn't listen hard enough. And it stopped happening because all I cared about was gaining power. I didn't give myself up to it like I used to.'

'You've learned fast,' said Cosmo.

'Of course, now I can stay here for longer no one will want me to,' said Effie. 'Because I am a galloglass. I understand that now, too.'

Cosmo shook his head. 'When will you learn to accept that you are loved?' he said.

'But Rollo—'

365

'Forget Rollo for now. Look at this.'

Cosmo reached over to the table by the lilies and picked up the stack of newspapers and magazines that were there. Each one had a similar headline. 'The Return of the Galloglass', said one. 'Why I Was Wrong About Galloglasses', said another. 'Why We Need Our True Heroes', said a third.

'What you did has had quite an effect,' said Cosmo. 'It's actually weakened the Mainland Liberation Collective. Putting that book in the library may even have averted war.'

'But how . . .?'

'These things are so complicated.' Cosmo shook his head. 'But people need to accept that the shades are simply neutral. We need the people who act for themselves – or, to be more accurate, on their own – just as we need people who act for beauty, or for usefulness, or for others. It's in combination that these things work. You can't start editing fundamental systems and removing the bits you don't like. If we were all aesthetes the world would be beautiful, but cruel. And if we were all protectors we'd smother each other to death. If we were all shapers there'd be nothing to shape. I realised recently that a Wizard Quest is, in a sense, the ultimate journey of the galloglass. In a Wizard Quest only the most wise go off on a long journey to see what they find, what knowledge they can bring back. It is undertaken alone, by one individual. Having the book in the library will make it better for us all. Most of all, it makes it possible to speak of the Flow, which will make every-one's lives a lot easier.'

'Suri said she wanted to be my mentor,' said Effie.

'That's right,' said Cosmo. 'Your power is very great, but you need to learn to control it. She will help you. You'll be coming here to the Lodge to study. If you want to, that is.'

'But you—'

'I will be on my Wizard Quest,' said Cosmo, nodding and smiling. 'It was my turn many moons ago, but I wanted to make sure you were all right first, child. And so you are. When I come back we can tell each other of our adventures. I trust you will keep the Diberi at bay while I complete my quest.'

'Of course,' said Effie.

'Well, then,' said Cosmo, patting Effie's hand, 'shall we join the party?'

Effie walked with Cosmo into the large drawing room. Suri smiled as Effie entered. There was something familiar about her eyes, as if Effie had seen them in another context, another person . . . *Will you give everything to me?* But surely . . . Effie's thoughts were interrupted when Rollo came straight over to her.

'I'm sorry,' he said. 'What I said before . . .'

'You accused me of being a galloglass and then said I shouldn't be allowed in the Great Library,' said Effie. 'Why? What did I ever do to you?'

Rollo sighed. 'It wasn't because of you.'

'Is this all about my mother? Because I'm actually getting quite tired of—'

'Sort of,' said Rollo. 'It's also about me. I don't expect you to forgive me immediately, but I thought you might be interested in this.' He handed Effie a piece of paper. 'You don't have to read it now,' he said, 'but I want to say thank you for putting the book back. It's made a difference to me as well.'

Effie glanced at the sheet of paper. It was the results of a *kharakter* consultation. Effie could see that Rollo was exactly the same as she was: a protector with a leaning towards galloglass. So that was why. It had never been about her. It was Rollo's fears about himself that had been his problem.

Clothilde appeared with a large slice of cake and a glass of fizzy fourflower water, both of which she gave to Effie.

'I'm so pleased you finally *know*,' she said. 'It's been driving me mad. I just wanted to tell you to go in the Flow rather than worrying about deepwater or playing tennis with the ring on. But you can't tell people. It ruins the whole thing.'

'Apparently now you *can* tell people,' said Effie.

'Yes, well, that's going to take some getting used to. But luckily there aren't any more young people around that need initiating after you lot. You were the last of the Dragon's Green kids to go in the Flow. So while you're here studying the rest of us can just focus on looking after the library and keeping the Diberi out. Pelham says there's one left from this recent batch, although she's pretty harmless. But we hear that there might be a new threat developing in London.'

'We can deal with it,' said Effie.

'The Mainland Liberation Collective have been driven out of Froghole at long last,' said Clothilde. 'And Millicent Wiseacre is being sent to the island in disgrace.'

'Great,' said Effie. 'I hope I don't run into her there.'

'Oh yes – I forgot about that possibility!' said Clothilde. 'Anyway, don't think about her now. Let's just focus on the celebration.'

Effie looked around the room. There were Cosmo, Rollo and Bertie chatting happily together. Pelham Longfellow was going to join them soon. And there were Effie's new classmates – or whatever she was supposed to call them. She once again admired the beautiful cheekbones, the cat's ears, fur and all the other ways they had made themselves look distinctive and interesting. She sensed the pure lightness that seemed to surround each one of them.

'I can't believe I once thought that people weren't doing much magic in the Otherworld,' Effie said. 'I can see it now, though. Everything's made of magic, isn't it?'

'Yes,' said Clothilde. 'It's how we can look the way we want, and live where we want. It's why everything's so beautiful. And you know now that we get more power the more we give to others. That's why there's no need for money here. And why so many people choose to serve others – like Bertie. I can't believe you once thought she was a maid! She's one of the most powerful elysians in this whole area. She mentors me.'

'I understand so much more now I've been in the Flow,' said Effie.

'I know,' said Clothilde. 'There's a lot that can't be put into words. You just have to feel it.'

Effie didn't stay in the Otherworld as long as she usually did. Although she still loved it there more than anything, she found that today she was keen to get back to her friends in the Realworld.

She walked to the portal on the Keepers' Plains in a happy daze, between two parties, on the threshold of something, although she wasn't sure exactly what. Studying at the Lodge. What was that going to be like?

The party at Maximilian's house was in full swing when Effie arrived. All her best friends were there. Raven introduced Effie to her new familiar, Neptune, and Lexy looked happier than Effie had seen her for a long time. She brought Effie a slice of carrot cake and a banana smoothie, and slipped a green tonic in Effie's pocket as well.

'What's that for?' Effie asked.

'To help you get in the Flow,' said Lexy. 'I've started reading about it already. You might need some homoeopathic sulphur as well. I'm not sure. Or maybe phosphorus. I haven't decided.'

'I'm so glad you're all right,' said Effie, putting down her cake and her drink and giving Lexy a big hug. 'Why didn't you tell us about JP? We would have helped.'

'I know that now,' said Lexy. 'But I didn't know how to put it into words. I didn't know if I was just overreacting to something other people might think was normal.' She shuddered. 'He really got in my head for a while.'

'Well, please, next time something like that happens, promise you'll tell me?'

'I will,' said Lexy. 'But I hope it's not going to happen again. That poem taught me something. To be an authentic person you have to be brave enough to act for yourself and not just hide behind the idea of doing good for others. If I'd thought that way more then maybe I would have told someone sooner. I just thought it would be selfish to make a fuss.'

'So JP's philosophy went against him in the end,' said Effie. 'I like that.'

Maximilian and Wolf came over.

'Meet my new brother,' said Maximilian, proudly.

'What?' said Effie. 'What do you mean?'

370

'My mum and Dill Hammer are getting married,' said Maximilian. 'And Wolf's coming to live with us.'

'Seriously?' said Lexy. 'That's amazing!'

Wolf handed Effie two keys. 'These are for your grandfather's place and the bookshop,' he said. 'You own the Old Rectory, and we need to discuss what's going to happen with the bookshop. No one's come to claim any of Leonard Levar's things. They're basically ours.'

'But why have you got the keys?' asked Effie, confused.

'Because my uncle was doing all that removal work for Leonard Levar. I took the keys when I left my uncle's place. He was knocking me about and after I epiphanised I decided I couldn't stand it any more. I lived in the flat for a while – I thought you wouldn't mind, and I meant to tell you, but everything was always so intense with the Diberi and then you had the Yearning and . . . Anyway, then I was living in the bookshop and—'

'When my mum discovered what was going on she insisted he come and live with us,' said Maximilian.

'I'm going to be over the road with Dill to start with,' said Wolf. 'But I think he's talking about moving in here, and me and Max having our rooms across the road. It'll be like a massive den.'

'A den of praying?' said Raven. 'And early nights?'

'Haha,' said Wolf. 'It's not like that.'

'I know,' she said, smiling. 'I'm only joking.'

'And you forget that I am a dangerous mage,' said Maximilian. 'I'll spice things up a bit.'

The friends sat down on Odile Underwood's big soft sofas

and carried on talking, teasing one another and planning the future. They were all Apprentices now, more or less – even though Raven and Wolf still needed official mentors. Professor Quinn had formally taken Maximilian on, and Odile was looking after Lexy. And Raven had discovered her art was hunter, just like Neptune.

Neptune jumped onto Raven's lap and started purring. He understood that a whole new chapter was starting for him too. Witches' cats have to work quite hard at meditation, witches' cats' prayers and spell-making of their own. And he and Raven were now a hunting team, which meant, in their case, hunting for the truth, solving mysteries and searching out evil. Neptune's days of hunting other animals were over. He and Raven were both going to need to spend a lot of time with the Cosmic Web.

Neptune now sensed the approach of a car. Yes, it was Raven's mother, Laurel, coming to take them home. She had her new girlfriend Dora Wright with her, and a big bag of doughnuts. He told Raven, and she put down her smoothie and got up to find her coat. But *wait*. Neptune sensed something else as well. Another person in the car with Laurel and Dora. Someone he had not yet met but who was going to make things very interesting . . .

The doorbell rang.

Raven went to answer it. In seconds Laurel and Dora were swept into the party by the other adults and given drinks. Laurel quite forgot to explain about the hitchhiker they'd picked up and her incredible story and if she could just find Wolf she'd tell him that . . .

Standing in the doorway was a girl of about ten.

'Hello,' said Raven. 'Are you all right?'

'I'm looking for my brother,' she said. 'My name's Natasha Reed.'

Acknowledgements

Thank you, as always, to my partner Rod Edmond, who read every draft of this book with his usual love and care, and who has remained the most wonderful companion on this adventure.

Thanks once again to my family: Mum, Couze, Sam, Hari, Nia, Ivy and Gordian, for all the love, support and happiness you have given me. And many thanks again as well to my extended *whānau*: Daisy, Ed, Molly, Eliza, Max, Jo, Murray, Joanna, Marion, Lyndy and Teuila. Ruth Troeller – happy 100th birthday. I wish I could have been there with you.

Many thanks to all my other friends, students and colleagues, in particular Amy Sackville, Teri Johns, David Flusfeder, Sue Swift, Alex Preston, Jennie Batchelor, Vybarr Cregan-Reid, David Stirrup, Bernhard Klein, Alice Bates, Steve Bates, Pat Lucas, Emma Lee, Charlotte Webb, Jean Balfour, Martha Schulman, Katie Szyszko, Sarah Parfitt, Gonzalo Garcia, Amy Lilwall, Tom Ogier, Roger Baker, Suzi Feay, Stuart Kelly and my wonderful new agent, Cathryn Summerhayes.

I am also extremely grateful for all the lovely people I get to work with on these books. Thanks so much to everyone at Canongate, particularly Francis Bickmore, Jamie Byng, Jenny Fry, Anna Frame, Alice Shortland, Neal Price, Megan Reid, Andrea Joyce, Jessica Neale, Caroline Clarke, Allegra Le Fanu, Becca Nice, Vicki Rutherford, Alan Trotter and Sylvie the dog. Many thanks also to Debs Warner for the brilliant copy-edit. And, as always, big thanks to Dan Mumford for the wonderful artwork.